old FASHIONED

THE BECKER BROTHERS, BOOK 4

Published by Kandi Steiner
Edited by Elaine York/Allusion Publishing
www.allusionpublishing.com
Cover Design by Staci Hart
Formatting by Elaine York/Allusion Publishing
www.allusionpublishing.com

To the ones who won't back down,

old FASHIONED

THE BECKER BROTHERS, BOOK 4

KANDI STEINER

who won't go quietly,
who won't give up.

To the fighters.

This one's for you.

ONE

JORDAN

Ever since I was twenty-three years old, there had been a fire burned into my memory.

I wished it was a metaphorical fire, one that drove me to excel and succeed and filled me up from the inside. I'd even settle for a bonfire that was memorable, one my friends and family had gathered around on an evening when everything felt right in the world. But for me, the fire was a living, breathing monster, seemingly small where I viewed it against a pale blue evening sky as it devoured a corner office in an old whiskey distillery on the edge of town.

A corner office, and nothing else.

A corner office I didn't know held my father inside it.

I'd been the only one of my family to see the actual fire, to watch the smoke billow and what was left of the flames lick at the roof of the building through the busted windows of that office. I hadn't thought twice about it, other than to think it was a small annoyance that had traffic backed up heading into town. I was on my way to Mom and Dad's for dinner.

It was such a small fire, already in control when I drove past it. The fire department had it surrounded, water spewing from their truck, the flames already weakening. I didn't know much about fires, but even I could tell that it was in no danger of spreading, that it was tamed, and I drove past it wondering if Dad would be called back up to the distillery to fill out paperwork, since he was on the board.

When I had opened the screen door from Mom and Dad's front porch, all three of my brothers were in the living room, playing video games and talking over each other at a volume that was always too loud for my taste.

None of them looked like me. My skin was darker, an umber brown that was light in the winter months and dark from the sun during the summer. Compared to their olive tan, it stood out, a reminder of our differences that we never really acknowledged. My onyx hair that curled tightly to my scalp was also a contrast to their sandy brown, straight locks.

But, the fact that the blood that ran through my veins was not the same as that which ran through theirs didn't matter. My *adoption* didn't matter. It never had.

We were brothers, an impenetrable force, a team forged in bad times and in good.

Mom had smiled when I arrived, wiping her hands on her apron before she crossed and kissed my cheek.

"Can you help me set the table?" she'd asked, hanging a hand on her hip as she gestured to the rest of my brothers with the other. "As you can see, this motley crew is useless. And your father had to stay late at work, something about exciting news." She rolled her eyes a little, because we all knew that *exciting news* to my father could mean anything from a promotion to him finding a washed dollar in his jean pocket.

I'd never forget that smile she wore when she turned back to me, the one that crinkled the edges of her eyes and spread from cheek to cheek. Because less than thirty seconds later, the home phone rang.

And I never saw my mother smile like that again.

I blinked, the memory of that summer night ten years ago fading as my laptop screen came back into focus. A dated software system filled the screen, Latin words on an old word processor file, a journal my father had kept for years before he passed.

A journal my brother had found on a hard drive not meant to be discovered.

A journal I was now trying to decode, as if it would somehow reveal all the answers to every question my family and I had asked since that fateful day in June.

I'd gone through months of entries before I'd discovered that my father had found a Last Will and Testament of the founder of the distillery. That had shocked me, since this entire town was rocked with surprise when Robert J. Scooter died and a Will *hadn't* existed.

It turned out one had, at least, according to Dad's journal.

But he hadn't mentioned it since that first entry.

I sighed, cursing under my breath when I checked my watch and saw it was almost one in the morning. I wasn't going to find anything more tonight — especially with so much on my mind. I safely ejected the hard drive and tucked it into my top desk drawer, the screen of my laptop modernizing again before I put it to sleep. I had to do it quickly, before my fingers hit the keys that would open my lesson plans for the week or, even more risky, my practice plans.

Tomorrow was the first day of high school for our small town of Stratford, Tennessee — and I had a team of football players to whip into shape.

I scrubbed my hands over my face, body aching as I lifted it from the chair I'd been living in all evening. It was normal for me to be anxious before the first day of school, the first day of *football*, but I was even more wired than usual.

Maybe it was the pressure of walking into a new season with two state championships under my belt. This entire town expected our team to keep winning, expected *me* to keep winning, which was a completely different kind of pressure than when you were the coach taking a team that rarely ever won all the way to state. That had been a driving kind of pressure.

This, however, was more on the crippling side.

Maybe part of my anxiety came from my youngest brother, Michael, moving across the country to New York City with his girlfriend. We'd all flown up to help get him settled, and while I knew *he* would be okay — mostly because Kylie would make sure of it — I worried about our mother, who was now in the house alone for the first time.

The same house she bought with my father.

The weight of responsibility I'd always felt for my mother pressed heavy on my chest, but I forced a deep breath, going through my nightly routine of brushing my teeth and flossing and lotioning from head to toe. When all that was left to do was crawl into bed, I splayed my large hands on the bathroom counter instead, staring at my reflection.

I didn't know the two human beings responsible for making the man who stared back at me.

I didn't know if I had my mother's eyes — gray-blue, with a brown burst surrounding the iris — or if I had my father's nose, the bridge slightly bent, nostrils wide. Was it his scowl that mine mirrored, thick eyebrows forever in a bent state of determination? Was it her freckles that broke through the dark complexion of my cheeks in the summertime?

Which one was black, and which one was white?

How did they find each other, and where were they now?

They were questions I'd asked myself hundreds of times throughout the course of my life, questions I knew I'd never have answers to. But one thing I *did* know was that I wasn't anxious about the first day of school because I felt pressure to win, or because my little brother was in New York, or because my mom was sleeping soundly on her own across town.

The truth was my anxiety was rooted in the newest addition to my staff.

A woman.

A very attractive, very distracting to young, hormonal boys, very newly divorced woman.

She would be the *first* woman on our staff, and the first new blood to come onto our team since I took over as head coach.

Everything I'd worked for, all the synchrony I'd developed over the years, all the trust and rhythm and comfort we'd grown accustomed to was about to be shaken up.

By the police chief's ex-wife.

Before I could fall into another spiral, I shook my head, pushing off the counter and swiping the bathroom light switch with my palm. I peeled my shirt off, stripped my sweatpants off next, and climbed into my flannel sheets in my boxer briefs, setting an alarm on my phone before I plugged it in and turned it face down on my nightstand.

Then, I laid awake for hours, tossing and turning, pretending that I was still in control and everything would be fine.

By the time I finally fell asleep, the alarm rang.

— ● —

Stratford, Tennessee, was a small map dot southeast of Nashville. It had a population of two-thousand-one-hundred-and-seventy-two people, according to the most recent census — and almost half of those residents worked at the Scooter Whiskey Distillery on the edge of town. It was where my grandfather had built his career, where my father had worked his entire life, and where two of my brothers worked still.

Noah was a barrel-raiser, with skillfully quick hands and muscles lining every inch of his arms. Logan was a tour guide, the face of our town to the tourists who passed through. And, before he left, Michael had worked in the gift shop.

It was a family tradition.

And though I was the oldest, and perhaps the one Dad *most* expected to follow in his footsteps, working at a whiskey distillery was the last thing on my mind growing up.

For me, it was all about football.

Mom had always told me that the first time I held a football, I couldn't even walk yet. Dad had been tossing one in the backyard with a friend of his, and when he missed a catch, it rolled over to where I was sitting on a blanket with Mom. She said I picked it up with both hands, stared at it with both brows bent, and then I looked up at her and smiled.

She said she knew right then that I'd play football.

What she *didn't* know was that I wouldn't just play it, I'd become *obsessed* with it. From the time I was on my first Little League team, football was my life. I couldn't wait for practices and games. I watched football whenever I wasn't playing it. I followed ESPN football stories like it was my job. I collected cards, ran drills on my own when the season was over, and was always looking forward to the next time I'd get on that field.

But where my teammates in high school dreamed of being scouted to a college and drafted into the NFL, my heart drew me to the behind-the-scenes work of it all. I wanted to dissect every play, watch every game, replay every tape, draw up my *own* plays, and — perhaps more than anything — I wanted to coach.

I never took for granted that my dream had come true, that I was doing what I loved most in the world and somehow managing to get paid for it, too. That's why a familiar buzz of excitement crawled under my skin as I pushed through the doors of the stadium locker room, eyes on my clipboard, words I would say to the team repeating in my head. It was only an hour until our first practice, and nothing compared to that feeling of starting a new season — not the ten days of summer camp, not the energy that coursed through every kid at tryouts.

Nothing.

It'd been a fast first day of school, my regular day filled with introducing myself to freshmen who were in my physical education class and catching up with the athletes in my weightlifting classes. I enjoyed teaching both for very different reasons. The freshmen were nervous, and I always jumped at the opportunity to make them feel welcome and comfortable in their new atmosphere — mostly by encouraging them to join a sport. And when the students I'd worked with came to me in weightlifting, athletes of all backgrounds with issues ranging from golf swings to softball pitching, the excitement that rang through me was palpable.

I *lived* for this, for discovering a physical limit and making a plan for how to overcome it.

But as much as I enjoyed teaching throughout the day, it was the first day of football practice *after* the school day let out that my heart really pounded for.

My head was still down when I pushed through the door to my office, using my back to open it. I kicked the door stop under it with my foot to prop it open, still not taking my eyes off the notes on my clipboard. I didn't realize my office wasn't empty, even after I sat down in the familiar, worn chair, the old leather splitting under my hamstrings, a soft *whoosh* of air from the cushion.

It wasn't until a soft clearing of a throat hit my ears that I looked up from my work and saw her sitting across from me.

Sydney Kelly was not the kind of woman you could pass by without noticing — she never had been.

I hadn't known her well in high school, but even then, every head would turn when she walked by, regardless of their sex or sexual orientation. She was riddled with unique features, from her jet-black hair — which was pulled into a high and tight ponytail right now — and almond-shaped eyes to the curious complexion of her skin. It was a golden brown, darker than the tans my brothers could achieve in the summer but lighter than my own. She never covered that complexion with anything but sunscreen, not in all the years I'd seen her around town. Makeup seemed to be nonexistent in her universe, which made the dusty pink of her plump lips and the severeness of her high cheek bones and the length of her black lashes that much more mesmerizing.

She was beautiful — dangerously so.

And she had *team distraction* written all over her.

I mentally cursed Principal Hanley, wondering how he didn't see this as an issue when he hired Sydney as our new athletic trainer. Of course, I'd voiced my concerns when we were reviewing applicants, but Dustin Hanley was close friends with Sydney's older sister, Gabriel. Dustin and Gabby had been in the same college when the Clarks first moved to Stratford. Apparently, the bond they'd formed in school had carried through.

What I had to say on the matter didn't seem to be a factor in the decision at all.

Not that I thought discrimination in *any* form was okay, but the truth of the matter was that teenage boys with raging hormones were hard enough to wrangle with a staff full of stalky, grumpy men.

With Sydney on the field, it'd be damn near impossible.

I stood abruptly, dropping my clipboard on my desk as I rounded it. "Mrs. Kelly, I apologize. I'm afraid I didn't see you there," I said, reaching out my hand for hers as she stood, too. She wore modest black leggings and a loose-fitting polo in our school's shade of red, but I realized in the moment that she could have been wearing a potato sack and she would still be a complete knockout.

I kept my eyes trained on hers to avoid the length of her toned arms, or the way her hips filled out those leggings, knowing full well that I'd be the *only* one on this team capable of doing so.

"Coach Becker," I said with my hand still extended. "Welcome to the team."

"No need to apologize, *Jordan*," she said my name with a smirk that set my nerves at attention, her eyes playful. "I'm glad to see you work just as hard as you did in high school. I don't think I'd ever seen that kind of focus before my first group project with you our junior year."

I chuckled as her soft hand slipped into mine, but she shook it firmly.

"And it's Sydney *Clark*, now," she added, her smile faltering before she snapped it back into place.

Clark.

Her maiden name.

Embarrassment flittered through me, along with a recognition. I couldn't believe I'd let her married name slip, especially after the scandal that *was* her divorce with Police Chief Randy Kelly. But, they'd dated ever since I'd known them — in high school and beyond. It was difficult to separate one from the other, anymore.

"Of course," I said, shaking my head as we released our grips. I slid my hands into my pockets, changing the subject away from her recent name change. "I didn't expect you so early."

"An hour before practice?" she asked, quirking one eyebrow. "I'd say that's more *punctual* than early. I figured you'd want to show me my office, let me get my table and supplies set up." She tapped the large duffle bag hanging off her shoulder.

"I guess I'm just used to the rest of my staff who like to roll up here ten minutes before the team starts showing up."

She smiled. "Well, then, let's just say I'm not like the rest of your staff."

You can say that again.

I motioned toward the hallway, guiding her out of my office and past the rows of lockers to the athletic training station. Once I flicked on the light, I stood at the entrance with my hands in my pockets. "We got a pretty decent amount of money from the boosters last year," I explained as Sydney dropped her duffle bag on the examination table, looking around her new space. "So, lucky for you, you're walking into an upgraded version of the mess that was here before." I pointed. "New ice bath, new whirlpool, extra storage, nice table for soft tissue work. We even got those fancy boot things."

"NormaTecs," she mused, crossing her arms as her eyebrows crept up. She eyed me with a smirk. "I didn't realize I was working for a team of professional athletes."

I grabbed the back of my neck with a shrug. "What can I say? When you win two state championships, you get a lot of money thrown your way. We had all new pads, new jerseys, new staff gear, end zone cameras, new iPads and screens for reviewing tapes. I was running out of ways to spend it."

She chuckled. "You poor thing."

I wanted to smile, too, but I was still rubbing my neck, staring at what I knew would be the source of every headache I'd have in the next few months.

"Sydney, listen," I said on a sigh, letting my hand fall. "I don't know how else to say this but to be frank with you."

Her smile fell, expression flattening as she straightened her spine.

"I'm worried about you being our athletic trainer."

Her eyebrows dipped, lips pursing. "Let me guess — because I'm a woman?"

"No," I said quickly, but then I rolled my lips together. "Well, honestly? Kind of." I held up my hands when she rolled her eyes. "But not because I don't think you're capable. It's just that... we're dealing with teenage boys here. They're rowdy, and — God help us — dominated by hormones that they can't control yet."

Sydney folded her arms over her chest, listening, her expression unreadable.

"I'm just saying," I continued. "There's a lot riding on this season. We've won two state championships in a row, and we have a lot of eyes on us."

"Meaning, you have a lot of eyes on *you*."

I swallowed. "Yes."

"And you think I'll be a distraction."

"Honestly? I know you will be."

Sydney smiled, shaking her head and looking around her new office before she took two purposeful steps toward me. "I understand your concern, but here's my side of things."

She paused, and I realized I'd never been this close to Sydney — not in high school, not in any of the years since. And there was an energy pulsing off of her, one that hit me like a wave of electricity low in my gut.

"If your players are distracted by a woman on the sideline, that is on *them* — not on me. If their parents didn't teach them that, then I'd wager that's *your* new job. I'm an athletic trainer, and a damn good one, which is why I got this job in the first place. I'm here to *do* that job, and the last thing I need is for my new boss to tell me that I might be *too pretty* to do it effectively."

"I didn't say you were..."

"Then what exactly *are* you saying?" she probed, taking another step. She didn't raise her voice, but the intensity between us shot up three levels. Her chest was a few inches from mine now, her eyes cast up, chin held high, jaw set. Those dark lashes brushed her cheeks when she blinked, waiting.

I catalogued every feature.

"What I'm saying is that you are the first new member to our staff since I became head coach seven years ago, and I'm making sure you understand that we set the standards high on this team."

"Great. Your expectations have been made clear. Can I have a while alone to set up my office now?"

I narrowed my eyes. "Do you have a problem with authority, Ms. Clark?"

"Only as much as you seem to have a problem with equality, *Coach*."

I blew out a frustrated breath, eyes rolling up to the ceiling as I debated whether it was worth fighting her over. I wanted to. *Oh*, how I wanted to. But the truth was I knew I'd already put my foot in my mouth, that I hadn't explained my concerns properly.

I *did* sound like a sexist asshole, and no verbal argument could win me out of that perception in this moment.

The only way for her to see that my concerns were valid was to witness them play out.

And I had no doubt they would — in less than an hour when that locker room filled with boys.

"Let me know if you have any questions as you get set up," I said, forcing a calm breath. "After practice, I'll get your sizes so we can order you staff polos and jackets for the games. The team should start showing up in about forty-five minutes."

I didn't say another word, nor did I wait to see if she had a last one to get in, either. Instead, I moved swiftly back down the hall, resisting the urge to slam my office door. I swiped my clipboard off the desk, attempting to focus, but I read the same line over and over again, all the while stewing on what I'd said, how I'd said it, and what she'd thrown back at me, in return.

It was less than an hour before the first practice of the year, and one thing was already abundantly clear.

It was going to be a long season.

TWO

SYDNEY

Thirty boys and three grown men stared at the giant, square trophy in Jordan Becker's hands as he carried it silently through the locker room. He sat it gently on the folding chair he'd propped in the middle of the room, placing his hand on the large, golden football that adorned the top of it. For a long while, he just stared at that trophy and didn't say a word.

The entire locker room was silent, too.

As much as I wanted to hate him for his rather rude welcome to me on the team, I couldn't deny that I respected him in that moment. He commanded attention — and he'd always been that way. I remembered him having the same presence in high school, though we weren't in the same crowd. One thing I'd learned was that he didn't speak often, so when he did, everyone knew it was important, and valuable, and necessary.

So many people filled the world with hot air, speaking before thinking, talking about nothing at all.

Jordan Becker was the exact opposite.

He was purposeful, severe — like the flood God cast down to cleanse the earth.

I stood straight in my little corner of the room, trying to blend while also knowing it was impossible. Until Jordan had waltzed that trophy into this room, I'd been about the only thing anyone could stare at. Eyes of each member of that staff widened when Jordan introduced me to them, and as the boys filed in one by one, their eyes stuck on me, too. They whispered to each other, smiling and elbowing each other in the ribs, and I could only imagine what they were saying.

Thank God, because imagining was still better than hearing it for real.

In retrospect, I knew Jordan wasn't wrong about the way the boys would react to me. The fact that it was sexist and *not* my fault didn't matter — boys would be boys, as they say. Still, this was my first day of work after years of being a stay-at-home mom — a job I didn't choose, but rather, was selected *for* me. If it wasn't for my sister's friendship with Principal Hanley from when they were in school together, I wasn't sure I would have been able to find a job as an athletic trainer after all the time I'd taken off. Before my daughter was born, I had been primed and ready to start my career, and I had offers waiting.

But things changed.

And no one in that locker room saw me as anything but someone new to the team. They had no idea that that day symbolized freedom for me. To them, and to most of that town, I was the bitch who divorced the sweet, amazing hero who kept this town safe. What they didn't know is that I'd been anything *but* safe in my marriage with him.

But in a small town, when the Police Chief is beating you with his words and his hands, you have no one to run to.

And you believe him when he says you're crazy, and that you deserve it.

I swallowed, shaking those memories off before they could slide in to ruin the first day of my new chapter. It didn't matter if no one else knew it, *I* knew it.

It was a new beginning.

A new era.

A tiny smile curled my lips at the realization, but as soon as Jordan lifted his head, I straightened again.

"Anyway."

It was the first word Jordan spoke, and I watched as confusion swept over the faces in the locker room — mine included. The boys glanced at each other, wondering if they'd missed something, while the staff of coaches stood behind Jordan with similar gazes.

"The past five years, this team has had a word of the season. Every day, we come back to that word. When we lose, when we win, when we practice, when we're on this field, and when we're off it — that word is our guide," Jordan explained.

His eyes were a storm in and of themselves, a swirl of gray-blue like an ominous sky with a burst of golden-brown around each iris. They locked on each of the boys looking up to him, as if he wanted to ensure they each felt seen. The way he stood next to that trophy, with his bicep muscles bulging out of his polo, his broad shoulders square and straight, his chin high, brows bent and determined, jaw square — he looked like he was about to take these boys into battle rather than onto a football field.

And with the way they looked at him, I knew they wouldn't hesitate to go to war for their sergeant.

"Our first year, the word was *work*. Then, *growth*. We took *growth* to *perseverance,* and then to *discipline,* and last year, to *determination.*"

That last word fired up the boys who I assumed had been on the team last year, and they chanted the word three times in different cadences before giving a deep-chested *ooah!* that echoed through the locker room.

Jordan smirked, but the curl in his lips faded as fast as it had come. "This season's word is different. It doesn't look motivational if you slap it on a poster and it probably won't make sense to anyone outside of this room. And that's exactly why I picked it. Because the truth of the matter is this: *we* are the unit. *We* are the team. And *we,* alone, are responsible for what happens this season."

There were a few nods, an unspoken understanding, the locker room so quiet you could hear my sneaker squeak against the floor when I shifted my weight.

"This season is going to be hard, but we're going to persevere, anyway," Jordan said after a while, glancing around the room. "Practices are going to be long and hot, but we're going to show up, anyway. There's a lot of pressure on us to perform, but we're going to excel, anyway. There are going to be days we all want to grumble or scream or throw our helmets or quit, but we're going to stay here and fight, anyway."

The more he used the word, the more fired up that locker room became. I watched the boys hold their heads higher, their brows furrowing deeper, their chests puffing out more and more with every word. I'd sat in the bleachers behind this team for years, every Friday night that we had a home game, watching Jordan lead them to win after win — but I'd never seen the *inside* of the machine, the one we watched work so effortlessly together on the field.

This was the making of a team.

This was magic.

Jordan left his perch by the trophy, walking around the room now. "You're going to mess up," he said, nodding. "Oh, trust me — you are. You're going to miss catches and tackles and run the wrong plays and look back on tapes wishing you'd done it all differently, but you know what?" He pressed his finger into one of the kid's chests. "You're going to get your ass back on that field on Monday, anyway."

There was a shuffling, a few kids rising to their feet with cries of *yeah!* and *that's right!*

"Your body is going to ache," Jordan said, raising his voice. "Your muscles are going to scream and beg you to stop and you're going to be pushed past your limits and everything inside you is going to tell you to quit. But you're going to keep going, anyway."

More standing, more cheers.

"Everyone out there," Jordan said, all but screaming now as he pointed to the locker room doors. "Is going to expect you to fail — expect *us* to fail. They're going to wait for us to crack under the pressure, to mess up, to fall short. But what are we going to do?" He looked around that room, and while I expected someone to answer, they all stood and waited, apparently well aware that it was a question Jordan would answer, himself.

And he did.

He smiled, shook his head, and thumbed his chest. "*We* are going to win, anyway. Can I hear you say it?" He held out his hands. "What are we going to do?"

"We're going to win, anyway," the room echoed back to him, softer than he wanted.

"What's that?"

"We're going to win, anyway!"

"When they tell you we lost our best players to graduation, what are you going to say?"

"*We're going to win, anyway!*"

"When they tell you there's no hope of us getting another state title, what are you going to say?"

"We're going to win, anyway!"

"This is not going to be an easy season," Jordan said to the humming room, all the boys on their feet now, shuffling, some of them clapping or stepping side to side. "We're going to have to work, and work hard. We're going to have to rise up against the odds. This town is supporting us, but the rest of this state can't wait to watch us fail. So, when the doubts creep into your mind, when your body hurts, when the scores don't look good or the fear strangles you, I want you to show up here, anyway. I want you to believe in yourself and in this team, anyway. And I want you to—"

"Win, anyway!"

Jordan smiled as the locker room erupted into cheers, and he clapped one of the boys on the shoulder. "Damn straight."

More cheers rang out, and I couldn't help but smile from my little corner of the room. It was the first day of practice and he'd already fired them up for the entire season.

That was a sign of a great coach.

"He's something out of this world to watch, isn't he?"

I followed the voice to my right, where the defensive coordinator had slid up beside me. Coach TK, as Jordan had introduced to me. He was a white man, with kind, hazel eyes and a smile that reminded me of my ex-husband's father. Coach TK was just as tall as Jordan, his stocky figure hinting that he, too, had played football in his youth, and he wore a baseball cap to cover his balding head.

"He's something, alright," I mused with a smile, eyeing Jordan with a mixture of annoyance and appreciation.

I couldn't deny that he deserved to be where he was, that there was no better man to lead our town's team to victory.

But I could still be upset with him for his presumptuous welcome.

"Now, before we hand out equipment and get our first day of practice under way, we have a new member on our staff," Jordan said, and as soon as the words were out of his mouth, all eyes were on me.

I smiled, pushing off the wall I was leaning against to stand straight.

"Please help me welcome Sydney Clark, our new athletic trainer."

Someone whistled, someone else yelled out, *"Oh, I'll welcome her, alright,"* and then the room filled with a mixture of laughter and cheers.

I frowned.

Jordan walked purposefully toward me, his eyes locked on mine, and that moment seemed to lengthen and stretch. There was something about that man's eyes, about the way he held himself, the confidence he exuded and the respect he demanded.

It left me breathless, awakening a part of me I thought had died forever, before he swiveled and faced the room of boys.

"I'm going to say this one time and one time only, and if it doesn't sink in, you will all run suicides for every time I have to repeat myself."

That shut them all up.

"You will respect Ms. Clark just as you respected Mr. Perry when he was in the position. There will be no foul remarks, no whistling, no slanderous talk, and no other behavior that your mother would classify as disrespectful and skin your hide for. If any of you fake injuries to get time on her table, or pull any kind of crap that makes her uncomfortable, you will have me to answer to — and trust me when I say the punishment will not be pretty. Am I understood?”

There were mumbles of *yes, coach* in response.

Part of me wanted to be annoyed that this even had to be a conversation, but the other part of me was glad he was setting the standards for his team from the start. He didn’t allow it to get past those first remarks made, and he was making it clear what was expected.

More than anything, it was a sign of respect for me.

One I appreciated.

“Good,” Jordan said, nodding once. “Ms. Clark has studied sports medicine in depth and had past offers to play with college teams.”

His eyes found mine then, and my brows folded. *How did he know that?*

“We’re lucky to have her,” he finished, with his eyes still on mine. I could feel the sincerity in them, the belief he held for the words he’d just spoken.

And something else.

Something else I couldn’t quite place.

But before I could dissect it further, he clapped his hands, barked out an order, and the team fled out of the locker room and onto the field.

—●—

They don’t tell you anything about motherhood.

When you’re pregnant, you *think* they’re telling you everything. You think the baby books and the unsolicited advice from family members and older mothers in town cover just about everything you’d need to know — and everything you *never* wanted to know, too.

You think you're prepared. You know that it will hurt, that the pain won't matter once that child is in your arms, that your life will never be the same. You know not to expect sleep, and that your breasts will swell until you feed, and that your priorities will shift to completely center your world around this new, tiny human you've created.

But what no one tells you is that from the moment that first cry rings out in the hospital, you will be terrified.

They don't tell you that you'll worry if you're breast-feeding long enough, or if you should breastfeed at all, or if you fed them the right food once they were able to eat solids. They don't tell you that as much as that kid's first steps will amaze you, they'll also make your stomach drop in fear. They don't tell you that for the rest of your life, you'll wonder how your actions affect that little human you made — are you screwing them up? Are you giving them a complex? Are you going to be the subject of their future therapy appointments?

Will they end up like their father, angry and impulsive and vindictive?

Or is there more of *you* in your child?

And if so, is that even a good thing?

It was enough to drive a person mad — which, I was convinced, was a permanent state of being for most mothers. We just knew how to *handle* our insanity, how to live with it and somehow get our shit done. You had to learn to quiet the fears and anxieties, to *fake it till you made it*, to do whatever it took to make ends meet and keep your home a safe place for your child.

Some days it was easy.

Some days it was impossible.

And every day, as a newly single mother, I worried.

"This is gonna be our year, Mama," Paige said, splaying her tiny hands over the laces of the football in her hands as she watched the Tennessee Titans press conference. They were her favorite team, and she idolized Mike Vrabel like he was her father.

In a twisted way, I wished he was.

"You think so, huh?" I asked, smiling at her from the kitchen where I was browning hamburger meat for dinner. I hadn't had the energy to do more than whip up a box of Hamburger Helper that evening, not after my first day of work. And it wasn't that Paige would mind — she was a kid, she didn't care. But it seemed I was always on a cycle of mom guilt, thinking I should be doing *something* better.

Or everything, really.

So, the fact that I hadn't come home and made a fresh, balanced dinner weighed on me a bit as I stirred the meat.

"I know so. Look at coach," she said, gesturing to the TV before her hands were on the football in her lap again. "He looks..." She stopped, struggling for the word.

"Confident?" I suggested.

"Yeah! And the rookies we drafted, the way the team worked together last season." She looked back over her shoulder at me with her crooked smile. "I can feel it."

I smiled back, tracing her features. I knew all mothers thought their child was the most beautiful kid in the world, but with my Paigey, it really was true. She had a full head of bouncy curls that would have made me and my sister both hate her and love her had she been our friend as kids. Her skin was a smooth tawny, her cheeks peppered with freckles that were like stars under her almond-brown eyes. She had a gap between her two front teeth that grew back in fully last year, and somehow it only made her cute factor go up.

She was only nine years old, and still, I knew I'd be in trouble once she started dating.

Another flare of anxiety over her having her heart broken seared through my chest, but I subdued it, draining the pasta noodles in the colander in the sink. "Well, if you believe it, then I do, too."

I *also* knew that all mothers thought their child was the smartest kid to ever exist, and once again, I was no different. Of course, with Paige, it was only pertaining to one subject: football. She watched games and listened to podcasts and studied football terms like it was her full-time job. She learned words that most kids her age couldn't pronounce, let alone understand, all in the name of being an expert in the sport she loved.

"You'll see, we're going all the way this season," she said, turning her attention back to the television. Then, a long sigh left her chest, and she whispered so low I almost didn't hear. "I can't *wait* to play football."

I furrowed my brows, torn as always with how I would explain to her that the likelihood of that happening was slim to none. She'd been watching football with her father every Saturday, every Sunday, and every Monday night since she was born. Somewhere around four years old, she started saying she wanted to play football. At the time, I thought it was cute, something she'd grow out of, but it turned out football would be one of the staples my daughter was built on.

She was hell-bent on playing football someday, and as a mother, that terrified me.

Again — normal.

Before I could decide if I wanted to respond encouragingly or realistically, my cell phone rang.

"Hello, sister," I answered, putting her on speakerphone as I mixed the fake, processed, powdered "cheese" with the noodles and hamburger meat. "Paigey, come sit at the table for dinner."

"But, Mom! Can't I just eat it in here? Coach is still talking!"

"Yeah, Mom," my older sister teased. "Coach is talking."

"Hush," I told her on a laugh, but when Paige hopped up and clasped her hands together, begging me with her signature pouty lip and big eyes, I was helpless.

I sighed.

"Fine," I said, scooping a good helping into a bowl for her. Paige hopped up and down in victory. "Set up the TV tray though, and use your napkin, Paige Marie, *not* your jeans." I gave her *the mom look* when she bopped into the kitchen, making sure she knew I was serious before I handed her the bowl. Once she was set up in the living room, I took my sister off speakerphone, pressing the device to my ear, instead. "Gray hairs, Gabby. I swear I'll have them before the year is up."

My sister chuckled. "Oh, come on. So your daughter is obsessed with football. It could be worse. She could be obsessed with boys like we were."

"Don't jinx it," I said, smiling when Paige tossed the football up in her hands between bites, her eyes fixed on the press conference. "How are you?"

"Oh, same old same here. It was a long night at the hospital, we had a three-car accident that was pretty nasty. I was dead on my feet by the time I got home this morning."

My sister, Gabriela, was older than me by five years. It was just a wide-enough gap to keep us from ever being in the same school together, but not too wide to where we couldn't share clothes. She was my best friend — thanks to our life traveling around with a mom in the military. Where the few friends we *did* make were left in the dust each time we were re-stationed, our bond never died. It only got stronger throughout the years, and Gabby was the only person I ever felt comfortable talking to about anything deeper than the weather.

Besides Randall, but I'd learned my lesson the hard way that not even he could be trusted.

"If you still lived here, I'd make you a glass of my famous sangria."

"Ugh," she dragged out the groan. "Don't tease me like that. It's not fair."

"What's not fair is that I can't walk two doors down and plop on my sister's couch anymore."

"You could," she argued. "If you moved here with the rest of us."

I grew silent at that, casting a glance toward my daughter before I made myself a bowl of Hamburger Helper and stepped out onto the back lanai. I still kept an eye on her through the sliding glass doors.

"You know it's not that simple," I said once I was outside.

Gabby sighed. "I know, I know. I wish it were, though."

I didn't have to elaborate, because Gabriela was the only one I'd ever opened up to about *everything* that had happened between me and Randy. Mom and Dad knew we were divorced, but they thought it was just because the love had faded over time and we'd been fighting a lot.

Gabby knew the truth — the bruises, internally and externally, that prompted my final decision.

The only reason Randy had even granted me the divorce I'd asked for was because he didn't think it would last, and because it happened on *his* terms. I'd threatened to hire a lawyer, to get my parents involved, to show people the photos I'd taken with the marks he'd left on me. So, to keep his reputation safe, he agreed to the divorce.

On the condition that I would never leave Stratford, so that Paige would be close to him.

So that *I* would always be in reach.

My heart squeezed. Growing up, Gabby and I were all each other had. With Mom in the Army and us moving every few years, we had grown up changing schools like most girls changed which Barbie doll was their favorite. After Mom retired, we came to Stratford.

I was a junior in high school at the time, and Gabby was just starting college after taking some time off. For a while, we called this town home, but when Gabby got into nursing school in Texas, our parents moved with her — mostly because Mom had been offered a full-time Army Policy Analyst position in Austin.

Under different circumstances, I would have gone, too.

But when it all happened, I was newly married, starting a new life of my own.

And I was pregnant.

That's another thing they don't tell you — how when you start a family of your own, the family you grew up with suddenly shifts to second place.

"So, how was your first day?"

I blinked, shaking free from my thoughts as I shoved a bite of our cheap dinner in my mouth. "It was... something."

"That bad, huh?"

"Not bad," I clarified, taking another bite and speaking around it. "Just... interesting. It felt good to be at work, to feel that part of my identity come back, but... well, let's just say my boss gave me a less-than-stellar welcoming."

My sister's voice hardened, and I could picture her brows folding together. "Who do I need to kill?"

I chuckled. "Easy, no need to bust out the nunchucks," I teased, referring to the time in sixth grade when she'd handed a kid his ass after he tried to put his hand up her skirt. She'd ripped his stupid toy nunchucks from his other hand and knocked him upside the head with them. "He was just predictably sexist with the intro, that's all."

"What do you mean?"

I rolled my eyes. "He went on about how he's worried about me being the new trainer because I'm a woman. He thinks he'll have trouble with the team being distracted."

"He said that?"

"In not so many words, yes."

"Well... don't hate me, sis, but... he's probably not wrong."

I sighed. "I know he's not, but the point is that it shouldn't be *me* he talks to about that. It's not my fault I'm a woman, and I shouldn't be held responsible for the teenage boys on his team getting distracted."

"Did he say anything to them about it?"

I shifted, poking at the noodles in my bowl until I had five of them stacked on my fork. "Well, yes, actually. He did. He set his expectations for how they should treat me before practice."

"Was he condescending then?"

I frowned. "No," I admitted. "Actually, he spoke about my accolades, and said they were lucky to have me."

"Wow," she said, mockingly. "What a jerk."

"*Anyway*," I said, ignoring her. "After that, it went fine. No injuries during practice, but I did meet with a few of the players who had injuries last season, to see where they're at in recovery. And I got my tables all set up. You wouldn't believe the equipment they have, Gabby," I added. "It's like a professional football team rather than a high school one."

"Well, that's what happens when you win two state championships in a row." She paused. "Who's the head coach again? Anyone we know?"

I flushed, though I couldn't be sure why, and I was *damn* sure happy my sister couldn't see it. "Jordan Becker."

"Becker…" my sister repeated. "I don't think I knew him."

"He was in my grade, younger than you," I explained. "But, his dad is the one who died in the fire at the distillery."

"Oh, shit…"

I frowned. "Yeah."

"No, I mean, *yes*, that's terrible, but what I said *oh, shit* to is his headshot." My sister whistled. "I just Googled him. Hot *damn*, sis. Your new boss is hotter than a Texas parking lot in July."

I snorted. "You're ridiculous. Although, I will say, you're not the only one who thinks so. You should have *seen* the Mom Parade at practice." I rolled my eyes, popping another bite of hamburger in my mouth as I thought back to practice that afternoon. "There's not even a reason for any of them to *be* at practice, but they're all right there in the bleachers, offering coach lemonade and telling him what a great job he's doing after every drill. One of them even dunked a towel into their ice chest and offered to put it on his neck."

Gabby laughed. "I don't blame them. Hell, I don't even have a kid and I'd find a way to fake it so I could be there to watch that man sweat."

"Gross."

"Don't act like you don't want to lick his chest."

"Again, gross," I said, but my cheeks flushed in betrayal. "He's my boss, Gab. And not that there are any official rules against it, but it's a *very* clear, unwritten rule that the head coach doesn't date anyone on his staff. Plus..." My voice faded, eyes finding my daughter through the sliding glass door. "You know my feelings on men. One psychopath in my life was enough. I have zero intentions of ever dating again." My voice faded. "And even if I did..."

Again, words were lost, but I knew Gabby understood. With Randy always around, watching me the way he did, the possibility of me dating anyone again was so close to impossible that I didn't even consider it.

He still felt like he owned me, and I knew better than anyone that if someone tried to play with his toy, they'd pay the price for it.

Inside, Paige took her own dishes to the sink and rinsed them, putting them in the dishwasher before she went back to continue watching the conference.

I smiled, the only piece of my heart left swelling at the sight. "It's just me and Paigey now."

My sister was quiet for a long while, and I knew she wanted to argue with me. She'd wanted me to join a dating website as soon as the divorce between me and Randall had been finalized. But she knew as much as I did that there was no use trying.

I was permanently broken, permanently turned off from love, and permanently happy being single.

"You know, you could go for full custody," she whispered. "Bring Paige here to be around her awesome aunt and amazing grandparents."

"In a normal situation like this, maybe," I conceded. "But, he's the Police Chief of a tiny map dot, Gab. Everyone loves him — including highly influential people, like Patrick Scooter, and the Mayor. You and I both know the power he has..."

She sighed, though it sounded more like the huff of a bull about to buck a cowboy off at the rodeo. "I hate him."

"That makes two of us."

"I have to get going," she said, a long pause hanging between us. "I love you, sis. Don't be too hard on the guys on the team. You're the first woman to be on the staff, in a small southern town, and in a sport dominated by men. Baby steps, okay?"

I smiled. "Okay. I love you, too, sis. Thanks for calling."

After she hung up, her words echoed in my thoughts, and I glanced once inside at Paige before I pulled up Google on my phone. I typed in my new boss's name, and when his stern face filled the screen — along with a Wikipedia article populating with all his stats — my stomach tightened.

Those eyes...

"Mom!"

I jumped, exiting out of the browser and shoving my phone in my pocket as my daughter bolted out into the yard.

"Can we go to the park and run drills?" she begged, holding up her football. "Pleeeease?"

"Maybe this weekend, okay? It's a school night."

She was tempted to pout, but knew better than to try that with me. Instead, she nodded. "Okay."

"Why don't you go run a bath and I'll braid your hair after."

Paige nodded, bounding back inside. My phone felt like a hot brick in my pocket, begging me to pick up where I left off, but I ignored it, taking my empty bowl inside to clean up the kitchen, instead.

As I ran the hot water, a pair of stormy eyes still burned in my mind.

THREE

JORDAN

Ten days blew by in a whirl, as they often did when the school year started. For me, it was always a blur of practice and plays and drills and tapes. It was school days filled with working my players in their weightlifting classes, and evenings spent getting them ready for the first game.

It almost seemed like I'd stepped in a time warp, because here it was, Friday night.

The first game of the season.

This was what I lived for — the smell of the turf, the energy of hungry athletes buzzing in the locker room before it exploded out onto the field, the hum of the crowd anticipating what will happen. It felt like coming home to me, pacing the sidelines as I watched my team, clipboard in hand and a piece of gum in my mouth for me to chew on when what I really wanted to do was scream like a maniac.

I had learned that trick after my first three games as head coach.

Still, tonight's game felt different than any game ever had before. Because as much as everything familiar and comfortable greeted me on that field, there was something else there, something quiet but menacing, soft but blatantly apparent.

Pressure.

The stadium lights felt like spotlights, all of them pointed at me as the residents of Stratford filled the bleachers. Everything in our town shut down on Friday nights during football season. You couldn't find a place open to get groceries or grab a bite to eat because customer or shop owner — everyone was right here.

I crossed my arms on the sideline, clipboard in hand as I watched the team warm up. My assistant coach and defensive coordinator were on opposite sides of our half of the field, running drills, while the Red Rock Raptors swarmed the other half. I watched them just as much as I watched my own team, wondering if they would be contenders this year. They had given us a run for our money last year, with a group of juniors growing stronger — juniors who were now seniors and ready to lead their team to victory.

"Your boys look good out there tonight, coach."

I smiled at the familiar voice coming from behind me, and when I turned, I was greeted by a crooked yellow grin.

"Let's hope they play good, too, eh?"

Elijah Braxton was the town fixer-upper. Any kind of maintenance job that needed done, he could do it. He knew plumbing, electricity, woodwork, and more. Whether it was a broken refrigerator or a tree falling on your house — he was the man to call. He was known for being a bit of a grump — except for when it was Friday night football, of course — and a bit crazy, too. He always wore the same fedora hat, one he'd owned presumably all his life, and he talked to himself while he worked.

Perhaps what *really* made him crazy was that he only charged what the person could afford for his services. If you were elderly, poor, or just going through a rough time, you could pay him in hugs and a fresh batch of snicker-doodle cookies, and he'd still fix your toilet.

He was a man with gumption, and I happened to like him very much.

I first met him when I played on this very field in high school. It was hard for me not to notice him, especially since there were very few black residents in our small town. I knew, because I was one of them, and especially as a child, I'd noticed the difference in my appearance compared to the other kids I played with in town.

And compared to the kids I watched on television.

And compared to pretty much every source of my cultural exposure.

I didn't know my exact genetic makeup, didn't know who my parents were or why my skin was caught somewhere between being as black as Eli's and as white as my adopted father's, but I knew I was different.

For a long time, I felt caught in the middle of something I couldn't quite put a name to.

I stopped trying to figure it out somewhere in my late twenties, deciding instead to just be me and let others put labels on me if they felt it was necessary.

I didn't need labels.

And I wouldn't live within the confines of them, either.

The point was that since the day I first saw him there, Eli had stood out in a sea of white in those bleachers. He was a little like me in a way that most other residents in that town weren't.

Ever since I'd been head coach, he'd been at every home game, and some of the away games, too. He was one of our biggest fans, and he was never shy to tell me what he thought of the team — or of my coaching.

The way our stadium was set up, there was a fence separating the track and field from the stands. Eli stood behind it, elevated just above me.

A few of my players' mothers interrupted me and Eli before he could say anything else, offering me words of *good luck* and inviting me to their house for a party after the game. I politely declined, and rolled my eyes at Eli's knowing smirk before turning back to my players.

We were the Stratford High Wild Cats, and Eli always called the moms who blatantly hit on me *The Stratford High Cougars.*

"Lost quite a few seniors last year," Eli said when we were alone again, his eyes on the field now. "You think you got boys who can step up and take their spots?"

"We'll find out soon enough," I murmured, leaning against the gate that separated the bleachers from the field.

He hung his arms over the top railing. "You got a lot of eyes on you this year."

I nodded, and to anyone who looked at me, I imagined I appeared calm and collected.

Inside, I was a tornado.

"Hope you did a better job working with the offensive line in this first week of practice," he said. "Even I could have sacked Rodgers in that first game last season."

I smirked, because this was always Eli's game. He'd play nice, give a few compliments or offer up a few generalized statements, and then he'd tell me what he was really thinking.

"Well, I tell you what. If Rodgers gets sacked tonight, consider yourself welcome to practice Monday morning to whip that O-line into shape."

"Famous last words, Coach."

I smiled over my shoulder at him, tapping the top of the fence twice before I made my way toward the water table. Sydney stood beside it with her thumbnail between her teeth, a giant bag of athletic training supplies on the ground at her feet. Her eyes were like cars on the highway, speeding back and forth, watching the players on the field like she was ready to grab that bag at her feet and sprint onto the green at a moment's notice.

She'd worked hard over the past week and a half, especially when one of our linebackers had a pretty severe turf toe injury. And, blessedly and most importantly, she'd stayed out of my way. Sydney showed up, did her job, worked with the guys who needed her and handled the ones who gave her a hard time without needing help from me.

I knew the twins on our defense — Bradley and Boone — would give her hell. They were by far the most girl crazy and tended to feed off each other as the team clowns. But, to her credit, Sydney was unfazed by them, and in just ten days she had a reputation with the team.

She was knowledgeable. They could trust her with their injuries.

What's more, they respected her — and they knew she took no shit.

I still felt a little guilty for the way I'd welcomed her onto the team, but it seemed to be all but forgotten between us. We didn't necessarily apologize or forgive, but we'd had civil conversation, and we'd done our jobs in the vicinity of each other for a week and a half now.

We were finding a rhythm, even if it was a little off tune to start.

"Nervous?" I asked, grabbing one of the plastic cups on the table and filling it with Gatorade.

"No," she answered quickly. "Just alert."

Her eyes never left the field, and I smiled, leaning against the table beside her as I took a drink. "I'm a little nervous."

Sydney snapped her attention to me, all but breaking her neck in the process. "You? Really?"

I nodded. "If you tell anyone, I'll deny it and fire your ass."

"You can't fire me," she shot back, but a small smile bloomed on her lips. "But I won't tell."

"Thanks," I said, watching our players on the field. "Two state championships… it's a lot to live up to. I mean, look around us," I said, but my eyes stayed put. "The entire town is here, and it's only the first game and already scouts are showing up, too."

Sydney glanced at the bleachers behind us. "It is a lot," she admitted. "The energy is palpable."

"Just wait until kick off."

Sydney looked at me, and my eyes found hers, and for a moment, it felt like an olive branch had been extended between us. In the lights from the stadium, her soft brown eyes were aglow, and I let them suck me in for the briefest second.

The corner of her mouth curled, and mine did, too.

"GIVE 'EM HELL, COACH!"

A roar of applause erupted behind us, and we both turned to find my brothers, Noah and Logan, banging on the fence and hooting and hollering like they were teenagers instead of grown ass men. They'd fired up the section of fans in the bleachers behind them, too. I smiled, waving to Mom as she passed behind them, shaking her head with flushed cheeks at her outlandish boys.

"I see the Becker brothers haven't grown up a bit," Sydney commented.

"We have too big of a reputation to live up to for all that."

She chuckled. "It does look like they're settling down, though. Bet that feels kind of weird, huh?"

I followed Sydney's gaze to where Noah and Logan were leading their significant others up the bleacher steps. Noah held Ruby Grace's hand — the hand that donned an engagement ring, and in just a few months would have a wedding band on it, too. Logan had his arm around Mallory, holding her at the hip, as if he was afraid she'd tumble backward down the steps if he let her go. I had a feeling it was the growing bump of a belly she had that made him so protective.

And though he wasn't there that night, I knew my youngest brother, Mikey, was building a new life with Kylie in New York City in that very moment, too.

"Yeah, I guess it is a little," I admitted, voice soft as I watched them. "But, they're happy. That's all that matters to me."

A longing for something unattainable sent an ache through my chest, and the way Sydney's eyebrows tugged together where she watched me, I was afraid she'd somehow seen it.

"What about you?" I asked, turning the attention away from me. "You have family here?"

Her eyes shot somewhere behind me, but then she pulled them back to the players on the field. "Yeah."

It was all she said — no explanation of who or where. But when I glanced over my shoulder, I didn't need another word. My eyes connected with our Chief of Police — Randall Kelly — who stood at the far edge of the bottom bleacher.

And their daughter stood next to him, her eyes wide with glee as she watched the field.

Randy didn't look as pleased. He wore a permanent frown, and his uniform, the black threads over bullet-proof vest and shiny gold badge over his heart giving him an air of arrogance and power. He watched me as if I had somehow offended him, so I offered a nod in acknowledgement.

He didn't nod back.

My brothers and I had our shares of run-ins with the law in this town — mostly over stupid bar fights or fights between ourselves. We were a rowdy crew, I'd admit that, but I'd never had Randy stare at me like that before.

Behind me, a whistle blew, and the sideline flooded with everyone but our team captain, who was already jogging to the fifty-yard line for the coin toss.

With one last glance at the town that came to watch us, I jogged out, too.

The coin was flipped.

And the game began.

— ● —

Three minutes before the end of the third quarter and our team down by three, my star running back limped off the field with what looked like a hamstring injury after a long run.

My heart tripled its pace as he hobbled in, and I sent in our backup for the next play. There wasn't enough time on the clock to assess his damage before the next play would take place. I nodded to Coach Pascucci, my assistant, letting him know to take over as I rushed to where Sydney was already bent over our player.

"Where'd you feel the pull?" she asked as I bent down next to her. She ran her hand along the hamstring of his left leg, which was in a bent position, cleat planted on the grass. "Here?"

He shook his head, swallowing as he reached down with his own hand and brushed the inside of his thigh.

As in, his fucking groin.

"I think it's more… here," he said, and his eyes flicked to mine before he laid back again, closing them altogether in a wince of pain.

I narrowed my gaze, standing again with a shake of my head. "Parker, get your ass up and get ready to go back on that field."

His shoulders deflated as he looked up at me, but before he could speak, Sydney's head whipped around, her eyes on me like lasers.

"Excuse me?" she hissed. "He will do no such thing, not until I properly assess the injury in the locker room."

"He's fine," I growled, barely glancing at her before I was barking at him again. "Parker. Up. Now."

"Do not move a muscle," Sydney said to him through her teeth, then she stood, jutting her chin up to face me. "I'm taking him back to do a full examination. If he's fine, I'll—"

"He *is* fine," I snapped. "He's being a smart ass and faking it to get time on your table. And he *will* pay for it in practice," I added, glaring down at a shrinking Parker.

"How do you know he's faking it?" she challenged. "It could be serious. It could be a strain or a stress fracture or—"

"You're kidding, right?" I folded my arms as I assessed her. "He limped off the field in a way that indicated a hamstring injury, now he's pointing to his groin." I blinked. "His *groin*, Sydney."

"Groin injuries are common in football," she pointed out, flatly. "I'm not clearing him to play again until I do a full assessment. So how about I do my job, and you do yours. Game's not over, in case you didn't realize."

I blew out a breath like a dragon, so hot I was surprised little flames didn't shoot out of my nose, too. But Sydney didn't allow me to argue further. Instead, she signaled for two of our players on the bench to help her, and as a group, they got Parker off the ground and on his feet, supporting him to the locker room.

I watched them go, grinding the gum in my mouth between my teeth before I let out a growl and snatched my clipboard off the bench in time for the next play.

Everything went downhill from there.

We were down by three when Parker limped off the field, and it was as if our offense couldn't get their shit together once he was gone. He was a natural leader, a key player, and without him, we suffered.

It didn't matter how hard the defense worked to keep the Raptors' score from climbing higher, our offense couldn't score. Hell, they couldn't even get us close enough for our kicker to get us into overtime with a field goal. I watched the clock run down on the last minute in the fourth quarter without Parker or Sydney returning to the field, and when the final whistle blew, I saw red.

We'd lost our first game.

At home, nonetheless.

It took every ounce of willpower I had to make it through shaking hands with the Raptors's coach and each of the players on their team before I was sprinting toward the locker room, ignoring the calls of my name and unsolicited advice from the bleachers. The team was still gathering their equipment off the sideline to limp their sorry, losing asses into the locker room when I pushed through the doors, full steam ahead until I was standing inside Sydney's office.

"We lost," I said, waiting until she brought her gaze to mine before I continued. "So, tell me. What's his big injury?"

Sydney blinked like she was bored, checking something off the clipboard in her hand. It was a bad time for me to realize that the red of our team polo blazed against her dark skin, or that the leggings she'd paired with it hugged her in all the right places, but I realized it.

And clearly, I wasn't the only one.

"He's fine," she said, checking something off on the clipboard before she set it on her desk. "I did my full assessment and had him work through a few exercises to make sure. He should be good to go for practice Monday."

"Well, isn't that great? He couldn't get back to finish out the game and get us a W, but at least he'll be okay for practice!"

I was blowing my top.

I was being irrational.

I knew it, but I couldn't stop it.

I was the calm one in my family, the sensible one out of all my brothers, no matter what was going on.

But when it came to football, my fuse was as short as my fingernails.

"Coach, this is my fault, not Sydney's," Parker said, raising his hand like he was in class. "I... you were right, I faked it. A few of the guys on the team dared me to. I waited until close to the end of the game because... well, I know we were down but... I guess I still thought we were going to win. I didn't think... I'm sorry."

Sydney's mouth popped open, and I couldn't help the smug smile that bloomed on my face.

Parker hung his head, staring at his hands in his lap as I stared a hole into his head. I *would* find out who made the stupid bet with him, and all parties would pay.

For now, I had a bigger fish to fry.

"Get out, Parker," I said simply, calmly — which should have scared him more than if I had yelled.

He glanced at Sydney apologetically, then back at me.

"*Out*," I hissed through my teeth. "And you better enjoy your weekend, because this field is going to be your own personal hell on Monday."

I didn't have to look at him to put the fear of God in him. He tucked his tail between his legs and hobbled out of the training room, as if he really were injured, and all the while, I kept my smug gaze on Sydney.

She inhaled a stiff breath, closing her mouth like she'd just realized it'd been hanging open this entire time. When her eyes met mine, there wasn't an ounce of apology in them.

"Got anything to say for yourself?"

Her head popped back like I'd slapped her. "Um… you're welcome for doing my job?"

"Your job." I snorted. "I told you he was faking it."

"And I told *you* that until I did a full assessment, I wasn't able to say whether that was true or not."

"We *lost,* Sydney," I reminded her, taking a full step into her space. Her chest puffed, but I puffed mine right back. "Because of you babying one of our star players."

"This is not *my* issue," she shot back. "Do not blame your loss on me because your so-called *star player* thought winning a bet with his buddies was more important than playing tonight. I did my job, and I will not apologize for it."

I didn't realize she'd been walking toward me until our chests brushed, the heat of her breath hitting my nose as she glared up at me. Anger rang in my ears, my fists clenching at my sides as I glared back. Our chests heaved, neither of us backing down, both of us sure in our stances.

Sydney's dark hair was pulled into a sleek ponytail, leaving nothing to distract me from the depth of her dark eyes. Time stretched between us in an immeasurable way as I fell into those pools. Her breathing softened a little, and without warning, my gaze fell to her lips.

They were nude, and smooth, and even when they were flattened into a frown, they were still somehow plump and full. I let my eyes focus on those lips for longer than I meant to, longer than was appropriate, and when they parted slightly, a hot breath slipping between them to assault my senses, I ripped my gaze back to her eyes.

Her dark eyes watched me in a completely different way now.

The step back that I took next came too late, and with it, each of us drew in a long breath. The air in that training office felt heavy and wet, like it was liquid instead of oxygen, and suddenly, I felt I'd drown if I stayed even one minute longer.

I glanced at Sydney once more before I turned, storming out of her office with anger still rolling off me in plumes. It took me ten steps to clear the hallway and step into the locker room — where a team of thirty boys and three coaches watched me with weary eyes and their heads hung, waiting to hear what I had to say.

And oh, were they in for a mouthful.

FOUR

JORDAN

My throat was sore, voice hoarse by the time I got to my mom's house. And when I slammed the door to my truck, still fuming as I made my way up the drive to Mom's front door, I was shocked to see Mary Scooter walking out of it.

Mary was Patrick's wife, and other than seeing her playing her role as the dutiful wife behind him all these years I'd grown up in Stratford, I didn't know much about her. One thing I *did* know was that since the fire, she hadn't set foot near my mother — probably because Mom was horrified that Mary didn't take her side on it.

Patrick, Mary, Dad, and Mom used to run in the same circle in high school. They were close friends, from what I'd picked up in passing conversations between Mom and Dad, but somewhere along the way, that had changed.

Still, Mary knew my Dad didn't smoke, yet she'd looked at my mom with the same sympathetic eyes the entire town did after the fire — like she felt sorry for her, like Mom was in denial.

Mary's eyes looked like she'd been crying, and she sniffed, nodding at me as she passed. "Jordan," she said.

"Mary," I replied, still confused.

"Good game tonight. Sorry about the loss, but you'll get them next time."

I forced as close to a smile as I could muster, and then she got in her car I hadn't even noticed parked among the others, and she was gone.

Mom was on the porch, and she pulled me in for a hug with a knowing look as soon as I was standing with her.

"Tough loss," she said.

I nodded. "What was Mary Scooter doing here?"

Mom's expression was unreadable, but she patted my shoulder — reaching up high, since she was so short in comparison — urging me inside. "Oh, no reason, really. She's just going through some things. We used to be best friends, you know."

"I know, but..."

"It's nothing," she assured me. "And please, don't say anything to Mallory about her being here. Okay?"

Mary was Mallory's mom — and ever since the big fallout between her and her family after she and Logan made their relationship official, they hadn't talked. At least, not to my knowledge.

Even when Mallory told them she was pregnant, there had been no reciprocation.

I nodded, though I didn't like keeping secrets. For Mom, I'd do anything. And if she was saying it was nothing to worry about, I believed her.

We made our way inside, Mom heating up leftovers from dinner while I made a drink. Everyone was gathered at the house — Noah and Ruby Grace, Logan and Mallory — but thankfully, everyone was leaving me alone for now.

It was a family tradition of ours, to have dinner at least once a week at Mom's, and any time that dinner fell on a Friday night during football season, they'd have dinner without me, come watch the game, and then we'd all gather here again after the game for me to heat up leftovers and for all of us to catch up.

Tonight, though, my appetite for anything that wasn't whiskey was nonexistent.

Later, Mom stared at the untouched plate of food in front of me, worry in her eyes as I sipped on the old fashioned I'd made. It was a bit strong, but already I felt myself cooling off, my temper settling.

It was me, Noah, and my mom at the table. Logan and the girls were in the living room, all three of them watching a documentary on Mars that Logan had been waiting on to air for weeks. I watched the screen from the dining room table in a numb state of being, all the adrenaline draining from my body to leave me feeling completely wiped.

"So," Noah said, sipping on his own glass of whiskey. He swirled the ice cubes around in it before setting it back on the table. "You wanna talk about tonight?"

Noah was the oldest of my brothers, but still four years younger than me. I remembered being wide-eyed and fascinated by him growing in our mother's stomach, back when I was the only kid in the Becker household. I had no idea what would come with being an older brother, only that my father had told me I would be responsible for him, that I would have to look after him, protect him, have his back.

And I had, from the very minute he was born.

Noah and I had our differences, though, and of all my brothers — I'd fought with him the most. He was bullheaded and always felt like he had something to prove.

Especially after Dad died, he was hell-bent on being *man of the house*. I had to literally wrestle him to the ground and kick his ass for him to calm down and see that we *all* had that title — and that it would take the entire team.

He was also the only one of us who really looked like Dad.

He had the same blue eyes, the same reddish-tone to his bronze skin. He was stout like Dad had been, where Logan and Michael were both lean and tall. They had Mom's eyes, and her smile, too.

"Not particularly," I answered after a minute.

Mom reached across the table and squeezed my hand. "It's one loss. One loss does not a season make."

I softened, squeezing her hand in return before I forced myself to take a bite of dinner. I knew if I didn't at least make an attempt, I'd break my mother's heart, and if anyone had a soft spot in me — it was her.

"I agree," I told her, taking a bite of sweet potato. "But, we should have won. We *would* have won, in my opinion, had a certain situation been avoided."

"You talking about Parker getting hurt?" Noah asked.

"He wasn't hurt."

Mom frowned. "He limped off the field. I saw the new trainer take him back to the locker room."

I ground my teeth together, forgoing my next bite and reaching for my glass, instead. "I know. But I saw it in his eyes even before he was taken back. He wasn't hurt, he just wanted to be rubbed down by Sydney. And like a fool, she fell for it."

Noah and my mom exchanged glances.

"I know I sound like an asshole," I admitted. "But, I told her not to take him back, to put him back on the field, and she refused. She dug her heels in like a stubborn woman."

"Jordan Solomon," Mom chastised.

"Sorry, Mom," I said quickly. "Male or female, it was a stubborn move and a blatant disregard for authority. She took him back, anyway, insisting she needed to assess the full injury, and then after the game, wanna know what happened?" I grinned, though I was far from happy about it. "He admitted it. A few of the players had dared him to fake an injury to get her to rub down his groin, and she fell for it."

Noah snickered and Mom swatted him across the chest.

"This is nothing to laugh about. First of all, that's awful that they did that to her. But, Jordan," she said, shaking her head as her eyes found mine. "Sydney doesn't know these boys like you do. If Parker had truly been hurt and she let him go back into the game, that would have been on *her*."

Mom looked older in that moment, as if the story I'd just told had somehow aged her. I knew the reality was that the last ten years had — ten years of raising four rowdy boys without her life partner to help. She'd recently cut her hair even shorter, the edges of it curling over her ears, and almost all of the soft brown was replaced by a silvery-gray. Her eyes were still a bright hazel, though — a swirl of green and gold.

"It's kind of funny," Noah argued after a moment.

"Regardless of whether it's funny or awful, it cost us the game. And I hear what you're saying, Mom, I really do," I said earnestly. "But, I have to figure out how to handle it and establish my expectations when I walk into that locker room on Monday."

"Hey now," Mom said, pointing her finger into my chest. "You don't know if you would have won that game had that Parker kid gone back out onto the field. For all you know, he could have fumbled the ball and made the score worse. There were other errors made far before he got hurt, like Rodgers throwing that interception that gave the Raptors their first touchdown. And *that* was probably caused by your offensive line not giving him time to make a smart throw."

A genuine smile found my face for the first time that night, because I could remember a time when Mom knew nothing about football and couldn't have cared less what the score was at the end of the night. But when I told her as a junior in high school that I thought I wanted to become a coach, she took a serious interest, and she was at every game, learning the rules, cheering me on, and — on my favorite nights — giving coach an earful of what she thought should be done to win.

Mom was our biggest fan, no matter what we did. And I knew it was a rare and special gift.

I sighed, still smiling, because her words were sinking in as they always seemed to do. "Do you ever get tired of being right?" I asked her.

She smirked. "Never."

Noah ran his finger over the edge of his glass, brows furrowed as he thought. "You know, I see where your frustration comes from. You saw what Sydney didn't see, because — like Mom said — you know those boys better than she does. Keep in mind, this is her first year on the team."

"It's also her first year back at work after being a stay-at-home mom for years," Mallory added, joining us at the table.

"What's wrong? Not interested in how we got a robot to Mars?" Noah asked.

Mallory rested her hand on her small, but rounding, belly. "All the orange makes me nauseous."

"Trust me, sweetie. *Everything* is going to make you nauseous for about another month, at least," Mom chimed in. "Let me make you some tea."

Before Mallory could argue, Mom was already up and in the kitchen.

"Seriously, though," Mallory said, her attention on me. "I don't know if you know Randy Kelly, but he's a prick. And she was *married* to him. Don't you remember that she was one of the smartest girls in school? She was *years* ahead of me and even I remember her sweeping the award ceremonies. She already had college credits when she graduated high school, and she graduated with her master's degree at twenty-two."

"What are you saying?" Noah asked.

Mallory shrugged. "I'm just saying. She wanted a career, and yet she never had one. She got pregnant before she ever had the chance to be a trainer like she'd wanted to be. And now, she's finally working, finally has the chance to prove herself — and all that after a divorce where you guys know as well as I do that she was painted as the villain." Mallory's eyes caught mine just as Logan came up behind her and squeezed her shoulders. She placed a hand over his. "Wouldn't *you* feel like you had something to prove — not just to the team full of boys you work with, and not just to this town, but to *yourself*?"

It wasn't a question she expected me to answer, and thanks to Mom delivering tea, I didn't have to. Ruby Grace joined us at the table and the conversation turned fully away from me and onto the upcoming wedding.

I sat quietly the rest of the evening, chewing on what Mallory had said, considering Sydney in a way I hadn't until that moment. I'd known she was married to Randy, of course, and that she had a kid. But I'd never considered the sacrifices she'd made — just like the ones my own mom had — nor had I considered what she must feel like as the only woman on a staff of men.

I'd pointed out that she could be a distraction, and now, I wanted to laugh at myself because I realized that was far from news to her.

She *knew* she'd be dealing with boys, that she'd be proving herself to men, that she'd be fighting an uphill battle from the moment she walked through those locker room doors.

And I'd been the General of the opposition.

More than that, what Mom and Noah had said sank in more and more the longer I sat there sipping on my whiskey. Sydney *didn't* know those boys as well as I did. And if Parker really had been hurt, she would have been responsible for letting him back on the field — even if it had been my call.

I sighed, disappointed in myself, and more than that, frustrated with where to go from here. I understood why Sydney took Parker back to do a full assessment. He was limping. He was claiming he was hurt. He was showing all the signs of not being okay to go back onto the field. It didn't matter that he was faking, to a responsible and professional athletic trainer, he was hurt.

And had it been our previous trainer, Perry, who'd done what Sydney had tonight, I would have appreciated him taking his job and the safety of our players seriously.

I'd judged her too harshly, and placed blame on her for something that was entirely Parker's fault.

And, maybe, partially mine, too.

"It'll all work itself out, Son," Mom said, leaning down to kiss my cheek as she passed by me and into the kitchen. I could tell when I glanced up at her that she saw the warring thoughts in my head even when I didn't speak them out loud. "Now, eat up. You're not allowed to leave that table until that plate is empty."

She patted my shoulder and continued into the kitchen, and I stared down at my full plate of lukewarm food as if it could somehow solve my problems.

I knew I, alone, was responsible for that.

I just had to figure out how.

—●—

Later that night, home alone with the glow of my laptop screen the only light in my living room, I felt another rush of adrenaline.

It had been more than a month of entries in Dad's journal since he'd mentioned the Last Will and Testament he'd found while cleaning Robert J. Scooter's office. Every night, I'd translated an entry from Latin to English, just to be disappointed that it spoke only of the new branding initiative or some other boring board discussion. It was frustrating, and more than one night of work on the journal had left me feeling deflated, like I was wasting my time looking for something that didn't exist.

But that Friday night, knowing I wasn't ready to sleep, I'd translated two more entries.

And what I found in the last one stole the last shred of hope I'd been holding onto that I'd get any sleep at all.

Something has been eating at me.

It's been over a month since I found Robert's will. I should have told Patrick about it, but I didn't. The truth is, I haven't told anyone — not even my wife.

The scary part is that I'm not sure why.

All I know is something is telling me to hold onto it, and — against every moral code I'm built on — I'm considering reading it.

I know it would be wrong. I know what is inside that sealed envelope is private and important. I should hand it over to his family, over to Patrick for him to read with their lawyer.

But... curiosity is eating me alive.

And something else.

It's hard to explain, which may be why I've kept it all to myself, but... I feel drawn to this document, like I found it for a reason.

It's as if a ghost is whispering in my ear.

But maybe it's just the devil.

FIVE

SYDNEY

It was an awful thing, to look around the park in search of blunt objects that could knock my ex-husband out, but it was all I could do in that moment.

It was all I could focus on to get me through the bi-weekly bullshit parade I had to endure with him, where he told me all the ways I'd fucked up by leaving him, and I sat there and pretended to listen, all the while counting down the minutes until he was gone and it was just me and Paige again.

I longed for sole custody of my daughter just as much as I hoped it would never happen. I never wanted to have to speak to Randy again. I wished so badly to leave him in my rearview mirror as a mistake I wished I'd never made.

But the truth was, I wouldn't even if I could.

Regardless of what we had been through, if it weren't for him, my daughter wouldn't exist — and I couldn't imagine a life without her.

I also knew it would *kill* her to be told she'd never see her father again, because as much as he was a class-A prick to me, he was a damn good father to her and always had been.

And so, twice a week, we met in a public space to trade Paige back and forth, and I endured my ex-husband's crap in the name of my daughter.

"Mayor Barnett approved a nine-percent raise for me," Randy bragged, puffing out his chest as he assessed my reaction.

Of which, there was none.

"I knew he would, of course," Randy continued, eyes skirting over the park a bit as if he was still on duty before they found me again. "I mean, after all the trouble he'd found himself in with the Scooters… all the drama with his daughter not marrying that politician…" Randy clicked his tongue. "It's been a mess to clean up."

I blinked, tracing my ex's features and remembering a time when I found him attractive. I could close my eyes and go back in time to high school, to the older, more-popular boy noticing me. And though it was a bit foggy now, I could still remember when he'd flash that smile of his — a dimple on each cheek — and I'd melt into a puddle on the tile floor. I used to look into those eyes and find safety and warmth. I used to run to those arms bulging out of his uniform as if they were put on this Earth only to protect me and hold me and make me feel loved.

I used to look into those green eyes and see my soulmate. I used to run my hands through that dark, coarse hair and get so turned on I could barely wait to get him home and undressed.

There was a time when I didn't even notice that his skin was white where mine was brown, a time when I thought it didn't matter.

Now, when I looked at that man, I didn't see a man at all.

I saw a monster.

Randy had never been obtuse in the years he abused me. The times he did hit me were few and far between, and usually spawned by a fight that I could easily look back on later and say I'd played a part in. It was the control he'd exercised over me that had been the real abuse, and my skin crawled the longer I stood next to him, knowing that as free as I felt, I'd never truly be free of that control he had.

"I'm sure it has been," I finally responded. "Especially since the police department is having *such* a hard time shutting down Patrick Scooter's little underground casino. Seems like if y'all could just do that, all of this mess would be gone." I tapped my finger to my lips. "But I'm sure it's not that easy, though, huh?"

Randy's mouth flattened. I was mocking him, and he knew it. My ex-husband was so elbow-deep in the dirty political shit of this town that he had proverbial flies hovering around him in a cloud — and it had been that way since he first joined the department.

It was always my theory for why he'd moved up so quickly in rank.

They knew he'd play dirty for them.

Patrick Scooter was the son of the founder of the whiskey distillery that Stratford, Tennessee, was built on. His father, Robert, had apparently been a stand-up guy. But Patrick? Well, I had my opinions about how he ran his business — how he ran this entire *town*. And the saddest part was that he didn't work alone, because he *couldn't* work alone. If Mayor Barnett and my ex-husband would have joined forces, they could have easily taken him down.

But to them, money and reputation talked.

Everything else was null and void.

"You know, it's a shame we're not together anymore," Randy said. "We could finally get that boat you've always wanted, take Paige out to the lake for long weekends in the summer..."

"Yep, it's sure too bad," I said, not feeling bad *at all*. If Randy should have known anything by now, it was that his money didn't mean a damn thing to me. I'd even told the judge I didn't want alimony, though it was owed to me. All I asked for was child support — and even *that* was nothing, in the grand scheme of things.

"How's your little *job* going?" he asked next, changing the subject away from his unethical nature. "I heard you pulled a kid out of the game for no reason and that's why the team lost last night."

I resisted the urge to grind my teeth together or scream or shove him backward so hard that he hit his ass right on the pavement. Instead, I blinked, took a long breath, and smiled.

"Parker is one of our best running backs. It was unfortunate that he was injured in the third quarter, and I'm sure the team missed him once he was gone, but his injury was one that needed closer assessment before he could be cleared to play again. As for why we lost, I have my own opinions about that, but I recommend you talk to Coach. He's the expert."

I chuckled internally at my sass on that last comment, but when I turned to my ex, he was watching me with disdain.

Randy *hated* that I divorced him, but I knew he hated even *more* that I was working. When I got pregnant, he made it very clear that I was expected to stay home and take care of Paige and the house. *They* were my job, now. It didn't matter that I had a passion for school, for learning, for the human anatomy and the way we push our bodies past their limits in athletics. It didn't matter that I'd already had an internship at the hospital two towns over, or that there was a junior college baseball team talking to me about coming on as their athletic trainer after Paige was born.

Honestly, *I* didn't matter to him — not really. He'd made me feel that way, made me feel precious and special and doted on, like I was his entire world. The moment I said yes to being his wife and that ring was slipped onto my finger, his true colors came out.

And I was already pregnant.

I shook off the ghosts threatening to join us in that park, turning my attention to where Paige was asking yet another little boy if he wanted to play catch with her. She held her football hopefully, her eyes wide.

"Oh, trust me, I plan on talking to Jordan. I'm sure this whole town does," Randy replied. "Last night's game was a mess, and if he has any hope of bringing another championship home, he's got a lot of work to do."

"Mmm," I answered, exhausted by trying to be nice to the man who'd been my own personal hell for years. My eyes flicked to where a gaggle of women were watching me and Randy more carefully than they were their kids, and I knew without a doubt they were gossiping about the divorce, likely painting me as the villain this town wanted to believe I was.

How could anyone leave sweet Randy Kelly?

He's such a great officer, and an amazing father.

She had nothing going for her. She was lucky to have him.

Why is she even staying in Stratford if she doesn't want to be with him?

But they didn't know me.

They knew nothing.

"Well, thanks for meeting up," I said dismissively. "I'll text you on Wednesday after practice to figure out where you want to meet."

"I could just come by to pick Paige up," he offered.

"No."

He frowned. "I used to live there, too, you know. That's my house, too."

"Not anymore. Public places, Randy," I said, a warning in my eyes. "Court's orders."

An evil smirk bloomed on his face, like he knew something I didn't, but instead of revealing his secret, he just offered me a wave and headed toward his truck in the parking lot. That smirk of his was one I knew well, and it elicited a deep wave of chills that cooled me to the bones.

As soon as he pulled out of the lot, I took what felt like my first breath since he'd shown up. My body was always tense when he was near, senses on full alert — as if I might need to run or fight at any given moment. I rubbed the back of my neck with a sigh, turning to find Paige on the playground.

When I did find her, my body tensed right back up.

"Shit," I said out loud, already jogging toward where she was standing at the opposite edge of the park. She still held tight to her football, but instead of pestering some kid her own age to play catch with her, she was talking animatedly to a very tall, very shirtless, very muddy Jordan Becker.

He wore an amused smile as he listened to my daughter, huge biceps crossed over his bare chest. His eyes flicked to me when I was ten yards away, and he smiled even wider before he turned his attention back to Paige.

"... You know what I mean? And, don't even get me started on the cornerback. The twin. What's his name?"

"Boone Parson."

"Parson!" Paige said, snapping her fingers together just as I came to a stop beside her. She glanced up at me with a grin. "Hey, Mama." Then, her attention was right back on Coach. "So, yeah, Parson. Does he butter his hands before the game? Because *honestly,* there were two times during the game last night where he could have had an interception if he'd just held onto the ball. *Two times,*" she repeated, holding up her fingers in a peace sign as if it wasn't sinking in yet. "Can you imagine what that might have meant for the final score?"

"Paige Marie, what on Earth are you doing?" I asked, grabbing her hand in mine until she looked up at me. "After all the *stranger danger* drills we've had, and you run up to a grown man on the playground?"

Paige's face screwed up in confusion. "Coach isn't a stranger," she argued, looking at Jordan before she glanced back up at me with her hand stretched toward him. "It's *Coach.*"

I pursed my lips — my classic *Mom Look* — and Paige shrunk an inch.

"Yeah, Sydney," Jordan said, tapping his chest with both hands. "I'm Coach. I'm not a stranger."

"You do not know Jordan personally," I said to my daughter, ignoring Jordan completely — mostly because he was still *very* shirtless and I did not know how I felt about that. "I understand that he feels safe because he is in a position of power in a sport that you love, but you still need to be safe, okay? You do not run up to an adult that is not your family without talking to me first. Understand?"

Paige dropped her gaze to her sneakers. "Yes, ma'am."

My heart ached a little at the sight, mom guilt sneaking in as it always did. I grabbed her shoulders and squeezed, moving her in front of me. "Now, go ahead and finish telling Coach how to make the team better."

Paige threw her head back, grinning up at me as Jordan barked out a laugh. For the next ten minutes, I listened to my daughter give every opinion she had on virtually every position on the team, as well as the plays that were run and the errors that were made in last night's game.

I had to fight back laughter when she said things like *buttered his hands* and *couldn't block to save his life*, knowing full well that she picked those phrases up from watching player discussions on ESPN. And when she struggled for the right words, Jordan helped her through them, suggesting what he thought she was trying to say. I knew she'd be cataloguing this conversation, adding it all to her football talk arsenal.

When she finally paused for air, I told her to go find someone to play with while I talked to Jordan, and that we were going to head home for lunch soon.

Like a bullet, she was off.

Jordan and I watched her sprint to the jungle gym, and I hung my hands on my hips, shaking my head. "I would apologize, but I love that little girl — quirks and all."

Jordan chuckled. "I would have been offended if you did apologize. That was the best football conversation I've had in years."

I smiled, glancing over my shoulder at him. The minute our eyes met, I remembered all too well the last time they had — when we were chest to chest and breathing fire at each other in the locker room, and when his eyes had stared at my lips...

I swallowed, but immediately after that tightness in my throat, I remembered what he'd said, how he'd blamed the entire loss on me. Judging from Randy's comment, the entire town now thought the same thing.

I frowned, clearing my throat before I turned back toward the playground. "Well, I better—"

"She said she wants to play," Jordan interjected before I could excuse myself. "Did you know that? That she wants to play football?"

I sighed, watching my daughter tuck the football into her chest and run with her hand out like she was blocking a defender. "I am very aware."

"You don't seem happy about it."

"I love that she's found something she's passionate about," I explained. "But… as her mother, I worry. If you haven't noticed, there aren't many girls playing football, and there isn't a single female player in the NFL." I turned to him with a frown. "How the hell do you tell your nine-year-old daughter that her dream of playing football professionally has practically zero chance of ever happening? How do you tell her that the sport she loves is *a man's sport* and she should try something else, like basketball or softball? And, that even if she *does* try one of those and happens to fall in love with it, she *still* has a very slim chance of ever doing it professionally, because female sports are not revered in America the way male sports are?"

Jordan's face changed several times as he listened to me, and when I finally stopped talking, he shrugged. "You don't."

"What do you mean *I don't*?"

"I mean, you don't tell her any of that."

I scoffed, crossing my arms as I found Paige on the playground again. "You're not a parent. You don't understand."

"No, I'm not, and I agree that I don't fully understand what it's like to be in your shoes," he said, moving until he was in my view. I let my eyes flick to his, but the rest of him was so distracting that I ripped my gaze away as soon as it had connected. "But, what I *do* know is that there's nothing in this entire world like that feeling when you're a kid — that feeling where you can do anything, be anyone, if only you work hard enough. There may not be any precedent set, not yet, but does that mean she can't possibly be the one to set it?"

I chewed my lip, watching my daughter laugh uncontrollably as she played football.

By herself.

"What if she were the first girl to play high school football for Stratford? Or the first to play for an NFL team? Hell, right now, there are girls playing football in college. Who's to say one of *them* won't be the first to play professionally, and suddenly, those doors you thought would always be closed for Paige open up."

I allowed myself to face him fully then, searching his eyes and smirking a little when I found nothing but sincerity there. "You really believe all that, don't you?"

"I do," he said confidently. "If there's one thing I've learned from watching my mother endure what she has, it's that women are a hell of a lot stronger than anyone gives them credit for. And if Paige has her heart set on playing football?" He shrugged. "I would never be the one to tell her that she couldn't do it." He paused. "Mostly, because I hate being wrong, so I wouldn't take that chance."

I scoffed, shaking my head and letting out a long breath. "I'm scared," I admitted. "She asked me if I'd let her play next year. She turns ten in March, and for her birthday, all she wants is to go to football camp next summer and play little league."

"I think you should do it."

I swallowed, all my mom senses prickling to life under my skin. "What if she's bullied? What if she gets hurt? She's never done more than toss a football around with her father, and he hasn't even taught her much but how to line her fingers up on the laces." I looked at Jordan. "I want her to have an equal opportunity, but you and I both know that's not usually how it works."

Understanding settled in his eyes, and he nodded, lips pressed together. "Well... I understand your concern, and I can't say that none of that will happen. She will probably get bullied. And as someone who has played football all his life, I'd say chances are pretty good that she'll get hurt, too." He paused. "But, isn't that the risk we take with everything? If all we did was play it safe... would that really be living at all?"

I'd never heard so many words out of Jordan Becker's mouth than I did in that park that morning. He was always a man of quiet reserve, but it was like I'd found the secret to splitting him wide open.

Football.

My eyes trailed from where his gaze held me, down his chest, bare and glistening and smothered with a reddish, clay-like mud. His body was that of a Greek god — broad shoulders, narrow waist, calves that were bigger than my head. I used the mud as an excuse to catalogue every hard ridge and deep valley of him, all the while pretending like I wasn't suddenly aware of how hot the mid-morning August sun was.

Mud covered him in patches on his abdomen and arms, and almost every inch of the skin on his legs. It specked his cheeks and forehead, matted his short hair, even peppered the inner canals of his ears. I let my eyes stray to his basketball shorts, which I would *hate* to be responsible for cleaning, before I found his eyes again.

His stormy eyes.

"So… did you have to fight your way out of the jungle last night or something?" I cocked a brow.

Jordan chuckled, grabbing the back of his neck. "Uh… I like to run in the mud."

I blinked. "I'm sorry, you what?"

He nodded behind where I stood, and when I turned, I found his Bronco just as dirty as he was. There was a bucket of soapy water and a large sponge next to it, along with a hose from the park's free car wash station.

"I don't know," he said when I turned back to him. "I went mudding with a friend in high school when I got my first truck at sixteen, and I guess that's where it all started. I used to take my little brother a lot, and then I started going by myself. And… well… one time when I was out there, I got stuck, and I had to run back to the main pit to find someone to come dig me out. At first, it sucked. But, then… something happened. It was like… I don't know, like I had this moment of total clarity, of a complete clearing of my mind. It was just me and my body, and even though I was sore as hell the next day, it was like I'd taken a hit of some magical drug rather than gone for a run." He smiled sheepishly. "Been addicted ever since."

I smiled, and for a long pause, our eyes connected the way they had in the locker room the night before. Only this time, there was no anger, no accusation. We were standing in an open park, and yet somehow it felt like we were in the smallest room, like the oxygen we shared was limited.

"Sydney," he said, swallowing. "I—"

"Mommy!"

Before Jordan could say whatever it was he had to say, Paige flung her arms around me, panting after the sprint she'd just made toward us.

"I'm hungry," she said. "Can we go eat lunch?"

I glanced apologetically at Jordan, but he waved me off.

"We sure can. What do you feel like having?"

"Hmm…" she tapped her finger to her lips, just like I'd done earlier, and my heart swelled. I loved little moments like that, when I saw pieces of me in her. "Macaroni and cheese!"

"And how about some chicken nuggets, too," I offered.

"Yes!"

"And broccoli."

Her nose wrinkled, shoulders deflating. "*Broccoli,*" she repeated, dragging the word out. "Yuck."

I chuckled, tugging on one of her braids before I steered her toward our car. "Greens make you strong, baby girl." I tossed a look back at Jordan. "See you on Monday."

"See you," he said, then he hollered at Paige. "I'll be sure to get onto Parson for you, Paige."

"Tell him if he wants anyone to draft the defense team he plays on for their fantasy football team in the future, he better get his act together."

That made us all laugh, and with one final wave at my boss, Paige and I climbed in the car, leaving Jordan with his mud.

And me with a burning curiosity over what he was going to say before my daughter interrupted.

SIX

SYDNEY

There was a different energy in the locker room that following Monday.

Gone were the smiles and the rambunctious boys from the weeks prior. No one looked excited as they tugged on their cleats and wrapped their wrists. No one was telling a loud story about a girl or making a joke about another player's mom. Instead, each boy filed in quietly, one by one, and got dressed without much of a word to anyone else.

They weren't exactly *defeated*, either. They didn't seem sad. No, it was more of a determined silence, as if they knew before Coach said anything that they had a lot of work to do, and they'd all shown up ready to do it.

I found the quietness welcoming as I worked, helping players with their bandages and doing some soft tissue work on those who needed it. I even checked in on Parker, who was sheepish and blushing when I approached him. He apologized and seemed sincere in it, so I dismissed him, deciding to let Jordan determine what his punishment would be.

When Jordan finally made his way into the locker room to stand in the center, I found my usual corner, trying to all but disappear and just observe.

He wore a permanent frown that day, his eyebrows folding so low I wasn't sure he could see at all. The quietness somehow silenced altogether when he stood in the center of the room, as if everyone were afraid that even a sneaker squeak would set him off like a ton of missiles.

I expected him to roar and growl and put the fear of God into those boys. At the very least, I expected an epic pep talk like the one he'd given the first day we'd all walked into this place. Instead, he looked at his clipboard, flipping through pages with all eyes on him for what felt like an eternity before he lifted his gaze and said three simple words.

"On the field."

Immediately, there was a shuffle of cleats and pads and heads hung as the boys made their way outside. And I learned that afternoon what all of them already knew.

If coach was quiet, there would be pain.

Suicides. Burpees. Bear crawls. Gut busters. Snakes.

Every football player's most-hated drill was called on that day, and I watched from the sidelines with a grimace as those boys sweated and screamed and cried and fell and threw up and still, every time, they got up and got back to work.

Not a single one complained.

Not a single one asked to stop.

Jordan didn't say another word after those first three in the locker room. The other coaches led the torture, with Jordan on the sideline watching like a king over his subjects. When more than two hours had passed, he found my gaze on the sideline, and he must have seen the worry etched in my features because he finally blew the whistle that signaled the persecution to stop.

I breathed out a silent sigh of relief along with the boys, who all hit the ground in sync, panting and groaning and catching their breaths. Jordan didn't say another word before he was heading back toward the locker room, and slowly, the rest of the coaches and players did the same, shuffling in with their helmets in hand and their heads held a little higher than they had been on the way out.

When we were all settled in the locker room, I checked in with each group of boys, making sure no one needed me before I found my corner again. Jordan seemed a little less tense, but not enough to make anyone in that room feel safe yet.

"We don't get time to rest in football," he said after a while, looking around at each player. "We don't get time to recover from a loss or come down from the high of a win. Because in four short days, we'll play our next opponent, and we have to be ready."

He paused, rolling his lips together.

"I'm not angry with your performance on Friday," he started. "I'm disappointed with the attitude you all had when you walked onto that field. You thought it would be easy. You thought that win was yours, like you'd already earned it before you'd even laced up your cleats. The Raptors?" He tongued his cheek. "They went out there ready to fight for that win, and they did, and they got it. And you know what else? *They* deserved it."

A few boys shook their head, and I wasn't sure if they were disagreeing with Coach, or if they were feeling the same disappointment he was.

"Regardless of how sore you are tomorrow, we have a lot of work to do, anyway," Jordan said quietly. "Regardless of how poorly or how well you feel like you played Friday night, we have to start all over tomorrow, anyway. And regardless of how entitled you may think you are to another championship, we have to fight like we've never had one, anyway. Because that's how this game goes. No one is promised a damn thing, and whoever is the hungriest takes the W. Understand?"

Nods across the room.

Jordan sniffed, looking around at his team. "We may be disappointed, but what are we going to do on Friday?"

At first, there was no answer, but then the kicker gently said, "We're going to win, anyway."

Jordan nodded, and then he said, "We may be embarrassed, but what are we going to do on Friday?"

"We're going to win, anyway," a few more players chimed in.

The energy started as a buzz, a soft flap of bee wings, and with every new question Jordan threw at them, it grew into a thunderous roar.

"We may be beat down!"

"We're going to win, anyway!"

Jordan stood, circling the room as his voice rose. "We may have a thousand eyes on us, waiting for us to fail!"

"We're going to win, anyway!"

"We may have an opponent ready to gobble us up and spit us out and show us we ain't shit!"

"We're going to win, anyway!"

Jordan started beating a rhythm on his chest, and the boys joined in, until it was a room of bodily percussion and a hum of energy so strong I felt it in my core.

"Tomorrow, we turn it around. Tomorrow, we get back to work." Jordan pointed his quarterback and team captain directly in the chest. "Tomorrow, we fight."

A roar of cheers, every player on their feet, and then in a circle where they chanted something I couldn't quite make out. When they threw their hands up in the air, Coach called practice, and every single player walked out of that locker room a completely different kid than when they had walked in.

I couldn't hide my appreciation.

"Sydney," Jordan said as he walked past me with his eyes on his clipboard. "A word in my office?"

He'd posed it as a question, but I knew it wasn't a request at all. There was something deep and demanding in that voice, in the way he said my name. I followed him without a verbal response.

My heart raced more with every step, neck heating as I prepared all my defenses for the lashing I was sure I was about to receive. If he tried to blame that loss on me again, I had a full list of errors to throw back at him.

Mostly thanks to my daughter.

When I stepped into his office, Jordan closed the door behind us, leaving his eyes on his clipboard as he motioned for me to take a seat in the chair in front of his desk.

I swallowed, doing as he asked, and once he was seated on the other side, he abandoned his clipboard on the desk and folded his hands together, his raging eyes somehow peaceful when they found me.

"I owe you an apology."

The breath I'd been holding blew out in a sharp exhale, my defenses easing, heart calming. Jordan watched me with a wrinkle between his brows, his jaw set.

I didn't say a word.

"I don't get riled up over much," he started. "If you ask anyone in my family, anyone on this team, they'd tell you that. I am generally calm, but when it comes to football, I'll admit that I tend to lose my good senses."

Still, I stayed quiet.

"You did nothing wrong on Friday night."

I couldn't help but scoff at that, because *obviously*.

Jordan smirked. "I know you already know that, but I couldn't see clearly until later that night. All I *could* see in that moment was our loss, and I felt the pressure of the entire town's weight on my shoulders, and I am ashamed to say I crumbled beneath it."

My own shoulders softened at that, and I opened my mouth to speak but he beat me to it.

"I'm sorry for blowing up on you, for questioning your decision and trying to assert authority in a space where I hold none. This is your area of specialty, and that's why we hired you. If I ever question your decisions again, feel free to kick my ass, and I know you probably could."

I laughed out loud at that, relaxing.

Jordan smiled, too. "Seriously, Sydney. I'm sorry. Not just for that night, but for my general attitude since you walked through those doors. You've done nothing but prove yourself, and still I have this urge to... protect you, or stick up for you."

A completely new heat crept up my neck at that, and I felt it tinge my cheeks, rendering me speechless once again.

"Which is stupid, I realize," he continued, holding up his hands. "But, I think it's part of how I was raised, and just part of who I am, in general. Regardless, I've made an ass of myself, and I was hoping we could start over. Call a truce."

I smirked. "I didn't realize we were at war."

"Well, this is me throwing the white flag, anyway."

A silence fell between us, and I sat forward, finding his gaze. "Thank you for apologizing. I think it takes a great man to do so in situations like this. And, if I'm being honest and fair, you were right."

His left eyebrow shot up at that. "I was?"

"Not about everything," I clarified. "I did my job, and there was no way for me or you or *anyone* to know that Parker was faking it, but... he was. And I couldn't see past his façade. I still think I would have done everything the same, but now that I know what these boys are capable of?" I smiled sheepishly. "Let's just say I won't be so easily fooled next time."

Jordan chuckled. "They are nothing if not a handful. Still," he continued. "I wasn't right. *You* were right. Yes, I know these boys, but regardless, you did exactly what you were supposed to do. We can't take injuries lightly, and I needed you to remind me of that. Parker took responsibility for his part, and he paid for it today on the field, but in the end, you did the right thing. So, don't consider yourself as easily fooled. Consider yourself as a professional trainer who I'm glad to have on my team, and thankful you put me in my place."

We shared a smile, and with that white flag waving between us, the truce was signed.

I stood, taking that smile as my cue that our conversation was over and I needed to wrap up work, but before I could take a step, he spoke again.

"I've been thinking," he said, standing with me. "About Paige. And... if you'd be open to it... maybe I could work with her. Teach her a few things, so that when she walks into summer camp next year, she'll be prepared."

My heart swelled and then fell into the pit of my stomach so fast that I was confused as to whether I thought that was the sweetest thing I'd ever heard, or the most terrifying.

"I'm trying to turn her *off* from football," I reminded him with a smile I hoped seemed casual and non-affected, crossing my arms. "Not provide her with a personal coach and source of encouragement."

"It's your call," he said with a shrug, sliding his hands into the pockets of his shorts. "But, one thing I've figured out with kids like her? Once they decide something and set their mind to it, there's no stopping them."

My smile slipped, lips pressing together as worry flittered through me like the wings of a thousand birds.

"You can either fight her on it, or you can embrace her dream and support it. Whether it hurts her or not, I can tell you just from hearing her talk on Saturday that she's not giving up on football — no matter how much you may wish she would."

I bit my lip, and Jordan rounded the desk as soon as he saw the anxiety I could no longer hide. His strong hand reached out, touching my elbow and holding it as he offered me a smile.

"No pressure, okay? Just think about it."

His thumb rubbed my forearm where he held me, and I looked down, marveling at the tenderness concealed in those calloused hands before he pulled away.

He swallowed when I looked up at him, and the energy shifted in the same way it had Friday night. But before I could latch onto it to dissect it, he stepped back, picking up his clipboard and effectively dismissing me.

"See you tomorrow," he said.

And I walked in a daze back to my office with every warning bell in my system ringing in sync.

SEVEN

SYDNEY

The week flew by in a cyclone of work and practice and evenings spent with Paige. I didn't even mind meeting up with Randy on Wednesday to swap, because all my energy and emotions were tied up in the team and the upcoming away game against the North Valley Hornets.

Monday's practice and talk from coach had changed everything, throwing the team into a new orbit that I couldn't help but marvel at. Every single player was fired up and ready to work when we met back in that locker room on Tuesday, and all week long, I watched with timid fascination as they somehow worked twice as hard as they had the first week and a half that I'd watched them before our first game.

Something had clicked, and no one was messing around anymore.

Of course, with harder work came more injuries.

I found myself busier and busier with each passing practice, and I had my eyes on almost every player for something or another. There were ice baths and compression boot treatments and soft tissue sessions and all the while, I was urging the players to rest as much as they could, knowing they wouldn't for a single second. I'd given out so many ice packs that our ice machine couldn't even keep up, and I had to run to the store to grab as many twenty-pound bags as our local grocery store had on hand.

So, when we loaded up on the bus to head to the game Friday night, I felt just as fired up and determined as the players and coaches did.

I sat in the front seat behind the driver, smiling to myself as I listened to the players talk about girls and cars and sports and video games and all the things that made high school boys tick. I smiled because I could easily remember a time when my worries had been as simple, too, and part of me yearned for that innocence.

Once everyone was accounted for and coach gave his speech, reminding the boys that we still had a game to play and they needed to be focused for our short, thirty-minute bus ride, we were off.

TK and Coach Pascucci sat together in the front seat opposite mine, already huddling over their clipboards and murmuring softly about plays, so Jordan took the open seat next to me. He let out a breath as we pulled out of the school's parking lot, dropping his clipboard between us and rubbing his eyes.

"Nervous?" I asked with a smile.

"More like *exhausted*," he said. "Is this what parenting feels like? Because if it is, I'm thankful I never went down that road."

I full-on laughed at that. "Oh, this is *nothing* compared to being a parent. Trust me."

"How do you handle it?"

I shrugged. "Yoga, gardening, running — anything where I can be alone with my thoughts and relieve stress. And I try to keep as much of myself present so that I don't lose who I was before I became a mother, if that makes sense. It's a big reason why I was excited to get back to work."

Jordan nodded. "Why didn't you work before?" Immediately, he paled. "I'm sorry if that was rude to ask. I just mean... did you want to wait until Paige was a certain age before you worked, or...?"

I attempted a smile, though my insides were on fire now with flashes of Randy striking like lightning in my veins.

"It wasn't exactly my choice not to work," I said, carefully.

Jordan's expression hardened, the gold around his irises catching the rays of sun as they filtered in the bus windows through the trees we passed.

Everything inside me begged him not to press, and without a word exchanged, he seemed to understand.

"Yoga, huh?" he asked instead, crossing his ankle over the opposite knee. He was dressed in black athletic slacks and a red polo with STRATFORD FOOTBALL embroidered on the pocket. The sleeves of it hugged his biceps, the hem of it tucked into the band of his pants where a belt was fastened.

He looked professional and somehow dangerous, too.

"Yep," I answered, nudging him. "Not as fun as running in the mud, I'd wager, but it's my own brand of release."

"I've never tried it," he confessed, popping a piece of gum into his mouth. I'd learned it was his game ritual, to chew gum, and I wondered if it helped him keep from blowing his top. He offered me a piece, too, but I declined. "Maybe we could do it with the guys during a Thursday practice sometime, if you'd be willing to lead us," he suggested. "Lord knows we could all learn to relax a little more."

"Maybe," I agreed with a smile, and then I turned to look out the window, because emotions I worked hard to keep down were bubbling up like a spring.

Jordan left me to gaze and think, pulling his iPad out and leaning over the aisle to talk to the coaches while I watched our little town disappear and fields of nothing take its place.

I loved the country.

Occasionally, we'd pass a house or a barn or a little fruit stand, but for the most part, there wasn't much between us and North Valley, and I surrendered to the solemn depths of my mind as we drove. Because it hit me in that very moment with Jordan's question that I was finally here, I was finally on the other side of the hell I'd endured, standing on my own two feet.

I was working.

I was taking care of my daughter.

I was remembering who I was.

I was living.

And, for the life of me, I couldn't decide why that made me want to scream in joy as much as it made me want to cry.

Thankfully, I didn't have time to dwell on it. As soon as we pulled up at North Valley's field, that same energy I'd felt in practice all week swept over us like a strong summer wind, and we got down to business.

There was something about Friday night football in Tennessee, an energy unlike any other in the entire world.

It was almost impossible to explain it to anyone who hadn't experienced it themselves, that cocktail of anticipation and excitement with a twist of anxiety. The passion for these teams ran deep in the blood of not just the students, but the entire town. There were painted faces and giant handmade signs and whistles and cowbells and synchronized cheers.

When it was game time, nothing else mattered.

Not for any of us.

I scanned the stands for my daughter, and when I found her sitting next to Randy with her wide eyes scanning our players as they warmed up, I smiled. She was pointing to each one of them and rambling on and on to her father — likely about who she thought should play, what their stats were, what part they played in last week's loss, and what they would need to do to turn it around.

Randy nodded and listened, but I didn't miss how much his eyes watched *me* instead of the players.

I was glad I took that moment before the game to find my daughter in the crowd, to watch the excitement on her face, because from the moment that first whistle blew, I didn't have another spare minute.

The boys played hard.

They had something to prove.

And there wasn't a single moment of that game that I wasn't wrapping or icing or working on sprains or joints or helping someone stretch out or checking them for concussions or watching a loud collision from the sidelines while I silently prayed nothing was broken in the process. I ran on and off the field more times than I could count, players on the ground with the stands silent until we both stood in unison and I got them to the sidelines.

It was a long and grueling game.

But when the final seconds on the scoreboard ticked down, we had twenty-eight points, and the Hornets had twenty-five.

We won.

It was an explosion of excitement from our sideline, benched players and all the coaches running out on the field to meet the team. I laughed from beside the bench, watching the high fives and hugs — not just with our own players, but with the other team's, too. It was perhaps my favorite part of football, that camaraderie that was shown to the opponent at the end.

"Mama!"

I turned to find Paige leaning over the railing of the stands, and I rushed to her, jumping up to high five her outstretched hand.

"We won, we won!"

I chuckled. "We did, didn't we?"

"If you ask me, it's because Coach and I had a talk." She looked up at her dad then, who was narrowing his eyes at me. "I know what I'm talking about when it comes to football, don't I, Daddy?"

"No one knows more, munchkin," he said, but his eyes still bore into me. I stood straighter, which I knew he hated.

He was so used to me cowering under that gaze.

"She told me you guys ran into Jordan at the park after I left," he mused. "How convenient."

I had to fight so hard not to roll my eyes, I barely had enough strength to respond. "He was there washing his car. Paige saw him and ran over to light into him about the game." I turned my attention back to her. "Which worked, apparently."

Her smile doubled, and she bounced a little, her wild curls hopping with her. "Can we stick around to talk to

Coach, Daddy?" She tugged on his sleeve. "Please, please, please!"

"They've got to load up on the busses, sweetheart," he said to her, rubbing her head to pacify her as she pouted. "And we've got important business, too."

"We do?"

He nodded, lowering himself nearer to her ear and whispering, "Ice cream."

Paige lit up at that, squealing and bouncing for a new reason. Randy chuckled and I couldn't help but laugh, too.

When our eyes met, we shared a brief moment of understanding.

A brief insight into what it felt like to look at each other *before*.

But as soon as it had come, it was gone again.

I hardened my gaze, his laugh slipped off, and with a quick hug and instructions to *be good*, Paige grabbed his hand and they were gone.

It was complete chaos for Jordan after the game ended. He was talking to local news reporters and shaking hands with administration and doing business with scouts and stealing players away for brief moments of either criticism or praise or both. It wasn't until we were back on the bus that he had a moment to himself, and as soon as he sat down next to me, he blew out a breath.

This time, it was with a smile.

"Congratulations, Coach," I said, nudging him with my elbow. "Looks like our year isn't hopeless yet."

"It's just one game," he said, falling back into the seat like he was wiped. "But *damn*, does it feel good to win."

He turned to look at me as the bus pulled out of the lot, and the stadium lights played with the shadows on his face until we slipped into darkness on the country road. I expected him to turn away, to give me a high five and lean over the aisle to talk to the other coaches about the game, but instead, he just stayed that way.

Watching me — like he was waiting for something, or like he was on the cusp of discovering something he'd missed all along.

"You're damn good at your job, did you know that?"

His words surprised me, and I couldn't fight off the blush that shaded my cheeks. I shrugged. "Just doing what needs to be done."

"No," he said, shaking his head. "Don't do that. Don't downplay what you did out there like anyone could do it. This is only your second game, and already, the boys on this bus feel more comfortable with you than they ever did with any other trainer we've had. Do you understand what that means?"

"Maybe it's because I'm a woman," I offered as a joke. "I give off those motherly, nurturing vibes."

"You do," he agreed. "But, that's not why they trust you. They trust you because you know what you're doing, and you prove it time and time again when you take them back for treatment. They know that if you say it's not safe to play, it's not. And if you say they're going to be okay, they will be. And if you say to rest or to ice or to do therapy, they know it's not just bullshit talk to fill the space. It's necessary." Jordan paused, frowning a bit. "You are a very impressive trainer, Sydney."

Emotion swelled in the middle of my chest like a lotus flower, sprouting up from the sticky mud that had stifled my self-pride for years. I hated how hot my ears were in that moment, but I loved the way it felt to have my hard work and talent acknowledged.

"Thank you, Jordan," I said — softly, almost a whisper. My eyes found his. "Really."

One corner of his mouth tugged up a centimeter, but otherwise, his expression remained the same. He nodded, still watching me, his eyes flicking back and forth between mine.

Those eyes that were too mesmerizing not to watch in return.

The air on that bus liquified, as if I could reach out and touch it and send a ripple flowing between where I sat and where Jordan was next to me. I felt it weighing in on me, warm and heavy, my breaths labored under the pressure.

I cleared my throat, ripping my gaze from his. I picked at my chipped nail polish a moment — polish Paige had painted on the night before I took her to her dad's. I'd found it funny and endearing that my football-obsessed little girl wanted to paint our nails together, and I smiled at the memory.

"You know," I said, picking a fleck of the red off before I looked at Jordan again. "Paige insinuated that you have *her* to thank for tonight's win."

"Did she now?" Jordan barked out a laugh, crossing his ankle over his knee. "Well, she was definitely part of it. You know, it was her idea to try Ingram at running back. She saw his speed and protection of the ball when he was warming up for last week's game." Jordan shook his head, as if he couldn't believe he'd missed it. "He's so young, you know. Freshman. I just didn't think he could handle that kind of pressure yet."

"And then he gets two touchdowns in his first game as a starter," I mused with a whistle. "Damn, my girl is smart."

Jordan chuckled. "That she is."

Darkness fell over both of us as we slipped past the last little part of North Valley, and I knew even though I couldn't see it, that same country I'd stared at on the way over was outside our windows now.

"I've been thinking," I said, biting my lip just in case I wanted to change my mind before I continued. "About what you said. About Paige."

"Yeah?"

I nodded. "I was wondering... would you possibly like to come by for lunch tomorrow? I hoped maybe you could sit her down, *really* explain what it would mean for her to play football. And I mean *really* explain it — the good, the bad, the ugly. I want her to understand everything she's getting herself into." I swallowed, the instinct I'd gained as soon as I became a mother flaring in my gut. "And if she's still serious after that... well... will you help her?"

Jordan smiled, but I balked instantly.

"I mean, if and when you have time, of course," I said quickly. "I know it's football season and you've got classes and practices and games, and a social life, I'm sure. I just... the other day, in your office, you had mentioned —"

"I'd love to."

Jordan was still smiling as I blew out a breath. "Yeah?"

He nodded with his eyebrows pinched together, like it was obvious. "Are you kidding? That girl's got grit. If she can play even half as well as she can chew my ass, I think she's got a real shot of making some serious moves in football."

I laughed a little too hard, covering my mouth with my hand as I shook my head. "I'm scared," I admitted.

"That just means you're a good mom," he said, and as if it was normal and casual and damn near instinctive, his hand reached over and wrapped around my knee with a squeeze.

It was a friendly touch, one of admiration and assurance, which was why I nearly squeaked out loud when a bolt of violent heat sprang from his touch up the inside of my thigh.

We both looked at where he touched me, then at each other, and in the same breath, he pulled his hand away and straightened while I tucked my hair behind one ear and looked out the window.

I squeezed my eyes shut, knowing I should respond, that I should say something — *anything*. But when I finally turned back to him and opened my mouth, he was already leaning over the aisle, a clipboard between him and Coach Pascucci as they discussed the game.

I internally groaned, letting my head fall against the window. The glass was slightly cool, a sign that fall was approaching — slowly, but surely.

My skin that touched it, however, was still burning hot.

EIGHT

JORDAN

One thing I had learned about Sydney in her time on the team was that she was tough.

She wasn't one of those people who had to try hard to give off that vibe, either. It wasn't as if she walked around scowling all the time, or puffed out her chest, or showed her scars and told battle stories. She didn't bark at anyone who came near her, and she didn't use force to get her point across when she had one to make.

She was effortlessly strong, in a way that was natural and pure.

I knew it from the moment she walked into my office. I saw it in the way she held her chin high, in the way her stoic eyes held mine, in the way she spoke — calmly and evenly, always. She didn't have to tell me that she'd been through shit for me to see it, and she didn't have to prove to me that she could handle herself.

Somehow, I knew that, too.

Last night, I watched her run on and off the field, her demeanor serious as she assessed each injury and determined next steps. She did it so quickly and confidently, and the players trusted her implicitly.

When I thought of Sydney, I thought of everything hard and resilient — rock, stone, iron, maybe even diamond.

Which was precisely why I was surprised on Saturday when I parked my Bronco in the driveway of a very soft, very feminine, very welcoming and modest two-story house on the north end of town.

It was a gray house with a yellow door and white trim. A colorful variety of stones paved the way from the driveway to the front porch, which was surrounded by a stunning garden of flowers and plants. I smiled at the three rocking chairs on the porch — two that were much like the ones my mom had, and one that was the same yellow as the door and about half the size of the other two.

It was exactly the right size for Paige.

There were remnants of a chalk drawing on the porch, too — a dragon and a castle, I thought. And as I lifted my fist to knock, I chuckled at the handmade Tennessee Titans wreath on the door.

"I'll get it!" I heard a tiny voice yell before there was the distinct sound of bare feet barreling toward the door. In the next moment, it flew open, and Paige grinned up at me with a crooked smile.

"Hey, Coach!"

"Hey, yourself."

"Mama said we're going to play football today!"

"That's not what I said," I heard from somewhere in the house, and I smirked, bending until I was level with Paige.

"We're going to *talk* about football, yes," I corrected, but before she could pout, I lowered my voice to a whisper. "But, I'd wager we'll end up playing some, too."

"I can already see you two will be the death of me," Sydney announced as she swung around the corner behind Paige — who was snickering now, like we had a secret.

My smile faltered at the sight of *Sydney at Home*, who looked *nothing* like *Sydney at Work*.

Her hair that was normally pulled into a bun on top of her head was wavy and unruly, pulled out of her face by a bright orange headband tied at the top of her forehead. It wasn't curly like her daughter's, but it was wild in its own way, barely tamed by that scrap of orange fabric. And the way she carried herself was different somehow, as if she were strolling in the park with nowhere to be. That guard she always hid behind, that shield that was always up seemed to not even exist at all.

She smiled at me as she wiped her hands on a rag, a tired smile on her face — along with a few smudges of dirt. I did a double-take at her overalls and gardening belt, my curiosity climbing as I noted the dirt stains on her knees.

"It looks like *you're* the one who's been playing football," I teased.

Sydney chuckled, opening the door wider so I could step inside the foyer with them. Paige was staring up at me with a giddy smile, bouncing slightly.

"I've been working in the vegetable garden out back," Sydney said, leading me through the foyer and into an open space that seemed to serve as the living room and dining room, both. College Game Day was on the television, and in the kitchen just off to our right, there sat a basket full of the evidence of that garden's existence. It was on the counter next to two dirty gardening gloves and a sheer.

"Wow," I mused, walking straight to it and picking up a carrot from the top. "Carrots, cauliflower, Brussel sprouts..." I paused, picking up a familiar herb. I turned to her. "Basil?"

Sydney nodded, folding her arms where she watched me. "You didn't call it a pile of leaves," she commented. "I'm impressed."

I chuckled, but before I could ask another question about her garden, Paige sighed, flopping down at the dining room table. "Mom's got a garden. There are carrots and stuff in it. Yeah, yeah, yeah, okay, we've covered it now, can we *please* get down to business here?"

She clasped her hands together in a plea, eyes wide and little feet dangling under her chair.

"Paige Marie, that was rude," Sydney said at the same time I burst into laughter.

"No, no, it's okay," I assured her, taking a seat across the table from Paige. "I like the excitement. You really do love football, don't you?"

Paige's face leveled, the most serious I'd ever seen her. "More than anything in the *world*, Coach."

"Except her mother, of course," Sydney said, kissing her daughter's hair — which was presently a wild fluff of half curl, half wave.

Paige waved her off with a groan, but smiled, too, and Sydney hung her hands on her hips.

"I'll pour us some lemonade and start working on lunch while you two *get down to business*," she said, offering me an apologetic smile before she made her way to the cabinet next to the sink. My eyes followed her up until the very moment she stepped on her tiptoes to reach the glasses, and I noticed the smooth, brown skin exposed between her tiny tank top and the overalls she wore over them. That gap between them gave me a view I'd never had before of her slim waist, and her hips as she wiggled to reach the top shelf.

I swallowed, tearing my eyes away and back to Paige. Who was watching me with a smirk.

"So," she said, glancing at her mom and back at me pointedly. "*Football.*"

"Football," I echoed, ignoring her smile that said she knew something I was trying to hide. "Let me ask you something, Paige — do you get your feelings hurt easily?"

"Nope," she answered quickly, nodding once before she sat up straighter in her chair. "I'm tough, Coach. I can handle anything."

"Anything?" I asked, leaning toward her as Sydney dropped off two glasses of lemonade on the table. She smiled at me before making her way to the basket on the counter, and again, my eyes followed her, watching her unpack each ingredient with care.

"Anything," Paige said, knocking on the table to pull my attention back to her.

"So, if you show up at football camp next summer, and all the boys on the team make fun of you and call you names and shun you out of their groups and make you feel like you don't belong, you can handle it?"

Paige rolled her eyes. "Please. I'm only nine years old and I know that boys are stupid and their opinions don't count for anything."

Sydney high-fived her daughter as she walked past to turn the volume down on the television.

I chuckled. "And if you go out there and work twice as hard as those boys who are teasing you, and end up being twice as talented, and yet, your coach still doesn't give you the same playing time as they get... can you handle that, too?"

Paige's confidence slipped. "That doesn't sound fair."

"It's not, but it's a very real possibility that could happen," I said, honestly. "And there's also a very big possibility that not only would you isolate yourself from having many friends by being a girl playing football, but that you could make a lot of sacrifices, work really, *really* hard, and still not be able to play past high school. And, even if you do get to play in college, as of this very moment, there is nowhere for you to advance to play football professionally."

Paige's eyes widened with every word I said, her little eyebrows tugging inward. It broke my heart to see it, and I could tell by the way Sydney watched us over her shoulder where she was cutting up the carrots that it worried her, too.

But, this is what she wanted. She wanted me to be real with Paige.

And I would be.

"I'm giving this all to you straight, Paige, because I believe you can handle it," I said, folding my hands on the table. "You want to know what else I believe?"

Paige didn't respond.

"I believe you *will* be better than a lot of boys on the teams you play on, and I believe you *will* excel in football. I think you will learn some of life's biggest lessons from it, and that it will become a part of you — a *permanent* part of you, one you'll never be able to erase. I think you'll breathe it in like it's the only oxygen that keeps your lungs working, and I think that no matter what challenges you face, you'll overcome them."

I leaned closer, leveling my eyes with hers.

"And more than anything, I believe you can have a happy and amazing life playing football. I believe you *could* play in high school, and college, and — truly — maybe even in a professional league. Now, I don't know what that would look like — not yet — but I believe just by your passion alone that it could happen. And if it doesn't work out that way?" I shrugged, smiling as I tapped her nose. "I know for a *fact* that you'd make a damn good coach."

Paige giggled at that, but as soon as her smile had appeared, it slipped away again. "Why can't girls play football professionally?"

Sydney and I exchanged glances, and she wiped her hand on her apron before walking over to her daughter. She bent down, swept her hair out of her face, and looked her in the eyes. "There are many reasons, Paigey. Some argue that women would get hurt, and it's a very valid argument. As you know from watching, there's a lot of danger with concussions and other life-altering injuries — whether you're a girl or a boy." Sydney sighed, glancing at me before she addressed her daughter again. "But, there are no rules that say a woman *can't* play in the NFL."

"Really?" Paige lit up.

"Really," I chimed in. "And, there are already *many* women working for the NFL as coaches, advisors, agents, trainers — like your mom — and more. There are a lot of ways to make a life in football."

We both watched her as she digested it all, and I resisted the urge to say more. It was a lot to throw on a nine-year-old. Hell, most kids her age had no *idea* what they wanted to do with their lives, and even if they *thought* they knew, they were likely to change their mind down the road.

But, I knew that look in Paige's eyes when she talked about football. It was the same one I'd seen reflected in my own growing up.

This wasn't just a phase for her.

It was everything.

After a long while, Paige looked at her mom, and then at me, and with determination in her eyes, she nodded. "I know it's going to be hard, and I know the boys are going to be tough on me, but I don't care." Her little hand balled into a fist on the table. "I want to play football."

I smiled, glancing at Sydney who looked over her shoulder at me with a mixture of pride and anxiety. I nodded slightly, locking my gaze on hers with a silent promise that I would help Paige, and that I would take care of her. And Sydney nodded back, as if she understood.

As if she trusted me unreservedly.

For reasons I couldn't grasp, I wanted to hold onto her gaze, to memorize the trust in her eyes and analyze the depth of it.

But, I tore my eyes away and looked at her daughter, who was watching me without so much as a single ounce of hesitation or concern for what she'd just decided.

"Okay, then," I said, standing. "Let's play."

—•—

Paige was just as tough as her mother.

She was also just as talented.

We spent every hour of sunlight in Sydney's backyard with a football, breaking only to eat lunch and to run in for bathroom breaks. From the moment we stepped foot on the grass and Paige showed me how she learned to line up her fingers on the laces of the ball and throw a perfect spiral, I knew I hadn't been wrong in my assumptions about her.

Football was ingrained in that little girl. It was already a part of who she was, and I knew without a doubt it would be a part of who she'd become, too.

Regardless of that belief, I didn't go easy on her.

We ran drills just like the ones I knew she'd run in football camp. I pushed her to her limits, testing her in everything from agility and speed to stamina and strength. When I asked what her top three desired playing positions were, she answered with quarterback, wide receiver, and kicker.

Three very different positions with very different sets of challenges.

Still, I gave her a crash introduction course in each, running throwing drills and catching drills and making her kick over and over until she started to complain that her foot was sore.

Sydney worked in her garden, did yoga on the porch, read over her notes in her training binder on our players, and read a thriller I recognized from Logan's bookshelf — all while keeping a close eye on us. When the sun began to make its descent, casting Paige's brown curls in a golden light, Sydney finally called it.

"Alright, you two," she said, standing as she slipped a bookmark between the pages of her book to hold her place. "I think that's enough for today."

I expected Paige to whine and beg for more time, but she put her hands on her knees, panting for a long moment before she stood and smiled at me victoriously.

"How'd I do, Coach?" she asked, squinting against the setting sun.

I ruffled her hair, the roots of it damp with sweat. "Killed it."

"Can we do this again?" she asked with wide eyes.

I glanced at Sydney, who worried her lip a little before nodding.

"Of course," I answered Paige, holding out my hand for a high five. "But you better work on these drills by yourself, too. Don't wait for me to get you going."

"I will! I promise!"

Sydney joined us from the porch, resting her hand on her daughter's shoulder. "Alright, Paigey. Go get washed up for dinner."

"Are you staying for dinner, too?" Paige asked me, folding her hands together. "Oh! And maybe to watch the Vols game, too?"

"Paige..." Sydney warned.

"Oh, Mama, *please*," Paige said again, turning her begging eyes to her mother.

Sydney pulled on one of Paige's curls, letting it bounce back into place before she spoke. "Jordan has been with us all day, sweetie. I'm sure he wants to get home."

"I don't mind."

The words came out too quickly, too honestly, and Sydney's eyes locked on mine as Paige tugged on her overalls.

"See? He *wants* to. Pleeeeeeease." She folded her hands together again and bounced, eyes hopeful and bottom lip protruded.

Sydney watched me for a moment longer, a question in her eyes I couldn't decipher before she addressed her daughter again with a sigh. "You're too cute for your own good."

"Yes!" Paige said, knowing without an affirmative answer that she'd won. She bounded off into the house without another look. "I'll shower fast and put the game on!"

She was gone before I could answer, and I chuckled, sliding my hands into my pockets. "I'm sorry about that," I said to Sydney, a little embarrassed. "I should have pulled you aside to ask you if you wanted company before I agreed like that."

"No, it's okay," she said just as quickly as I had, and I smiled at the sight of a blush on her cheeks. "I don't get the chance to cook for guests very often. I like it."

"Yeah?"

She nodded.

For a long while, we stood there, toe to toe, in her backyard as the sun lit up the sky with vibrant pinks and violets, her eyes on mine and mine watching her, in return.

"Need some help in the kitchen?" I finally offered.

At that, she gave a short laugh out of her nose. "I'd love that," she said, but one brow quirked high as she let her eyes roam down the length of me. "But you need a shower first, too."

"What? Am I a little sweaty?" I asked, inching toward her.

Sydney's smile flattened, her eyes wide before they narrowed in warning. "Jordan... don't you dare."

"Oh, come on," I teased, reaching out for her before she could escape. She squeaked and writhed in my grasp as I crushed her in a hug. "See? I'm perfectly dry!"

"Ewww," she dragged out, swatting at me in laughter until I let her go. She shook her head, shoving me toward the door. "Shower. Now. Before I change my mind and kick you out."

I was still thinking about the way she felt in my arms, about her eyes, and her smile, and about the way that smile filled her entire face that afternoon as I washed away the day in her shower. I had to wash with her shower gel, which smelled like her, and dry with a towel that did, too.

And it was when I had my nose in that towel, when I took a deep inhale and soaked in her scent, that I realized what I was doing.

My eyes shot open, and I saw myself reflected in the foggy mirror in her bathroom.

What the hell are you doing?

You shouldn't stay for dinner.

You shouldn't have been that close to Sydney.

You should leave.

Now.

I knew why I wanted to stay for dinner, regardless of whether I was ready to admit it to myself or not. It was because I didn't want to leave *Sydney at Home*. It was because I'd had a glimpse inside her life, and now I wanted to know more.

I wanted to know *everything*.

It was because I liked the way she felt in my arms, and the way she smelled, and that she had a garden and that she did yoga on her back porch.

It was because I found her beautiful, in every way possible, and I wanted to be with her for as long as I could be.

My expression hardened at my reflection in the mirror. Everything about the man staring back at me screamed question after question, warning after warning, accusation after accusation. It was a dangerous line I was tiptoeing on. There didn't need to be a written rule for me to know that there were lines between me and Sydney that couldn't be crossed — not with me as head coach and her as the athletic trainer.

But who said it had to be more than a friendship?

I could stay for dinner. I could get to know Sydney, admire her beauty and loveliness without acting on it.

I wasn't doing anything wrong.

I searched the eyes I'd searched my entire life for a long moment, something between shame and stubborn denial washing over me the longer I did.

But before it could permeate my skin, I ripped my gaze away.

I finished drying quickly, ignoring the voice inside me that always warned me when I was on the precipice of doing something stupid. I told myself I wasn't breaking any rules, that I had no intentions other than to be helpful and polite. I told myself I was a welcome guest, that Sydney and I worked together and could be friends, that I was here to help *Paige*.

Surely, that was okay.

I repeated my excuses over and over as I dressed in a pair of basketball shorts and a t-shirt I always kept in my car just in case — namely for when I went to Mom's straight after practice or a game and showered there.

Then, I threw my towel in Sydney's dirty hamper and joined her in the kitchen, ready to help.

I didn't look at my reflection again.

NINE

SYDNEY

It was nine-oh-eight when I popped the cork on a bot-tle of red wine, and I sighed out loud at the sound of it, filling my glass a little past the line of what was ladylike before I held up the bottle with my eyes on my guest.

"Wine?" I asked.

Paige was finally in bed, conked out cold after what was likely the most exciting day she'd had in her young life. She was still talking animatedly about football and how her day with Jordan had gone when I'd tucked her in, and I'd listened to her intently, even as she spoke through her yawns. When I'd paused at her door to tell her I loved her before turning out the light, she'd taken the opportu-nity to melt my heart.

"This was the best day ever, Mom," she'd said before she closed her eyes and rolled over. "Thank you."

I couldn't help the smile that little girl brought out in me with that statement, nor could I disagree with her that it had been a good day.

But, I was still exhausted — physically and mentally

— and my anxiety had worked my nerves to the point of being nearly shredded.

Mama needed a drink.

Jordan smirked at my offer, leaning his elbows on the counter from where he stood on the other side of it. He still looked freshly showered even a couple hours later, his hair slightly damp, skin clean, the faint scent of my body-wash wafting off him. I flushed a little bit at the thought of him naked in my shower, but turned my attention back to the bottle in my hand and away from my boss's nudity.

"Any chance you have something a little stronger?" he asked.

I gave him an incredulous look before I set the bottle of wine down and pressed up onto my tiptoes to reach into the cabinet above my sink, retrieving a bottle of Scooter Whiskey.

In this town, *everyone* had a bottle somewhere in their house.

Jordan's smile climbed at the sight. "That's more like it. Now," he said, rounding the counter to join me in the kitchen. "What are the chances you've got an orange, some cherries, some—"

"Simple syrup and some bitters?" I chuckled, retrieving two glass tumblers from the cabinet next. I shoved the cork back into the bottle of wine I'd just opened as best I could. "I knew I liked you for a reason. Two old fashioneds coming right up."

His mouth dropped. "I was totally kidding. You really have everything to make one?"

"It's one of my dad's favorite drinks, too," I explained with a shrug. "I don't know when I started doing it, but I always have the ingredients on hand — just in case."

Jordan watched me silently as I made our drinks, and when the final garnish of the cherries were dropped into the glasses, I handed one to him and held the other up in a toast.

"I can't believe I'm saying this," I said with a sigh. "But, to football."

"To football," Jordan echoed, holding up his own glass. "And to you — may God give you the strength to keep up with that little girl in there."

"And send me a few angels to help, too."

We clinked our glasses together with soft laughter, each of us making our own noises of appreciation after the first sip.

A moment of silence fell between us after that, and I kept my eyes on my glass, but could feel Jordan watching me.

"You really are a great mom, you know," he said. "I should know. I have a great mom, too."

I smiled. "I'm just trying to keep my head above water."

"Do you feel a little better about her playing football after today?"

"No," I answered quickly and honestly on a laugh. My eyes found his, then. "I mean, I guess I feel *marginally* better, because I know she has you to help, and I feel like she at least understands what she's getting into. But... I don't think she'll *really* understand until she's in it. You know?"

Jordan nodded.

"I mean... I don't have to explain this to you. But, it's already going to be tough for her in ways that aren't fair or reasonable. She has hair that doesn't straighten and skin that's too dark to be white but too light to be black." I swallowed, picking at what was left of the polish Paige had painted on my nails. "In this town, and sadly, in a *lot* of towns, that's something that will create hurdles for her."

Jordan let out a long exhale, his eyebrows pinched together as he chewed on what I'd said. "I understand what you're saying. Trust me, I grew up in an all-white family in practically an all-white town. I get it." He stood a little straighter, tilting his head before his eyes found mine. "But, she will persevere through any challenges she faces. And I do mean *any* of them. I know that just after spending one afternoon with her, and I'd wager you know it, too."

Warmth spread through my chest like a spring on a summer day. "I will never understand how she got so tough."

Jordan scoffed. "That one's easy. You're her mother." We shared a smile. "So, since we're on the topic, what exactly *is* your nationality?"

I chuckled, because it was a question I got with everyone's eyes when they first saw me. They didn't understand the color of my skin or the shape of my eyes and most of all, how they existed in the same human.

I nodded to the dining room table behind Jordan, where we both took a seat before I answered. "Well, my mother is Filipino," I started. "My father is a Neopolitan ice cream cone, as he always liked to put it. His father is African American, his mother is a Caucasian woman from many different descendants." I shrugged. "So, I'm somewhere between all of that. What about you?"

Jordan was smiling as he listened, but the curve faded when I asked him to tell me his background. He scratched his neck, looking out the sliding glass door at the dark backyard. "I wish I knew."

A long, quiet moment stretched between us, and I glanced at where his hands rested on the table — one wrapped around his drink, the other beside it with nothing to hold. I debated reaching out to let him know I was there, but thought better of it, standing to make my way over to the Bluetooth speaker in my living room, instead. I put on a mellow playlist before rejoining him at the table.

"How old were you when the Beckers adopted you?"

"I was a baby," he answered quickly, and I noted the way his shoulders relaxed now that the conversation was on the family he'd been with all his life instead of the one that created him. "I don't remember anything before I was with them. Honestly, I didn't really understand that I *wasn't* truly their son — not until we went to the lake for the first time."

I tilted my head, confused.

"I was five. It was the summer before kindergarten. I don't remember a lot, but I do remember that Noah was only a baby, one or so, and we went out to the lake with Mom and Dad. I was swimming with some other kids, and one of them pushed me into the water and was making fun of me. He asked me where my parents were so I could run and cry to them, and I pointed to where Mom and Dad were on the shore with Noah, and the kids all laughed. They said, *'That can't be your parents. They're white!'*"

My stomach knotted so tightly I placed a hand over my gut to soothe it.

Jordan just shrugged, wiping the sweat from his glass before he took a sip. "So, on the ride home, I asked Mom why I looked so different from her and Dad and Noah. And I'll never forget that look they shared, the one that told me I'd missed something, that there was something being hidden from me."

Jordan paused for a moment, and I took a sip of my old fashioned, waiting.

"They told me everything that night, and from that moment on, I understood. And it didn't make me feel like any less a part of the family," he clarified, but then his eyes found mine, the gray-ish blue that surrounded his brown iris glowing in the low light of my kitchen. "But, it did open a new door in my mind, one I didn't even know existed. I realized I was theirs, but not really *theirs*. They were my mom and dad, but I had *another* mom and dad, too."

I nodded in understanding.

"So, yeah. It opened a new door. And I've walked through that door frequently ever since that day, looking for answers that I know will never come."

My heart ached with the desire to hug him.

It hit me so fiercely and unexpectedly that I nearly followed it. I uncrossed my legs and made to stand before I realized what I was doing and stopped myself, taking a deep breath, instead. There were no words to say in that moment — none that would be anything other than hot air to fill the space. So, I didn't say a word. I just sat there with him and let him know he wasn't alone.

"It's strange, because I had a similar awakening when we camped when I was a teenager, too. Only that time, I had been hanging out with a brother and sister who were black. But, they treated me differently, like I didn't actually belong with them." His eyes found mine. "It's like you were saying with Paige, and I'm sure you've been there, too. It's like I'm stuck in this strange in-between of not being black enough, but not being white enough, either."

I nodded, a grim understanding. "I know that feeling well."

"I couldn't have asked for a better family, though," he said after a moment with a small smile. "I'm proud to be a Becker."

I laughed softly. "You boys are as thick as thieves. Always have been. I think I'd heard of every single one of you before I even started my first day of school here."

"Hey, to be fair, I'm usually the one *wrangling* those trouble-makers — especially Noah. Lord knows Ruby Grace couldn't have come a moment sooner to settle that hothead down."

The mood lightened with the mention of his brothers, and we chatted about each of them. A big part of me was curious about the fire that had taken his father's life, but after having one already-heavy conversation, I skirted around my curiosity and stayed firmly in the friendly territory.

"Speaking of siblings, how's Gabby doing?" Jordan asked after a while.

I smiled at the mention of my sister, who I knew would likely lose her mind if she knew Jordan was in my kitchen at this hour of the night. "She's really good, loving the nursing life — though I'll never understand it. She works all night, long hours, dealing with people who usually treat her like she's a problem rather than a help." I shook my head. "Makes me appreciate people who work in healthcare more."

"Where's she at now?"

"She and my parents are all in Austin," I said, frowning as my finger traced the top of my glass. "Mom got a civilian job there working as an analyst, and I guess since we were all moving around together growing up, Sis just wanted to go with them."

"You didn't?"

I shrugged in lieu of an answer, my heart screaming *I did.*

Jordan was quiet for a while before he asked, "Was it hard, moving around like that when you were younger?"

I tilted my head, considering. "Yes, and no," I said honestly. "It was hard not staying in one place long enough to have real friends, but... my sister and I were so close, you know? And it always felt like an adventure, moving from place to place, always having something new to discover."

"I can't even imagine," Jordan said. "I've been in this town my whole life."

"There are worse places to be."

Jordan leaned back on a nod, watching me with a tired smile.

Conversation flowed easily between us after that, and so did the whiskey. As we talked, we went through two more old fashioneds, and the more we sipped, the easier it was to open up. I told him more about my upbringing, about the trouble I would get into with Gabby, a little about my parents. He knew about my mom's military job, but had no idea that my father built and sold custom furniture made of solid wood wherever we were stationed. So, we talked for nearly an hour about the places I had lived and traveled to growing up, about Mom's deployments and various job duties, and I even showed him pictures of my father's favorite projects.

I'd just finished sharing a story about me and my sister getting in trouble for swimming in an old quarry in Alabama when I glanced at the clock and realized it was almost midnight.

I sighed, opening my mouth to tell Jordan it was probably time we both get some sleep, but then the song changed, and he closed his eyes and smiled, letting out an appreciative noise through his nose.

"Wow," he said, shaking his head before he opened his eyes. They found mine instantly, and he stood, reaching one hand down to where I sat.

I stared at his hand, quirking a brow before I glanced back up at him like I had no idea what I was supposed to do with it. But he curled his fingers with a smile, nodding behind him to the living room like it was a dance floor.

"What?" I asked, feigning ignorance.

"Dance with me."

I laughed.

"Seriously," he said before I could call him crazy. "There's a great story that goes along with this song, and I want to tell it to you."

Well, shit.

That got my attention, and I took one last sip of my drink before I slipped my hand in his, ignoring the way it covered mine easily with warmth as he tugged me to the living room. When we were in the space between my couch and love seat, he twirled me, pulling me into him with ease before I had the chance to stumble or fall.

Jordan Becker.

A good dancer.

Who the hell would have guessed *that*?

For a moment, we just swayed — one of his hands on my waist and the other covering my hand where it rested on his chest. I held my other on his shoulder, listening to the song. It was one I didn't really know. I recognized it, and vaguely recalled my parents listening to it when I was younger, but past that, I had no idea why this song had made Jordan Becker pull me into my living room to dance.

"Do you know who this is?" he asked.

I shook my head.

"Eric Clapton," Jordan said with another smile. He was like a completely different man in that moment, one I'd never met before. The coach with the clipboard didn't exist, not in that living room. He was somewhere else, sleeping or planning plays, and the man who swayed with me was the *real* Jordan Becker. It was like spotting a Siberian tiger in the wild.

I wondered how many people had ever seen him with their own two eyes.

"Wonderful Tonight," Jordan said, just as the chorus began to play. "This was my mom and dad's wedding song."

I smiled, my heart squeezing as he twirled me out and back in. "It's beautiful."

Jordan nodded. "It is. And they didn't just dance to it at their wedding. Every night after dinner, Dad would help Mom clean up in the kitchen, and then he'd pull her into the living room, put on this song or sometimes another one that they loved, and dance with her."

I stopped swaying, gaping at him. "You're kidding."

Jordan didn't miss a beat, sweeping me back up in the rhythm with him. "Dad was a smooth cat."

"I can see that," I said, chuckling. "So, *every* night after dinner?"

"Every night," he repeated, and his smile slipped, ghosts dancing in his eyes just as much as we danced in that room. "When he died, I think that was the hardest part for her." He had a far-off look as a moment passed between us. "I mean, my brothers and I, we were dealing with our own shit, you know? Noah was on this kick about who would be the man of the house. Logan was going crazy trying to figure out where he should step up and take

Dad's place in running the house, paying the bills, cleaning, caring for the lawn, doing taxes, all that. Mikey was so young... he was just trying to hold on, to understand that he'd lost his father."

I squeezed his shoulder where I held him.

"And then one night, after dinner, Mom was in the kitchen cleaning up, and she had these big tears in her eyes that she was trying so hard not to let fall. My brothers and I sat at that table feeling helpless and run down. It was the first time I think we'd ever really felt off-kilter as a family."

I nodded in understanding.

"And then, Logan got up from his chair, went into the living room, and put on this song." He smiled. "I'll never forget the way Mom froze in the kitchen, her eyes widening at the sound of it. And Logan went in there and reached for her hand, and took her back to the living room, and he danced with her."

Tears welled in my own eyes, and I rolled my lips together to keep them from falling.

"And I swear, it was that dance that brought us back together as a family," Jordan said, his voice softening to a whisper. "Every time we have family dinner at her house now, we take turns dancing with her after. And it's like Dad is still alive, like he's there with us, like *he* was the one who pulled us all together that night, as if to remind us that we always have each other, and he's never really gone. And you know what?" He chuckled. "This song never gets old."

My heart broke at the same time it surged with emotion. I didn't know how to react to Jordan opening up to me. I didn't know how to feel with his hand on my waist, with his other hand holding mine over his chest, with his stormy eyes searching mine as the music played between us.

But I leaned into him.

I leaned into his life, into his story, into everything and every person who made him who he was today. I leaned my body into his, leaned my heart into this soft man with the hardened edges. And when we both stopped swaying, when the music seemed to grow so loud it permeated our skin, when his fingers trailed their way up my ribs, over my arm, and framed my chin before tilting it up toward him, I leaned up on my toes.

His exhale was shaky when it touched my lips, but then my eyes closed, and his mouth found mine, and my living room exploded into a universe of stars.

The kiss was timid at first, our lips barely touching, sticking together in a hesitant embrace before we pulled away again. It was like we were each testing the other, giving them the chance to back out. My heart tripled its pace in my chest when our eyes met, and then, he kissed me again.

This time, his mouth was harder when it found mine, and more sure, his arms wrapping around me as he pulled me into him and kissed me like he was always destined to do so.

We both inhaled — the kiss, the night, each other — and his hands framed my face, holding me to him as if he was afraid I wasn't real, that I'd fade in an instant if he didn't hold onto me for dear life. He kissed me long and tender, and yet feverishly, too. We were lips and breaths and moans and then our mouths opened at the same time, and his tongue found mine, and an electrifying heat I hadn't felt in years zipped violently from where we touched through every nerve in my body, ending at one point of contact between my legs.

It was that rush of heat that kicked my brain into gear, and I realized with freezing cold awareness what I was doing.

I was kissing Jordan Becker.

I was kissing Jordan Becker — my *boss*.

I was kissing someone.

Period.

I broke away as if his kiss was a knife in the gut rather than the sweetest ecstasy. Before he could even frown, I was already out of his grasp, backing away with my hands over my mouth, eyes wide.

When he registered what he was seeing, his eyes went wide, too.

"Shit," he muttered, holding up his hands and taking a step toward me. I backed away just as much. "Sydney, I'm sorry. I—"

"It's late," I interrupted, turning away from him and bolting toward my dining room table as I cleared my throat. I immediately picked up our glasses, dumping what was left inside them into my sink and tossing the garnishes in the trash. I kept my eyes on my hands as I washed the glasses, as if I couldn't have tossed them into the dishwasher, instead.

"Sydney," Jordan tried from behind me.

"Thank you for today," I said, heart racing, mind blurring. I didn't know why it was happening, and I *hated* it, but in that moment?

All I thought of was Randy.

All I thought of was that Jordan and I couldn't happen, that Randy would never *let* it happen, and that perhaps more than anything, I wasn't ready for it to happen.

"I'm pretty tired," I continued, still washing. "I think we both better get some sleep."

The water was scalding hot on my hands but I didn't move to change it. I just scrubbed and scrubbed until the soap was a frothy foam of bubbles on the sponge and the glass in my hand was clean enough for the Queen herself to drink from.

I could still sense Jordan in my home, hear his breaths, feel the mixture of longing and regret swirling inside him the same way they moved in me. But slowly, without another attempt to speak to me, he gathered his belongings, and with one last look in my direction that I didn't return, he let himself out my front door.

And I fell to the floor, the water still running as I backed myself into the cabinet and squeezed my eyes shut, running my hands through my hair.

What have we done?

TEN

JORDAN

Was it possible for a hangover to last forty-eight hours?

If anyone would have asked me on Monday afternoon thirty minutes before football practice, I would have responded with a resounding *yes*.

My head still pounded, gut churning like I was in danger of forfeiting what little I'd been able to eat at any given moment. I knew there were bags under my eyes and that I was in rough shape as I ran over my plans for the day's practice.

And I also knew that *none* of it had anything to do with the alcohol I'd consumed.

I hadn't been drunk — not at Sydney's, not in the car on my way home, and not the next morning. If anything, I'd nursed those drinks to make them — and the conversation with Sydney — last.

I wasn't hungover from the whiskey.

I was hungover from her kiss.

I'd been in that state of absolute worthlessness since I left Sydney's house on Saturday night, spending the rest of the weekend ruminating on my actions, and even more on her *reaction*.

I'd kissed her.

Like a damn fool, I'd kissed her.

And she'd torn away from me like I was the devil himself.

Here I'd been chastising my team the past few weeks, telling them to be respectful of Sydney, and it had been *me* who had crossed the very line I'd put in place. She'd trusted me — not just here on the field and at the school, but in her home, too. I was there to work with Paige, to reassure Sydney that it was all going to be okay, and instead, I'd put her in the worst-possible situation.

I felt like a predator, and even more, like a joker.

Because the worst part of it all was that I really did think she wanted to kiss me, too.

I'd thought I'd read the signs right, that she'd leaned into me and looked up at me with eyes that silently pleaded for me to break the rules and lower my mouth to hers. I thought she'd opened up to me, and that I'd opened up to her, in return, and that we'd crossed into a new territory that could no longer be defined by our roles on the Stratford High School football team.

I'd thought we'd shared something that night — hell, that entire *day*.

What. An. Idiot.

I'd run over my mistake in my head for the rest of the weekend, and nothing could save me from my thoughts. Not even taking the Bronco out mudding or dinner with my family on Sunday night brought me relief. Mom commented on how I was even quieter than usual, but I couldn't even open up to her about what had happened — *that* was how stupid I felt.

More than that, I felt irresponsible.

I decided long ago that relationships were not for me. I knew too well how they could fail, how one partner could be left behind, how the pain that came with love almost always outweighed the pleasure. I never wanted to be in that line of fire, and more than that, I never wanted to be responsible for someone else's demise, either.

Football was the love of my life, and I was happy with that.

So, when I'd crossed that line with Sydney, I'd done so not with the intention to hook up with her, to have a one-night stand, to have something *casual*.

I'd done it with the knowledge that I didn't *do* anything half-assed.

I wanted her. I wanted to court her and date her and take things slow and worship her and eventually call her mine.

I wanted all those things knowing that she'd already been through hell once, judging by the ugly breakup with her and Randy, and that I would likely put her through it again, because that was just the way love worked.

Round and round and round these thoughts went in my head, all weekend long, like a carousel of torture that ran on its victims screams — of which there were plenty. Even working through more of Dad's journal entries hadn't distracted me from what I'd done and what it would mean.

And all along, I'd been dreading this very moment — when we'd have to be at work together, and it wouldn't be the same as it was when we worked together just three days ago.

Another heavy sigh racked my chest as I tried to soothe my anxiety with a deep breath, and at that very moment, my office door swung open and slammed shut again before Sydney plopped her ass down in the chair on the opposite side of my desk.

"Alright," she said, tying her hair up in a knot on her head before her eyes locked on mine. "Let's get this awkward conversation out of the way now, shall we?"

It was unfortunate that I'd just exhaled instead of inhaled, because I held my breath from the moment she sat down, waiting for her to continue.

"So, we kissed," she said, as if we were discussing a player who got hurt on the team and what to do about it instead of everything I'd worried about for the past forty-eight hours. "I think we can both agree that we were tired, it'd been a long day, we had been drinking and we were talking about some pretty heavy things and neither of us were thinking clearly."

I kept my mouth shut, because while I *could* agree with some of that, I didn't agree with the last part.

I was thinking *very* clearly when I pressed my lips to hers.

"The first thing I want to address is..." She paused, rolling her lips together. Her eyes that had been so fiercely on mine fell to something on my desk — an object serving as a focal point, I imagined. "I just don't want you to think that you did anything wrong, because you didn't. I..." She swallowed. "I also took part in what happened, and it was not one-sided or anything."

Her eyes flicked to mine, but they didn't stay there long.

"That being said, I have a lot on my plate right now with my recent divorce, and with Paige, and I just..." She sat a little straighter, finally looking at me again. "Frankly, I do not have the capacity to be... like *that*... with anyone right now. And I think we both agree that even if I did, it shouldn't be my boss. I know there are no written rules or anything, but you and I both know that I can't... *we* can't..."

I remained silent, though I was very aware of how tight my chest was at those words.

"Anyway, I wanted to come directly to your office this afternoon so we could just put this all behind us. What do you think?"

My eyes bulged, because it was my time to speak and I hadn't even *breathed* since she'd walked into my office.

I started there, inhaling a stiff breath before I nodded, schooling my features. "Yes. Of course, totally."

"So, we're in agreement, then?" she asked. "We can just pretend like it never happened?"

"Like what never happened?"

Her jaw dropped a little, but then she let out a relieved sigh on a smile when she realized what I'd done. "Exactly."

I faked my best smile in return while my stomach continued to tie itself into knots. But, the longer I watched her, the more I knew I had to say. "Sydney... I really am sorry."

She held up her hand quickly. "Please, don't. You don't need to apologize. It never happened. Okay?"

I frowned, but nodded, nonetheless.

"Does this mean..." I started, but then paused, re-framing what I wanted to ask. "I was hoping... just because I know she was excited about it, and I don't want her to think I bailed on her or anything... would it be okay if I still worked with Paige from time to time?" I held up my hands. "Not all the time," I clarified quickly. "Just... you know, whenever it works out. I just would love to keep working with her and help her get ready for camp next summer."

Sydney smiled, letting out a long exhale that was calmer than any breath had been in that room since she walked into it. "Of course," she said. "You're always welcome."

I returned her smile, and though there was still something new and uncomfortable that existed between us now, at least the conversation was had, and we could begin to put it all behind us.

My chest tightened again, as if it was protesting that I had just agreed to forget what was honestly the best kiss of my life, but I ignored it, standing instead.

"Welp, I'm going to go get these boys fired up for another week of practice."

Sydney stood abruptly, too. "Yep, I'm going to go get my tables set up and ready. I've got a few injuries to follow up with today and I'll give you a report of who we need to keep an eye on by the end of practice."

"Sounds good," I said with my eyes on my clipboard as we made our way out of my office. "Oh, and can you do some soft tissue work on Martinez's right shoulder?" I added. "He's been rubbing it after almost every throw, and the last thing I need is a second-string quarterback who can't perform if he's subbed in."

"I'm on it," she assured me, already heading down the hall toward her office.

And just like that, it was back to work.

Like nothing ever happened.

— • —

And so the week went.

Everything was back to normal, in the sense that they were *far* from normal, but at least we were pretending.

My days passed with teaching my P.E. classes and weight-lifting, evenings passed at practice with me and Sydney dutifully dancing around each other, all the while being "normal," and at night, I fell back into my routine, meal prepping and running and working through entries in Dad's journal.

Part of me wondered if it really was only me who felt like we were pretending. Sydney seemed fine, as far as I could tell. She was focused on the field and in her office, not skipping so much as one beat after our conversation on Monday.

I wondered if anyone could tell that I was on the opposite end of that spectrum.

It drove me mad that I couldn't drop it, but I tried my best, reminding myself of our conversation.

It was a mistake.

We were tired and tipsy.

It's not a big deal.

It never happened.

On Thursday night, I was successfully distracted, my nose buried in my playbook as I mapped out my strategy to take on the Conway Chargers. It would be another away game for us, and though the team was on a high from the win the week before, I knew it would be important to keep them focused and run the plays that we were nailing over and over in practice.

I wanted to play this game safe and bring home another win without any fanfare. That was my goal.

My eyes were starting to blur with all the x's and o's when my phone buzzed on the coffee table where my feet were propped. I scrubbed my hands down my face, moving my playbook to the side and smiling when I saw my baby brother's face on the screen.

"Well, if it isn't the city slicker," I answered, kicking back on the couch again.

"Hey, old man," Mikey teased back. "I was worried I might not get an answer, what with it being eight o'clock and all. I know that's past your bedtime."

I smiled, though my chest ached a bit, too. Mikey was the first of us to move away from Stratford — likely, the *only* one who ever would — and the Becker clan felt a little unsteady without him here.

"How are you?" I asked.

"All is good over here, just getting settled in still. The art gallery is pretty cool, and Kylie has been volunteering. She got a job helping out at the hospital, too. When we're not working, we're exploring the city. Kylie's dad put together a list of all her mom's favorite places from when she lived here, so we've been working through that."

I smiled. "That sounds fun. And you sound good."

"I am good," he replied, and I could hear the smile even though I couldn't see it. Then, I heard a faint *hi, Jordan!* in the background, and my smile grew. "Kylie says hi, by the way."

"Tell her I said hi back, and to keep you in line up there."

"Like you even have to tell me, that's my number one job," I heard her reply, like she'd stolen the phone from Mikey altogether.

I chuckled.

"What about you?" Mikey asked. "How's the season going? You ready for tomorrow night's game?"

I blew out a breath, tapping the playbook beside me with a longing look. "Working on getting ready, anyway. I mean, the team seems pumped, coming off a win last week, but with that giant L from week one still fresh in everyone's mind, I don't think anyone is unaware of the fact that this is an important game."

"One loss doesn't make a season, Big Bro."

"You sound like Mom. And I know," I agreed. "But, it does serve as a pretty heavy weight on our shoulders."

"How's it working out with the new trainer?"

My throat constricted, heart stopping before it took a nose-dive into my gut and resurfaced again, beating faster. "It's fine, everything is fine, why would you ask?"

There was a pause. "Uh... well, because you seemed kind of worried about it when you were here? I mean, when you found out about her joining the team and all. I just was curious if it had been an issue."

"Oh," I said quickly, and my next breath came easier. "Yeah, she's been great. I made a bit of an ass of myself when she first joined, basically saying in not so many words that I was worried she'd be a distraction on the team."

"Jordan..."

"I know," I said before he could continue. "Not my proudest moment. But, I was stressed coming into the new season, and to be honest, I *was* worried that the guys would be distracted by her. And, to be clear, they are — but that's not her fault. She's doing her job, and doing a damn fine job of it, too. At first, the guys were all gaga for her, but they respect her now. She feels like part of the team already."

"That's awesome," Mikey said, but there was a hesitance in his voice. "Now... are you going to tell me why you reacted like a kid getting caught with his hand in the cookie jar when I asked you about her?"

I opened my mouth to argue, but he cut me off before I could speak.

"And don't pretend like it's nothing, because I know you better than that, and to save us both time we should just skip the part where I have to beat it out of you."

I wanted to be annoyed that my brother knew me so well, but I couldn't help but smile, because I was this way with all of them, too.

We could see through the bullshit when it came to each other, and that was part of what made our bond so strong.

I sighed. "I don't even know where to begin."

"How about you start with whatever is on your mind right now."

I worked the inside of my cheek. "I kissed her on Saturday night. She freaked out and basically kicked me out of her home. Then on Monday, she stormed into my office and said it was a drunken mistake and we should forget it ever happened."

"Ouch."

"And I agreed," I continued. "Even though I don't *actually* agree."

"I see."

"And I hate it," I added, chest aching with the realization that I really, really *did* hate it. "Because we had a friendship, you know? I felt like... like I could talk to her, and like she was opening up to me. And we would joke with each other, and we worked well together, too... and now?" I sighed again. "We're just dancing around each other, pretending like I didn't cross the line and that everything is back to normal, when we don't even *have* a normal, anymore."

Mikey was quiet for a long time, then he asked one simple question.

"Do you still want to kiss her?"

I frowned. "It doesn't matter if I do or not."

"I guess what I mean is — when she said it was a mistake and you guys should forget about it, did you take that opportunity to tell her that you *didn't* feel like it was a mistake, and that you'd like to try being more than friends?"

"Mikey, she told me we should forget about it."

"I realize that," he said. "But what I'm asking is does she know you feel this way?"

"It doesn't matt—"

"It does!" Mikey's voice was loud and firm, and I shut my mouth in response. "She told you it was a mistake, that you both were drunk, and you agreed and said yeah, let's forget about it. What if there was a little bit of hope in her that it *wasn't* a mistake? What if she was waiting to see what *you* said?"

I frowned.

"Look, I know you, Big Bro, and one thing I know is that you don't misread signs when it comes to women. You are not an asshole, and you wouldn't so much as *think* about making a move on a woman unless there was a real connection and consent. You've always been the gentleman, and you've always taken things slow with the women you've dated — and what's more, there haven't been many. So, if you crossed the line and kissed Sydney, I know for a fact that it was because you felt something, and you wouldn't have felt something if *she* hadn't felt it, too."

A little balloon of hope filled in my chest, but I popped it quickly. "It's not that simple."

"It could be."

"I can't just…" I threw my hand out, as if to show him all the reasons why. "*Confess* that I wanted to kiss her and that I *still* want to kiss her and that I think about her every damn minute of every day. This isn't high school. We *work* together, Mikey. She technically works *under* my supervision, which makes me her boss, in a way. She's already working against the odds as the only female on an all-male staff in a male-dominated sport, *and* she's back to work for the first time in years. *And*," I continued, running out of breath. "She has a daughter, and an ex-husband, and there are just a lot of complications at work here, okay?"

My little brother didn't respond for a long time. It was just me, breathing heavily, waiting for him to argue with me so I could fight him some more on the topic. But instead, after a long pause, he made a noise of understanding.

"Well," he said. "It sounds like you have your answer."

My chest was still rising and falling at a rapid rate, but when the urge to fight him left me, I was left in a hollow sadness wishing he would keep going, keep telling me reasons I was wrong.

"Just pretend like it never happened and things are back to work as usual," he continued. "She forgets about you, you forget about her. No harm, no foul. It was just a kiss, right?"

A long, slow exhale left my chest. "Right," I agreed, though my voice was soft and unsure.

Mikey didn't say anything, letting the silence sit between us, and I chewed on everything he'd said and every point I'd thrown back at him for the rest of our phone call. When we were all caught up and promised to talk again soon, I hung up the phone and stared at the blank screen of my television.

"It was just a kiss," I repeated out loud, to no one and to whoever might be listening — myself, included.

Then, I picked up my playbook, and got back to distracting myself from all the lies.

ELEVEN

JORDAN

Fall began to make its descent on our little Tennessee town over the next two weeks. The days cooled to a beautifully perfect seventy to seventy-five degrees, and the evenings welcomed us with a crisp wind that brought chilly nights. It wasn't quite cold enough to get the fireplace going yet, but it was getting there, and I reveled in the fact that I could wear leggings and a long-sleeve shirt without sweating.

Margaret's Bakery boasted the arrival of pumpkin bread and apple cider, Charlie Warren was already setting up his pumpkin patch on the edge of town, and I knew the corn maze wouldn't be far behind.

And most of all, football season was in full swing.

It was our first home game since the one we'd opened the season with, and the Stratford stands were packed. We'd won all three of our away games since then, and our fans were anxious to see if we'd deliver a W at home tonight. Winning in any capacity was great, but winning in your own house was another level of high — and I could feel the pressure our players were putting on themselves to deliver.

"Alright," I said after wrapping our quarterback's left ankle. I tapped the toe of his cleat. "Try not to get sacked, and I'll re-wrap at halftime, if necessary."

Rodgers smiled, thanking me as he hopped up from the bench and jogged out to join his team warming up on the field. I packed away the tape in my training bag, looking over my notes on all the players to make sure I hadn't forgotten anyone. My pre-game responsibilities felt natural to me now, and I loved that I had a routine.

"Coach!"

I followed the sound of someone calling out to Jordan, smiling curiously when I found an older man I recognized from when he'd helped Randy work on our busted pipe in our kitchen one afternoon years ago. He had dark brown skin and soft, kind eyes — and a crooked yellow grin that widened the longer he stood there. He wore a fedora on his head, one that matched the suspenders he wore, and he tipped it at Jordan as he made his way over to the sideline, leaning over the railing that separated us from the fans in the bleachers.

"What say you, Eli?" Jordan asked, pressing his back to the gate next to where Eli stood. It made it where they could stand next to each other and talk, but he could still keep an eye on his team, too.

"I say I'm looking forward to you bringing all those W's you've gotten on the road home tonight."

Jordan raised his eyebrows, gaze following the throw Rodgers had just made to Smith on the field. "If all goes according to my plan, that's exactly what you'll see." He glanced up at Eli before his eyes were on the field again. "Missed you at last week's game."

Eli grumbled. "Yeah, well, they had a plumbing emergency down at the nursing home Friday evening. I couldn't very well leave Ms. Betty Collins without a properly working toilet, as I'm sure you well know."

Jordan chuckled at that, and I found myself wondering who Betty Collins was, and my curiosity climbed the more I watched them together. That was, until the Mom Parade made their way to the fan side of the fence.

I rolled my eyes at the way they leaned over it, giving glimpses of their cleavage, their eyes light and playful as they talked to Jordan. They asked if they could get him anything, if he needed a shoulder massage before the game, if he wanted to hang out *after* the game — and any time Jordan gave them an incredulous look, the women hid their intentions under a flurry of laughter, as if they were joking when we all knew they'd jump at the chance to have Jordan in their bed.

I didn't like the way my stomach soured at that thought.

I couldn't stop watching, and I wondered if he felt it, because as soon as the parade moved on, Jordan's eyes met mine, and I tore my gaze away like I'd been caught.

After that, I kept my focus on my own tasks, working through my pre-game checklist as the clock wound down toward kick off. Just beforehand, Jordan sidled up beside me.

"Ready to go?" he asked.

"Yep," I answered, eyes still on my notebook. "Everyone is wrapped up and massaged and iced and ready to rock."

"Good," he answered, watching the field.

I glanced at him, feeling like he was a complete stranger. That's what it had felt like ever since... well, since the night we both pretended never happened. We worked together the same as we had before, and to everyone else, I imagined we looked just fine.

But it was different.

We didn't joke, we didn't talk about anything of substance, and we definitely didn't spend any time getting to know each other better. He'd come over to help Paige twice since that night, and both times, he'd avoided me like the plague, and I'd done the same, leaving him to work with her and asking him to stay for dinner knowing full well that I didn't actually want him to and he wouldn't out of respect for our agreement.

We were putting it behind us, acknowledging it as a mistake and pretending like it never happened — just like I'd suggested.

And still... I longed for the version of us that existed before that night.

I also longed for a day when I wouldn't accidentally find myself staring at his mouth, remembering the way it felt pressed against mine.

A blush heated my cheeks as that thought found me, and I cleared my throat, glancing at the stands behind us and back at him. "Was that Elijah Braxton you were talking to?"

Jordan smirked, but didn't take his eyes off his players. "Indeed. He's a big football fan, comes to every game — even the away games, when he can." One eyebrow climbed as he faced me. "And believe me when I say that when we lose, he's the first one to let me know what he thinks about it."

I chuckled. "Well, at least if we *do* lose, you'll also have plenty of... *support,* too." I nodded to where the women who were just talking to him were gathered in the front row of the bleachers.

Their smiles grew when Jordan looked at them, and he had a brow cocked when he turned back to me. "I don't think I want the kind of support that crew would offer."

I bit my lip against a smile, not sure why his reaction to them made me happy. "Anyway, you better get out there," I said just as the referee blew the whistle signaling that it was time for the coin toss.

Jordan watched me for a long moment with a curious gaze, but then he nodded, jogging out onto the field without another word.

And the game began.

It was a wondrous sight to behold, the way Jordan could hold his shit together through one of the most nerve-racking games I'd ever witnessed. There was a lot on the line in this home game, and we volleyed back and forth with the Salem Serpents, scoring a touchdown only for them to answer with one, in return.

We'd go up by three, then down by three, up by seven, then down by three again. Back and forth, over and over through every single quarter of the game.

And all the while, Jordan paced the sideline calmly and coolly, chewing his gum, a permanent scowl on his face as he talked to the other coaches behind his clipboard and pulled players to the side to whisper in their ears each time they came off the field.

Me, on the other hand?

I was a mess.

My knuckles were white from how hard I gripped my notebook all game, and though I would never wish for a player to get injured, not having anything to take my focus off the field put me even more on edge. I would check in on the players I was working with from time to time, but for the most part, I wasn't needed — not for anything other than support.

When the two-minute warning came at the end of the fourth quarter, coach huddled up our offense, speaking with a low, firm voice in the middle of the circle. I couldn't hear what he said, but when the players ran back onto the field, I saw the fierce determination in their eyes.

We were down by three with the ball on our twenty-seven-yard line, and two minutes to score.

I didn't breathe for those two minutes — not when we made a forty-yard pass in a third and eleven situation and not when our offense was a wall against their defense, trying to push the last few yards into the end zone with less than forty seconds left to play. But when we finally broke through and scored, I gave my burning lungs the oxygen they needed and screamed like a banshee, jumping up and down on the sideline.

I could hear Paige going wild behind me, too, and I found her in the stands, giving her an air high five. Randy was there next to her, but he didn't seem in a celebratory mood. Instead, his eyes were hard on me, disapproving.

He didn't like that I was happy.

Nothing could get under my skin at that moment, though — least of all him. And I blew a kiss at Paige just as our boys lined up for the extra point kick. It was good, and then we were up by four.

But the Serpents still had thirty-two seconds to play with.

It was the longest thirty seconds of my life, watching them make conversion after conversion, lining up quickly after each play to get the next one in before time ran out. They were on a mission to win in the last stretch, and our defense was on a mission to stop them.

When they snapped the ball with four seconds left to play, their quarterback launched it long, eyes on their best receiver who was just ten yards from their end zone.

But he didn't catch the ball.

Boone Parson, our cornerback, did.

Every player on our sidelines jumped in the air when the interception happened, the stands going crazy behind us as we all rushed the field. The rest of the defense hoisted Parson up onto their shoulders, and he held the ball over his head in victory.

I was all smiles and laughs and cheers and a racing heart as I watched. Jordan remained calm until he shook hands with the other coach, and then, for the first time all game, emotion showed on his face. He thrust his fist into the air, joining in on the celebrations as the entire town of Stratford roared their approval.

We'd won four games in a row, and our first one at home.

The Stratford Wild Cats were on fire.

It was a high unlike any I'd ever known, winning a home game — especially one that close. The energy was still buzzing through me when my job was done in the training room and the players had all gone off to celebrate their win. The other coaches were still laughing and reminiscing over their favorite moments of the game when I rounded into Jordan's office.

"Okay, I have a serious question," I said, plopping down into the chair across from his.

He glanced up, smiling when he saw me as he kicked back in his chair. "I'm sorry, but I'm not signing autographs at this point in time."

I stuck my tongue out.

"What's up?" he asked, still smiling. I had a feeling that smile would be glued to his face all weekend.

"How the hell do you go to *sleep* after a game like that?"

Jordan barked out a laugh.

"I'm serious," I continued, shaking my head with my hands extended toward him. "I mean, my heart is *still* pounding."

"It was amazing, wasn't it?"

"Absolutely unreal," I agreed. "Paige is staying with her dad tonight, and I just cannot imagine a scenario where I go home, make some tea, and go to bed. Like... I feel like I could run a freaking marathon right now."

Jordan smiled as he took in my enthusiasm, but the longer he watched me, the more that smile fell. His eyes flicked back and forth between mine like he was warring with something, and he opened his mouth, shut it again, then finally spoke.

"Maybe you don't go home then," he suggested. "At least, not yet."

"And where the hell should I go?" I asked on a laugh.

But when Jordan's expression sobered, the storm swirling in his eyes, my own smile fell, too. There was a new energy in the room, one that had snuck in without me noticing, but now, it was all I could feel.

The air was hot.

The office was smaller somehow.

Jordan's eyes pierced me like the blade of a knife, and without rhyme or reason, I leaned into the edge.

"Come with me," he said — and it wasn't tentatively or hesitantly, but confidently, like there was no other choice but for me to agree.

My heart that had been racing stopped altogether, chest tightening as if to warn me this was a bad idea. And I knew it, too — I knew by the way it was suddenly difficult to swallow, and the way my neck heated the longer he watched me that way.

But no matter how bad of an idea I told myself it was, I couldn't suppress the louder voice inside me that said *go*.

So, I stood, and with that buzzing, electric energy still hanging like live wires between us, I ignored the danger and submitted to temptation.

"Let me grab my bag."

— ● —

JORDAN

"OH MY GOD, OH MY GOD, OH MY GOD!"

I couldn't stop laughing at Sydney's outbursts as we tore through the Tennessee mud in my Bronco, the full moon above us and my headlights lighting the way. She held on to what I referred to as the, "*Oh, shit*" handle with one hand and gripped the center console or the dashboard with the other — depending on which way the Bronco was moving.

My abs were on fire like I had been doing crunches instead of just laughing, but I couldn't stop, and I reveled in the sound of *her* laughter the longer we were in those woods.

Sydney went from screaming in terror to cackling in uncontrollable laughter and back in the span of sixty seconds. I focused on keeping us steady and safe, flooring it over the ramps and spinning my tires to fling up mud, all the while ensuring we never got deep enough to get stuck. When I finally pulled us onto one of the dirt trails for a break and the Bronco evened out, Sydney slumped in her seat, breathing like she'd just run for her life.

"Oh, My-Lanta," she said on a long breath when I pulled over, putting it in park in one of my favorite meadows. "Is it possible to be sore from mudding?"

"Hey, you said you had a lot of energy to expend. Tell me that didn't do the trick?"

"It did," she agreed, shaking her head. "But, it also maybe gave me a heart attack or two."

I chuckled, turning the keys in the ignition until the engine ceased, and then all the noise was gone and we were blanketed in a silence only nature could provide. Slowly, as my ears adjusted, the faint sound of the few katydids still hanging around in the cooler nights made their way through the silence. In the summer, the music they made together was deafening, a sign of warm weather. But in the fall, hearing them was rare — especially once it actually got cold.

I grabbed my jacket from the backseat, shrugging it on and climbing out of the driver seat as Sydney watched me curiously. There were other creatures talking to each other all around us — maybe birds, maybe coyotes, maybe insects. I couldn't be sure of all of them, but I knew they made up my favorite symphony.

When Sydney joined me outside the truck, I walked over to her side, offering my hand and nodding to the front tire.

She cocked a brow. "What?"

"Hop up," I answered easily.

She looked at the wheel, at the muddy hood, and back at me with her brows drawn together. "On the hood?"

I smiled, grabbing her hand in mine and giving her a boost as she lifted herself up. "Trust me, you won't hurt it."

She still seemed a little hesitant, even when she was sitting on the hood, but when I climbed up on the other side and sat next to her, leaning back against the windshield with my eyes on the clearing ahead of us, she relaxed, reclining until her back hit the glass, too.

It was chilly — not so cold that it was uncomfortable, but enough so that I was glad I had my jacket. Sydney wore a Stratford High Football hoodie, and she pulled the hood of it up, tucking her hands in the pockets and crossing her legs where they splayed out in front of her.

"This is beautiful," she said, eyes wandering over the meadow. It was a phenomenon I didn't really understand, how in the middle of mud and trees and a forest there could be a break in all of it where the grass and plants and flowers bloomed freely.

"You should see it in the springtime," I said, letting my eyes travel up to where the stars peppered the sky. On a dark night, you couldn't count them all to save your life. But tonight, the moon was full and bright, its glow stealing the show in the sky. "There are all these wildflowers, and if you sit here long enough and are quiet, you'll see deer and rabbits and warblers and all kinds of creatures. I even saw two foxes once." I smiled at the memory. "You ever see a gray fox before? Bastards are too cute for their own good."

Sydney laughed. "I take it you come here often, then?"

"It's my spot," I said comfortably, proudly. "I love mudding in the truck, and I love to get a good run in to burn off any frustration or stress, but this? Sitting here and being still for a while?" I shook my head. "There's nothing more peaceful."

We sat there on the hood of my truck, the damp coolness of the forest on our skin and our eyes cast upward. For a long time, neither of us said anything, and somehow, it was the best conversation we'd had in weeks.

"I'm sure you don't need me to tell you this," she said after a while. "But, you're a really great coach, Jordan. Those boys... hell, this whole *town*. We're lucky to have you."

I shrugged, humbled, but my chest filled with a sense of pride hearing those words from her. "Thank you," I said. "I just love football, and I care about my team. And I think when those two things are true, anyone can be a good coach."

"False," she said quickly, rolling onto her side. She propped her head up, elbow on the windshield and hand cradling her cheek. "It's more than just loving the game and you know it. You're talented. You see things that others don't. You know a player's weakness before they do, and what's more, you know how to *conquer* it. You command respect, and you know what to say when they're down and defeated and what to say to keep them focused when they're on a high, too. You make tough decisions when it comes to who to play where and when to take someone out, and you don't apologize for anything — not even when you lose — because you know you have a plan, and you believe in it."

I let my head fall to the side until my eyes met hers, and I swore I'd never felt so exposed in my life. I'd been given compliments on my coaching before, but no one had ever put it into words the way she just had.

"They're like family to me," I told her. "Not just the players we have now, but any player who I work with." I paused, wetting my lips as I tried to find the words to explain. "I've always wanted to coach, and I got started as soon as I could after high school. I wanted to make a difference — not just for our school and football, but for these boys — individually, you know? We're in a small town, and some of these kids don't exactly have the best role models at home. I want to be there for them to remind them what they are capable of, what they have inside them, to push them when they need to be pushed and encourage them when they need to be encouraged. And to tell them I'm proud of them," I added. "Because I might be the only one they ever hear it from."

Her eyes softened, brows folding together.

"But as much as I want to make a difference, I'm also fucking *terrified* of messing it all up — of messing *them* up."

"You have no reason to be scared," she assured me. "You're the best coach I've ever known."

"How many have you known?"

"That's not the point."

I chuckled, letting my eyes wander back up to the sky. "What about you?" I asked. "How did you end up in athletic training?"

"Oh, that's easy," she said quickly. "I love bodies."

I snorted.

"No, but really, I have always had an interest in the way we push ourselves as humans, especially in sports. I knew I had an interest in anatomy and the medical side of things, but I didn't really want to be a *doctor*, you know? So, when I went to college, I focused on sports medicine and fell in love."

She paused, and I turned toward her again, sobering a little at the distant look in her eyes.

"When I was finishing my master's, a small junior college baseball team asked me to come on as their trainer. Fresh out of school." She smiled, but her eyes were sad. "I couldn't believe it. But it was the first time in my life that I felt like everything I'd done was right, like it had all led to that moment."

"That's amazing, Sydney," I said earnestly. Principal Hanley had told me a little about her background, about her previous offers to work with a college-level team, but this was the first time I heard it from her.

She swallowed. "Yeah, well... I never accepted the job, so..."

"Why not?"

Sydney's eyes found mine, and she shrugged with the smallest, most innocent smile on her face. "I got pregnant."

My heart squeezed.

Part of me considered reaching over to grab her hand, or pull her into me, to hold her and let her know I understood. But the truth was I *didn't*. I didn't know what it was like to have a child, to give birth to another human, to have something happen like that where every priority in life shifted.

"They said they'd wait," she continued, her voice soft. "They said when I had Paige, I could come work for them whenever I was ready. They'd hold the spot. Do you know how unheard of that is?" Her eyes welled with tears. "But Randy insisted we get married, and what I didn't realize was that when I agreed to be his wife, I also agreed to live by his rules."

My face hardened. I didn't know a thing about Randy other than what he did for a living, but in that moment, watching the look in her eyes... I knew he'd hurt her.

That was enough for me to be pissed.

"That's bullshit," I said after a moment. "That's not how marriage is supposed to work."

"It was how it worked in his eyes," she said, sniffling. "And I was so young... so afraid. I was going to be a mother and I could barely take care of myself, you know? But Randy was there, saying he could take care of everything. I could just focus on Paige, be a mom, and he would take care of us both. And I loved him, and it all sounded so nice," she admitted, and then she bit her lip and let out a bitter laugh. "And it was. Until it was hell."

This time, I couldn't resist the urge that overcame me, and I reached for her, pulling her into my chest and folding my arms around her as if I could shield her from something that had already happened. I didn't even know what *it* was, what the hell she referred to entailed. All I knew was that I wished in so many ways that I could somehow snap my fingers and go back to high school and grab her in the hallway, pull her into a closet, warn her of the choices she was about to make.

But then, Paige wouldn't exist.

And Sydney wouldn't be the woman she was today.

As much as life hurt like hell, those painful lessons somehow seemed to have beautiful ramifications, like everything that happened was for a reason we could never fully see or understand until years down the line.

Sydney was stiff and hesitant in my arms at first, but then she relaxed, exhaling a long breath and letting me hold her. She was so small in my arms, and everything inside me ached to keep her safe.

We laid there with her wrapped in my arms and my chest tight for a long while, the soft sounds of the night surrounding us. I didn't dare speak, not for the fear of spooking her out of my grasp with the mere sound of my voice. It was just like all those other times I'd sat in that meadow and tried to be perfectly still and quiet so as not to scare away the fauna.

She relaxed more and more into me as the minutes passed, and I held her tight, rubbing my hands over her back to soothe her. Then, out of nowhere, a soft and low *hoot, hoot* broke through the silence.

Sydney lifted her head, looking at me before she looked up at the trees behind us. "What was that?" she whispered.

It came again, and I smiled, sweeping the mess of hair that had fallen from her bun behind her ear. "I think it might be a saw-whet owl," I answered, just as soft. "They're rare, I've only ever heard one once before."

Sydney smiled, laying her head back on my chest, and we listened to the owl until it quieted or left us, though we couldn't be sure which.

"You know... I had a huge crush on you in high school."

My eyes shot open at her admission, and I peeked down at her. "You're shitting me."

She laughed, shaking her head. "Nope. I thought you were soooo cute." She dragged out the syllables. "My friends did, too. But, you were so quiet, so elusive."

"You make it sound like I was some broody bad boy."

"To us, you were."

I laughed through my nose. "I was just minding my own business."

"Rare in this town."

"I had a crush on you, too, for whatever it's worth."

"Wait, really?" She looked up at me, a pleased grin on her lips. "I wasn't sure you even knew I existed."

"Are you kidding? Have you *seen* you?" I shook my head. "Besides, you were new in town. You know as well as I do that you can't be new in town and everyone not find out who you are."

"Why didn't you ever say anything?"

"Why didn't *you*?" I shot back. She stuck out her tongue, then laid on my chest again, her breaths coming easier now that we'd moved off the topic of her ex-husband.

We laid there silently, the night getting cooler around us. And with her wrapped up in my arms like that, I found myself thinking about the night I promised her I'd forget about, about the kiss we tried to swear never happened.

"I like this," Sydney said after a while. "Talking to you

like normal again." She leaned up to look at me. "It's been kind of... awkward, hasn't it?"

I didn't answer, though my heart leapt into my throat.

"It's just nice to not feel like there's something weird between us," she continued.

"But there is."

Sydney stiffened, and my heart beat hard in my chest — once, twice, faster and faster, as if urging me not to stop until I'd said what I'd needed to.

"There *is* something weird between us," I said again, leaning up until my chest was even with hers, until our eyes were level and she could see the sincerity I hoped I was conveying. "That's why you feel it. And it's not just weird, it's rare, and unique, and intoxicating and terrifying, too."

Sydney's throat constricted, her mouth parting as she listened.

"We're both trying to pretend like I didn't kiss you when I did," I said, though my heart was so heavy in my ears I couldn't be sure I'd actually said it loud enough. "Like I didn't *want* to kiss you. But I did."

Her eyes flicked between mine.

"Like it was a drunken night or a mistake," I continued. "When we both know the truth is that I kissed you because I wanted to, because I *needed* to, because it felt like the only thing I could do in that moment."

"Jordan..." Sydney whispered, but it wasn't a warning — more like a plea.

"And I've wanted to kiss you every day since then, too."

Her lips trembled as she pressed them together, and I hadn't realized her hands were on me, not until I felt her fist twist in the fabric of my jacket, like she was in danger of falling off the hood of my truck if she wasn't latched onto me.

"Sydney," I said, soft and low. "It wasn't a mistake for me. It wasn't an accident. And I don't want to keep pretending like it is. But," I added, swallowing. "I *will* respect if that's the way you see it. If you truly want me to forget it ever happened, I... well, I'll find a way. But only if you can look at me, right now, look me right in my eyes and tell me that's what you want."

Her face crumpled, and for a moment I was worried she was about to cry, that I'd pushed too far, that I'd listened to my baby brother's advice like a fucking idiot and was about to pay the ultimate price.

"Was our kiss a mistake?" I asked again.

And with her eyes still welled up, she shook her head.

My heart slammed in my chest. "Do you want me to forget it ever happened?"

She shook her head again, and already, our hands were reaching for each other, our lips parting, closing the distance between us.

"Can I kiss you again now?" I whispered.

She nodded, and I tilted her chin up, taking her mouth with mine like it had always belonged to me.

And in a snap, all the energy in that forest rushed to the point where our lips met.

TWELVE

SYDNEY

Everything that had been dead inside me came to life when Jordan Becker's mouth claimed mine.

It happened in a rush, in an instant, in a shock so violent and powerful that I felt it like an earthquake in my soul. Desire that I hadn't felt in years pooled heavy and hot in my gut. My heart that had only beat in fear and suspicion began to beat in urgent want, instead. My hands that I thought had forgotten how to touch a man reached for Jordan like he'd always been mine.

And in the midst of it all, the way he kissed me made me realize I'd never really been kissed before.

I'd never had strong hands holding my face like that — in a way that commanded I was his but also ensured I was cared for. How was it possible that his lips were hot on mine, that his teeth sent sharp pangs of pleasure and pain through me each time he bit down on my neck, that his hands gripped me hard enough to leave bruises and yet *still* he was somehow tender, somehow hesitant, somehow gentle and sure all at once?

I pressed my hands into his chest as the night came alive around us, feeling its energy as I straddled him on the hood of his Bronco. The more we moved, the more we both became covered in the fresh mud he'd conjured up on our ride out to the meadow, but I couldn't find it in me to care.

My kisses grew harder, more insistent as I rolled my hips, and when the heat of me met his growing erection, I smiled in satisfaction.

In two quick and fluid movements, I broke our kiss and stripped my hoodie over my head, letting it fall somewhere on the ground behind me. I already had my long-sleeve shirt up and over my head when Jordan's hands gripped hard on my waist, stilling me where I was grinding against him.

"Sydney," he panted just as I lowered my mouth to his again.

I stole his next words, and he moaned, holding me tighter as I kissed him and rubbed the seam of my leggings against the growing bulge in his pants.

He cursed into my mouth, breaking our kiss with his hands grabbing my wrists and holding me away from him.

"Syd," he said again, and for some reason, that little shortened version of my name made the urge to kiss him even more intoxicating. "Maybe we should slow down."

"Shut up and kiss me," I said, breaking the grip he had on my wrists and wrapping my hands around his neck.

My fingers gripped at the base of his head, pulling him into my kiss, and he bit down hard on my lip, releasing it with a pop before he held me away again.

"Woman," he warned, but he was smiling, panting. "I'm serious. I don't want this to be just..." He frowned. "I want to court you, get to know you, take you on a date."

"You can take me on a date later," I said, rolling my hips against him. It was the only place he wasn't holding me still, and his eyes rolled up toward the full moon above us with the friction I created. "Right now, I want you to *touch* me."

I couldn't believe those words came from my mouth, that the desire breaking free had been bottled up in my cold, lifeless heart. It was like I'd been broken and sewn together with a thin piece of yarn, and all Jordan had done was tug one end of it, but it'd been enough to unravel me completely.

With my request, Jordan gave up resisting, and his mouth claimed mine again, both of us panting and moaning, licking and tasting, rolling and flexing until the need inside us was so fierce we nearly died beneath the weight of it.

"Wrap your legs around me," Jordan said, lifting my ass like I weighed nothing. I did as he asked, and in a feat of strength that he made look easy, he held me to him as he hopped down from the hood of the truck.

His lips were still hot on every inch of me he could reach, kissing my lips and neck and chin and jaw as he walked us to the back door of the Bronco. He felt for the handle blindly, and then the door was open and I was on my back, Jordan sliding into the space between my legs with the door still open behind him.

When he lifted to take off his jacket, he thunked his head hard on the ceiling, and I laughed, loving the smile that bloomed on his face, too.

"Think it's funny when I get hurt, huh?"

"No," I answered, leaning up on my elbows. "Think it's funny that we're about to fuck in the backseat of your truck like a couple of high schoolers."

"How do you know I'm going to fuck you?" Jordan asked, slowing his movements as he tugged his t-shirt up and over his head.

I didn't even try to hide my hungry gaze as I devoured every newly exposed inch of him, remembering when I'd seen that chest and abdomen speckled with mud in the park.

"What if I'm just going to touch you?" he continued, trailing a fingertip over the swells of each of my modest breasts where they were pushed up in my bra. "That's what you want, right?"

He made a path with that finger up my neck and over my chin, running it along my bottom lip before I sucked it into my mouth and released it with a pop that had his eyes rolling.

"If you can resist fucking me right now, I'll wash your truck tomorrow."

He smirked. "Is that a bet?"

"I don't know," I asked, sitting up fully. I reached back to unfasten the clasp on my bra, letting my breasts spill out as I tossed it on the floor of the truck. "Is it considered a fair bet if you know you're going to win?"

I tilted my head, leaning back on one hand and tracing my nipples with the other. They each puckered under the touch, and Jordan watched with his mouth parted, stormy eyes snapping to mine.

In an instant, he was on top of me again.

His kisses were slow but hard, purposeful and breathtaking. He sucked the skin on my neck on his way down to my chest, and then he palmed my right breast in his hand, appreciating the weight of it with a groan before his lips closed over the peak.

I arched into the touch, into his mouth, into *him*, and slowly, subtly, as if we were in a movie or the pages of an epic novel, time slowed, and every sense awakened to that man and that moment.

His pace softened, and he took his time with each of my breasts, sucking and licking and kissing and touching. I was so heavy with need when he finally backed off of me to stand again, and he kept his eyes on mine as he unfastened his belt, slowly stripping out of his sneakers and then his pants.

The bulge in his boxer briefs had me biting my lip, and I fell back into the seat, lifting my hips until I could shimmy out of my leggings, too. I pooled them at my ankles before I tugged off my sneakers and socks, then I peeled the leggings the rest of the way off — just in time to watch Jordan grip the band of his briefs and tug them down in one swift motion.

Then, he stood, his erection springing to life between us.

My lips parted as I squeezed my knees together, suddenly shy. It wasn't that I was naked physically in front of my boss, it was that he'd already stripped me bare emotionally before a single article of clothing had been removed.

Jordan seemed to sense the shift in energy, too, as he slowly climbed back into the truck with me. He settled between my legs, and each inch of my skin he touched on the way fired shots through my nervous system until he hovered over me, our bare chests somehow hot and slick in the cool night.

For a long moment, his gray-blue eyes searched mine, and in that light, I couldn't even see the burst of brown around the iris. They were just two icy pools sucking me into his depths.

He swept my hair away from my face, still marveling at me like I was the most beautiful creature in the entire universe. "Where did you come from?"

His voice was just a whisper, and yet I felt it deep within me like he'd screamed to the world.

"Just finished my walk through hell."

"Does that make this purgatory?" he asked on a smirk.

I smiled, too, reaching up to press my lips to his. "I think that makes this heaven."

He frowned, leaning into my kiss with purpose, one arm holding him balanced over me while the other gripped my hip with force. I bucked my hips, and with the motion, the slick heat between my legs coated his shaft, eliciting a sharp breath from us both.

"Syd," he said, panting and pressing his forehead to mine as he stilled. "I..." He swallowed. "As much as you're right about me not being able to resist fucking you right now, I don't have a condom."

My heart stopped for a second, but it kicked back to its quick pace in the next breath. "Are you clean?"

"Yes," he answered automatically. "But..."

I swallowed, each half of me warring with whether I was ready to expose the next bit of information. But the desire pulsing through me won over the part of me that was somewhat ashamed.

"I can't get pregnant," I assured him with a soft shrug. "After Paige, I..." I swallowed. "I had a surgery..."

I didn't have to tell him what kind of surgery for him to understand.

Those words hung heavy between us, and the fact that no one knew that about me — not even my ex-husband —

was written in my expression. I knew it, because without me even having to say it, I could tell *Jordan* understood that no one else knew. His brows bent in a sad understanding, and he kissed my forehead before his lips trailed to each of my cheeks and back to my mouth.

The tender moment lasted only a moment before it was replaced with urgency again, and I felt myself open to him — my mouth, my heart, my legs — until the tip of him was at my entrance and all it would take was a nudge of my foot in his backside, or a flex of his hips, to answer all my needs.

Jordan's breaths were shallow, his shoulders shaking where he held himself above me, and he broke our kiss, his mouth hovering over mine.

Then, on an excruciatingly slow roll of his hips, he entered me, and everything that wasn't Jordan Becker faded to black.

Pain ripped through me in a flash, the sensation of being spread open after having that part of me empty for so long. I cringed against it, and Jordan kissed me, distracting me as he slowed his movements and made his way deeper inside me as gently as he could.

Each moment brought more ecstasy and less pain, until I was denting his flesh with my nails, bucking my hips to meet his, my kisses hungry and desperate and hot. I reveled in the way his back arched with every thrust, in the way his glutes tightened with each flex inside me. It was animalistic, the way he held me to him, the unbridled passion that flowed between us as he took me in the back of his truck. The rough fabric of his seat scratched my back as I scratched his, and pain danced with pleasure in equal measure with each passing minute.

Before I realized what I was doing, I'd pressed my hands into his chest, pushing him off me long enough to have him sitting in the seat and me climbing into his lap. He was barely out of me before I sat on top of him again, the length of him sliding in deeper, making both of us pause when he was all the way in as if we'd lost all breath completely.

The windows of that old Bronco were steamy and hot, but every now and then, a cool breeze would reach us from the forest, and I'd shiver and shake, the combination exhilarating.

Slowly, I began to move, my thigh muscles burning as I grabbed his shoulders and rode him. His hands were free to roam, and roam they did, gripping my waist and my hips and my breasts before they were cradling my face to his again.

I threw my head back on a gasp when he bucked into me, realizing that when he worked his hips in time with mine, a depth I never knew existed was reached. Each new thrust pressed a spot deep inside me that sparked my orgasm, like two rocks slicked together over a bundle of straw, just waiting to catch fire.

Jordan's mouth latched onto my neck, sucking and licking his way down to my breast, and when he sucked my nipple between his teeth and bucked his hips at the same time, I cried out in a moan I was sure couldn't have been mine.

"Oh, *God*," I groaned, and the muscles in my body ceased to work. I sat there on top of him without moving, completely useless, but Jordan kept working.

He wrapped his arms around me, hugging me to him so that every new thrust of his hips didn't just make him penetrate me deeper, but also had my clit rubbing against his pelvis, that fire closer and closer to catching with each flex.

"Jordan," I whispered.

"Oh, fuck, *Sydney,*" he answered on a breath, my name long and desperate on his lips, and then he was pumping harder, faster, and I knew he was close, too.

His desire fueled mine, and I exploded, thighs clenching around him as I let my orgasm take me under. The spark that finally caught was more like a nuclear blast, one so powerful that I trembled and moaned like I'd left my body entirely in that moment. I floated above it, feeling everything and nothing at all, a powerful sensation of every nerve being ignited at the same time everything inside me numbed.

Jordan came right behind me, burying his head in my chest with a groan and gripping me so tight I could barely breathe as he stilled. I felt his hot release inside me, and I somehow found the strength to move when he couldn't anymore, riding him until we were both spent, collapsing into each other in a panting tangle of limbs.

The symphony of the forest came back to life, insects and birds singing in the night as our breaths evened out, our bodies hot and slick but still wrapped up in every possible way.

When I finally mustered the energy to peel myself away from him enough to look into his eyes, Jordan ran both hands back through my hair, tugging on it slightly until my chin lifted and his mouth met mine.

"Alright, you little devil," he said, kissing me hard before he pulled back on a smile and ran his thumb across my bottom lip. "Now that you've had your way with me, let's talk about that date."

THIRTEEN

SYDNEY

"**O**H, MY GOD, YOU KINKY LITTLE FOX!"

I covered my mouth to suppress my laughter at my sister's outburst the next day, casting a glance at Paige in the living room to make sure she hadn't heard anything. College Game Day was on, so of course, I was invisible to her.

"I can't believe you hooked up with your boss," Gabby continued, whisper-yelling at me. She was at Mom and Dad's for the day, and I'd told her to find someplace private when we got on the call. "In a friggin' *Bronco* in the damn forest, for God's sake."

I bit my lip against my smile, both loving and hating the giddy feeling inflating my belly like a hot air balloon. I loved it because it was fun and exciting, but I hated it because I knew as soon as it took over, anxiety would sweep in to knock me out of breath.

"You're ignoring the pressing question, dear sister, which is..." I glanced at Paige, making my way through the sliding glass door and onto the back porch before I continued. "What the hell do I do now?"

"What do you mean?" Gabby asked. "You bang him again — preferably in a bed this time, but hey, no judgment if exhibitionism is your thing."

I wished she was in the vicinity to smack her.

"Gab, be real. Do you not see every single thing wrong with this scenario? Because they're like flashing neon lights to me."

"So what, he's your boss," she said, as if that didn't matter. "First of all, there aren't any *official* rules that say you can't date."

"No," I agreed. "But it's *very* much implied. And could you imagine? I'm the first female to ever be on this staff, and rumor gets around that I'm sleeping with the head coach? And, on top of that, I'm already the villain in my divorce with Randy."

I lowered my voice on that last part, as if someone would hear me and the gossip that Stratford was so well known for would begin before I had the chance to thwart it.

Gabby sighed. "Yeah... I guess you have a point. What if you kept it on the down low? I mean, do you think it's serious?"

Her question made my stomach tie violently into a knot the size of a basketball. "I don't know," I answered honestly. "I mean... I guess I'd probably be naïve to believe it is, wouldn't I? I'm a single mom with the Police Chief as an ex-husband." I scoffed. "Pretty sure *no one* is lining up to enter into a relationship with me."

"First of all, Paige is not baggage. If anything, she adds to your hot factor because she's adorable and sassy and fun," Gabby said, and I could picture her holding up her stiletto-nailed fingers as she counted off. "And secondly, *you* are a catch. Your dumbass ex-husband is in your past, and he has no effect on who you are now."

I sighed, flopping down into one of the lounge chairs that was usually in the sun. Today was an overcast day, though, as fall as it could feel, and I wrapped myself up in my long cardigan sweater against the cool morning air. "Maybe it's me who's scared," I admitted. "Maybe the thought of opening myself up to a man again makes me shrink in terror."

"That breaks my heart, sis."

I shrugged, though she couldn't see me. "It's true."

A long silence passed between us before Gabby spoke again. "Well, I hope that one day you open yourself up to the possibility of letting yourself be happy again. But, if this is really how you feel, then I say keep it casual. Have the conversation with Jordan and let him know where you're at."

"Casual..." I repeated, testing the word on my lips. "As in, a booty call, a hookup, a friend with benefits that no one knows about."

"Exactly."

I wrinkled my nose. "Why does that make me feel dirty?"

At that, Gabby barked out a laugh. "Welcome to the modern world of dating, where no one is happy and everyone pretends to be fine with no strings attached."

My stomach soured, but I didn't know what other option there was. Jordan couldn't possibly want something serious with me, and even if he did, we couldn't possibly *be* serious. We worked together, I had a kid, and my ex was a psycho.

Three strikes, as they say.

"You also don't have to make any decisions right now," Gabby added. "You know?"

"Yeah..." I agreed, but my chest tightened as if to say *you better make some decisions before we have a panic attack, bitch.*

Suddenly, Paige jumped up from the couch inside and ran to the front door, voice loud and boisterous as she greeted Jordan. He was smiling down at her, giving her a high five for something she was telling him.

In the other hand, he held a bouquet of flowers.

"Shit..."

"What?" Gabby asked.

"Jordan just got here. He's working with Paige today."

"Yeah... you told me that. But why the curse word?"

"He brought flowers."

"Shit..."

We were both silent for a moment, and Jordan's eyes found mine through the window. The way the sunlight shined through the thick clouds that day illuminated those blue eyes of his, and the brown around his iris looked almost gold.

He crooked a sideways smile, and I melted.

"Wish me luck," I told her, and as soon as she did, I ended the call.

"... and I've been working on kicking. I really like it, actually. I always thought I wanted to be a quarterback, but you know, *so* many games come down to whether or not the kicker can make a field goal or an extra point, you know? And I was just thinking, *man*, I'd love to be that person who wins for my team."

Paige was still rambling on as she and Jordan joined me in the backyard, Paige circling Jordan with a football in her hand, hair a wild mess.

"I think you'd make a great kicker," he said, listening attentively.

"Really?"

He nodded. "We can work on more drills that will help you get strength and accuracy today. Sound good?"

"Yeah!"

He smiled, but then his gaze was on me, and the heat that came from it had me sweating instantly.

"Paige, why don't you run inside and braid your hair," I said with my eyes still on Jordan.

"Mom," she complained.

I snapped my eyes to hers. "No whining, Paige Marie. If you're going to be outside playing, you'll want it out of your face, anyway."

"But it takes *forever* to braid."

"Jordan and I need to talk about some work stuff real quick, anyway. Now, go braid your hair and then you can keep watching Game Day until he comes to get you."

Paige pouted, but did as I said, and Jordan's smile climbed a little when we were alone.

Just being near him had my body reacting, like every nerve was waking and reaching for him instinctively. The memory of his lips on mine, of his hands on my hips, of his thighs — big and strong beneath me as I rode him... it all came back to me in a series of flashes, and I blushed so furiously I thought my face would ignite.

"I know you already have plenty of flowers in your garden," he finally said, taking a few steps toward me and holding out the bouquet. "But... well, I was brought up to bring a woman flowers when you care about her, and for no reason at all. So..." He shrugged, grabbing the back of his neck with his free hand. "I hope you like daisies."

I smiled, taking the bouquet when he offered it to me and inhaling the sweet scent. It was a beautiful gathering of Michaelmas daisies, all in rich purples and mauves, with little pops of yellow Goldenrod surrounding them.

"They're beautiful," I said.

Jordan smiled, reaching down to take the bouquet from me and setting it on the table. Then, he grabbed both of my hands, pulled me to stand, and without a single hesitation, pressed his lips to mine.

It was a soft and sweet kiss, his hands cradling me to him as he inhaled me like it was his first breath since he'd dropped me off back at the stadium after two o'clock this morning.

My breath was deep and long, too, and I melted into his touch, into that kiss, into the sweet feeling of having a man hold me and want me and bring me flowers.

But then my anxiety poked me hard in the ribs, and I pulled back quickly.

Checking inside to make sure Paige hadn't seen us, I quickly put space between me and Jordan, blushing as I gestured for him to sit.

"Uh, we should talk."

Jordan smirked, but sat in the chair that was a bit too small for his six-foot-whatever frame, anyway. He crossed one ankle over the opposite knee and folded his hands over his abdomen, kicking back in a relaxed fashion. "Okay," he said. "Let's talk."

I frowned. "Do you have to do that?"

"Do what?"

"That," I said, waving my hand at him as I took the seat opposite where he sat. "Look all effortlessly handsome and casually relaxed."

He chuckled. "I am relaxed. I'm happy to see you," he said easily. "Should I not be?"

I frowned again, a deep sigh leaving my chest as I leaned my elbows on the table. I stared at my hands as I spoke. "Look… last night was…" *Amazing. Incredible. The best sex of my life.* "Fun. But, I think we should talk about what we do from here."

I chanced a glance at Jordan, who cocked a brow.

"So… we should just keep this between us, I think. I'm sure you agree. With our jobs and everything… well, it's complicated. Plus, there's Randy…" I didn't elaborate there. "And I think we both know it's nothing serious, and we can have fun without anyone knowing, right? So…" I swallowed, because the more I talked, the more Jordan's smirk climbed. "Yeah. Casual."

I waited, and Jordan tilted his head to the side, assessing me before he leaned over the table toward me. His hands reached for mine, and they covered mine completely, his thumbs smoothing the skin on my wrist as his eyes found mine.

"Sydney, while our first time together being in the back of my Bronco might not insinuate it, I'm an old-fashioned kind of guy," he said, licking his lips as a soft sort of laugh came from his nose. "I don't know *how* to do the whole casual hook-up thing."

I sighed. "That makes two of us."

His smile grew a little at that, but then he was serious, his hands squeezing where he held mine. "This isn't a *keep it on the down low, let's just have sex and not tell anyone* kind of thing for me. I like you, Sydney. And I told you this last night — I want to get to know you. I want to *date* you." Jordan's eyes were sincere when he tipped my chin up so I'd look at him again. "If you're mine, you're mine. And I'm going to make sure everyone knows it."

My stupid heart shattered into a million butterflies, each one of them tickling my ribs as they fluttered about.

But I herded them all back into their cage, brows bending together as I squeezed Jordan's hands in return.

"As much as I want to say the same, I think we both know this is more complicated than that."

"How so?"

"Well, for starters, I have a kid — a kid who *just* survived the divorce of her parents." I shook my head. "I'm not ready to tell her about us, because I don't think she's ready to hear it. Especially because she's grown so close to you in her own way, and I don't want her to worry about that being broken."

Jordan frowned, but nodded. "That's fair."

"And," I continued. "You're my boss. And before you even make the argument that neither of us signed a contract saying we wouldn't date," I said, holding up my finger to halt where he'd started to speak. "It doesn't matter. The fact still remains that I'm your employee, and the first female on this staff, and if word got around that we were intimate, I would be judged for it, and you would not be."

The more I talked, the more Jordan scowled — but it wasn't in anger, rather in a deep, unsatisfying understanding.

"Plus, Randy..." I started, but shook my head, not wanting to dive into it. "Well, let's just say I know he wouldn't be okay with me having a boyfriend, and I don't want to deal with that right now. Not when I'm just settling into being free of him."

Jordan blew out a long breath, squeezing my hands. "I understand."

He looked so hurt, so defeated, and it killed me.

I leaned into him, looking him in the eyes as I said, "I like you, too, Jordan. And I'd love to get to know you more, to see where this goes... but, I have to be realistic, and we have to go slow."

"I don't know how to not treat you the way you deserve to be treated."

I smiled, heart swelling. "You can, just... can you also live with knowing I'm yours, but keeping it between us for now?"

His lips twitched into a smile when I said the words *I'm yours*, and I smiled in return.

"So, dating on the down low."

I nodded. "As secret as if it were an affair."

His mouth screwed to the side at that, but he considered, nodding after a moment. "Okay. But, I have one condition."

"State your condition, Coach."

Jordan chuckled. "You have to come to my brother's wedding," he said. "As my date."

"Jordan..."

"It's not until November twenty-sixth," he said before I could argue. "That's a full two months away. By that time, playoffs will be over and we'll be in the offseason, so you won't have to worry about the team for a while. That gives us two months to warm Paige up to the idea of us."

"But Randy—"

"Randy is your *ex*-husband," he reminded me in earnest. "He doesn't get to hold power over you anymore."

My heart squeezed — both in warmth and in warning — and I chewed my lip, considering his proposal.

"What do you say," he asked after a moment, peeling his hands from mine before he extended one. "Do we have a deal?"

I fought against my growing smile, shaking my head. "You're ridiculous."

"I'm serious when it comes to making promises and keeping my word," he amended for me. "I'll agree to your half of the deal, if you agree to mine."

My mouth pulled to one side, but I reached for his hand anyway, and he shook it firmly as if he'd just sold me a car.

"Fine, I'll be your wedding date," I said, but I quickly held up a finger at his victorious smile. "*But*, I still want to have a discussion before we tell Paige. Or anyone else, for that matter."

"Tell me what?" Paige asked, bounding outside with her hair braided and football in hand.

"I told you to wait inside," I warned her, standing with Jordan, already missing the warmth of where his hands had been in mine.

"It was a commercial break, and you guys were taking *forever*," she said, dragging out the word.

"Well, let's get you warmed up, Miss Impatient," Jordan said, holding up his hands for the ball. "Hit me."

Paige grinned, tossing him the ball before she ran out into the backyard, and just like that, they were in practice mode and she'd forgotten what she'd heard when she'd walked outside — that was the blessed attention span of a nine-year-old in all its glory.

I made my way back inside, cleaning up the dishes from breakfast as I watched Jordan run drills with my daughter under an overcast sky. Every now and then his eyes would find me, too, and he'd smile, and I'd smile, and my heart would race in an exhilarating stampede of excitement and fear.

Autumn was upon us, alright.

And I had a feeling the leaves wouldn't be the only things falling in the upcoming months.

FOURTEEN

JORDAN

Up until that point in my life, each month had fit into a category.

When I was younger, they were separated by school months and summer months.

When I graduated high school, things blurred a little, and I began to measure them by the seasons, noting the different weather each month could bring.

When I got the coaching job at Stratford High, and every year since, the months had simply been divided into three: football season, off season, and summer training.

October, in my old life, would have fit right into the middle of football season. I would have greeted it with a nod and an otherwise non-affected state of determination to keep doing what I'd done in September and drive my team closer to the championship.

But now, it wasn't just October, the last month of football before we found out if we were going to the play-offs or not.

It wasn't just October, cool weather and colorful leaves and homecoming and Halloween.

Now, it was October, the first full month of Sydney Clark being mine.

It didn't matter that no one knew it but me — which was surprising, because it wasn't my usual game to play. But after our discussion at her house the morning after our game against the Serpents, we fell into a rhythm, into a sort of dance where we kept our distance and remained professional at school and around Paige, but blurred those lines when we were alone.

We had a secret, and I found no one really needed to know that I was kissing her lips each night — as long as that fact remained true.

Currently, on the Monday night after our homecoming game against the Ranchwood Rockets — whom we absolutely *crushed* — Sydney was on my couch in an oversized t-shirt and a pair of boy shorts, her hair loose and wavy where it framed her face, and she was popping candy corn into her mouth. She had her legs outstretched, feet in my lap, and I rubbed them as we finished the second movie in our Halloween movie marathon that night.

First was *Casper: The Friendly Ghost.*

And now, *Hocus Pocus.*

Turned out neither of us were big horror fans.

I tried to keep my attention on the movie, chuckling as the kids tricked the witches and the parents were put under a spell to dance all night. But I was more focused on my hands moving over her arches and pads, on the little groans of approval that she let slip from time to time, and on the unbelievable four weeks I'd had with that woman on my couch.

I wondered if she realized it, too — that one month ago in her backyard, she'd said she'd be mine.

Or maybe I was just a lovesick fool and should be ashamed that I even *cared* that it had been one month.

Still, though, I'd held my stern outward appearance at school and kept quiet around my family as per usual, when I was with her?

I couldn't pretend.

I massaged up her calf a little, smiling as I recounted the time we'd spent together. I didn't know which I'd loved more — watching her work with appreciation from a distance, sneaking kisses when the other coaches had yet to show up to the locker room, learning her as a woman on the nights Randy had Paige and I got Sydney to myself, or marveling at the role she played in Paige's life as her mother when I spent afternoons practicing with that little girl in their backyard.

I was learning her favorite flowers and memorizing the look of determination she wore when she worked in the garden. I was learning about her childhood, about her parents and her sister, about her life traveling before finally settling down in Stratford just in time to finish high school. I was learning who she was when she was with Randy, how she'd changed since, and the ways in which she would *never* change — like the fact that she was, had always been, and always would be a woman who was curious about the way things worked, like the bodies of the players she worked on and the vegetables she tended to in the garden and her daughter, who threw her for a loop because she changed and grew each day.

It was like slowly peeling off buttery flakes of a pastry, discovering new tastes with every layer, and I cherished each morsel.

The more I got to know her, the more I struggled to understand Randy — who, up until that point, I had respected. It wasn't that Sydney ever spoke ill of him, but she didn't need to. I knew all I needed to know about him, the way he treated her, and their relationship by how she responded to being treated the way she always should have been.

Every game he came to with Paige by his side, I would chance a glance at him, wondering how he could have been so stupid as to let her slip away.

He always met my gaze with the same intensity, as if he knew something I didn't.

As I became more familiar with Sydney, I revealed my own layers to her, too — letting her pass through walls I never realized I had built and fortified.

My smile faltered a bit as that thought settled in, because I realized one subject I'd yet to even broach with her was the death of my father — specifically, the hard drive and the journal and my discoveries so far.

And I knew it was on purpose.

That part of me — the young man who was left without a father, with questions never answered — he was tender and raw and I did everything I could to never expose him. The need to protect my father's legacy and my brothers and my mom and *myself* was so deeply sewn into my being that it had sprouted roots.

But, something in my throat tightened that Monday night on my couch when Sydney leaned up, kissing my cheek before she scampered off to use the restroom down the hall.

I paused the TV, grabbed my laptop, plugged in the external hard drive, and opened the journal I'd been neglecting since Sydney had stolen my time and attention.

Not that I'd complained.

"Uh-oh," Sydney said when she plopped back down on the couch beside me, leaning on the arm of the couch with one elbow. "Don't tell me you got another new trick play idea or the sudden urge to watch defense tapes. We were just getting to the good part."

She smirked, nodding toward the TV where the witches were paused on the screen, and I reached over to squeeze her knee.

"I want to show you something."

Sydney rolled her eyes, but scooted closer, wrapping her arm under mine and reaching for her phone. "*Fine.* But I'm setting a timer, and after twenty minutes, no more football talk until the movie's over. I don't care how close we are to playoffs."

"It's not football-related."

Sydney paused where she was reaching for her phone, her little mouth popping open into a soft *o*. "I'm sorry, I don't know how to hide my shock."

She was teasing, but when she saw the sincerity on my face, her brows tugged together.

"What is it?"

My heart stopped altogether on my next breath, and I held it, turning my laptop until she could see the screen.

I watched as Sydney's eyes roamed, her frown deepening the more she looked. "I don't understand... what am I looking at? It's like..." She reached for the computer, pulling it into her own lap for a closer look. "It's like an old processor or something. Is this Windows Vista?"

"Mm-hmm."

She frowned more, shaking her head at the document I had open. "And this is... well, part of it is in Latin, I think? But..." Her eyebrows softened, lips parting. "It says your father's name. It says... it's talking about the distillery." Sydney's eyes slowly found mine. "Jordan, what *is* this?"

I swallowed, realizing the jolt of nerves in my stomach wasn't because I was afraid to tell Sydney about what my brothers and I had found.

It was because I'd found someone I *wanted* to share it with.

"It's my dad's journal."

The tension between her brows released, her eyes widening. "Your... your dad's *journal*?"

I nodded, pointing to the hard drive plugged into the side of my laptop. "It's a long story, but... well, essentially, Logan and Mallory found this old, burned up, useless computer when they were tasked to clean out a storage closet at the distillery. He managed to get the hard drive out of it, and used this external hard drive," I said, tapping the large silver square. "To host it, I guess. It pulled up dad's computer as if we were logging onto it, but the problem was... it was password protected."

Sydney listened intently, her eyes ever-widening.

"Mikey's girlfriend — well, she was his friend at the time, but that's another story — she's smart, and has always had a fascination with coding and such. So, the two of them worked on trying to break into it. One day... they did."

"Whoa..." Sydney looked back at the screen. "And they found this?"

"Among other things. It was mostly work files and emails and such, when they first started looking, but then Mikey found the journal. And see," I said, reaching over to scroll on the mousepad until the beginning entries were on the screen. "At first, it's just a normal journal — and really, it's more like a daily log. Boring stuff. Him going to meetings, notes on what he needs to accomplish that week, random reminders. But then, something strange happens."

"He starts writing in Latin," Sydney finishes for me, scrolling down to the first entry in the old language.

"He starts writing in Latin," I echo. "My brothers were confused, but I remember when Dad got on this kick about how so many of our words are based in the Latin language, and how he read an article that if you learn Latin, it's a gateway to learn pretty much any other language in the world. I remember him listening to the tapes and studying this giant book he'd bought on it. And I got into it, too," I added with a shrug. "It was kind of fun. Challenging. And it was time with my dad, you know?"

Sydney's mouth pulled to one side, and she reached over, grabbing my hand.

"Anyway, I told my brother's that with some time and some online translation tools, I thought I could go through and figure out what he was writing... see if it was anything important."

"That's what I guess I'm missing here," she said, glancing at the screen and back at me. "I mean, I think it's cool that you found your dad's journal, but you're just... reading it? Kind of seems like an invasion of privacy. Don't get me wrong," she said quickly. "I'm sure it feels good to be close to him in a way again, and have access to what he was thinking each day, but..."

"It's not about that," I explained. "Think about it, Sydney. When Logan found the laptop, it was in a box that had been stuffed in a corner, covered by other tubs and boxes, in an old storage room that *no one touched* for almost ten years. And in that same box, there were charred things from my dad's desk — a picture of our family at the lake, a paper weight with a favorite quote of his, and some other things."

"Well..." Sydney looked like she was afraid to say her next words. "I mean, that makes sense, doesn't it? With the fire..."

"The fire was in Robert J. Scooter's old office. Why would my dad's things be burnt, if they were in *his* office? And why, when the Scooters cleaned out my dad's office, did they not give any of the things in that box to our family?"

Sydney's expression went blank, and she gripped the edges of the laptop harder as she sat back on the couch. "You think you'll find answers in the journal."

"Honestly, I don't," I confessed. "But... I guess there's a part of all of us that hopes."

"Have you found anything yet?"

I chewed my lip, taking the laptop from her long enough to pull up the entry where dad had mentioned he'd found Robert J. Scooter's Last Will and Testament. I turned the screen back to Sydney, watching as she read over what I'd translated.

"Jesus Christ..." Her eyes found mine. "I thought there wasn't a Will. I thought..." She shook her head, glancing at the screen and back at me. "There wasn't a Will. That's what the Scooters always said. I remember my dad telling me the story of the distillery when we moved here, and telling me about Patrick Scooter and his father and how he died from a random infection on a seemingly harmless injury and... and... *there wasn't a Will.*"

I cocked one brow on a sigh. "Well, it seems there *was* a Will... which leads me to believe that maybe there is something to be found in this journal, after all."

Sydney stared at the laptop for a long pause. "Does your mom know?"

"No one knows except me and my brothers," I said. "Maybe their significant others, at least Michael's girlfriend, Kylie, for sure. And, now... you."

She looked at me then, her almond eyes wide and glossy, lips parted, chin quivering.

Anxiety flickered like a lantern in my chest. "I'm sorry," I said quickly, shutting the laptop. "Was that too much? God, you probably think we're crazy, all the conspiracy theory bullshit—"

"I don't think you're crazy," she said quickly, turning to face me completely once the laptop was on my coffee table. Her eyes were sincere, her hands slipping into mine. "I think you're right."

I squeezed her hands in mine.

"Thank you, Jordan," she whispered, gaze searching mine. "Thank you for telling me, for trusting me."

I nodded, heart pounding slow like a fist was wrapped around it as she crawled into my arms. She kissed my neck, my chin, my jaw, all over until our lips fastened together and I pulled her tighter into my chest.

In that moment, I felt it — our hearts fusing together, our souls opening the door to each other's, finding a room, making it home.

And in the same breath that I found relief and warmth, I was also overwhelmed with a sickly cold terror.

Because suddenly, it was real.

We were real.

And I couldn't decide why, in the pit of my stomach, there was the gnawing notion that none of it could possibly last.

FIFTEEN

SYDNEY

"I'd like to make some toast," Paige said, holding up her champagne flute filled with Welch's grape juice and holding her chin high.

Jordan barked out a laugh, but lifted his glass, anyway, and I did the same, smiling at him from across my dining room table.

It was Saturday night, and less than twenty-four hours before, the Stratford High Wild Cats had clenched our spot in the Tennessee Division I High School Football Playoffs.

"To Coach," she said, addressing Jordan. "You were a loser at the beginning of the season, but that didn't stop you, and just like I heard Mom saying when she was making fun of you to Aunt Gabby one night, *you found a way to win, anyway!*"

Jordan laughed again, cocking a brow at me as I kicked Paige under the table. "You were making fun of my word of the season, huh?"

"Shh, I'm not done," Paige said before I could defend myself. "To the players, who have worked their butts off."

"That's right," Jordan said, pride beaming off him like a ray of light.

"And to my mom."

Paige turned to me, then, her little eyes that looked so much like mine crinkling at the edges as she lifted her glass toward me.

"The strongest woman in the whole wide world, and the best athletic trainer Stratford has ever seen."

Jordan held his glass toward me. "Hear, hear." Our eyes met, and he smirked, making me blush.

"Thank you, sweetheart," I said, heart squeezing as we all met glasses in the middle of the table.

"Here's to winning not just our first playoff game, but *all* of them, and bringing another trophy back to Stratford!"

We clinked our glasses to the tune of a little *yeehaw* from Jordan and some giggles from me and Paige, then we all took a sip, setting our glasses back down and digging into the celebration dinner I'd made for us.

"That was quite a speech, Paigey," I said, leaning over to help her cut her steak.

"I've been practicing." She sat straighter, turning to Jordan. "Now, before we get too much into the celebrations, we need to talk about that defensive line and their low sack record. Jones is too big and powerful for him to not have *at least* ten this season."

Jordan smiled, listening intently as Paige continued on, offering her suggestions and advice on virtually every single player and coach and play by the time we'd finished eating. I couldn't get a word in edgewise — not that I minded. My heart was full sitting at that table with my animated, passionate daughter and my kind, patient...

Whatever he was.

My stomach flipped, and I sipped down the last of my champagne before I stood, starting to clear the table.

"Cake?!" Paige asked excitedly, clapping her hands together and bouncing in her chair as she looked up at me.

I laughed. "In a little bit. Why don't you go play in your room for a while."

"But, Mom," she groaned, her little nose wrinkling as she thrust a hand toward the television. "The Vols are playing Alabama. This is like the most important game of the season."

I hung a hand on my hip, balancing the stack of plates in the other. "Jordan has spent the entire day playing football with you," I reminded her. "Ever think that maybe he needs some adult time? You can watch it in your room."

"Actually…" Jordan said, raising one finger up. He grimaced when I looked at him. "I really want to watch this game, too."

"See?" Paige said, dragging out the vowels. "Come on, Mom. We're celebrating tonight, remember? Football and cake and then I *swear* I'll leave you guys alone." She clasped her hands together. "Pleeeeease."

Jordan mimicked her, poking out his bottom lip until I rolled my eyes and tossed one of the dirty napkins at each of them to the sound of their laughter.

"I am so outvoted in this party of three and I am *not* okay with that."

"Thank you, Mama!" Paige stood on the chair to kiss my cheek before she leapt down off it and scampered into the living room, calling for Jordan to follow.

He stood, helping me carry the rest of the dishes to the sink, and when he glanced over my shoulder and found Paige glued to the television, he wrapped his arm around my waist, pulling me into him subtly.

"For the record," he said, whispering in my ear with his hot lips brushing my neck. "I really *am* looking forward to adult time."

His hand slid down, cupping my ass and squeezing it before he released me, and a flush burned through me as I bit my lip and swatted him away. He just grinned at me over his shoulder, and then he plopped down on the couch next to Paige, both of them kicking their feet up on the coffee table.

My hands were on autopilot as I washed the dishes, throwing some directly into the dishwasher after I rinsed them and spending time scrubbing the others. I found comfort in the warm, soapy water, glancing at Jordan and Paige in the living room from time to time, my thoughts wandering.

It melted my heart to see them together.

Jordan had been so comfortable with Paige from the start, and she was the same with him. It was like they were best friends from the very moment they spoke in the park. Paige counted down the days until she could spend an afternoon in the backyard running football drills with Jordan, and he never seemed to mind her stealing a Saturday of his. In fact, if I had to put money on it, I'd say *he* looked forward to it just as much as she did.

My stomach soured as Randy floated into my mind, as he still tended to do, this time as I compared his relationship with Paige to the one Jordan was building. It wasn't that he and Paige weren't close, or that Paige didn't look up to him and love him dearly, but I couldn't help but note that they'd never spent time together the way she and Jordan had. Randy had always put work first, from the very moment he was promoted to Chief of Police, and Paige and I had taken the backseat willingly, lovingly, with understanding and grace.

I wondered what they did when he had her for half the week.

I always did my best not to pry, not to ask her about her father when I already knew we'd put her in a tough position being the daughter of divorce. And, to Paige's credit, she never volunteered what they did. It made me wonder if she ever talked about *our* time together, or if she kept that between us, too.

She was a tough kid, and though I *knew* the divorce had affected her, she was the kind who wanted to handle it on her own. We almost never talked about it, or about her dad, or about how things used to be.

Paige was a survivor, and she looked forward, with her eyes on the brighter horizon, always.

My mind was still spinning when I sat next to Jordan on the couch, eyes blurring on the television screen with a football game on that I really couldn't have cared less about. Instead, I sipped the wine I'd traded in my champagne for, thinking about Randy, about my own father, and eventually, about Jordan's.

When I'd been at his house Monday night, not even a week ago, he'd revealed a secret to me that no one else in this town knew — one only he and his brothers shared. I hadn't had a good night's sleep since then, because while I was digesting what he'd told me about what they'd found at the distillery, I was also digging through my foggy memory, straining to recall what *I* had heard that night.

It had been late by the time Randy had come home — to *this* home, our new home at the time, one we'd bought with the help of his parents and my own when I'd come home from college earlier that summer. I wasn't even a full two months' pregnant with Paige, but I remembered holding onto my belly when I tiptoed down the stairs, pausing when I heard his hushed voice on the phone with someone in the kitchen.

The fire had been all anyone could talk about, all the local news could show that evening, and there was little information getting out. To this day, I'd never known what made me stop and listen at the foot of those stairs for a while before I made my way down the hall and into the kitchen.

Randy had ended the call quickly, and though he'd tried to smile and be gentle with me at first, his anger showed the more questions I asked.

He assured me it was an accident, that I was crazy, that it was started by a cigarette and they'd be closing up the case easily. He growled at my questions, when I asked how a cigarette could have started such a fire without John Becker noticing and being able to get out. *Was he sleeping?* I'd asked. *Was the door locked? How was he the only one to perish?*

That hadn't been the first night my husband had raised his hand to me.

But it had been the first time he'd let it fall.

He'd told me to mind my business, reminded me that I knew nothing about what was going on and that I was better suited to tend to our *home life*.

He'd said I was crazy, and I remembered that clearly because it was the first time he'd said it, but it wouldn't be the last.

What I *didn't* fully remember was why he'd said it in the first place, why he was struggling to explain himself, getting angry with the more questions I asked.

The memory was foggy, but every now and then, when the smoke cleared, I swore I remembered holding my daughter where she slept in my belly, my heart racing out of my chest.

And my husband's hushed voice in our kitchen whispering something about *homicide.*

— • —

JORDAN

On the Thursday before our final playoff game — *the* game that would determine if we went to fight for the championship — I rallied up the boys, got them ready for practice, and sent them out on the field to work drills with Coach Pascucci and Coach TK.

"Sydney," I said, eyes on my clipboard as I made my way to my office. Everyone else was making their way outside. "A word in my office?"

I kept my face neutral, though my neck was hot, and no one suspected a thing as I continued on to my office without checking to see if she followed. The coaches were already on their way out, and the boys shuffled out behind them, their energy palpable with so much riding on tomorrow night's game.

I sat in my chair, and when Sydney entered the office, I told her to close the door behind her without looking up.

When she did, and we were alone, I dropped my clipboard, stood, and rushed to her.

She was in my arms in the next breath, giggling and whispering for me to get off her as I kissed up and down her neck, over her chin and jaw, her cheeks, before I claimed her lips and silenced her protests.

"Are you mad?" she whispered, but she was still smiling.

"Crazy about you, that's for sure."

I continued my assault of kisses, but she pressed one hand into my chest and shoved, putting space between us.

"Do you actually have something you need to see me about, or did you just interrupt work to make out?"

"Is *both* a reasonable answer?"

She rolled her eyes, but her smile was light and playful.

I gestured for her to sit, and then I leaned my ass on the edge of my desk, folding my hands in my lap as I looked down at her. The longer the silence passed between us, the more my heart raced in my chest.

"What?" she asked when I didn't say anything. Then, her smile slipped. "Oh, God. Did something bad happen?"

"No, no," I assured her, shaking my head, but the words were still lodged in my throat. I was equal parts excited and terrified over what I wanted to ask her. "Do you have plans for Thanksgiving next week?"

Sydney blinked, brows folding together in confusion. "Um... well, I have Paige. But, we're not going anywhere, just staying home, doing a little dinner with the two of us."

"Come to Thanksgiving at my house, instead." I paused. "My *mom's* house."

Sydney's eyes shot wide, her skin paling, lips parting in shock.

"Hear me out," I said before she could answer. "Mom loves having a big Thanksgiving, and everyone will be in town since the wedding is the Saturday after. Paige will have me and my brothers to watch football with, and you could meet everyone before..." I swallowed. "Noah knows I have a plus one to the wedding, but I haven't told him who it is yet. And I just thought..."

Sydney's expression morphed slowly into a soft smile. "Jordan, I'd love to join you and your family for the holiday."

"Really?" I let out a long, relieved breath.

She nodded. "Yes. But... can we just..."

She paused, standing and moving until she was between my legs, and my hands moved to her hips instinctively while her own pressed into my chest.

"For now... can we just tell everyone we're friends?"

My shoulders sagged.

"Not for much longer," she said quickly. "I just... I want to talk to Paige first, and with playoffs in full swing right now, and the holiday, and the wedding... it's just a lot." She swallowed. "I also think I need to tell Randy. He needs to hear it from me."

"You don't owe him anything."

"I know, but... it might save some drama in the long run." She shook her head. "I'm scared, for many reasons, and I know it's asking a lot of you, I know this was my part of the deal, but... I'm asking, anyway. I need a little more time. Okay?"

The next breath that came through my nose was short and hot, but I nodded, though my chest was tight. "Okay," I agreed. "But, if I'm being honest, I don't think my family will buy it."

She smirked at that, lacing her arms around my neck and pressing a kiss to my chin. "I don't think so, either. But, I appreciate you letting me do this the way I need to. I'll talk to Paige as soon as we make it through this busy time, okay? And then..."

"And then you'll be mine."

Her brown eyes searched mine, and she shook her head, pressing up on her toes to kiss me long and slow before she whispered, "I already am."

SIXTEEN

JORDAN

"No, Betty, you're supposed to break the wish bone *with* someone," Ruby Grace explained to Betty Collins, who was holding both sides of a broken turkey bone in her hands. "And whoever gets the bigger piece is the one who gets the wish."

"Exactly. That's why I broke it on my own — better odds that way." She pointed the bigger piece of the bone at Ruby Grace. "That's just simple math, sweetheart."

Betty was a feisty old woman who'd been brought into our life courtesy of Ruby Grace and her time at the nursing home. She and Mom had become fast and furious friends, and she quickly became part of our family.

Ruby Grace rolled her eyes, but smiled still, taking the pieces of bone from Betty to toss out before she continued working on the stuffing she was making.

Mom had been trying to shoo her out of the kitchen all morning, repeatedly pointing out that Ruby Grace was a bride-to-be and should be relaxing two days before her wedding — not cooking. But Ruby Grace insisted she wanted to be in the kitchen, and Mallory and Kylie were helping, too.

I'd never seen Mom so frazzled at a Thanksgiving before. The poor woman didn't know what to do when she had actual help in the kitchen.

"Can I help with anything, Mrs. Becker?" Sydney asked, already reaching for a knife where sweet potatoes were waiting to be diced up for the casserole.

Mom swatted her hand away, and then instantly reddened, covering her mouth with wide eyes. "Oh, dear. I'm so sorry. I just…"

I chuckled, grabbing my mom by the shoulders with a tender squeeze. "Why don't you come hang out with your sons in the living room and let the ladies work? I can't remember the last time you took a Thanksgiving off."

Her bottom lip trembled, and Sydney glanced at me with caring concern before she smiled at my mom. "You know what? I would actually *love* a little tour of your garden, if you wouldn't mind? I saw the beautiful violas and pansies out front, and Jordan said you have a garden in the back."

Mom shifted her weight, glancing up at me before a small smile bloomed on her face. "That's where all the squash came from, and the pumpkin."

"You have a pumpkin patch?" Sydney shook her head. "Now you *have* to show me."

At that, a genuine smile found Mom's lips, and she patted Mallory on the back. "Alright. You ladies let me know if you need me, I'm going to take Sydney for a garden tour."

They all smiled at her, and I mouthed *thank you* to Sydney as they passed by me, headed out the front door.

As soon as Sydney was gone, all four pairs of female eyes were on me.

I inwardly groaned, knowing this was coming. Mom hadn't said much when I asked if Sydney and Paige could join us for the holiday. I'd proposed it under the pretense that it was Paige's first Thanksgiving since the divorce, and that Sydney's family lived in Texas, and that we had grown a friendship since she started working for the school. I'd mentioned how I'd been training Paige for football camp next summer, and that I knew they'd fit right in.

I knew Mom didn't buy my story, but she'd smiled knowingly and not asked a single question — bless her.

My brothers' significant others and Mrs. Betty Collins on the other hand...

"So," Kylie said, one eyebrow cocked. "Seems Mikey and I have missed a lot since our move to New York. Care to fill us in?"

Mallory and Ruby Grace exchanged looks before their smiles grew, Betty tapped a dirty spoon on the palm of her hand, and all of them waited for me to answer.

Just then, a roar of cheers and groans came from the living room.

I hooked a thumb over my shoulder. "Sounds like the game's getting good, I better go see."

"Jordan Becker!" Ruby Grace chided, throwing the top of a cut up celery stalk at me. "Don't you dare leave without spilling the tea."

I dodged the greenery and smiled, making a notion like my lips were sealed before I ducked out of the kitchen to the tune of four dramatic huffs.

I chuckled, knowing they would all be in there going crazy trying to figure out what Sydney and I were, but they knew by now that I was not the kiss-and-tell type. I wasn't the *anything*-and-tell type. I preferred to keep my private life just that — private.

At least, that's what I kept telling myself.

I rounded into the dining room, glancing out the front door where Sydney stood in the front yard with my mom. Mama was bent down, showcasing something as Sydney leaned over and nodded, her brows pinched in concentration.

And my heart pinched at the sight.

That's when I realized that while it wasn't out of the ordinary that I didn't want to talk to the girls about Sydney, that wasn't what had my chest tight.

It was that I *wanted* to talk about her.

Hell, I wanted to talk to *everyone* about the woman, and that was completely opposite of who I'd always been. The truth was if I had it my way, I'd likely talk more than I had in my entire life if I had the chance to tell someone, *anyone,* about the time Sydney and I had spent together.

But here we were, two months in, and the truth was I didn't know where we stood.

Until I met Sydney, I'd avoided dating with the general consensus that love was dangerous, and when you engaged in a relationship with someone, you put yourself and, maybe more importantly, *them* at risk. I'd watched my friends' parents go through divorce, watched my brothers break hearts and even get theirs broken in return, and above it all, I'd seen the unbreakable love my parents shared shattered by tragedy.

And maybe deep down, I'd always been afraid *I* wouldn't know what to do if I ever found "the right woman." I didn't know if I could treat her the way my father had treated my mother, if I could put her first, be patient and caring and kind.

With Sydney, it was effortless.

I treated her like gold because in my eyes she *was*. I didn't have to try to care about her, to put her first, to love her.

I did it all because it was as if there was no other choice, and all my life I'd been preparing for this moment with her.

My chest tightened again, because though I was fairly certain that *I* wouldn't be the one to hurt her, I didn't have a shred of assurance that she wouldn't do the same to me. Not because she wanted to — but because I swung into her life when I knew things were complicated, when I knew she wasn't ready, and when I knew we had an army of circumstance working against us.

That afternoon in her backyard, she told me what she could give me, and what she couldn't.

When I asked her to join us for Thanksgiving, she'd asked me for more time.

And now, it was two days before Noah's wedding, and we hadn't come back to that conversation to discuss *her* part of the deal.

I'd done what she needed me to do — stayed quiet, kept our relationship a secret, respected the boundaries she'd put in place. She assured me the time was coming, that she needed to do it *her* way, and I believed her.

But I wanted her so badly I couldn't bear the weight of not knowing if she felt the same way I did any longer.

And I knew I had to ask her tonight — before the wedding, before I had the chance to fall any further.

Though I knew in my gut it was already too late.

Another roar came from the group in the living room, and it shook me out of my daze. I chanced one last glance at my mother and Sydney together before I leaned over the back of the couch where Noah and Mikey sat. Logan was in Dad's old recliner.

And Paige was smack dab in the middle of the floor, sitting on her knees, eyes glued to the television.

"I *told* you the Cowboys didn't have a chance against the Bills' defense," she said, looking pointedly over her shoulder at Noah. "This isn't 2007."

"Were you even *alive* in 2007?" Mikey asked.

Paige turned back to the TV with a flick of her wild, wavy hair that had me stifling a laugh. "Doesn't matter if I was or not. I clearly know more about football than any of you do."

Noah's mouth popped open, him and Mikey exchanging glances before they looked over their shoulders and up at me.

Logan chuckled. "I like this kid."

"Me, too," I said, and Paige smiled back at me with pride.

A battle of emotions roared on inside me as the cheers roared on at the AT&T Stadium. I both loved having Sydney and Paige at my mother's house for Thanksgiving and loathed it, because I'd never brought anyone home with me before, and because they fit in like they'd always been here, and because I knew without having to ask that my mom was already falling in love with Sydney — her heart easier to win than my own — and that my brothers would already go to war to protect Paige, if they had to.

It was the weekend before my brother's wedding, and we were all gathered in the same place for the first time in months — Mikey and Kylie home from New York, Ruby Grace no longer separated from Noah with her Ameri-Corps contract, and Mallory and Logan closer than ever with a baby on the way. Mom was at the head of it all, watching her family grow, and all the while, I thought I'd been flying under the radar, watching from a distance with nothing to add but a hug or a small piece of advice from time to time.

But I was here with someone I loved, too.

Even if she had no idea.

And maybe what scared me most was that having her and Paige here was a reciprocation, the missing piece I didn't realize I'd wanted so badly. For months, I'd spent days and nights in their home, learning who they were as a family.

The fact was that Sydney and Paige already felt like *my* family, too.

My stomach rolled more with every minute, and I wondered how I'd be able to eat. I was just about to make my way into the kitchen to pour an old fashioned that I hoped would settle my nerves when Mikey threw one arm over the couch to look at me again.

"So," he said. "One week from tomorrow, you'll be fighting for that trophy again. How you feeling?"

I blew out a long breath, leaning over the couch again and clasping my hands where they hung between my brothers. "The team is ready. They're strong, talented, and thanks to Sydney, all in a pretty healthy shape, too. But," I added, scratching my jaw with my eyes on the television. "Pressure gets to them. I saw it in the first home game, and again twice after when we played our biggest rivals. They get sloppy, and don't play smart. If that happens next week, we don't have a chance."

"You know what *I* think?" Paige said, standing and flopping down in the middle of the couch between my brothers, her chin turned up toward me.

"No, but I bet you're gonna tell me."

"You need to ask Rodgers to get them in the zone before Friday."

I cocked a brow, waiting, because I knew she wasn't done.

"What I mean is, he's the quarterback, right? And the team captain. But, he's a quiet guy — kind of like you, Coach. And I think that's why the team respects you so much. They know that when you say something, it's because it's important. And, well, I think it's like that with Rodgers, too. I think if you pulled him aside and asked him to step up this week, and suddenly their leader was speaking out, telling them the errors he sees, suggesting what they need to pay attention to?" Paige shrugged. "We'd win for sure."

"That right?"

Noah shook his head from beside her. "You're going to be president one day."

"Nuh-uh," she said, looking at him matter-of-factly before she smiled up at me. "I'm going to be a football player."

It wasn't long after that that the girls announced that dinner was ready. We called Mom and Sydney in from the garden, tore my brothers and Paige from the television, and all gathered around a feast that could feed at least three times the amount of people in attendance.

When we were all seated, Mom held out her hands, and I took her left while Noah took her right. Sydney was next to me, Paige across from us, and we all linked hands, connecting to each other around the meal that brought us together.

"I'd like to say grace, if that's alright," Noah said.

Mom smiled and squeezed his hand, and we all bowed our heads.

"Heavenly Father, thank you for the blessings you have bestowed upon this family. We are so blessed to be able to be here together in this way, to share a meal and spend time together when life can so easily slip away from us."

I swallowed, my throat tightening with emotion.

"I know I speak for everyone when I say we're missing a big piece of our puzzle today, but we know Dad is up there with you, probably watching the games and yelling at the big HD screens they got up there."

We all chuckled.

"So, give him a big hug for us, and tell him we love him and we miss him. And Lord, I want to thank you for our amazing mother, who has filled this home with love and wrangled us rowdy boys for our entire lives, and for my brothers — who I can always count on."

That emotion I'd felt before surged through me again, and I cleared my throat to ease the swell.

"I want to thank you for Kylie," Noah continued. "Who has put up with us for years and still manages to like us."

Kylie giggled.

"And for Mallory, who put up with us all being jerks to her because of her last name, and somehow still manages to love us and forgive us, anyway."

"And for *y'all* seeing past that last name, seeing me for who I really am, and loving me, too," she added.

"We pray you will keep her and Logan's baby safe and healthy inside that little oven of hers," Noah said. "And deliver him or her safely to us."

"Her," Logan whispered, and at that, all of our eyes popped open and locked on him, though he was looking at Mallory, who smiled and squeezed his hand.

"*Her?*" Mom cried out, her eyes flooding with tears.

Logan nodded, and the whole table buzzed with a mixture of congratulations and excitement.

"Shhh," Noah said, calming us. "Still praying here."

We laughed, closing our eyes and bowing our heads again.

"I want to thank you for Betty Collins, and for bringing her into our family when we needed her most."

"You're welcome," she chimed in, and we all chuckled again.

"And for our new guests, Sydney and Paige, who fit in like they've always been here, and already bring us joy, and make our oldest brother smile — which is honestly really weird and kind of unsettling, but we'll get used to it."

"I *told* you to stop being so grumpy all the time," Paige said to the tune of another flurry of laughter, but my throat was so tight I could no longer swallow, and I blinked my eyes open, looking at the place where my fingers intertwined with Sydney's.

"And Lord, I want to thank you for my incredible fiancée, who will be my wife in less than forty-eight hours from now. I have waited my entire life to find a woman like her, and you delivered her just like I always knew you would. Thank you for making me a patient man, for helping me see why it never worked out with anyone before, and comforting me in those dark times to know that the light was on its way. It wasn't easy," he said, and there was a murmur of agreement, but my eyes were floating up to Sydney's.

And hers were open, too — staring back at me.

"But it was so, so worth it. If there's anything this family has taught me, it's that love is the most important thing, and it's worth fighting for — no matter the risk."

Sydney's eyes were wide and glossed, a little pinch between her brows as she watched me and I watched her, nothing being said, but everything spoken just the same.

"Thank you for our blessings, Lord. And thank you for this meal. Amen."

"Amen," we all echoed, and while my mom instantly went into how great Noah's grace was and then began peppering Mallory with baby questions now that we knew the gender, Sydney and I continued watching each other, and I wondered if she felt what I felt in that moment, too.

I couldn't wait any longer.

I needed more from her. I needed her to claim me, to assure me that I wasn't crazy or alone in what I was feeling, to make what we had between us *real*.

And I would ask for it.

Tonight.

—•—

SYDNEY

After dinner, everyone helped clear the table, and then we all separated into little groups without really noticing it.

Jordan and his brothers were watching football in the living room with Paige, who I imagined was in hog heaven with so many people around who loved the game like she did. Before he retreated there, Jordan had pulled me to the side, asking if we could talk after I put Paige to bed tonight. My stomach was in knots wondering what it was about, but he assured me it was nothing bad, so I tried to trust him in that.

Jordan's mom, Laurelei, along with Betty and Ruby Grace were gathered at the dining room table, now filled with the contents of Ruby Grace's wedding planning binder. They were drinking wine and laughing as they went through last-minute preparations.

Mikey and Kylie were in the backyard, sitting together at a little bonfire they'd made while Mikey played the guitar.

Mallory and I were in the kitchen cleaning up, and we cracked the window so we could hear what Michael was playing. He was actually quite good, and I wondered to myself if he would ever consider making a career from music.

He and Kylie were so young, just nineteen years old, and I smiled from time to time thinking about how everything felt so possible at that age, and yet it also felt like nothing had to be figured out at all — not yet.

When I was nineteen, I was in college, with my eyes set on the future. I envisioned working with athletic teams across the country, learning more about the human body every day, and more importantly — how to keep athletes healthy and on the field or court where they wanted to be.

My stomach sank, as it often did when I thought about what could have been. Then I shrank from guilt, knowing that if it had turned out that way, I wouldn't have Paige.

I blinked the thoughts away as Mallory handed me a freshly cleaned casserole dish covered in warm soapy suds. I ran it under the cool water from the faucet, rinsing it completely before I set it to dry on a towel we'd laid out on the counter.

"I can handle this, Mallory," I offered for the second time since we'd started cleaning up the kitchen. "If you want to go help the other ladies with the wedding plans."

She scoffed, cocking an eyebrow at me before she got to work on the next casserole dish. "I know you don't know me very well, but trust me when I say wedding planning is nowhere on my list of things I'd like to do in my spare time."

I chuckled. "Not your cup of tea?"

"Let's just say the only time I like to get serious about what colors to pick for something is when it comes to dying my hair. At least, it *was*, until this little gal decided to start blooming and I started thinking about what color to paint her room."

She patted her stomach with a soapy hand, smiling at me before she was back to work on the dish. I took her in then, noting the fading pink and orange at the tips of her dirty blonde hair, the septum piercing in her nose, the fierce and beautiful makeup she wore on her white skin, the sliver of tattoos peeking out from where she'd shoved the sleeves of her sweater up to her elbows along with the lotus flower right behind her ear. She was unlike any girl I'd seen around this town, and I kind of loved it.

"Besides, you can't get rid of me that easily, not when we're all dying to know more about you — specifically, you and Jordan."

The blood rushed from my face, and I took the dish from her hands, rinsing it without responding. My heart was racing as I tried to find the *right* words to say — or really, any words at all. If only she knew I'd been asking *myself* questions about me and Jordan for the last two months, and especially the last week, wondering more and more every day what we were, how we could be *anything at all* considering our circumstances.

The gravity that pulled me into Jordan — effortlessly and completely — also sent me spiraling in the next minute, down a rabbit hole of uncertainty and warning. Nothing had changed since we first made our agreement. He was still my boss. I was still the first and only female on a staff of men in a small town. I still had a daughter who was fresh off my and Randy's divorce.

And I still had Randy, though I wish I could be severed from him forever.

If anyone would understand that, it would be Mallory, I realized sickly.

I didn't know her very well, as she had just pointed out, but thanks to Randy getting drunk one night and bragging about it, I knew that he'd made a move on her when she was younger.

Too young.

And that he'd embarrassed her in front of a room of men.

I shivered at the thought, lost in another time, and when I didn't answer, Mallory smiled, bumping my elbow with hers. "Hey, don't sweat it. I know what it's like to want to keep things private for a while." She handed me a plate before working on the next one in the stack beside her. "Logan and I, we couldn't tell anyone when we were together — not when there were so many... complications. And things were so messy for a long time. I hurt him," she admitted. "Badly. But we found our way, eventually."

I still didn't say anything, not wanting to own up to me and Jordan being more than friends, even though I *knew* it was silly to think everyone in that house didn't know.

Except for Paige — at least, I hoped.

Besides, my mind was on another topic now, one that I couldn't ignore.

"Oh," Mallory said, dropping the plate she was washing into the sink of soapy water and bending at an awkward angle, her hand on her lower back.

"Are you okay?" I asked, drying my hands like I was about to have to spring into action.

Mallory waved me off. "Fine. I've just been getting some back pains recently. But honestly, compared to the first trimester?" She shook her head. "This is heaven. I have more energy finally, and the nausea is gone — at least, for now. I've been craving some really strange food combinations, like — have you ever had French fries dipped in a malt from Blondies?" She mouthed *oh my God*, her eyes rolling up to the ceiling. "And it seems to feel better when I'm standing or moving around rather than sitting. But, otherwise? I'm feeling dandy."

I chuckled, placing a hand on her shoulder. "I really hate to be the one to burst your bubble, but this is the honeymoon stage of your pregnancy. Enjoy it while it lasts, because around the next corner is a whole lot of *fuck this shit*."

She burst out laughing, returning her hands to the soapy water as I readied myself beside her to continue rinsing.

We were quiet for a pause, and I frowned, my rib cage shrinking in on my lungs as I considered what I was about to say to Mallory. I couldn't explain why I wanted to, or why I felt comfortable enough to. Honestly, I *didn't* feel comfortable.

But I *needed* to talk to her.

I needed to get this out.

"Mallory," I said, keeping my eyes on my hands as I rinsed a plate and she handed me another one. "I owe you an apology."

Mallory paused. "What for? I told you I *want* to be in here doing dishes. Please don't make me go talk about ribbons and seating charts."

I couldn't find it in me to smile. Instead, I pinched the bridge of my nose with my wet fingers, leaning a hip against the counter. "No, no... it's not about now. It's about..." I sighed, looking at her with remorse. Suddenly, I didn't have the words.

"What is it?" she asked, her brows bending together.

My stomach fell to the floor before settling again, and I forced a breath. "Mallory, I am not proud of how long I put up with Randy's shit. Our relationship turned sour so early, early enough that I should have known it would never be okay, but I stayed, anyway."

Mallory's face went blank at the sound of Randy's name, and she'd turned back to the water, working on scrubbing the spatulas and serving spoons. She handed them to me to rinse without looking at me again.

"I was young," I said. "Not that that's an excuse, but... I... I didn't know how bad everything was, how much he was hiding from me. I had clues, but..." I was stumbling, and I shook my head, trying to clear the fog. "What I'm trying to say is though I am ashamed of how long I stayed with him, and what I put up with, I am the most ashamed of the fact that I knew he disrespected you, and I did nothing about it."

Mallory's hands went shock still in the water, and she slowly withdrew them, still not looking at me.

"I don't know everything," I said, lowering my voice to a whisper as I checked over my shoulder to ensure no one was listening to us. "But I heard him talking to his friends about that night in your dad's casino. He said... *awful,* inappropriate things about you, and about other girls who were far too young for him. And I..." I teared up, shaking my head as I lowered it in shame.

"It wasn't that bad," she said softly, but her eyes said differently. "He pulled me into his lap, made some lewd gestures and pretty much said I should call him when I turned eighteen."

"How old were you when it happened?"

She swallowed. "Fourteen."

I shook my head, my stomach rolling with the threat to overturn the dinner we'd eaten. "I did nothing," I whispered, ashamed. "I *stayed* with him and I didn't come to your defense and I... I was young and scared and confused," I tried to explain, but it all felt weak and pathetic. "I am so sorry."

In a flash, Mallory had dried her hands on a dish towel and framed my shoulders with them, bending her neck until I looked her in the eyes.

"Listen to me," she said sternly. "You do *not* apologize for him. You understand? It is not your fault. What he did to you, what he did to me, what he did to anyone — it is on *him*, not on you."

My eyes welled with tears, but I sniffed them back, unable to respond. It was true what I'd said about not knowing everything. I only had pieces of the puzzle I tried to put together for years. Randy was good at hiding things.

He was good at manipulating me to think I was crazy, too.

But I knew he'd done something inappropriate to Mallory, something that had made everyone in that underground casino that Patrick Scooter liked to run out of his house laugh and jeer and encourage him to push more. But I didn't know how old she was — just fourteen.

He was twenty-one at the time.

"You are not responsible for his actions. Do you hear me?" she said, pulling me back to the moment with her.

Mallory waited until I nodded, though I wasn't sure if I agreed.

"I know we have both been through a little bit of hell with that man — you much more than me, I'd imagine. But, as sick as this sounds, I'm not sorry for what he did to me. He opened my eyes that night, Sydney. He gave me a backbone, and for the first time in my life, I started standing up to what was wrong, and standing up for what is right. And look at you," she said, shaking me a little. "You are an incredible mother, and a bad ass athletic trainer — *on a team of men*, might I add. I can tell just by looking into your eyes that you are stronger because of what you have been through. Am I wrong?"

I rolled my lips together. I didn't have to answer.

"You and I?" Mallory whispered. "We are fighters, Sydney. We are warriors. Survivors. You *never* have to apologize to me, okay? You just have to keep fighting. *That* is what you owe me — not an apology, but a fight. Because if we don't fight? Then he wins."

I swallowed, and Mallory glanced over my shoulder at the dining room before she forced a smile and pulled me in for a hug.

"Now, pretend we were talking about baby stuff," she whispered through that smile, pulling back on a chuckle. "God, thank you. It feels good to talk to someone who's been through this stuff."

"Uh-oh," Jordan said, grabbing for the whiskey on the counter to refill his glass as he smiled at us. "Baby talk, huh?"

"The good, the bad, and the *very* ugly baby talk," Mallory confirmed, and she winked at me as I tried to school my features.

When Jordan's eyes met with mine, I knew I was doing a terrible job.

I somehow managed to get through the rest of the evening, but when Paige had had her pie and it was halftime on the late game, we took the opportunity to leave — much to her dismay. Jordan could sense that something was off, and I could feel how badly he wanted to touch me, to hold me, to reassure me.

And I wanted the same.

I hugged everyone goodbye — getting an extra-long hug from Jordan's mom — and Jordan promised to be back bright and early in the morning to help with wedding set-up and final preparations. And of course, the guys would be going out for what Noah claimed would be a "tame" bachelor party tomorrow night.

When we were piled into the car, Jordan and I listened to Paige go on and on about the football games and about every one of Jordan's brothers and the girls and his mom, too. She talked a lot about Betty, who she wanted to hang out with more, and I smiled and asked questions when appropriate, letting her run the conversation until we pulled into the drive, with Jordan watching me with worry in his eyes the entire way home.

When we got there, I took Paige upstairs and got her ready for bed. She was already softly snoring by the time I shut out her bedroom light after reading to her for not even ten minutes, and I tiptoed down the stairs, finding Jordan on the couch.

He stood when he saw me, his brows folding together, mouth in a thin line.

But I said nothing.

I just crossed the room and collapsed into his arms, knowing that as much as it would hurt, I had to tell him what I knew about Randy and Mallory, too.

When he wrapped me in those strong, warm arms of his and kissed my hair, rocking me gently, I struggled against the urge to cry.

And I prayed he would understand.

SEVENTEEN

Jordan didn't speak for the longest time.

I'd lit a candle — one that smelled like lavender and made me feel slightly better — before launching into what had happened with Mallory in the kitchen. I'd told him about what I'd known about Randy, what I wasn't sure I'd known, what I'd questioned.

And I felt ashamed, knowing that Jordan now knew how weak I had been, what I had put up with, what I had let happen to me and my daughter before I'd found a spine and left.

The candlelight flickered across his face, which was severe, his brows nearly touching in the middle of his forehead and making a wrinkle so deep I wondered if it'd stick forever. I wondered if he was judging me, deciding he didn't like what I'd uncovered. The only source of comfort I had that that was *not* the case was that he still rested his giant hand on my leg where I sat next to him.

After a long while, he swallowed, letting out a long breath. "So... did he..." He frowned even more. "Did he assault her?"

I shook my head. "No. At least, not that I know of. But he made her uncomfortable. From what I gathered, he basically pulled her into his lap and made some comment about them having sex when she turns eighteen."

"Jesus fucking Christ," Jordan said, and he finally stood, no longer able to sit still with what he'd just learned. He paced back and forth in my living room while I sat on the couch, watching him. "I wonder if Logan knows."

"I'm sure he does."

"Then I'm surprised Randy is still breathing."

I didn't have anything to say to that.

He continued pacing, and my heart had stopped beating altogether before I finally reached for his hand, pulling him to a stop. He looked down at me with that same severe look he gave the team when he was pissed.

"Are you mad at me?"

At that, his face crumbled, and he collapsed into the couch next to me and immediately pulled me into his chest.

"What? Of course not," he said, blowing out a hot breath and shaking his head as he rocked me. I clung to him like he was the only thing holding me to the Earth. "You didn't do anything wrong, Sydney. This is all on him."

"But I didn't tell anyone," I pointed out. "I didn't fight him on it or question him more when my gut *knew* something was off. I was scared, and he *was* the police, so I didn't know where to go... and I just... I feel so awful."

I buried my face in his chest as he gently quieted me, holding me tighter.

"Sydney," he said after a long while, pulling back until he could look me in the eyes. "Do not feel guilty for his actions. You did not play a role in what he did to Mallory or anyone else. You were a victim, too."

I sniffed, still feeling like he was wrong but not wanting to argue it.

"There were so many things I heard over the years," I confessed on a whisper, searching his eyes as that foggy memory from the night his father died flittered in like a wisp of smoke. "But nothing that was ever concrete. Nothing that I couldn't dismiss with just a few questions of whether I was crazy or not, of whether I had really heard what I thought, or if I was being dramatic."

Jordan swept my hair from my face. "He knew what he was doing. He knew his power."

I swallowed. "The night of Mallory's grand opening of her art studio last year... do you remember that?"

He nodded.

"That was when I knew," I said on a shaky voice. "We went to it, and Mallory saw him and I saw the look in her eyes and I *knew* I was right, that he had done her wrong. And then when I came back from the bathroom, I overheard him and one of his officers making a joke about it." I shook my head, tonguing my cheek. "He said something about how he wished she would have been down for the deal, because judging by her piercings and tattoos, he bet she was a freak in the bedroom."

Jordan's jaw clenched shut, and he looked away from me briefly, as if he needed to look at something else to calm himself and keep from shooting off that couch and flying across town to confront Randy right now.

"I told him I wanted a divorce the next day," I said. "Not to his face. I didn't stay, because I knew he wouldn't let me go if I did. I got a lawyer, made sure everything was on paper just in case anything happened, you know? And I wrote him a letter and got on a plane with Paige to go see my parents and my sister for Christmas." I shook my head. "My dad called Randy, and I don't know what was said, but honestly, Jordan, I think the only reason he signed the papers and granted the divorce was because I agreed to stay in town, to not move Paige away, and he knew..." I sniffed. "He knew that if I stayed, he'd still have power over me."

Jordan softened, pulling me into him again on a sigh and resting his chin on the crown of my head. "He will never hurt you again. I promise."

Tears finally broke free at his words, because I knew that he meant them with every fiber of his being. I knew that if it came to it, Jordan Becker would go to war for me, for Paige, for us.

And I wasn't sure I deserved it.

He held me for a long while before I sat up straight again, swiping the tears from my face and letting out a long, slow exhale. "Anyway, enough of this," I said, forcing a smile. "You wanted to talk about something."

"Sydney..."

"Please," I said, nearly crying again. "I really don't want to talk about this anymore."

He frowned, but nodded in understanding. "Well, what I had to talk about can wait, too."

"No, please, you wanted to talk first, and then I sprung this all on you, and—"

"Hey," he said, his knuckles finding my chin. He tilted it up, those blue eyes searching mine while I traced the rim of gold around his iris. "I am always here for you. Okay? Always. You are not a nuisance, and I *want* to be this person for you." He swallowed. "I want to be your everything."

My chest tightened, a mixture of the most intense longing and desire I'd ever felt swirling in a tornado with all the anxiety and warning sounds my body could release all at once.

"Jordan..."

But before I could speak, his lips were on mine, the warm swells both comforting and demanding as he took the words I was going to say and swallowed them whole.

I pulled back, breathless, fingers trailing down his chest before I grabbed his hand and stood. He followed me down the hall to the guest room, where we could be alone without the possibility of waking Paige since my room was next to hers.

When I closed the door behind us, the only light came from the horizontal slits in the closed blinds, and they cast streams of white across his face, his chest, his arms, his hands where they reached for me and pulled me in again, the next kiss tender and sure.

Just like that, we were done talking.

— ● —

JORDAN

Something about the way the night settled over both of us in Sydney's dark guest room was different than any time we'd been alone before.

The moment that door closed behind us with a quiet *snick*, the moment her hands reached for me in the dark, and mine reached for her, and our mouths connected, comfortable and instinctively, it sent a charge through me like an electric current. I felt that energy spread like warm oil, slicking up every joint, seeping into every crevice, filling me up whole.

I cradled her face in my hands, my eyes closed as I tasted her, memorized her, my heart aching from what she'd confessed in the other room. The urge to protect her and keep her safe tore through me in the next moment, and I pulled her into me, crushing her in my embrace as I strengthened the kiss.

Sydney gasped, and as soon as her mouth opened I was walking her backward, kissing down her neck and over her collarbone until the back of her knees hit the bed.

"Lie down," I whispered, and she reached blindly back, hands finding the bed as she sat and stared up at me, her chest heaving.

Without a word, I reached down for the hem of her sweater, peeling it up and over her head as she lifted her arms to let me. Then I kissed her, pushing her back until she was flat on the bed, and I kissed down, down — over the swells of her breasts, the muscles of her abdomen, the smooth skin above the band of her leggings.

My fingers dipped beneath that band, and Sydney lifted her hips, helping me peel them down her thighs and calves until they rested at her ankles. I kept my eyes on hers as I pulled them the rest of the way off, letting them fall to the floor.

She hadn't been wearing anything beneath them.

The urge to groan in approval ripped through me, but I suppressed it, because though she was nearly naked now and my erection was so strong it pitched a tent in my pants, there was something more to this moment than lust, something more than my hands on her thighs spreading her legs as I kissed a trail from her ankle to the sweet spot at the apex of them.

I couldn't take away what she'd been through. I couldn't go back in time and steal her away from Randy before he had the chance to make her his, before he took that chance and used it to fuck her up instead of cherish her. I couldn't *unhurt* her.

But I could show her what she meant to me.

My heart thumped hard in my chest — once, twice — reminding me that I had things I needed to tell *her*, questions I needed to ask, answers I had to have. But I quieted it with a soft kiss on her clit, one that elicited a gasp from her lips and an arch of her back off the bed.

It could wait.

Knowing what we were and what we weren't, hearing her claim me, explaining that I needed to claim *her*, that I needed more, that I needed all of her — it could all wait.

Tonight, I would *show* her what I felt.

And when the time was right, I'd tell her, too.

My hands grabbed at the creases where her hips met her thighs, and I tugged her down until her ass was half off the bed, the weight of her in my hands as I paid homage to her pussy. I ran my tongue flat and hot from bottom to top before sucking her bud between my teeth, gently sucking, just enough to make her squirm before I released it again.

Sydney's hands found my hair, and I buried my face more, letting her guide me where she wanted me. I listened to the words she wasn't saying, to the way her hands tightened in my hair or loosened, to the way she moaned or stayed silent. My tongue was the student, eager and devoted, and her body language taught all it needed to know.

She was panting heavily and squirming so much she'd nearly fallen off the bed when I adjusted her, making sure she was secure before I removed one hand from where I held her and tickled her entrance with my fingertips. She groaned, leaning up on her elbows, her eyes hooded from where she watched me.

I kept my eyes on hers, my tongue flicking her clit, and in one thrust, I pushed two fingers deep inside her.

She arched in a mixture of pleasure and pain, flying back down on the bed and gripping the sheets. She twisted them wildly as I curved my fingers inside her, holding back the screams I knew she wanted to let loose so we didn't wake Paige. Her hand pressing the back of my head more into her and her legs shaking around it told me what her screams couldn't, and I kept pace, flicking and flexing and pushing in and out until her entire body erupted into an earthquake of trembles, her breaths short and loud, climax ripping through her.

She collapsed in a heap on the bed as I slowly withdrew my fingers, kissing my way up her body until I found her mouth. Sydney held my lips to hers, the kiss hard and desperate and appreciative, and then she bit my lower lip as I stifled a moan.

"Take these off," she whispered, tugging on my athletic pants, and I stood, eagerly answering her plea.

I peeled my long-sleeve shirt over my head, making quick work of my pants and briefs next, all while keeping my gaze locked on hers. Sydney tugged her sports bra over her head, too, and then crawled back until her head was on the pillows, and we both sighed in relief when I was on top of her, sliding between her legs, our bodies hot and slick where they met.

I was already lined up at her entrance, and all it would take was a flex of my hips to bury myself inside her. But we both paused, our breaths heavy and loud as Sydney ran her fingers back through my hair, and I held my weight on my elbows, balancing over her, our eyes searching each other's.

Everything that existed in the fundamental part of who I was screamed for me to tell her I loved her.

It echoed like my body was a chamber, like if each cell yelled loud enough, Sydney would hear it whether the actual words came or not.

And maybe she did.

Maybe she understood, as her brows bent together, and her lips parted, and she lifted her head off those pillows enough to connect her mouth to mine. Maybe she knew it all along, and that kiss was quieting me, as if to tell me I didn't need to speak it out loud at all.

Maybe she felt it, too, as her thighs tightened around me, and she pressed her forehead to mine, our breaths hot and heavy where they danced between our lips. Maybe our bodies and souls were having entire conversations without a single whisper as her heels gently dug into the back of my thighs, urging me on, begging me to push inside her.

And when I did, the rubber band of energy around us warped, stretching to its max before it snapped back with a pop that had us both letting out a shaky, longing sigh.

Sydney's hands pulled and gripped, her nails scratching and digging, as if she couldn't get me close enough, like any centimeter of distance was too much. And I worked between her legs, pulsing, in and out, my lips on her neck, her breasts, her chin and jaw before we were kissing again, the pressure crushing.

I came with my mouth fastened to hers, and she rolled her body in time with mine, taking my release inside her without either of us slowing. Even when I was spent, when every drop was spilled and my body ached to collapse, I continued, slowing my pace but staying inside her with our kiss just as demanding as before.

I love you.

I want you.

Be with me.

Those words were never spoken, but they rang loudly through that room as if the walls had come alive long enough to say them for us.

We were slick, fastened together from lips to chest to hips, and still, I moved, flexing in and out of her until I started to get hard again, and Sydney rolled me onto my back. She straddled me with her hands on my chest, and took control, easing us into round two before round one had even fully ended.

Until the night turned to morning and I had to sneak out of her house, we made love.

And for the first time in my life, I understood the meaning of that phrase.

EIGHTEEN

JORDAN

"Icannot believe *this* is what you wanted to do for your bachelor party," Logan said the next night, looking around the old treehouse our father built when we were kids. It was out in the middle of nowhere, in an oak tree by the creek. Each corner of it was decorated differently, reflecting what our interests were at those ages, and we sat in our respected areas. "I mean, it's your last night as a free man. Shouldn't we have taken you to Nashville? Hit up some live music bars and some strip clubs?"

Mikey stopped where he'd been strumming on his guitar, cutting out the sound with a thump of his hand on the shell. His corner of the treehouse had been filled with music, even though he was only around six when Dad built it. Even then, we all knew Mikey would be a musician.

"To be fair, I'm still underage. I'd bet it's my fault we aren't out at the clubs."

"Nah," Noah said, clapping our youngest brother on his shoulder before he kicked back on his bean bag again. He rested his hands behind his head, looking up at the makeshift constellations Dad had made him on the ceiling. His area was filled with maps and sailboats, a reflection of his dream at the time to sail around the world.

I wondered if it was still a dream, if maybe he and Ruby Grace would do it together one day.

"It's not you, Mikey," he continued, his eyes still on the ceiling. "I wanted something low key. I mean, to be honest, I don't consider this the last night of me being a *free man*. The truth is, my heart was taken off the market the moment I met Ruby Grace."

Logan smiled at that.

"If anything, this is my last night of a chapter I'm excited to end. I think my real freedom, my real life starts when I marry that woman tomorrow."

"Yeah, but still, you don't want to see some titties?" Mikey asked.

Noah looked at all of us with an unreadable expression. "Does it make me the biggest pansy in the world if I say the only titties I want to see for the rest of my life are hers?"

There was a chorus of soft laughter from each of us, but not much of an argument, which was a testament to what we'd been through in the last few years. There was no doubt in my mind that had this night happened five years ago, we *would* have been at a strip club — whether Noah wanted to go or not. We would have snuck Mikey in, if we had to. Back then, none of us were settled down, and it wasn't even on the radar.

Now, we were different men.

All thanks to women we never saw coming.

"I would tease you about it," Logan said. "But the truth is, I'm in the same boat."

"Me, too," Mikey chimed in.

"I'll *bet* you're in the same boat, Logan. Especially now that Mallory's boobs are getting baby-ready, if you know what I mean," Noah joked, waggling his brows.

Logan pointed a finger at him from his corner of the treehouse — which was filled with books — and narrowed his eyes. "Talk about my girl's baby-ready boobs again and we'll be fighting, brother."

Noah threw his hands up on a laugh. "I told you, I've got my own boobs."

"Can we change the subject?" Mikey interjected. "Now I'm thinking about *both* your girl's boobs and I don't like it."

There was another shuffle of laughter, and then Noah was refilling the whiskey in our glasses. We were drinking a bottle from one of the single-barrel releases last summer — on the rocks, of course, Noah's favorite way. And Mikey was indulging in *his* favorite drink, a rootbeer float, since he'd volunteered to be our designated driver.

The conversation flowed on, and I stayed mostly quiet — which no one questioned me about since it wasn't unusual, thankfully, even though tonight's silence had more weight than my norm. My chest was still tight from Thanksgiving, from the night I'd spent with Sydney, from the feelings for her that were growing and stirring in my gut with the need to tell her and to hear her reciprocate, too.

I knew when she opened up to me about Randy last night that it wasn't the time, but I hadn't seen her today, either, and Noah's wedding was tomorrow. She would be in our family photographs forever. She would be there for one of the most important days of my little brother's life. This wasn't a family dinner or a public date, it was more.

Having her there as my plus one *meant* something to me.

And it was driving me mad that I didn't know if she felt the same.

Part of my brain told me to shut up and relax, to take her actions as reassurance. She'd spent the entire day with my family yesterday, and then we'd spent the entire night wrapped up in each other after she came to me with something she didn't go to *anyone* else with. She trusted me, felt comfortable with me, opened up to me. And over the last two months, we'd explored each other, discovering just as much about one another as we did about ourselves in the process.

But this was new for me.

I'd never opened my heart to someone before, and I worried about what I was feeling, what *she* was feeling, and where we would go from here.

If we would go anywhere, at all.

I wondered if I read all the signs wrong, if I was in too deep when she was wading in the shallow end, if we would be able to survive working together if whatever this was between us didn't work out.

And I knew she was wondering how we would survive working together if whatever this was between us *did* work out.

I was worried about one thing, and she was concerned about another.

How could we meet in the middle with those two facts being true?

This was the constant whirl of my thoughts over the last twenty-four hours, and I couldn't shake loose from them, no matter how I tried.

"So, Jordan," Mikey said, snapping me back to the moment with my brothers. "You going to fill us in on the Sydney situation willingly or do we have to beat it out of you?"

I blinked, trying to think of the right words to assure them that there was nothing to talk about, but Logan rolled his eyes before I could speak.

"Oh, come on. Mikey told us that you kissed her earlier this season, and though he *also* told us she didn't want it to ever happen again, I think it's pretty clear after yesterday that it has."

"A lot, I'd wager," Noah added with a smirk.

I narrowed my eyes at Mikey, who threw his hands up. "Hey, we're brothers. Don't act like y'all didn't talk about me behind my back when I was going through my shit with Bailey and Kylie."

I sighed at that, because it was true, and because if my brothers didn't worry about me, *I'd* be worried. We were a family unit tied together with bonds as strong as steel, and we watched out for each other, ready to fight if necessary or be there as a shoulder to cry on.

And we *hated* to cry.

But we were never too proud to. It was one of the many things our father had instilled in us — that it was okay to have emotions, and it didn't make you less of a man.

"Come on, guys," I said on another sigh, looking through the binder of old football rookie cards I'd once collected. It felt good to keep my eyes there instead of meeting their gaze. "You know I'm not a man of many words."

"So just use a few of them," Mikey offered.

I scowled, but closed the binder with a heavy breath. "I don't know. Obviously, we're not just friends."

"Quite," Logan said, and I narrowed my eyes at him before continuing.

"We... were intimate, after the first home game win," I said, feeling a little uncomfortable airing our personal business like that. But it was my brothers, and I knew I could trust them. "And I thought that was it, you know? That we were going to cross over the friendship line. And we did, but... it was different for me than it was for her."

"Meaning?" Noah probed.

"Meaning we had a conversation the next day about how she didn't want to tell anyone, and she didn't want it to get too serious."

"Yikes," Logan said on a whistle. "And you said?"

I shrugged. "I was honest, told her I didn't do the *hook-up* thing. So, we made a kind of deal, I guess. That we'd keep it on the down low, not make a big deal of it, but that I wanted her to come to your wedding with me." I looked at Noah then. "And I basically implied that if we made it to this point, we would know if we were serious or not, if we should tell people, claim our relationship."

"And?" Noah asked.

"And..." I sighed. "I know how I feel, and I *think* I know how she feels, but I'm not sure. And I want to ask her, but I'm afraid to push, but I also can't wait much longer, because I think I'll go fucking crazy if I do."

They were all silent for a long moment, and finally, Noah asked, "What's the rush? I mean, would you be okay to not push it, to wait until she's ready to broach the subject with you?"

"I just don't like this game," I confessed. "Why are we not telling anyone, running around in secret, keeping it from our families and making it feel... dirty? You know?" I shifted uncomfortably. "This isn't how Dad taught us to be with women, and I don't like how it makes me feel."

"And you're scared."

I looked at Logan, who'd said the words I didn't want to admit.

I swallowed. "And I'm scared."

"I was the same way with Mallory," he said with a nod of understanding. "I understood our reasonings for needing to go slow and keep it to ourselves for a while, but after a certain point, I just... I needed to know I wasn't fooling myself."

"Exactly," I said on a breath, feeling understood. "And she's got her reasons — good ones — for us to keep it quiet. I mean, she's the only woman on a staff of men in a small town. People would talk if they found out we were together — and not about me, because that's not how it works."

"So shitty..." Mikey murmured.

"I know. And I couldn't protect her from that, though I could try. *She* has to be ready for it. She also has to be ready to tell Paige, who is just getting used to the idea of her parents being divorced, I'm sure."

"And then there's Randy," Logan said, his expression hard, and when his eyes met mine, I knew that *he* knew what Sydney had confessed to me last night.

"And then there's Randy," I echoed.

"What about him?" Mikey asked, confused. "So what, she was married before. They're divorced now. It's not like she's cheating."

"That's not it at all. It's more that Randy is a shithead," Logan said for me. "And he has been on a power trip since he first became an officer shortly after high school. I'd bet anything that he does whatever he can to constantly remind her of his power."

I hadn't thought of it that way, and I tilted my head to the side. "You think that's it? I mean, I figured she didn't want to upset him, because from what she's told me, he has anger issues and their relationship wasn't the healthiest. But... do you think she's afraid he'd do something to put her or Paige in jeopardy?"

"That's exactly what I think," Logan said.

We all fell silent, chewing on that, and finally I blew out a breath. "I don't know. I get that, but she knows I would be there for her through that. We could figure it out together. And honestly, I think I'll go crazy if I don't just *hear* it from her that she's feeling the same way I am. I know she's showing me with actions but... it's different."

I looked up at the stars above Noah's corner of the treehouse, trying to explain it.

"I'm already afraid of how I feel, like I'm an aerial artist that just flung off my hoop into the air and I have no idea if her hands are outstretched and ready to catch mine or if I'm going to freefall to my death. I'm more anxious than I've been my entire life, and I don't want to be stupid." My throat closed in on itself before I said my next sentence. "If she's not in it, I need to let her go."

There was another long pause, and we all sipped from our glasses, letting the whiskey settle in as if it could help us problem solve.

"I think you should tell her," Noah said. "Tomorrow. Just put it all out there."

"I agree," Mikey chimed in. "I mean, at this point, the possible gain is worth the possible risk. You just said it — if she's not where you are, then it's better to stop it now, before you both get in deeper."

I nodded, and Logan told me with his eyes that he agreed, too.

"Thanks, brothers."

They offered small smiles, and then the conversation was changed — blessedly — and they let me slip back into my quiet state.

Somewhere around midnight, as we were packing up and getting ready to leave, Mikey stopped in the middle of the treehouse, looking around at each of our corners.

"I wish Dad could be here tonight," he whispered. "And tomorrow, for you, Noah." He looked at our brother then, whose face crumpled a bit.

"I do, too," Logan said.

"He's here," I reminded them, clapping the two oldest ones on the shoulder. We all stood there, taking in what our father had built — not just with wood, but with his blood, sweat, and tears.

He'd built that treehouse.

And he'd built us, too.

My chest tightened, and I hooked an arm around each of them, reminding them that no matter what, we had each other. Then, I echoed the truest belief I had.

"He's always here."

— • —

Later that night — or rather, *very* early the next morning — I lay wide awake in my bed, one arm under the pillow behind my head, eyes on the ceiling.

I couldn't sleep, and I wasn't surprised.

Talking with my brothers had my thoughts running laps in my head again, and when I glanced at my phone screen where it lay on my bedside table and saw that it was nearly three in the morning, I huffed, tossing the covers off me and storming to the kitchen to get some water.

I needed to sleep. I was one of the groomsmen in the wedding tomorrow — or rather, *today*, and it would be a long day. I drank half a glass of cold water, looking around my little house and debating whether I should get in a quick twenty-minute, high-intensity workout and take a hot shower to see if those two things combined would make me pass out.

But then my eyes landed on my laptop where it sat on my coffee table, and on the external hard drive next to it.

Digging into Dad's journal this late was a bad idea. I was tired, and I needed to be focusing on sleeping, not on staring at a computer screen.

Then again, I knew even with a workout and a shower that sleep wasn't anywhere *near* within reach, so I refilled my glass and padded into the living room, pulling the computer onto my lap and plugging in the hard drive.

I scrubbed my hands over my face as the screen loaded, typing in Dad's password when the login page popped up. I had his journal open in the next minute, and then I lost myself in translating the Latin entries, in the boring day to day my father had experienced at the distillery.

I hadn't realized how long I'd been working.

I hadn't realized how much time I'd made up for, how much of his journal still remained when I dove into it that night.

I hadn't realized that after just ninety minutes, I'd be staring at the last entry.

It was marked at the top with the date of his death.

My stomach lurched — so violently that I shot up straight, gripping the edges of the laptop as my eyes scanned that date in the top right-hand corner over and over again.

It was the last entry.

And this one wasn't in Latin.

My heartrate accelerated, and the first thing I thought was *why didn't we think to scroll to the bottom, to start here instead of at the beginning?*

The next notion was more consuming, though, and I let it take me under — because these were my father's last private thoughts before his life was snuffed out like a match flame.

And I was about to read them.

Journal,

Ah, my old friend, I've enjoyed our secret conversations in the ancient language, but I'm afraid there's no time for me to practice that art today, for I have discovered something far too exciting to take my time in divulging.

As you know from previous entries, I recently discovered the Last Will and Testament of our founder — Mr. Robert J. Scooter. What I might have failed to mention before is that there was no record of this Will when he passed, and for that reason, I did something I'm afraid I should be ashamed of.

I read it.

For months, I have combed through each page — of which there were many — researching the legal terms I did not understand and making notes of my own, searching for something my father believed would have existed in Robert's Will — had there been one.

And he was right.

I needed to be sure, so even when I first discovered the pages that dictated how the company shares should be split in the event of Robert's death, I did not let my hope and excitement guide me. Instead, I read and re-read and made notes and researched until I was so certain that nothing could be refuted. And I discovered the missing piece to a puzzle my father never solved in his lifetime.

Robert left my father, and our family, fifty percent of the company stock.

Half.

Part-ownership.

Journal, even when I had the proof, I worried about whether or not to bring this information to Patrick Scooter. As you know, we haven't exactly been best friends throughout the years, which I attribute largely to his father's affection for me and how much he entrusted to me when it came to the distillery. I would also have to admit to Patrick that not only had I found the Will, but that I had not come to him with it directly, but rather read it on my own without permission.

Nevertheless, I felt I had no other choice.

It was time to set things right.

Oh, I was nervous. My hands are still shaking as I type this, but now, from an exhilarating joy and anticipation rather than an uncertainty. To my utter amazement, Pat not only listened to me and agreed that I was correct in my interpretation of the Will — he insisted that we rectify the situation immediately.

He's going to name me as partner.

He's going to backpay my family for the years of income we should have been receiving, immediately include me on business decisions I was only a small voice for before, rewrite the staff organization chart, and for the first time since his father's death, he seemed open to hearing my ideas for the future of this distillery.

I guess now, he has no choice.

What's more, he wants me to move into his father's old office — the one I've been cleaning out for months. He insisted it was what his dad would have wanted, for me to follow in his footsteps, to "take my place at the table," so to speak.

As I write this, I have already gathered most of the belongings in my office to transfer over, and Patrick has asked me to meet him in his father's office after our four o'clock board meeting to discuss next steps.

Again, I am trembling with excitement and disbelief. I can't wait to get home to tell Laurelei and the boys.

This is it, Journal.

This is the day my father's legacy is revived.

This is the day my family's life changes forever.

There was no sign off, just those last nine words dangling at the end of the page, and I read them over and over again, heart pounding out of my chest with the dark truth that my father never could have understood they held.

Our lives *had* changed forever on that fateful day.

But not in the way they were supposed to.

Black invaded my vision as I stared at the screen, my head foggy, chest so tight I couldn't squeeze a breath out to save my life.

Half of the company was ours.

Half of the company had been left to my grandfather, to my father, to *us*.

There was never supposed to be a Will, and yet my father had found it. He'd brought it to Patrick. Patrick *knew* what was inside it.

And on the day of my father's death, he'd asked him to meet in the very office where he perished.

Every nerve in my body stood on end, my chest fluttering with the rapid beats of my heart, head pounding with questions and accusations circling like an F5 tornado. More and more questions popped into my head with every new re-read of the entry, and sweat gathered on my forehead, my gut churning, breaths shallow once I finally found them.

All the years we'd searched for answers, and now we had them.

And I knew sleep was the last thing I'd be able to do now.

NINETEEN

JORDAN

On the outside, everything was perfect.

It was perhaps the most beautiful November day Stratford, Tennessee, had ever seen. An unusual front of warm weather had swept in overnight, leaving us basked in a cloudless sky of sunshine and a comfortable sixty-seven degrees. It was just warm enough for women to not have to wear a jacket over their dresses, and just cool enough for the men in tuxedos to not sweat.

Perfect.

I stood by Noah's side at the altar, along with Mikey and Logan, and when the entire congregation turned to watch Ruby Grace float down the aisle in her floor-length, cream-colored lace dress — I watched him. His eyes welled with tears at the sight of her, and he bowed his head, trying to fight them off before he lifted his eyes to her once more and I watched two tears slip in parallel lines down each cheek. His smile was the size of his entire face, though he covered it with one hand, in utter disbelief that the stunning woman walking toward him was about to be his forever.

Perfect.

Ruby Grace's sister and best friend stood behind her, and I watched them get just as emotional as my brothers during the ceremony as we watched Noah and Ruby Grace pledge their undying love to one another. They held each other's hands as Pastor Morris spoke of eternal love and sacrifice and compromise and I knew without a doubt that they barely heard a word of it, because they were lost in each other's eyes, in the dreams they had built together, in the ones yet to come.

Perfect.

It all seemed to come and go in both slow motion and the quickest hour of my entire life. I was wrapped up in every moment, until Pastor Morris declared that they were now husband and wife and Noah could kiss his bride. When he did, the church roared with applause, and Noah turned to the crowd, thrusting his hand holding Ruby's into the air while he yanked his opposite fist into his side in a victorious pump. He'd landed the girl. She was his, and he was hers, and their new life together started now.

Perfect.

On the outside, at least.

Because on the *inside*, under the rib cage that held my lungs and heart in place, and under the skull that protected my brain, and inside the deepest part of my gut?

It was total and complete chaos.

As I'd predicted, sleep hadn't come for me the night before — not after what I'd discovered. I hadn't been able to eat this morning, either, because the mere thought of food made my entire body heave in protest. Every nerve, every cell that made up the man I was was focused on that journal entry, on what I'd read, on what my father had left behind as the final clue to solve the mystery of his death.

And the worst part was that I knew I couldn't tell anyone.

Not yet.

It was Noah's wedding day — a day he'd been planning for and looking forward to for months. It was a day Mom had dreamed of for his entire life. It was a day to celebrate love and union, not to make my entire family sick with the knowledge that Robert J. Scooter had a Will, and we were in it, and Dad had found it, and Patrick knew about it, too.

And the last request he'd made was for Dad to meet him in the office he'd taken his last breath in.

All of it compounded right on top of the feelings that had been stirring inside me over Sydney — the *original* reason I couldn't sleep last night. So, while I forced my best smile for my brother and did everything in my power to be present, to celebrate, to let it all go until the day was over, I was powerless to fight the wave of anxiety that took me under over and over again.

After the ceremony, Ruby Grace and Noah stood near the doors to speak with all the guests in the receiving line. Mom stood on one side while Ruby Grace's parents — Mayor Barnett and his wife — stood on the other, each of them greeting the guests with a handshake or a hug and a *thank you so much for being here.*

My brothers and I stood off to the side, waiting for the time when our next job duties would kick in. We each had our role to play in the day, and the next step was transporting the bride and groom to the outdoor reception that would be hosted at the Mayor's mansion.

I had my hands in my pockets, watching Noah's genuine grin, wondering how the hell I would tell him and my other brothers what I'd found when Sydney stepped into view.

"You know, as much as you look at home in Stratford High colors, I *really* like you in a navy tux," she said, her hand finding the flax yellow daisy boutonniere fixed to my lapel. She adjusted the pin to stabilize it, pressing both hands to my chest before her cheeks flushed and she folded them together at her waist, instead.

She wore a long-sleeve, vermilion floor-length dress with a V-cut neck and an open back that exposed her lean muscles. Intricate lace details covered the bodice, the sleeves made entirely of the same lace, and the long, flowing skirt was a crepe fabric that had a slit up to her left thigh, showing her toned legs beneath. When I let my eyes wander over each inch of her face, noting the light and delicate makeup she wore, my stomach took flight on the wings of a dozen hummingbirds. Her eyes were highlighted with golds and pinks and slanted into the shape of a cat's with liner, and the way she'd braided her hair over one shoulder left the delicate slope of her neck begging for my lips to graze it. The longer I stared at her, the more my chest ached with the yearning urge to reach for her and pull her into me.

Perfect.

I knew I still wore that forced smile I'd put on that morning along with my tuxedo and bow tie, because when our eyes met, Sydney frowned.

"You look beautiful," I told her on a whisper, and my heart burned in my chest with the truth of it. "So, so beautiful, Sydney."

She smiled, but her eyebrows were still bent together, her eyes searching mine.

I wondered if she could sense it, my heart breaking — both from my feelings for her and from the discovery of my father's last entry early this morning. I wondered if just by looking at her, she could feel my pain.

She didn't ask if I was okay, but as my mother signaled that it was time to make our way outside for the bride and groom's exit, Sydney looped her arm through mine, holding my bicep as she snuggled in close.

"I'm right here."

Her words were softer than a whisper, but they brought me my first steady breath of the day, one that pushed out all the stiff air in my lungs and made room for a new, fresh, clean inhale of assurance.

And with her on my arm, I somehow found the strength to walk through the church doors and continue the celebrations, all the while holding the biggest secret I'd ever had buried where no one could see.

— ● —

SYDNEY

I hadn't been to a wedding since my own, which had been small, and private, and far from glamorous. It was just me, Randy, and our families — including Paige, who was already growing in my belly at the time.

It was *nothing* like this.

While the church ceremony had been modest and simple, the reception at Mayor Barnett's home was nothing short of extravagant. Their home was something out of *Better Home & Gardens* magazine, the classic, all-American southern house — complete with a porch that wrapped all the way around. I couldn't say for sure how many acres they had as part of their land, but it was at least three, and a giant portion of it had been transformed into the nicest event space I'd ever seen.

At the center of it all was a dance floor, planks of wood fitted together in the middle of their yard as if it had always existed there. It was framed by gold and all around it were round tables with lavish floral centerpieces, candles of all sizes, and photos of Noah and Ruby Grace throughout their relationship.

While the tables surrounded the dance floor, at the head of it stood a small stage with a full string band — one that was currently playing the sweetest, most beautiful rendition of "From The Ground Up" by Dan+Shay while Ruby Grace and Noah shared their first dance in the center of the floor. He held her tight, her eyes cast up toward his as they swayed, both of them whispering softly to each other so no one else could hear.

Strings of gold and white twinkle lights criss-crossed above it all, casting the cool November night in a warm evening glow. There were pyramid flame heaters surrounding the tables and placed strategically between them, so that there was plenty of space to move around but also that no guest could ever possibly get cold.

Every detail was thoughtful and refined.

My eyes found Jordan's where he sat beside me, and he offered a wink before his gaze was on his brother and Ruby Grace again. The smile he'd been trying to hold all night fell once more, along with my gut, because I knew something was off — thought I didn't know exactly what it was.

Throughout the evening, as we listened to Logan and Ruby Grace's sister, Mary Anne, give their speeches, and as dinner was served, and as the band played soft music as we all conversed at his family's table — I held his hand in mine under the table. He felt so distant that I'd squeeze that hand from time to time, and he'd squeeze in return, letting me know he was still there, when for all intents and purposes he seemed universes away.

And I knew I was the reason.

Here we were, two months from the morning he'd sat at my patio table and told me that he would agree to keep our relationship between us if I agreed to be his wedding date this evening. And while I had followed through on my end just as he had his, I knew that to him, me being here meant more than just *me being here.*

He wanted all of me.

And what I'd realized this weekend was that I felt the same.

Maybe it was walking with his mother in her garden, listening to her tell stories of Jordan growing up. Maybe it was watching his brothers with Paige, the wide smile on her face and the stars in her eyes. Maybe it was that night, when I'd come to him with my deepest shame, and he'd accepted me fully, holding me and kissing me and making love to me until the morning light slipped through my guest room window.

But I knew it was more than that, too.

It was the way he was with Paige, the way he already cared for her as if she were his own. It was the way he saw all my scars and kissed them with reverence, as if they were what made me beautiful. It was quiet nights on his couch and lively afternoons in my backyard and secret kisses stolen in the locker room at work when no one was looking.

Somewhere, in the middle of all that, my fear and anxiety over what would happen if we were ever publicly together had faded. Somehow, the sense of knowing no matter what, we'd get through it together had taken its place. And some way, I'd fallen in love with the last possible man on Earth who I should have.

My stomach still tightened and rolled at the thought of what the town would say, the gossip that would fly. I still worried over Paige, though part of me knew she'd likely be excited about us being together, about Jordan being a part of our lives.

But the biggest hesitance still grew from the knowledge that my ex-husband was an angry, powerful man.

And I knew he wasn't ready to let me go yet.

I squeezed Jordan's hand, and he squeezed me back, his eyes catching mine just as Ruby Grace and Noah finished their last dance. The string lights above us seemed to fill his gray-blue sky eyes with stars, and my throat tightened, heart nearly pounding out of my chest with the need to tell him how I felt.

And I decided, right then and there, that tonight was the night I would turn my back on my fears, on what was holding me back, and I would finally break free of the chains my ex-husband had shackled around my wrists.

Jordan seemed to sense the erratic beats of my heart, because he leaned in close, whispering, "Take a walk with me?"

I nodded, and we politely excused ourselves from the table as the band picked up the mood, launching into a popular, upbeat country song that had the floor already flooded with guests ready to line dance.

Jordan didn't hold my hand as we weaved our way through the tables, the music softly fading out the farther we made our way across the yard. There was an extravagant garden and gazebo between the wedding reception and the Mayor's home, and we strolled through it quietly — him with his hands in his pockets, me with mine clasped behind my back.

For a while, we were silent but for the sound of our shoes on the stones lining the garden path. The vines and trees and bushes stretched so tall and wide that we were eventually hidden completely, the reception like another world altogether.

It was then that Jordan stopped mid-stride, and I turned, finding a mixture of pain and fear in his icy eyes.

My heart sank. "Jordan..."

"I know you can tell I've been off today," he said.

I bit my lip, but nodded, moving toward him. My hands tentatively reached for where his were in the pockets of his slacks, and he withdrew them, threading them with mine. My heart picked up its pace, the beat of it loud in my ears as I shook with the words I wanted to say.

I love you.

They were on the tip of my tongue when Jordan looked around us, as if he were afraid we'd been followed, before lowering his voice to a hushed whisper. "I found something last night." He shook his head. "This morning. Whatever four AM is considered."

My mouth was already open, ready to speak my truth, but I closed it slowly at his words.

"Found something?" I asked, confused, and suddenly, I was tracing back through my memory of the day, wondering if I'd read everything wrong.

Jordan nodded, looking around again before he pulled me over to the beautifully carved marble bench by the rose bushes. When we were both sitting, he let out a shaky breath, his eyes on mine.

"I've been sitting on this all day, but it's eating me alive, and I just have to tell someone. I *can't* tell my brothers — not yet. And, well..." He shrugged. "You're the only other person I trust."

My heart swelled, and I squeezed his hands, letting him know he *could* trust me — and that I trusted him, too.

"You know how I showed you my father's journal? The one I'd been going through?"

I nodded, and at the mention of his father, my pulse ticked up another notch.

"I couldn't sleep last night, I... I just had a lot on my mind," he added quickly, dismissing that part of his story. "So I started working on the journal to tire myself out. But before I knew it, an hour and a half had gone by, and suddenly, I was on the last entry."

I blinked. "Like, the last entry in his journal... ever?"

Jordan's expression tightened as he nodded. "Yes. Written on the day of his death."

A violent chill shot through me, so powerful I trembled where Jordan held me.

"And," he added. "This one wasn't in Latin. It was in English."

I shook my head, confused. "But... I don't understand. Wasn't that the whole point of him writing in the journal? Like... he wanted to learn the Latin language, I thought?"

"He did, at least... that's what we think. And I didn't understand it either, not at first." He swallowed. "Not until I read it."

His energy was flowing off him in tidal waves, and I was wrecked by each and every one of them, my body reacting like I was in danger of falling off a cliff at any moment. "What did it say?"

Again, Jordan looked around us, then he lowered his voice so much I had to bend in closer to hear him. "Dad read the Will he found, Sydney. The one Robert J. Scooter left behind. And we were in it. My grandfather, my dad, all of us. We were supposed to get fifty percent of the company shares when Robert passed."

My jaw hinged open, and my eyes found his, mirroring the terror I saw reflected in them.

"Patrick knew," he continued. "My dad wrote in that last entry that he'd gone to him, that he'd told him and showed him the Will and everything."

"So Patrick *knows* about it?"

"He knows," Jordan confirmed. "And he told my dad he wanted to rectify it immediately, make him partner, announce it to the whole board and the company and pay our family what we were owed. All of that."

I shook my head, so confused that I ached all over trying to reach for understanding. "I don't get it. If he knew, if it was all right there in the Will—"

"He told my father he was giving him Robert's old office," Jordan continued.

"The one he'd been cleaning out, right? Where he found the Will?"

Jordan nodded. "Exactly. He said that it's what his father would have wanted, and he told my dad to meet him there after their four o'clock board meeting to discuss next steps." Jordan's face went ashen. "He wrote in the entry that he'd already packed up some of his things to move over, that he couldn't wait to get home to tell Mom." He swallowed. "To tell all of us."

My hands ripped from where they were holding Jordan's, and I shook my head in disbelief. "No..."

"Yes," Jordan said, and he spoke the words out loud that I knew we were both thinking, but I was too afraid to breathe to life. "Sydney, I think Patrick Scooter murdered my father."

Those words hung between us like the razor-sharp blades of a thousand knives, like if either of us moved a single centimeter, we'd be sliced to ribbons.

I couldn't be sure how long the silence stretched between us with my vision fading in and out of blackness before I leaned back, letting out a long, cooling breath and pressing a hand to my forehead.

"I know," he said. "It's a lot. I think this is why Dad was writing his entries in Latin. I think he was covering his tracks, in case someone found his files and tried to read them."

I shook my head, speechless.

"And I need to tell my brothers," he continued. "But... I couldn't tell them yet. Not today. Not when we're celebrating Noah and Ruby Grace."

"When will you tell them?"

"Tomorrow," he said, definitively. "At least, I think. I mean, I don't know how I could sit on this any longer. It's not proof, by any means," he admitted. "But... it's *something*, right? It's written evidence that Patrick knew about the Will, that he has never told us about it even though he knew, and that he'd asked my father to meet him in that office on the evening of his death." He shook his head. "I'm no lawyer, but I'd say there's a leg to stand on there somewhere."

My gut twisted, and I sat upright, facing Jordan again as I steeled myself. "Jordan, there's something I need to tell you. Something that... oh, God," I said, tears flooding my eyes as I pressed my hand to my forehead again. "Something I can't be entirely sure of, but that I feel like I have to tell you."

His brows bent together, and he pulled my hands into his again. "What is it?"

I blew out a breath, holding onto the next. "That night... the night of the fire. I... I was pregnant, and Randy came home late, and he was talking on the phone to someone in the kitchen, and... I don't remember everything, okay? And it's all a little fuzzy and I don't know if this even *means* anything, and—"

"What did you hear, Sydney?"

I swallowed. "He was just... he was so *angry* when I asked him questions. I wanted to know how that was the only room in the whole distillery that burned, how your dad was the only one who died. And I didn't understand it being caused by a cigarette, you know? I mean, was he sleeping? Or so focused on something that he didn't see it catch fire? And when it did, wouldn't he have fled the room? Like... was it *locked*?"

"These are all the questions my family and I have plagued ourselves with for *years*. For an entire decade."

"I know," I said, and my voice was strangled with emotion. "And... Jordan, I swear I heard him on that phone call... I heard him say something about *homicide*."

Jordan's face washed over, all emotion gone before his nostrils flared and he scowled hard. "You *heard* that?"

"I think... No, I mean, I *know* I did. Yes."

For a long moment, he was quiet, and I wondered if he was angry with me. But then, he smiled, shaking his head as he released my hands to run his back through his hair.

"Sydney... do you know what this means? We *have* something. We have my dad's entry, and now, your testimony. This is it. We can get a lawyer, we can—"

"Testimony?" I echoed, already shaking my head. "Jordan, I can't... I can't testify against Randy."

Jordan's frown grew. "Why the hell not?"

"You *know* why," I told him. "You know how he is, how he's controlled me, the hell he's put me through even *after* our divorce."

"He doesn't own you."

"He might as well!" I argued back, fear crippling me in a completely new way now. "Look, I told you what I told you so you can have reassurance, so you and your family can hold onto that and... and... I don't know, work with a lawyer to find out more. But, I can't testify."

"But, it's the right thing to do. You have to!"

"I *can't*!" We both looked around, lowering our voices again. "What about Paige, huh? You *know* she comes first in my life. How could you even ask me to do this?" I shook my head. "He is a white male in a position of power, Jordan. The goddamn *Chief of Police*," I reminded him. "Do you not see how at his mercy I am? How he could turn this story around on me in a snap, make it look like I'm crazy, like I'm an unfit mother and take my daughter from me forever?"

Jordan opened his mouth to argue but I stopped him.

"And even *if* it somehow works, we go to court and I testify and the judge rules in our favor. Then what? Randy goes to jail for life, and Paige has no father?"

Jordan's mouth closed again at that.

"Don't you see how complicated this is?"

"If he goes to jail, it's because he deserves to. And Paige is strong enough to understand what's right and what's wrong."

I scoff. "That's a very naïvely simple way to put this situation."

He gawked at me incredulously. "It *is* simple — right or wrong. There is no in-between."

My bottom lip trembled as I tore my gaze from him, crossing my arms over my racing heart. He didn't understand. He didn't feel every motherly warning going off in my body, every cell of my existence flying into self-preservation and survival mode at the thought of confronting Randy with this.

"You know, I don't know why I'm surprised," Jordan said, standing and turning his back to me. "If there's any risk involved, you're out, right? Just like with us. We can be a team in secret, fuck in secret, *love* in secret, but when I need you to be my teammate for real, it's too much, isn't it?"

He turned on me then, and I shrank under his hard gaze.

"It's okay for me to sacrifice, for me to give, for *me* to put my values on hold in order to be what you need. But when *I* need you, and *you* have something to lose, suddenly, you don't want to play?"

My nose stung, and tears blurred the details of his face. "That's not fair."

"Maybe not, but it's the truth."

I shook my head, and Jordan dropped back to the bench, grabbing both of my hands in his and pulling me forward desperately — into him, into us.

"I *need* you right now, Sydney." His eyes flicked back and forth between mine as a tear slipped free and rolled down my hot cheek. "Please."

Moments before, I'd been ready to look into those eyes watching me and tell this man I loved him. It was all I could think about all day long.

Now, my body warned me of a threat, of danger for myself and my daughter, too.

And those two emotions went to battle inside me, breaking down everything in their path to fight for who would win out.

It was too much — the discovery Jordan had made, the confession I'd told him thinking he would understand, the demand he was making of me, the guilt I felt that I couldn't give it to him, the island I was stranded on as the only one between us who understood my choices, who knew what it was like to give *everything* to protect Paige.

I couldn't make the decision in this state — not now, not tonight.

"I'm sorry," I croaked, and I pulled my hands from his, covering my mouth as my eyes squeezed shut and released another flood of tears. I was already up and off the bench, flying through the garden and across the lawn to where I'd parked my car, and I didn't look back to see if Jordan was following me.

Maybe because I knew he wouldn't.

I'd gone into that evening with the intention to hold his heart in my hands, to promise to keep it safe, to tell him I wanted him — *all* of him — and I wanted him to take all of me, too.

I was supposed to tell him I loved him.

I was supposed to claim his heart as my own.

Instead, I'd left it shattered on the stony path of a cold, dark garden.

And I'd never hated myself more.

TWENTY

JORDAN

The next evening after Sunday dinner at Mom's, I sat at the firepit in her backyard surrounded by all my brothers, and I told them what I'd found.

I felt numb going through the story, telling them what I'd already told Sydney the night before and feeling my heart split open a little more with every thought of her. I wished she was there with me, telling *her* side of the story, but I kept that to myself.

Even if I didn't understand her choice, I respected it.

I wouldn't tell anyone what she'd told me.

Still, *I* knew now, and the fact that she'd overheard Randy on the phone that night talking to *someone* about homicide only fueled my justice fire.

We were going to take someone down for my father's death, though I wasn't sure who yet.

But we had to be smart about it.

We had to have a plan.

"We can't tell anyone else about this," I told my brothers after their initial outbursts at the news and the silence that had followed. I waited until each of them were looking at me to continue. "Least of all Mom. She'll kill him."

"Are you kidding me? *I* might fucking kill him," Noah seethed, fuming like a dragon.

"That would solve nothing," I reminded him, bluntly but as gently as I could. "The biggest mistake we could make right now is letting our emotions get the best of us. We have to be smart."

There were quiet nods, though I could tell by the way my brothers wore identical scowls and flat-lined lips that no one was happy about the agreement.

"And I want to tell Mom just as badly as you guys do, but it wouldn't serve her any good right now. Until we have someone in handcuffs or substantial proof, she doesn't need to know."

"I just don't understand," Mikey said, shaking his head. "How could Patrick *murder* someone like that? A father, just like him — and someone who grew up with him in that distillery? Someone his own father loved?"

"Maybe that's just it," Logan said. "I mean, you heard what Jordan found in Dad's last entry. Patrick never really liked Dad. He saw him as a threat."

"And look at all the illegal shit Patrick Scooter does without blinking an eye. His underground casino has gotten half this town into debt they'll never see the other side of — Ruby Grace's dad included. I mean, he found a way to pay it off, but he's the *mayor*. What about everyone else?" Noah shook his head. "I think, in his eyes, he owns this town and everyone in it, and he can do whatever he damn well pleases."

"He *had* to have known that Will existed," Mikey chimed in.

"I don't know," I volleyed. "If he did, why would he have had Dad working in that office *knowing* there was a

Will hidden somewhere in there? And besides, we don't know that Patrick is the root of this. All we know is that he asked Dad to be in that office at the end of the day."

We all fell silent at that.

"Wouldn't Robert's lawyer have had the Will, too, though?" Logan asked after a while. "I mean, it has to be notarized. I imagine *someone* had a copy — a lawyer, a financial advisor, whoever. That one in his old office couldn't have been the only one."

"Money speaks, brother," Noah said quietly. "My gut tells me if Patrick didn't want that Will being read by anyone, he'd pay just about anything to get agreement from all involved that it never existed."

Again, silence.

It was a tornado of emotions for each one of my brothers, one that had already ripped through me. I was on the other side of it, sitting calmly in the rubble, thinking of how to rebuild. But right now, they were in the thick of the storm, and I knew all too well how disconcerting that was.

"I think I need to tell Mallory," Logan said after a moment.

I frowned.

"It's her *father*, for Christ's sake," he pleaded with me. "I don't feel comfortable making a plan to confront him without her being in on it."

My chest tightened at the thought of someone outside of my brothers knowing what I'd found, but I understood what he was saying. Mallory's father was the main subject of the discovery. It was only fair that we told her what we found.

"Alright," I conceded. "But, I think right now, we need to all stay calm and quiet about this. I'm going to look into getting a lawyer, see what our options are."

"It has to be someone outside of town," Noah said. "I don't think we can trust anyone here."

"Definitely," I agreed, then I ticked through the list of what we each needed to be doing. "Logan, you fill Mallory in, maybe she'll know something more about that night, or at the very least know how we can get Patrick to admit to whatever happened. Mikey, I want you to comb through the last few journal entries, make sure I didn't miss anything. And Noah," I said, looking at him last. "You are going to go on your honeymoon and forget about this until you get back."

He scoffed, ready to argue, but I shook my head firmly.

"I mean it," I said. "You just married the love of your life. There's nothing to be done right now, not until we get a lawyer and make a plan — and we won't do that while you're gone. Okay? I know it's going to be hard to do, but you need to focus on Ruby Grace and enjoy your time with her." I exhaled long and slow. "I have the State Championship game on Friday night. You'll be back from your honeymoon on Sunday. Let's just agree to meet up then, and we can talk through the next steps. We've waited ten long years, guys... we can wait another week."

My brothers all exchanged looks, but in the end, they nodded in agreement. One thing I'd learned as the older brother was that it was my responsibility to help them see reason when all they wanted to see was red. It wasn't always an easy task, but they trusted me — and as long as that was true, I knew they'd listen, even if they didn't agree.

"I need to come up with a reason why Kylie and I can't go back to New York," Mikey said.

"No, don't do that. Go back. You have work and she does, too. We need to keep everything normal. But I'll book you a flight to come back home next Sunday, okay?"

He frowned, but nodded. "I want her to come, too."

"Okay," I said. "I'll get you both a ticket."

We were silent for a long while, each of us staring at the fire where its flames licked away at the evening settling in around us.

"Do you think we'll get what we need to take him down?" Logan asked after a long while. "I mean... do you think we'll actually get justice for Dad?"

No one answered, because none of us knew for sure.

All we *did* know was that we had to try.

—◆—

I hadn't realized how much of my focus had been on what I'd found in my dad's journal until I'd finally told my brothers and relieved myself of being the only one who knew.

As soon as I did, every ache inside me turned its attention to the hole Sydney had left.

The week passed by in slow agony, with my days spent working with my athletes in weightlifting class, my afternoons spent at practice getting them ready for Friday, and my evenings spent on the phone with one or more of my brothers, trying to calm them and reassure them that everything would be alright. Before I knew it, it was Friday night, and I was on the field watching my team warm up in preparation to play the biggest game of their lives so far.

And while I should have been focused on *that*, I could only think of Sydney.

I could only feel numb.

The naïve part of me thought that if I kept busy all week — and I did — there wouldn't be time to be broken up over Sydney.

But she didn't need to be the center of my day to be present in every moment of it.

She was like a slow leak, forcing her way between all the crevices of my broken heart and slowly, centimeter by centimeter, wearing it down and causing it to rust so much so that I wondered if a stiff inhale would make it shatter altogether.

Seeing her at work killed me, but it wasn't as bad as it would have been if I couldn't see her at all.

Every afternoon when I walked into my office, she was already set up in hers, working away and getting our boys in top shape for the game on Friday. We didn't speak about what had happened Saturday night at the wedding. Hell, we didn't speak at *all* other than in staff meetings or in the locker room when everyone was present and she needed to update me on an injury.

We avoided each other at all costs.

But when our eyes *did* meet, it was like standing in a blue-flamed fire.

I knew she was hurting. I knew she couldn't have been sleeping or eating much more than I was managing to. I wanted to ask her a million questions. I wanted to hear her say a million things that would take what happened at my brother's wedding away and give us the chance to start over. I wanted to pull her into my office, pull her into *me*, hug her and kiss her and tell her everything would be okay.

But I couldn't, because *nothing* was okay right now.

We were both fucked up, but what mattered even more than that was that we were both set in our ways.

She believed she was right.

I believed I was right.

And there was no in-between, not for either one of us.

I struggled with understanding her, especially after everything she'd told me about what Randy had done to her over the years. Here was the perfect opportunity to get him to answer for his evil, and she was too coward to stand up and make him pay.

I knew Paige complicated things, and that she was worried his power was too much, that we could never win.

But Paige was smart. She was kind-hearted. *She* knew right from wrong, and I believed in my gut that if she knew the full story, if her mother explained it to her, she would be okay. Maybe not immediately — but eventually. She was a tough kid like that.

Then again, did I have a right to say that, to believe that, when I'd never been a father? How could I ever fully understand the position I'd asked Sydney to put herself and her child in? How could I know what it feels like to make a decision that affects not only you, but a growing child, who will likely grow up differently *because* of that decision?

The answer was that I couldn't.

And could I really say that we had nothing to worry about when it came to Randy, that the justice system would prevail and the bad guys would lose and the good guys would win?

Because, realistically, what proof of that did we have *anywhere*?

If anything, the daily news only supported *her* side of it — that right and wrong didn't always matter, and sometimes, good people got fucked over.

But, it wasn't her views on what the right thing to do in this situation was that upset me the most. That wasn't what drove the nail deeper and deeper into my splitting chest, making breathing damn near impossible.

It was that I came to her with something I hadn't told anyone. I trusted her. And when everything was said and done, I looked her in the eyes and told her that I needed her.

I need you, Sydney.

And she'd denied me.

My ribcage hollowed out at the reminder of it, but it was a stinging pain I was beginning to get used to — like chronic back ache after a sports injury. I subdued it as best I could, focusing on the clipboard of plays in my hand as I talked to Coach TK in a hushed voice, our eyes on the players on the field.

It didn't matter now, what had happened between Sydney and me.

It was over.

We were over.

And maybe what hurt the most was that we had never really begun, at all.

I wished so badly to live in this moment that — *before* Sydney — had been all I could dream about. I was at the State Championship game. My boys were warming up on the green turf of Tucker Stadium at Tennessee Tech. We were about to play the other top high school team in the state of Tennessee, to have the chance to prove that *we* were the best. The massive arena was filled with screaming football fans, with our entire town, everyone showing up to support us and cheer us on to another W.

This was all I'd wanted.

Until Sydney.

I felt her warmth even when she was on the complete opposite side of the benches from where I stood — which was where she aimed to be at all times, it seemed. She was keeping her head down, working on players, wrapping and taping and doing soft tissue work and ensuring we were ready to play.

"Time to get focused, Coach," Elijah Braxton said from behind me, clapping me on the shoulder with a knowing look, like he could see I was a mess.

We'd been allowed to bring more people onto the field than we needed, and he'd been one of the fans we'd invited to be on the sideline with us. He was helping in whatever ways he could, getting water for the guys and helping run warm-ups, but for the most part, he stayed out of the way, watching.

And when he looked at me, looked at Sydney, and then gave me a knowing, sympathetic smile — my heart burned like a dying star.

I glanced at Sydney then, and our eyes met for one brief second before I jogged out onto the field for the coin toss.

In that one moment, we seemed to say a thousand things.

But I couldn't understand a single one of them.

I heard Eli's words like bell tolls in my ears when the coin was tossed and our players lined the field for kickoff. And with all the effort I had left, I shoved everything out of my head that wasn't football. It was a skill I'd practiced and perfected when I was younger, when Dad had died and I was trying to figure out how to take care of Mom and be there for my brothers and somehow still get my career as a coach off the ground, too.

It was a numb state of mind, one that felt like I was floating underwater, or like being tethered to the Earth but suspended in outer space.

Somehow, I slipped back into that zone for the next hour and a half, and I didn't emerge from it again until we were jogging into the locker room at halftime.

We were down by a touchdown.

I had to figure out a way to get my boys back on track, to get them fired up, to get this win.

So, I put on my game face and walked into a silent locker room with all eyes on me, waiting.

It was when I locked gazes with a pair of almond brown ones that I found the strength to speak.

TWENTY-ONE

SYDNEY

If I looked at the facts alone, I was still alive.

I was still breathing, inhaling oxygen and exhaling carbon dioxide, and it had been like that all week long. I was still waking up each morning — though I wasn't sure it counted as *waking up* if I hadn't ever fallen asleep — and I was still getting Paige ready for school, and going to work, and coming home, and making dinner, and hanging out with her until bedtime, and then climbing into bed myself just to do it all over again.

I was showing up.

I was holding it together.

I was alive.

Those were the facts.

But if I broke it down to the molecular level, it was all a lie.

No one saw the tears I drowned in every time I took a shower, but that didn't mean they didn't happen. No one saw the hollowness I felt in my chest, or the ache that ripped through me as my heart broke every time I laid eyes on Jordan — but they were there, regardless.

My past had trained me to put on a warrior face, to stand tall and strong no matter what, and I was doing just that.

But inside, I was crumbling.

The week I'd spent without Jordan since that wedding had been nothing but a numb blur of daily tasks and motions that convinced me I was going to be okay. I told myself that the more time that passed, the less it would hurt, and one day, it wouldn't hurt at all.

That felt like a lie, too.

To his credit, Jordan hadn't reached out to me. He hadn't texted me or called me or asked for anything from me at all. It was the right thing to do — a clean break.

But it was the last thing I wanted.

Every time he walked into his office, I wanted to walk in right behind him, shut the door, and leap into his arms. Every time I stood next to him on the field, I wanted to lace my fingers with his, tell him I was sorry, that I loved him, that I wanted to be with him. Every time our eyes caught, I looked away as fast as I could, but every cell inside me begged to keep his gaze.

I wanted him. I wanted us.

But I knew deep down that I couldn't give him what he needed.

It was more than just the fight we'd had in the garden Saturday night. It was true that I couldn't testify against my ex-husband, that I couldn't be what Jordan wanted me to be when it came to finding justice for his father. There was too much at stake — my daughter, my safety, our future.

And past that? Jordan was right about me.

I was a coward.

He'd held up on his end of our deal, and I'd failed on mine. The first time he asked me to be there for him, I bailed. I was ashamed, but I wouldn't hide from that truth, either.

I couldn't be the woman he deserved.

I had a child, and an ex-husband I was still tied to. It went so much deeper than my reputation on the team and in our small town.

In the most fundamental ways, we were wrong for each other.

And *that* was a fact I couldn't ignore.

The State Championship game had snuck up on me like a snake in long-leaved grass, but it was a distraction I welcomed. It was easy to lose myself in the excitement of the players, to focus on getting them ready to play and keeping them iced and bandaged and warm throughout the game. Even in the locker room at halftime, I'd been able to stay distracted, working on the players and tuning out the sound of Jordan's voice as he motivated them to go out there and get us the win in the second half.

But when the last seconds of the game ticked down, when their team had one last Hail Mary throw chance to come back and score a touchdown and take away our three-point lead, when they *missed* that chance and the crowd roared and our team exploded off the benches and flooded the field to celebrate our win, everything in me stopped.

And all I could do was find Jordan.

The level of noise that stadium erupted into was unlike anything I'd ever experienced. It was dizzying, the roaring cheers and the sea of people crashing onto the field and swallowing it up. In a matter of seconds, it went from where you could see every yard of green on the field to where you couldn't see a single square patch of it.

It was absolutely surreal.

We weren't in our little hometown. No, we were on a *college* team's field, in a stadium twenty-times the size of our small one back home, and we had the entire state watching.

Watching us win.

We won.

It sank in more and more as adrenaline coursed through me, and I searched the crowd frantically, trying to find Jordan. There were already swarms of players and reporters and fans on the field, but I looked toward the middle of it, knowing he would have jogged over to shake hands with the opposing coach before anything else.

There were too many people, and the more that flooded the field, the more my chest tightened. I wanted to find him, but why? What would I do? What would I say? *Congrats on the win, Coach*? Nothing was right, nothing was *enough*, and yet I couldn't stop myself from seeking him out. It was as if I didn't have a choice at all.

I was still searching for the right words to say once I *did* find him when there was a little clearing in the field, and there Jordan was, jogging back toward our sideline as reporters chased after him.

He kept his head down, speaking from the corner of his mouth to a few of them but focusing on getting back to where his team was. I imagined he was telling them he'd talk to them at the press conference, or that he just wanted a moment with his players. But they were relentless, all wanting a piece, and when he looked up and saw me staring at him from ten yards away, he slowed to a walk, and then to a complete stop.

It was only a few seconds, if even that.

It was just a small, microscopic moment.

He looked at me. And I looked at him. And all the noise, the chaos, the thrill of the win faded, along with the crowd around us. Time was like an elastic band between us, and I knew he felt it, too — like those few seconds were hours, instead. He just watched me, and I watched him, and we somehow said everything, but nothing at all.

The corner of my mouth lifted, and his did the same.

You did it, I told him with my eyes.

We did it, he told me with his.

I swallowed.

His jaw clenched.

Tears flooded my eyes.

His brows drew together.

Then, as fast as the moment had come, it was gone.

I saw it — the moment Jordan decided not to run to me. His right knee jerked forward automatically, his body leaning into the motion, but he stopped himself, and pulled back, and in his eyes I saw the truth I'd reminded myself of all week reflected back at me.

This was it for us.

We were over.

All of that happened in a matter of seconds, though it felt like an entire lifetime to me, and then all at once, the universe snapped back into action, and Jordan was enveloped first by a few of the players giving him a Gatorade bath from our bright orange water cooler, and then by the sea of reporters.

They swallowed him whole, taking him out of my sight, and I turned before another tear had the chance to fall.

I couldn't be sure how much time passed on that field after that. I checked in on players, talked to reporters, high-fived the other members of the staff and accepted an emotional hug from Principal Hanley, who told me he *knew* he made the right decision hiring me.

He also said the job was mine as long as I wanted it, and he was happy to see that Jordan and I worked together so well.

I ignored the fire in my chest at his words, encouraging him to go talk to the other coaches while I found my daughter. And as soon as he shook my hand and made his way deeper onto the field, Paige slammed into me full speed, wrapping her arms around my waist and screaming while I tried to keep my balance.

"YOU DID IT! YOU WON! WE WON! WE WON!"

She was hysterical, jumping up and down and squeezing me and jumping up and down again and then running in circles around me. Seeing her excitement brought the first genuine smile I'd had all week, and it somehow hurt, as if my face had forgotten how to activate those muscles altogether.

"I can't believe it!" she said, panting, her hands on top of her head as she looked up at me with wide eyes. "I mean, we were down at halftime and I thought for *sure* that was it! And then you guys came back out and *wham*!" She made a one-two punch motion with her fists. "Sacks here, tackles there, *two* interceptions and a field goal kick to gain the lead. And they just crumbled! They couldn't catch us once we were on fire like that!"

I chuckled, rubbing the crazy hair on her head. "I bet it was because you were in those stands cheering."

"I mean, I *do* think I'm a good luck charm," she said with a crooked grin. "But, this time, it was the team. And Coach! Oh my gosh," she said, as if she'd only just realized she was on the field. Her eyes scanned it wildly. "Where is he? Can I go find him and congratulate him?" She looked up at me before I had the chance to answer and clapped her hands together. "Please, please, please, pleaseeeee."

My next breath was stolen by my rib cage squeezing in on itself, but I looked back, finding Jordan standing with Principal Hanley, the reporters talking to the players now and leaving him be.

"Alright," I said. "But hurry over there and then come right back. Stay where I can see you."

She'd barely acknowledged my rules before she sprinted into action, and I kept my eyes on her as Randy sidled up next to me.

The moment he did, I felt sick again.

"Congratulations," he murmured under his breath.

I knew he was being condescending and didn't actually mean it, but I thanked him anyway.

We stood next to each other in silence, both of our eyes on the field. My stomach rolled when the scent of his cologne caught on the breeze. It was a scent I used to love, one I used to find comfort and love in. Now, it just made me ill.

I watched Jordan smiling down at Paige as she jumped around in front of him, animatedly telling him all her thoughts on the game, no doubt, and my heart ached so fiercely in my chest I had to press a hand over it.

Randy watched me from the corner of his eyes, then he looked at Paige, at Jordan, and back at me.

"Is there something you need to tell me, Sydney?"

His voice sent a chill down my spine, though I wasn't sure why.

"I have literally had nothing to say to you since the day I left you, Randy."

"I don't know, sweetheart. I think you *do* have something to tell me."

"What are you getting at?" I asked, hoping the long sigh from my chest gave away that I was bored and not interested in fighting with him.

"I ran into Marty at Buck's the other night," he said. "You know Marty. Barrel-raiser down at the distillery."

"Yes. And?"

"Well, he was at Noah Becker's wedding last weekend," he said, and then my heart stopped at the same time a wicked grin climbed on his lips from my peripheral view. "But I guess you already know that, since he told me *you* were there, too."

It took every ounce of willpower I had left to calm my breathing in that moment, to not let him see that I was intimidated by his menacing gaze, by the threat that lay beneath the innocent words he'd said out loud.

"I'm not doing this with you," I finally said, and I took a step toward Paige, but before I could walk away, Randy grabbed my wrist and ripped me around to face him.

Pain shot up my arm, and panic zipped through me before I subdued it, meeting his eyes with fierce determination to not let him see me scared of him ever again.

"Paige is nine years old, Sydney. Do you think she hasn't been telling me that *Coach* has been over nearly every weekend?"

My heart raced, but I didn't say a word.

"First of all, I didn't agree to Paige playing football. I'm still her father, in case you forgot."

"Randy," I said as calmly as I could when he gripped me tighter. Every cell in my body was slipping into survival mode, and I used every ounce of strength I had to remain calm.

But before I could ask him to release me, Randy pulled me in closer, eyes dark and narrowed.

"Are you fucking Jordan Becker?"

His words were a slap to the face, but I didn't flinch.

"Randy," I said calmly again, glancing around to make sure no one was watching us. Everyone seemed to be distracted by the win, but my heart ricocheted within my ribcage regardless. I lowered my voice to just above a whisper. "Let go of me."

He blew out an angry breath through his nose, his grip tightening even more on my wrist as I winced. That seemed to wake him, and he blinked, like he'd been in a fog. His eyes caught somewhere behind me, and he released me immediately, smoothing his hands over his uniform — which he didn't need to be wearing, but I knew he did because he needed that power, always.

Randy's eyes caught at the same point behind me before he found my gaze again. "We'll talk later," he said, and then he turned and left without even saying goodbye to his daughter.

And I let out a shaky breath that I covered with both of my hands, squeezing my eyes shut and releasing two tears down my hot cheeks. I tried so hard not to let them fall, but my body was acting of its own accord, the relief and anxiety crashing into me all at once like a tsunami.

I didn't have time to get it together before Paige was at my side, and then I heard Jordan, too.

"Sydney?" he asked, touching my elbow, and I nearly broke at the contact — so gentle and calming and sure.

So unlike Randy's.

"Are you okay?"

I swiped the tears from my face, not looking at him as I reached for Paige's hand. I knew if I saw concern on his face, if I saw care in his eyes, I would break completely.

"I'm fine," I said as calmly as I could. "I'll see you at school on Monday. Come on, Paigey."

I put on my best smile for her, steering her toward the locker room. I needed to get my stuff. And then I needed to get the hell out of here.

I'd driven separately from the team for the two-hour road trip so that I could take Paige home with me after the game, and I was thankful for that fact as I packed up my athletic bag and slung it over one shoulder, listening to Paige go on excitedly about what she'd talked to Jordan about. She was still going as we made our way across the parking lot reserved for the players and coaches and their families, and when we climbed into the car, she buckled up with a giant smile.

"I'm so happy for you, Mama. You're an amazing trainer. You know that?"

I smiled as best I could, heart still racing. "Well, coming from you, that's a high honor. Thank you, sweetie."

"One day, I'm going to be a player on that field," she whispered, looking out the window. "Just wait and see."

I was still trying to hold it together as she smiled, finally quiet as I started up the car. But as soon as I backed out of the parking space, she was on again.

"We should have Jordan over tomorrow to celebrate. Oh! Mama!" Her mouth popped open, eyes wide as she looked at me in the rearview mirror from where she sat in the back seat. "We could make him a cake!"

I covered my mouth as another wave of emotion surfaced, threatening to take me under. But I inhaled a hot breath, holding it together as best I could and smiling back at Paige before I took my eyes to the front. "Maybe, sweetheart. I'm sure he wants to celebrate with his own family tomorrow."

"Well, we could invite them, too," she offered. "They had us over for Thanksgiving, after all. Or, if not tomorrow, then Sunday. Whenever works for him. But we *have* to celebrate. We won the State Championship!"

I reached back and squeezed her knee in lieu of an answer, then I plugged in my phone and turned on her favorite country song, blasting it so loudly she couldn't hear the first sob that choked through my façade.

—●—

JORDAN

It was late as hell, but the two-hour bus drive back to Stratford was anything but sleepy or quiet.

The energy wafting between the players was palpable as they relived every moment of the game, sang our fight song loud and proud, and passed the trophy around to take pictures and rub it for good luck going into the next season. They were already posting all over social media, making phone calls to their girlfriends or their families they had to leave behind at the stadium, and to the ones who hadn't been at the game at all. And of course, I heard talkbragging about what the sports articles were already saying about the game in the online blogs.

I half-listened to their merriment, half-zoned out in the front seat, with my eyes losing focus on the yellow dots peppering the two-lane highway that led into our town.

Thankfully, none of the other coaches pestered me — likely because they knew after talking to reporters that I was absolutely spent — so I had silence amidst the chaos for the entire ride home.

I spent most of it thinking about Sydney.

Again, I wished for the focus I'd had before I met her. I imagined a completely different scenario for this night had I never known she existed, where I would be celebrating with the guys and taking silly pictures with the trophy and handing out accolades to those who deserved it.

As it stood, I was saving all that for Monday, when — hopefully — I'd be feeling more myself.

I wondered if it was partly everything going on with my father, knowing that the day after tomorrow, I'd be meeting up with my brothers to discuss where we'd go from here.

We'd all been sitting on what we'd found all week long, powerless to move forward without knowing what our options were, and now that I'd spoken with a lawyer in Nashville, I knew the odds weren't in our favor.

We had something, that was sure, but if it would hold up in court was another question entirely — one the lawyer couldn't answer without doing more research.

She said she'd get back to me, and to not do anything drastic in the meantime.

But she didn't know my brothers.

Still, even as my heart squeezed with the thoughts of my father, I knew my misery tonight was wrapped up in Sydney. It was in the way I wanted to run to her when we won, how I wanted to pick her up and spin her around and celebrate with *her* more than anyone else in the world. It was in the way we found each other on that field, in the long moment that passed between us, in the tears that flooded her eyes before we both turned away.

And it was in the way I'd seen Randy holding her wrist, the way she'd panicked and fled the field, the way she couldn't even look at me.

I hated the power Randy had over her, and the way he could make her feel like shit on what should have been one of the best nights of her career so far. He'd had enough sense to leave before I made my way over to where they'd been standing, but he also knew that I'd seen it.

If I had it my way, I'd take him down right along with Patrick Scooter.

With my mind racing the entire drive home, I had a feeling it would be another sleepless night as we pulled into the high school parking lot. There was a small crowd waiting for the bus — friends and family and students who had beat us back to the school and were now holding giant signs that welcomed us home as three-time champions — and I stood in the aisle when we parked, addressing the team.

"Before you leave, all the equipment needs to be off this bus and put away *correctly* in the locker room, understood?"

There were murmurs of acknowledgement, but most of the focus was on the crowd outside, and boys were already hanging out the windows and shouting down, starting the fight chant.

I smiled, standing aside and waving them off the bus. "Alright. Go have fun."

They were a boisterous wave of noise and body odor as they flew out the bus doors and down to where the crowd waited for them, and the coaches and I stood back and waited, chuckling to each other when we finally made our way off, too.

I kept to myself while everyone celebrated, having already hugged Mama and Logan at that stadium after the game. They were staying in a hotel overnight, not wanting to make the late drive back, and Mama had already insisted that we celebrate tomorrow.

She didn't realize there was so much more to do than celebrate.

I took my time in the locker room, taking the equipment from the guys as they dragged it in and sending them on their way. I didn't mind staying back to organize it all and make sure it was in the right place.

They needed to be out living it up.

I smiled as the last of them filtered out, remembering a time when high school football felt like everything to me. I couldn't dream of a day past graduation, of a season more important than the one I played my senior year.

Those boys would remember this night for the rest of their lives.

When I was finally ready to leave, it was nearly three in the morning, and I was the only one left on school property. At least, that's what I thought as I locked up the locker room behind me and made my way across the field to the staff parking lot.

But parked next to my Bronco was a Stratford Police squad car.

The lights weren't on, but it was idling quietly, and when I was just a few feet away, the engine cut off and Randy stepped out of the driver side.

He looked manic — his hair out of place, eyes red, a bottle of something concealed in a paper bag wrapped in one fist. He took another swig of it as I approached, and a shit-eating grin spread on his face.

"Congratulations, Coach," he slurred as I threw my athletic bag in the back of my truck. I leaned against it when I was empty-handed, crossing my arms over my chest.

"Thank you," I managed, doing my best to keep a level of calmness in my voice. "Something I can help you with tonight, Randy?"

"Oh, fuck off with your niceties, Becker," he spat, shaking his head. He pointed one of the fingers wrapped around the paper-bagged bottle straight at me, closing one eye as if he was aiming a gun. "You're fucking my wife, aren't you?"

It was an instant reaction, every nerve standing on end as my chest fluttered with the *fight or flight* adrenaline kicking into gear. The hair stood up on the back of my neck, but I remained where I was leaning against my truck, simply blinking when what I really wanted to do was ram my fist into his jaw.

"I didn't realize you were married."

He growled at that, running at me but stopping with a few feet between us, his finger now pointing in my face. "Don't try to be fucking smart with me. I'll arrest you right now and take your ass *all* the way down, you understand me?"

"What exactly would you arrest me for, Randy?"

"Anything I goddamn please," he spat with a smile. "Don't you see? *I* make the rules here, and if I say you were driving drunk, or resisting arrest, or carrying a gun that you tried to pull on me?" His smirk climbed. "Then you were. No one questions me. I'm the Chief of Police, you worthless motherfucker."

The urge to connect my fist with his face strengthened, but I crossed my arms over my chest tighter, willing myself to calm down. Hitting him would only give him fuel for all the fire he just threatened me with, and as fucked up as it was, I knew he wasn't bullshitting.

He *could* get away with any of the things he'd just listed.

It was my word against his, and as one of the few men of color in this town, I knew the odds weren't in my favor.

Suddenly — and all at once — everything Sydney had said to me at Noah's wedding clicked.

She wasn't a coward for being afraid of Randy and the power he possessed.

She was smart. She was aware.

And she was a mother doing what she could to protect Paige from the man standing in front of me.

My heart sank at the realization, and I reminded myself to stay calm, to not agitate him, to play by his rules until I was out of this situation.

So, I waited, knowing he had something he wanted to say — and I just hoped once he'd said it, he'd leave me alone.

"Now," Randy said, straightening. "Are you, or are you not fucking Sydney?"

My jaw clenched, because the way he spoke about her was as if *fucking her* was all she was good for. He had no idea what he'd lost when she left him, and he never deserved her in the first place.

"Not that it's any of your business, but yes, Sydney and I were dating," I confessed — mostly to see the look of incredulousness on his face. But I didn't have a smug smile to meet him with, because my heart was already breaking before the next words made their way out. "But, we're not anymore."

Randy narrowed his eyes, as if he didn't believe me. When he found no sign of a lie, he must have been satisfied, because he smiled again, taking a long swig from the bottle wrapped in that bag before he took a few steps back. "That's what I thought."

I cocked a brow.

"I don't know what happened between you two, but I hope you realized that you will *never* have her." He stopped walking backward, tilting his head to the side a little, his red eyes narrowed in on mine. "Sydney is *mine*, do you understand? She always has been, she always will be."

My fists clenched where they were tucked into my sides, but I held back, biding my time until he would be gone.

"Stay the fuck away from her, Becker, or I swear to God, I'll take you and your entire family down." His wicked grin split his face then. "And believe me when I say I *can*."

With another slug from the bottle, he opened his door, pointed at me one last time, and slipped inside the squad car, slamming the door shut behind him.

Then, he revved the engine to life, flicked on the blue and red lights and an ear-splitting siren, and peeled out of the parking lot, leaving me in his dust.

TWENTY-TWO

SYDNEY

Paige and I slept in the next morning, which was usually impossible with Paige, but all the excitement from the game had kept her up late and led to her passing out hard when I finally got her tucked in.

We woke around eleven, and then she insisted on making me chocolate chip pancakes — which always ended up being more work for me than for her. But, she was adamant that we celebrate, and I was in need of a distraction from the way my chest was slowly ripping open, so I obliged.

The kitchen was covered in flour and smudged chocolate and bits of batter when we finished. We ate in the living room, still in our PJs, leaving the mess in the kitchen while we watched College Game Day.

When we were done eating, Paige asked if she could drag all her art supplies into the living room to make a card for Jordan. And of course, I told her yes, because what else could I say? I didn't have the heart to tell her he likely wouldn't be by as much as he had been.

Would he?

I wondered if maybe there *could* be a friendship between us, one that was comfortable and safe and where no lines would be crossed. Would he want to still come over and work with Paige? To stay for dinner? To be with us?

The answer, I knew, was that he would love those things — but that now that we'd crossed the line into being more than friends, we could never just tiptoe back over it as if nothing had ever happened.

My chest was tight, tears pricking the corners of my eyes as I watched Paige sprawled out on her belly in the middle of the living room floor making a card for Jordan. Her little legs swung in the air, and she'd stop every now and then to look up at the TV before she'd get back to her task.

It was too much for me to bear, and so I slipped outside, dialing my sister's number as soon as the sliding glass door was shut.

"Well, if it isn't the State Champ!" she greeted enthusiastically. "Please tell me you're extremely hungover from all the celebrating you did last night."

She chuckled, but my eyes flooded with the tears I'd been trying to hold back, and a soft sob broke through my lips and the silence I'd met her with.

"Oh, Syd," she said sadly. "What happened?"

For the longest time, all I could do was cry while my older sister listened helplessly on the other end. But finally, I found my breath, and I told her everything — from our agreement and the amazing two months we'd spent together to Thanksgiving and the wedding and the last week. When I'd said all I could think to say, I quieted, sniffling, waiting for her response.

It was her turn to be silent.

"Please say something," I finally pleaded, wiping my nose on the back of my sleeve and tucking my legs under me. It was cold outside, and I'd wished I'd grabbed a blanket or a jacket.

"Do you want me to bullshit you, or be honest?"

I cringed. "Honest."

She sighed. "Sydney, you deserve to be happy. Do you realize that?"

Another wave of tears assaulted me, and I closed my eyes, resting my forehead on my knees and holding the phone tightly to my ear.

"First of all, Randy does not *own* you. I know it can feel like that, but he doesn't. Jordan would protect you if he tried anything, and I think the bigger part of you knows that." She was quiet for a long pause. "Did you... did you really hear him say something about homicide that night?"

I sniffed. "I think so. I mean, I was pregnant, there were a lot of hormones going on and I was tired and we fought and..." All the muscles in my body tightened. "And that was the first time he hit me..."

I knew without her saying a word that my sister had her fists tightened at that, because no one in my family knew of the abuse until I left Randy.

As it so often goes.

"So, I don't..." I continued, sobs still breaking up my sentences. I forced a calming breath as best I could. "I don't know, my memory is foggy. But... I really think I did."

"Then you have to testify."

My jaw dropped. "Gab... I *can't*. He'll make me look crazy. He'll turn it around on me. And even if somehow they *did* believe me over him, and let's say he goes to jail, then what? What do I tell Paige?"

"The truth," she said. "Being her mother doesn't always mean hiding the bad things from her, Sis. Sometimes, it means *showing* her the bad things — leading her to them and teaching her how to handle them. This world is a fucked-up place, and you know that more than I do." She paused. "I don't know what would happen if you did testify, if the Beckers took Randy and Patrick and whoever else to court to get to the bottom of all of this but... I *do* know that if you stood with them, you'd be doing the right thing. And I know that's what you *want* to do."

My stomach rolled so violently I nearly lost my breakfast, and I shook my head against the urge to throw up. "But..."

"I know," she said, and I knew I didn't need to finish my sentence. "It's terrifying. You've been in survival mode for so long that this goes against everything you stand for. But, Sydney, do you really think you'd be okay to just sit back, lose the first guy to ever truly care for you, and watch him fight for justice for his entire family without you there on his side, helping?"

My face warped with emotion, and I shook my head, laying my tear-stained cheek on my knee. "No," I whispered. "But, Paige..."

"Mama?"

My head shot up, and Paige stood in the doorway, her little face so sad it nearly broke my heart as she took in the sight of me crying.

"Hey, baby," I said, wiping my face. "I have to go, Sis. I'll call you later," I told Gabby, and I ended the call, forcing a smile and patting my lap — signaling for Paige to come join me.

She padded over slowly, crawling into my lap as I wrapped her up in a fierce hug.

"Everything's okay, sweetheart," I told her as I rocked her. "Mama's just having a bad week, that's all."

"Is it because you and Jordan broke up?"

Shock zipped through me, and I couldn't hide the expression on my face as I pulled back to look at my daughter.

"Come on, Mom," she said, rolling her eyes. "Did you really think I didn't know?"

I covered my smile with my hand, amused. "Know *what*, exactly?"

"That you and Jordan are boyfriend and girlfriend, but that you thought you were hiding it from me and everyone else. But, I'm smart, Mom. I see the way he looks at you."

"And what way is that?"

"Like he *loooooves* you," she said, drawing out the word and tapping my nose with her fingertip. We both giggled, and then she looked sad again. "But he hasn't been here all week, and you haven't been sleeping, and I knew something was wrong when you guys were acting weird at the game yesterday. You broke up, didn't you?"

I sighed, but nodded, deciding it was no use to hide it from her now.

"Why, Mama? I like Jordan. I like having him here with us. He's nice, and we play football, and he was nice to you, too, wasn't he?"

My heart squeezed in my chest, and I let out another breath, trying to find the words to explain it to her, all the while trying to digest the words my sister had said to *me*. But before I could figure it all out, there was a loud, pounding knock at the front door — so loud we heard it all the way through the house and out the back door.

Then, a muted voice from around the other side of the house.

"Open up, Syd. It's me."

"Daddy?" Paige looked at me, surprised, before she jumped off my lap and sprinted through the house to the front door.

When I caught up to her, my heart stopped altogether.

She was looking up at where Randy stood on the porch, telling him how we'd made pancakes that morning to celebrate the big win, but I couldn't take my eyes off my ex-husband. He was a complete disaster — his hair sweaty and matted to his forehead, eyes bloodshot, hands trembling where he patted our daughter's head with an affectionate smile.

He'd been drinking, or worse, and when his eyes met mine, I knew without a doubt that he'd come looking for a fight.

"Paigey, why don't you go make a pancake for your dad, huh?" I asked her, smiling and smoothing down her wild curls as she grinned up at me.

"Okay!" she said, and bounded past me and back into the kitchen.

I narrowed my eyes at Randy then, standing in the doorway so he knew he wasn't invited in. "You're not supposed to be here."

"It's my fucking house."

I ignored my urge to argue that point. "What do you want?"

"You know what I want," he seethed back, and then his eyes traveled the length of my body in my thin pajamas.

I crossed my arms over my chest in disgust.

"You're drunk," I whispered, careful as to not let Paige hear. "Go sleep it off."

"I talked to your boyfriend last night."

I stilled at that, and Randy's grin grew even more wicked where it grew on his ashen face.

"Oh yeah, we had a *great* little chat at the high school after he'd unloaded the bus. You see, when I saw the way you were looking at him on the field, when I started putting the pieces together from everything Paige had been saying about him, I knew something was up." He shook his head, as if he pitied me. "You were at his brother's *wedding*, Sydney. I'm not stupid."

"It's none of your business who I date."

"Funny," he said on a laugh. "That's what Jordan said, too. But he *also* said that you guys broke up." He tilted his head at that. "And you know, it got me thinking... what has our poor daughter been subjected to all this time that I've been gone? First, being allowed to play football — a dangerous sport, mind you — without her father's consent. And her mother bringing strange men around... sleeping with them in our home... going through toxic breakups..."

I moved to slam the door in his face and dismiss him, but his hand caught it quickly, and he stepped a foot over the threshold, his nose inches from mine.

"I *know* you fucked him in this house, in *our* house," he spat. "How *dare* you?"

"Your daughter is inside," I reminded him, hushing my own voice while he raised his. "You're drunk, Randy. Go home."

"I'm reporting you to child services, you ungrateful bitch."

I gaped at him. "What is *wrong* with you?"

"I'll tell them you're an unfit mother, that you're fucking strange men in the house when Paige is awake and can hear it all, doing drugs, partying all night."

"Literally *none* of that is true and you know it."

"It doesn't matter if it's true or not," he seethed. "Now, you can make this all go away if you just agree to have dinner with me."

At that, his eyes softened, and I struggled with not letting my jaw drop farther at his audacity.

"You know me," he said quietly. "You know how I grew up with nothing, how I worked so hard to get everything I have now. And you..." He shook his head, looking at me with reverence. "You were my crowning jewel. You were the best part of my life. I don't want to live without you anymore."

It was the same shit he'd pull on me after he hit me or we had a fight. He'd bring up his childhood, blame his parents or his abusive older brother for his behavior. He'd tell me I was his everything, that I was the one thing that kept him going, that made everything okay.

But I saw through the lies, eventually.

I was nothing but a prize to him, a toy he could control and play with when he pleased.

One dinner, Syd," he begged. "Give me a chance to remind you what we had. We can try again. We can—"

He was reaching out for me to caress my cheek, but I backed away, trying again to shut the door on him. "Randy. Stop."

"Come on, sweetheart."

I cringed, backing away from his touch again. "Randy, you need to leave. I mean it. If you don't, I'll—"

"You'll *what*?" he challenged, his eyes wild now that he hadn't gotten his way. The stench of whiskey rolled off of him in plumes thick enough to fog the entire town as he latched onto me, his hand wrapping around my wrist and crushing it the way he had last night at the game. "Call the cops? I *am* the cops, sweetheart."

"Daddy?"

We both ripped around in time to see Paige's bottom lip protrude, tears flooding her eyes as the pancake she'd just made slipped off the plate she was holding and flopped onto the floor.

"It's okay, sweetie," I assured her. "Just go up to your bedroom and—"

"Daddy, let go of Mama," she said through her tears, and then she had her hands wrapped around my arm, trying to pull me away from Randy.

"It's okay, honey," I told her again before I narrowed my eyes at Randy and whispered. "Let. Me. *Go.*"

"Not until you agree!"

Paige was crying harder now, and Randy's grip tightened on me so hard that I winced and crumbled forward at the pain shooting up my arm.

Suddenly, Paige let out a scream, and then she wrapped her little hands around Randy's arm, instead, and with all her might — she bit him.

Randy yelped, yanking his arm back and holding it in shock. It was just enough time for me to shove him backward as hard as I could manage, and I didn't wait to see if he fell or regained his balance before I slammed the door shut and locked it. I ran to the sliding glass door next, making sure it was locked, too, and then I rushed back to where Paige was at the front door.

She had giant tears rolling down her cheeks and more building in her eyes when I pulled her into me, and I sank down to the floor, my back against the front door as my daughter sobbed into my chest.

From the other side came a cynical laugh. "This isn't over, Sydney," Randy sang. "You belong to *me.*"

I squeezed my eyes shut, and Paige held me tighter, shaking and crying in my arms. I couldn't be sure how much time passed before I heard the car door to his cruiser slam shut, and then the squealing of tires as he pulled away.

I let out a gasp, my hands frantic where I smoothed Paige's hair and held her to me and assured her everything was alright. But I knew it was a lie. Things were *not* okay, and they hadn't been for a long time.

Through the beats of my heart pumping loudly in my ears, I heard Mallory's voice from Thanksgiving night.

We are fighters, Sydney. We are warriors. Survivors. You never have to apologize to me, okay? You just have to keep fighting. That is what you owe me — not an apology, but a fight.

Because if we don't fight? Then he wins.

The truth of her words cut me like the hot blade of the sharpest knife, taking my next breath with it. But when I did inhale again, it was calmer, deeper, more resolved as I felt my battle gear slip over me like the armor of a knight.

She was right. Jordan was right. My sister was right.

The Becker family needed me.

Jordan needed me.

And I needed him, too.

I'd run before. I'd been scared, and manipulated by the power I felt Randy still held over me. I worried for my daughter, but now I could see plainly that it was *him* who was putting her in danger — not me.

I had to make things right with Jordan.

I had to apologize, to tell him and his family everything I knew, to link arms with all of them and charge into battle — *together*.

We had to fight.

And more than that — we had to *win*.

—◆—

JORDAN

I forced the biggest smile I had as Mom aimed her ancient digital camera at me, and Logan smirked from his side of the table, knowing I was hating every moment of this.

"Hold the cake a little higher so we can read it," Mom said, waiting until I did so before she lifted the camera to her eye again. She didn't even need to — it had a digital screen. "Okay, say *champions!*"

"Champions," I murmured through my smile, and Logan covered his laugh, which earned him a poke in the side from Mallory.

"Thanks, Mallory," I told her, narrowing my eyes at my brother. "At least *someone* has my back."

"Oh, come on, Bro," Logan said, hopping up from his chair and wrapping my head under his arm. He rubbed his fist into my skull before I shoved him off. "You're a three-time State Champ! Lighten up a little."

I smiled, but shoved him off again until he was sitting next to Mallory again. It was just the three of us and Mom tonight, a small celebration with Mom's famous barbecue ribs and a giant cake that we'd likely take to Betty at the nursing home after, because there was no way four people alone could eat it.

Mallory eyed me from the other side of the table, and when our gazes met, she nodded with a slight smile and understanding. I knew then that Logan had told her what we'd discovered, and I wondered if she was just as anxious as I was for my brothers' arrivals tomorrow. Noah and Ruby Grace would be home from their honeymoon in the Exumas, and Mikey and Kylie were flying in around noon.

Mom thought they were all coming back to celebrate the win, and that was the way I wanted to keep it.

Mallory held the small of her back as she waddled into the kitchen, returning moments later with a knife and serving set. She began cutting into the cake when I heard the wheels of a car on the gravel drive that led to Mom's house. When I looked out the front door window and saw Sydney's car, I was up off my feet in seconds.

"Who's that?" Mom asked, but I was already out the door. I didn't even bother grabbing a jacket, just jogged down the front porch steps and stood there, waiting.

Sydney had barely parked before Paige was out of the car, and she bolted straight to me, crashing into me with a force I never would have expected from the size of her. She wrapped her arms full around my waist and hugged me tight, burying her face in my shirt.

"Hey," I said, and I knew instantly that something was wrong, because Paige wasn't spouting off something silly or sarcastic.

She was crying.

She hugged me tighter as her little shoulders shook, and I looked up at Sydney just as she got out of the car.

Her red, blotchy face told me she'd been crying, too.

"Hey," I said again, softer now, holding Paige tight. "It's okay. Everything's okay."

I heard the screen door open behind me, and I looked up, meeting Mom's worried gaze. I didn't have to say anything for her to understand, and she made her way down the steps to join us.

"Hey, sweetie," she said to Paige, running her fingers through Paige's wild curls before she reached out her hand. Paige looked at it, and then up at Mom. "Why don't you come inside with me. We just cut some cake, and I saw an *especially* big slice with your name on it.

Paige sniffed, rubbing her nose with the back of her sleeve before she looked up at me. I nodded, encouraging her with a confident smile, and she took Mom's hand, who gave Sydney a soft nod of acknowledgement and me a sympathetic smile before she led Paige inside.

I watched them walk all the way inside, and as soon as Mom shut the wooden door inside the screen one and gave us privacy, I turned back to Sydney.

The sight of her made my knees buckle.

Her hair was tied into a messy nest on top of her head, and her eyes were swollen, bloodshot, the stains of tears still marring her cheeks. She looked so small and meek, so sad and defeated, and her eyes welled with more tears the longer we stood there — which just broke me even more.

"I'm so sorry," she whispered as the first tear slipped from her left eye and down her cheek. Another one followed it as her face crumpled. "To just show up here, after everything... I'm so sorry."

I shook my head, crossing the distance between us and pulling her into me without another word. She choked on a sob once she was in my arms, and every cell in my body stood at attention, like I'd have to fight to defend her at any moment.

"Don't apologize," I told her, holding her so tight in my arms I worried I'd crush her. My lips were right by her ear, and I resisted the urge to kiss the skin beneath it. Instead, I cradled the back of her head and wrapped my other arm full around her, holding her to my chest. "You never have to apologize for coming to me. I will always be here."

"But, I was so awful to you last weekend," she cried into my shirt, and her shoulders shook violently before she could speak again. "I was wrong, Jordan. You were right. I *was* a coward."

"Shhh," I tried to tell her, but she shook her head, pulling back from my embrace to swipe the tears from her face and look me in the eyes.

"I was," she instead again. "It was all just so over-whelming, so sudden, and the last thing I expected. I thought when we went on that walk..." Another wave of emotion flashed on her face, but she rolled her lips together, fighting against it before she whispered, "I wanted to steal you away to tell you that I loved you."

My shoulders deflated, but my heart swelled with hope.

"And then you told me what you found, and then we were talking about lawyers and testimonies and..." She shook her head again. "It just got so big and real *so* fast and I didn't know what to do and I ran," she confessed on a breath. "And I'm so sorry. But I *do*, Jordan. I do love you. And I'm not running anymore. I want to fight. I *need* to fight. With you, with your family, with *my* family. I'm done with this town and its corrupt powers. And I won't let you fight them without me."

I pulled her into me again, this time not fighting it when my heart urged me to kiss her hair. I held my lips there, closing my eyes and breathing her in.

"Sydney, I understand now," I told her. "Randy... he was waiting for me when I left the field last night. He threatened me, threatened *you*, and Paige. I understand now why you were scared." I swallowed. "It scared *me*, too. He has a lot of power, there's no denying that. And I don't want you to put you and your daughter in jeopardy just to—"

"No," she said loudly, pressing her hands into my chest and looking up at me. "He does *not* have power — not over me, or over Paige — not anymore. I decided that, and I will do whatever it takes to ensure it's true."

I searched her eyes, riddled with pain and terror, as I swept her hair back from her face. "What happened?"

Her bottom lip trembled. "He came to the house today, drunk or hungover or both. And angry. He was *so* angry," she whispered, shaking her head. "And he threatened me, said he would convince child services that I was an unfit mother, doing drugs and bringing random men home."

My jaw clenched. "That's fucking bullshit."

"I know, and *he* knows that, too — but as he liked to remind me today, *he is the cops*," she said, mimicking his voice. "And he has every powerful man in this town wrapped around his finger, waiting to do what he asks — whether to pay back a debt or to keep their *own* dirty laundry from being exposed."

"That motherfucker…"

"And he grabbed me," she continued on a sob, showing me her arm that was already bruising. "And said I could make it all go away if I gave him another chance, and then Paige saw us, and she was crying and screaming at him to let me go but he wouldn't." She closed her eyes, crying, shaking her head like she couldn't believe the story she was telling me was real. "And then she was pulling at me, and she *bit him*, Jordan." Her eyes met mine. "She bit him, and I pushed him out, and then he was still going on from the other side of the door." She sniffed, scowling. "He said he *owns* me. And I decided right then and there that this all has to end. I don't know how, but I know I would rather die trying than to give in to his bullshit even one more day."

My chest was on fire with rage, and it was nearly impossible to cool it down, to remain calm after hearing her story. I forced a long, slow exhale, closing my eyes for a while before I opened them and found her staring back at me again.

"I'm supposed to trade off with him on Tuesday," she said softly. "I can't... I *won't* hand my daughter back to that monster."

I nodded, pulling her into me once more and hugging her tight. When she looked up at me again, our lips were just inches apart, our breaths warm where they met between us.

"I'm in love with you, too, Sydney," I whispered, and with the words, more tears glossed her brown eyes. "Do you know that? I love you with everything that I am, and I give you my word that he will *never* hurt you or Paige again. Ever. You hear me?"

She nodded, and when she pressed onto her toes to kiss me, I tasted her salty tears on those sweet lips.

We held each other tight, kissing like the world was ending and this was our final moment together. It *felt* that way — like we were on the precipice of the biggest storm, one we weren't sure we would live through.

"We have to take him down," she said, definitively. "Him, and Patrick, and whoever else is responsible for your father's death. We have to get justice, Jordan. We must."

I nodded, framing her face with my hands. "My brothers will be here tomorrow. I've been trying to get a lawyer but..." I sighed. "I think Patrick knows we're onto him, or *someone* knows, because every time I get a lawyer willing to talk to us, they pull out the next day or even hours later, saying there's a conflict of interest."

She frowned. "He can't *possibly* have that much power over that many lawyers. Did you go to people outside of Stratford?"

I nodded. "I even talked to two in Nashville. I don't know, Sydney... I think we're in deeper than we realize."

Her eyebrows tugged together, a defeated sigh leaving her chest as she watched me. "What do we do?"

A breeze rolled in over my mother's front yard, whipping Sydney's hair about and stirring up something deep inside me. It felt like the heavens were taking up arms with us, like my father had just dropped down and landed beside me, ready to fight.

"Tomorrow, when Noah and Mikey are here, we assemble the troops. We make a plan," I said.

My chest caught fire again, puffing out, my heart racing loud and heavy in my ears as Sydney watched me. I saw the same fierce determination reflected in her eyes, and another gust of wind blew through the trees and through my soul, too.

"Then, we go to war."

TWENTY-THREE

JORDAN

On Monday evening, after the workday was done and the sun had already set over our small, sleepy town, Patrick Scooter walked us back through his immaculate home and into his office.

It was a dark and royal room, with deep mahogany bookshelves that lined three of the walls, and the only one *not* lined with books boasted a floor-to-ceiling glass window that I imagined had an impressive view when the sun was shining.

I was glad you couldn't see anything out of it now.

Patrick was annoyed we were there — that much was clear. His annoyance seemed to grow when Mallory opened the blinds that covered the large window, and cranked a wooden handle to the right of it, which opened the bottom at a small angle to let a cool breeze in.

"There, that's better," she said. "It's always so stuffy in here."

"It's cold outside," her father argued. "And close the blinds, I don't want anyone being able to spy in on us."

Mallory rolled her eyes, sitting across from her father in one of the chairs opposite his side of the desk. "No one is *watching* us, Dad. It's Stratford, Tennessee, for Christ's sake, and dinner time on a Monday."

Patrick grunted, but didn't argue further, and my heart raced in my ears as I kept my eyes on him and away from the window Mallory had opened.

Noah and Logan were with us, and Logan sat in the chair next to Mallory, while Noah and I stood behind them. We were all quiet, letting Mallory do all the talking for now — as we planned.

If we knew anything right now, it was that we *had* to stick to the plan.

Patrick Scooter hadn't changed much in the years since my father had passed. He had an old western feel about him, almost never seen without one of his many cowboy hats donning his head of white hair. His face was long and lean, but hard at the edges, and the wrinkles in his tan skin were deep and severe. Mallory told us that he used to be nothing but kind to her when he spoke, a farce that she began to see through as a teenager.

It didn't seem to be that way now.

I wondered how *she* felt — being in the same room with her father for the first time in almost a year. After she told him she was with Logan and she turned down the job he tried to give *her* first, inviting that it go to Logan. Instead, he'd ripped away the small art gallery in town that he'd bought for her and exiled her from the family. Everything had changed then, as she'd told us, and he stopped putting effort into the charade of pretending he and his daughter had a good relationship.

He hadn't even wanted anything to do with them when he found out Mallory was pregnant.

What was possibly even worse was that Patrick seemed to control his wife, Mary, who had watched me carefully when we first arrived at the house. She looked worried that I'd mention how I'd seen her at Mom's earlier in the season, but I'd made a promise to my mom that I'd never say anything, and I'd kept it.

Still, I could see the pain in Mallory's eyes, and the longing in Mary's, like she wanted to hug her daughter and kill all the drama that had separated them.

But one look from her husband, and it was clear who was calling the shots.

It made me even more sick when Patrick sat back in his chair and steepled his fingers, waiting. Because he hadn't asked to see his daughter when he found out she was pregnant, but when she fed him the lie we'd come up with that pertained to Scooter Whiskey Distillery business — of course, he found the time.

He was a piece of shit.

And by the end of this night, we'd prove he was a murderer, too.

"Thanks for agreeing to meet with us," Mallory started, all business as she rested her hands on her baby bump.

Her father eyed her stomach with distaste before letting out a long, bored sigh. "Well, you tell me you've discovered something that could cost the distillery millions unless it's handled, and you've got my attention." He pointed at Noah and Logan. "Now, I can understand why you two are here — you both work for me, and I imagine you have knowledge on whatever this *thing* is that Mallory has found. But *you*," he said next, pointing his nubby finger at me. "I'm a little confused as to why you're here, being that you've never worked at the distillery, nor have you ever wanted anything to do with it from what I can gather."

I didn't have time to answer before Mallory spoke again. "You'll understand why soon. Now, should we get down to it?"

Patrick's mouth pulled to the side, and he watched me a moment longer before he finally waved his hands over the desktop as if to say *please, let's get this over with.*

And Mallory must have agreed, because she wasted no time with baiting him, she just reached into her messenger bag and pulled out the charred remains of my father's laptop that she and Logan had found last year.

My heart immediately accelerated to a gallop, but I held a steady expression.

Mallory sat the laptop gently on the desk between her and her father, and instantly, the color drained from his face.

Noah smiled beside me, and I had to fight to keep that same smirk from showing up on my face, too.

We got you, you bastard.

"So," Mallory began. "As you know, you and Uncle Mac thought it would be hilarious punishment for me and Logan to clean out the old storage closet last year. And, oh, Dad..." she said, shaking her head. "I'm a little disappointed in you, that you didn't think about *what* could be hiding in those old, dusty bins and boxes — especially when you had something this big to hide."

Patrick's eyes were wide, and I could see him searching the corners of his mind for a reasonable excuse.

When he finally tore his gaze away from the laptop and looked at Mallory, it was with feigned ignorance. "What is this piece of junk?"

"Don't play dumb," Logan said. "It's my father's laptop — or, what's left of it. We found it along with a box of his belongings. Funny," he said, tonguing his cheek. "You told my mother that the box you gave *her* was everything you had of his."

Patrick scoffed. "So, you found this and *took it* without telling anyone?" He shook his head, reaching for the cord phone on his desk that I wanted to roll my eyes at because it felt like a prop in an old sixties' movie that he'd wanted in his office just for show. "That's stealing. I'm calling the cops."

"You might want to hear us out before you get law enforcement involved," Mallory said, placing a hand over her dad's on the receiver. "Unless you want to be in hand-cuffs."

"*Me* in handcuffs?" Patrick repeated, laughing incredulously.

"You murdered our father," I said.

For the first time since we entered that office, Patrick Scooter looked at me — *really* looked at me.

"You killed him. And we demand to know why."

Patrick opened his mouth, ready to deny it by the looks of his features — as if he pitied me — but Noah stopped him.

"We were able to recover the hard drive in the lap-top," he said. "And we broke into that, too."

"Great," Patrick said with a dismissive wave of his hand. "Even more evidence to slap you with in court. That's confidential information."

"Oh, we agree," I said. "In fact, I'd say the journal my father kept at work was *extremely* confidential — especially after what we found written inside it."

Patrick's face went white, and I took notice of the slight tremble in his hands as he folded them over his stomach again, leaning back in his chair. He was pretending like he knew about the journal, like we had nothing on him, like he was still in control.

But his body was betraying his façade.

"You know, I remember when *your* father died," I said. "I was young, but I remember. And even though I didn't quite understand what a Will was, I knew it must have been a big deal, because this entire town was shaken up that your father didn't have one." I paused. "But he *did* have one. Didn't he?"

Patrick's lips were sealed together, and he watched me — emotionless.

"Yeah... see, it seems my father *found* that Will when he was cleaning out your father's old office. But," I said, smiling as I pointed at him. "You already knew that, too, didn't you? Because my father *told you* he found it."

Patrick shifted in his chair, eyeing the phone like he would reach for it at any second to make a magic phone call to save his ass.

But it was too late for that now.

"He also told you that he read it," I continued. "And that *in* that Will, your father left half of the company to... well, I don't need to finish that sentence, do I? Should I let *you* tell us what was said in that Will?"

Patrick stood abruptly, slamming his fists on the table as he shook with anger, his face red, eyes bulging where he leaned over the desk and pointed at me. "You don't have *shit*, little boy — and that's what you are. You're nothing but a scared little boy messing around in matters you don't understand."

"We have our dad's journal," Logan reminded him. "And his last entry says that *you* asked him to meet you in your father's old office. After business hours. After the board meeting." Logan sat calmly looking up at him. "And in case you forgot, that was where he died."

"You think a *journal* is going to hold up in a court of law?" Patrick asked, laughing. "You could have written it.

You could have faked it to frame me. There is no Will, and your little *discovery* is flaccid, at best. You have *nothing*."

"How was the fire contained to only *that* room?" Noah fired back at him. "Started by a cigarette that everyone in this town *knows* my father never smoked? And even if it *was* a cigarette, how was he unable to get out of the room once the fire started?"

Patrick straightened, wiping his hands over his chest as if he'd just spotted some dirt there before he sat back down calmly. "Your family has been told this time and time again, Noah. The fire department thinks he might have dozed off after a long day at work."

"And he didn't wake up when the room was on *fire*?" I shot.

"Look, we all have questions about that day, okay?" Patrick said. "But this... *CSI* game you're playing at here is silly, and childish, and frankly, a waste of my time. I think we're done here."

"You are so predictable, father," Mallory said, and it wasn't a biting or sarcastic remark. It was quiet, sad, like she truly was disappointed that he was still the same man who had hurt her, too.

She shook her head before she stood, and then she left the room abruptly.

Patrick looked between me and my brothers, as if to ask what we were still doing there. But then, Mallory came back in and shut the door behind her again.

This time, she wasn't alone.

Sydney stood beside her, tall as she could, with her eyes set in a narrow line focused on Patrick Scooter.

Patrick pinched the bridge of his nose. "Jesus Christ, what *now*?" He looked at Sydney, thrusting an open palm toward her. "What could you possibly have to add to this?

Oh, wait, let me guess." He snapped his fingers. "You found something buried in your ex-husband's files! An old diary, right? Or a Magic 8-Ball!"

He was toying with us, and Noah surged forward, but I planted my hand flat in the middle of his chest to stop him.

"Calm down," I told him under my breath, and Patrick chuckled at the outburst, amused.

"On the night of John Becker's death, I heard my husband talking on the phone in our kitchen. He was whispering about something, and for the longest time, I had blocked out that memory, that entire night, because..." Sydney swallowed. "Because that was the first night my husband struck me, and I wanted to forget it ever happened."

Patrick looked bored as he listened to her, and I clenched my jaw, wondering how someone could ever become so callous.

"But, the fog has cleared since our divorce, sir. And I know what I heard that night. I know he was in our kitchen, talking on the phone in hushed whispers. Talking on the phone with *you*," she clarified. "And I heard him saying that you needed to trust him, that you needed to keep your mouth shut, and that he didn't need to remind you that it wouldn't be easy to cover up a homicide."

Silence fell over that little study, and for a moment, as I watched Patrick, I thought that maybe we'd struck a chord.

But then, he laughed.

"Seriously?" he asked, pointing a thumb at her as he looked around the room, like it was some sort of prank being pulled on him. "*This* is the so-called *evidence* you have that you think will win the case?"

That was it.

I couldn't remain calm any longer — not with that snide son-of-a-bitch making jokes like my father's death was funny.

I slammed my fist on his desk, then reached forward, gripping him by the neck of his button-up and yanking him out of his chair. His face was inches from mine when I roared, "ADMIT IT, YOU BASTARD. YOU MURDERED OUR FATHER."

Patrick laughed, and I reared back to punch him square in the jaw before Logan and Noah yanked me back, freeing Patrick from my grasp as they contained me.

He was still laughing as my brothers tried to calm me, but then he dusted off his shirt where I'd held him, and smiled at us. "You know what? You're right."

Everyone went still.

Everything went silent.

"I *did* kill your father. Is that what you want to hear?" He shook his head, looking me and both of my brothers in the eye — boldly, unapologetically. "I killed John Becker. There. There's the answer you've been looking for. Does it make you feel *any* better? Because no matter what you do, no matter what *proof* you think you have, it doesn't matter," he said, exasperated. "The case is ten years old. It's already been solved. It's closed. It's over. The journal you found, this..." He gestured toward Sydney. "*Scorned* ex-wife of our Chief of Police testifying? It's nothing. It won't hold. I have lawyers, and police officers, and board members and firefighters who were there that night, and all signed witness accounts and official reports of what happened. Randy *did* help me cover it up," he confessed, more like a brag. "And he was damn good at it, too."

He pressed his palms on top of his desk, leaning over it with a sympathetic expression, like he felt *sorry* for us.

I surged forward again, but my brothers held me still.

"While I expect this sort of behavior from *you* lot," he said to me and my brothers before turning to Mallory. "I'm disappointed in you. I raised you to be smarter than this. And regardless of how you feel about me, I expected better."

To her credit, Mallory didn't react to his insult. Her gaze was steady while I felt completely unhinged.

He turned back to us, standing tall, voice booming. "I am Patrick fucking Scooter, you dimwits. I own this town and everyone in it. You won't win. Do you hear me? You will *never* win."

He stood even straighter, somehow, before sniffing as if he'd just realized he'd let himself get a little carried away during a board meeting.

"Now," he said. "If it will make you feel better, I can write you a check for two-hundred-thousand dollars. That's more than just a little something to help your mom, and we can put this all behind us."

I roared, and my brothers no longer held me back.

"You heartless sonofabitch!" I yelled first. "How dare you! That's our *father*. He was your friend!"

"You have the nerve to offer us *money* for his death?" Noah barked.

Logan was right behind us, and being that he was the peacekeeper of our family, I was shocked when he lunged at Patrick and I had to hold him back. "He *trusted* you," he screamed, his eyes glossing with tears. I knew he was angry they were showing. "He came to you with what he found and you betrayed him, betrayed your own father and his dying wishes!"

Mallory grabbed his arm, and her tender touch seemed to rein him in just enough not to kill her father, but it was still complete and total chaos. We were all flying toward him, screaming, asking him how he could live with himself, how he could do this to us, to his daughter, to someone who used to be his friend. It was like a tornado unleashed in that study until an unfamiliar voice broke through it with a high-pitched scream.

We all fell quiet, turning to find Mary Scooter standing in the office doorway.

"That's enough," she said, chest heaving as she looked at her husband and then at the rest of us.

"Mama…" Mallory said, standing.

It was quiet as her mother looked at her — *really* looked at her, not the way she had when we first got to the house, but as her daughter. Her eyes took in Mallory's swelling belly, and then she covered her mouth as tears flooded her eyes.

"This is business, Mary," Patrick said to her dismissively. "We'll be done soon, I assure you."

"No."

It was one, simple word, but when it came from that little woman's lips, it felt like an earthquake.

Mary looked so much like Mallory, or maybe it was Mallory who looked like her. The angle of their eyes, the slope of their noses, the pinch between their eyebrows as they watched each other in that room. Mary was shorter than Mallory, and her hair was a dark brown where Mallory's was naturally a dirty blonde. But it was there, the resemblance, and it was almost like they'd just noticed it in that moment, too.

I'd rarely heard Mary speak in all the years I'd known her. She was soft and quiet, always standing behind her husband and smiling, playing her part.

But in that moment, she stood on her own — for maybe the first time.

I felt it.

Everyone in that room did.

"Enough," she repeated, shaking her head. "I've had enough. Of your lies, your corruption, your... *power trips*. This is our *daughter*, Patrick." She pointed at Mallory like her husband must have forgotten that fact. "She's pregnant. We're going to be grandparents. And whether you like it or not, Logan is the father, and that means the Beckers are our family, too."

"They most certainly are *not*," Patrick argued.

"We have to make this right!" she screamed back at him, shaking her head. "I never knew... not for sure. I always wondered, but I never questioned you about that night." She looked as if she'd seen a ghost. "That's me, right? Always content to sit back and let you run the show, to tell me what part to play. But... I heard everything just now," she confessed. "Everything, Pat. And I swear to God that *I* will testify against you if you do not make this right."

Patrick's mask crumbled a little at that, and he seemed genuinely surprised and hurt as he stared back at his wife. "Mary..."

"No, don't even try," she said, holding up her finger. "I love you, Patrick Scooter, but I will *not* watch anyone suffer any longer, paying the price of a *scorned man* who never got over his first love rejecting him."

Patrick's face drained at her words, and the rest of us exchanged confused looks.

"Oh, they don't know that side of the story, do they, sweetheart?" Mary asked, and she seemed to be growing a bit of a backbone right before our eyes.

"That's enough," he warned her, but she was on a roll now.

"He was in love with your mother," she said to Noah, to Logan, but her eyes avoided mine. "All through high school."

"Mary," Patrick warned again, his voice climbing.

"But Laurelei saw Patrick as a friend. She always had. And when she and your father fell in love, it drove Patrick mad."

Mallory watched her dad like she didn't know him at all. "Is that true?"

He didn't answer. His eyes were murderous as he watched his wife betray him.

"Oh, it's true," Mary answered for him. "Believe me. As the woman who loved *him*, watching him love *her* was a heartbreak I'll never forget. Laurelei was my best friend," she said, her eyes blurring with tears, and I thought back to the night she was on my mom's porch. "I knew he liked her, but I didn't realize how bad it was until she rejected him."

"That's why I saw all those pictures of you with Laurelei when you were younger," Mallory whispered, shaking her head. "You weren't just *friends*. You loved her."

"He wouldn't let it go when she turned him down," Mary continued. "Why? Because of all the men she could have fell in love with, she fell for John Becker — the sacred little barrel boy Patrick's father loved more than his own sons."

"He was a liar, and a brat, and a disrespectful little shit and he didn't deserve her!" Patrick cried out, slamming his fist on the table. "He didn't deserve her," he echoed again. "And he *damn sure* didn't deserve half of my grandfather's company."

"Which is exactly why you told our family lawyer to never speak of your father's Will, isn't it? Because he had one, and you knew what was in it, and you paid everyone off who you needed to in order to keep that a secret."

Mary was fuming, and the rest of us could only watch, wide-eyed.

"I wouldn't have done what I did if it hadn't been for *you*, you lying bitch, and you know it!" Patrick fired back, and then to everyone's shock, he pointed a finger at me. "Because of *him*."

The silence that fell over us was sticky and wet, but it lasted only a split second before his finger was on his wife, again.

"I told you to *get rid of him*, but you couldn't do that, could you? No. You couldn't part with your bastard child, so you took him to Laurelei. To *my* Laurelei. And to *him*, to John fucking Becker, to the one man you knew I hated. You told them our biggest secret and left me forever in debt to him. It's because of *you* that I hated him so much. It's because of *you* that I did what I did to get rid of him."

Mary's bottom lip was trembling, a tear staining her cheek, but she held her head high, returning her husband's gaze before she finally looked at me for the first time that night.

When she did, my heart leapt into my throat.

"What is he talking about?" I asked. At least, I thought I did. The voice that came from me didn't sound like my own. It sounded distant, like it was in another universe altogether.

"Jordan, I am so sorry you had to find out like this. I never intended to tell you at all," she said, her voice shaking, face crumbling. I swore she shrunk seven inches in that single moment.

"Tell me what?"

Sydney reached for my hand, grabbing it in hers with a squeeze, but I couldn't look away from Mary as my pulse continued to race.

"I'm your mother, Jordan."

She whispered the words, or else the beating of my heart in my ears was so loud I *registered* it as a whisper. Either way, I said nothing in return, but I felt my brothers watching me closely with bent brows.

"I... God, I am so sorry to tell you this way," she said, sniffing back the tears pooling in her eyes. "I was lonely, upset, betrayed by Patrick and his undying love for Laurelei. And I am as ashamed to admit it today as I was ashamed to engage in it then, but... I cheated on Pat."

Mallory's jaw dropped along with my stomach.

"I did it because I was sad, or maybe to get his attention, to..." She sniffed, shaking her head. "To *feel* something. I was so numb. And then there was this sweet, caring, funny, kind, *amazing* man making me feel so special."

She shook her head with glossed eyes, as if she was remembering another version of who she used to be.

Who she could have been.

"But," she continued. "When I got pregnant, he sent me away, and no one knew. They all thought I was at rehab, that I'd been drinking too heavily and admitted to Patrick that I needed help and he'd sent me away. And when I came back, I was better than ever, and everyone congratulated me and suddenly I was being asked to speak and to run events and I found purpose again. And the baby." She stopped, correcting herself. "*You.* You were the wake-up call I needed. I know it doesn't make sense but... I came back to me and Patrick being stronger than ever before."

She shook her head, as if none of that mattered — and in this moment, it didn't.

"But, he was adamant that this all remain just between us. So, when I returned, I told him that I gave you to a family in Idaho." She rolled her lips together, her voice soft again "But... I couldn't part from you. I couldn't bear the thought of never being able to see my son grow up. So, I went to my old best friend, and I asked her for the biggest favor of a lifetime."

I could feel Noah and Logan watching me, but all I could do was stare back at this woman — this *stranger* — who suddenly, I realized, had features that were reflected in me. I saw the freckles on her nose, and the curve of her eyes, and the wrinkle between her furrowed brows.

They were all things I saw in myself, too.

My throat was tight the more she spoke, and Sydney squeezed my hand, reminding me she was there.

"Laurelei and John were having trouble getting pregnant at the time," Mary explained. "And I knew she wanted to be a mother so badly, and I knew she would help *anyone* — no matter what — because that's the kind of woman she has always been." Mary sniffed. "So, she did. She helped me. And she helped you."

My head was swimming, and Mallory and I exchanged a glance that held just as many questions as we'd walked into this room with at the beginning of the night.

We were brother and sister.

That was *my* mother standing on the other side of her.

But who was my father?

I didn't have time to ask, not before Mary brought our attention back to the matter at hand. "I'm sorry you had to find out this way, and I know you must have many questions. But right now," she said, turning back to her husband. "I don't care what your reasoning was for what you did, you need to make this right."

"*Fine*," he seethed, looking at all of us then. "What do you want? You want money? Name your price."

"We don't want your *fucking* money," Logan said. "We want you to rot in prison for killing our father."

"You and everyone who helped you," Noah chimed in. "We want names."

"And we want the shares of the company that we are rightfully owed," I added, though my chest was tight, because now I wasn't sure which *we* I fit into.

I'd wondered for so long who my biological mother was. I never would have imagined that once I found out, I'd feel an invisible tear from the family I'd known my entire life.

Patrick laughed, shaking his head at us. "You're delusional if you think I would *ever* give you *any* part of my company. You're lucky I even let you pieces of shit *work* for me. And I promise you this," he added, thumbing his chest. "I will *never* go to prison — especially not for your worthless father and the end of his worthless life. Like I said before, you don't have any proof — none that would matter. None that would stand up against what *I* have built. Did you forget what I said earlier?" He sneered. "You. Will. *Not*. Win."

"Wow, that's a *good* one," a female voice said from outside the office window, and Patrick jumped, shock falling over him.

Noah and Logan exchanged a smirk, though I couldn't quite find it in me to join them.

"Who is that?" Patrick asked quickly, running over to the window. Just as he did, the light of a giant camera blasted in at him, and he shielded his eyes.

"Can I quote you on that? It would really add a menacing, *evil bad guy* tone to the piece."

The light disappeared, and Patrick was searching in the yard, wild-eyed and confused. He looked back at us, panicking. "Who was that? What's going on?"

Then, the door behind Mary opened wider, and Mikey stepped through it.

Along with Miranda Hollis.

Miranda was a writer for our local newspaper — *The Stratford Gazette* — and thanks to Mallory helping us make a plan, we knew if we got her involved, we'd be able to slam the door on this case once and for all. She was famous for writing scathing articles about Patrick Scooter and she had for years — though, admittedly, none of them held much weight.

This one, however, would be a home run for her.

Mallory had blackmailed her father with Miranda before, telling him that if he didn't give Logan the position he was owed at the distillery, she would go to Miranda and tell her everything that happened when she was fourteen years old and Randy Kelly sexually harassed her in the basement of Patrick's underground casino.

With Miranda's father in politics and a place of power even *Patrick* couldn't touch, he would do anything to keep Miranda out of his business.

But that time was over now.

Patrick's face went sheet white at the sight of her, and he looked around the room like a cornered animal, trying to find a gap in our legs to escape.

"Hi there, Patrick," Miranda cooed, holding up the digital recorder in her hands. She had short brown hair and glasses too big for her face, the frames of which lifted a bit as she grinned at Patrick.

A burly man holding the large video camera that had blinded Patrick through the window came in behind her, and she pointed at him over her shoulder.

"Have you met my friend, Shadow? He works in Nashville for Channel 2 News. As you know, we don't have a video crew for our little newspaper here in town, but when Sydney came to me with this juicy story? Well, I just *had* to be prepared. And we've been listening outside this *entire* time, my dear."

Patrick just shook his head, over and over, his eyes scanning the room in disbelief.

"Oh yeah, buddy," Miranda said. "You're going *down*."

For a moment, Patrick just stood there, stricken, with everyone's eyes on him. Then, he laughed, though the worry slipped through every crack in his façade. "This is absurd. I didn't agree to you recording me," he pointed out. "You can't air this, let alone use it in a court of law."

"You *would* think that, wouldn't you?" Miranda asked. "But, you see, Tennessee is a one-party consent state, and everyone in this room consented to me recording them other than you. Therefore, this video and audio is protected, and *yes*, it can be used in a court of law."

Patrick looked to Mary, and Miranda nodded.

"Yes, even your wife — which solidifies this more than anything."

Patrick eyed Miranda, and then the deepest, most primal growl ripped from his throat. He was like a cornered animal, and in a flash, he crossed the room, ripping open the top drawer of his desk and whipping out a pistol.

His eyes were wild and murderous as he raised it. Sydney gasped, and Mary reached for Mallory, holding her close as if to protect her and the baby. But Patrick didn't have time to pull the trigger before Logan and Noah pounced on him, sending him flying to the floor and the gun spiraling away from him. I grabbed it, emptied the chamber, and held both the bullets and the gun in my hands as Patrick writhed in my brothers' grips.

"Oh, please say you got that, too," Miranda said, giddy as she turned to Shadow. "That will look just *perfect* on the evening news. Oh, by the way, Patrick," she said to him next. "The cops are already on their way. And not your shady Stratford cops either — who, by the way, we've been investigating undercover for years now. We already have a case building against Randy Kelly, and this is just the icing on the cake." She smiled victoriously. "You're all going to pay for what you've done."

Noah and Logan looked at each other, at Mikey, at me, and in that moment, the weight we'd carried on our chests for a decade was lifted, and I swore I felt our father in that room with us.

Noah smiled, still holding Patrick firmly, and Logan looked up at me with tears in his eyes.

"We did it," he said, shaking his head. "We did it, brothers."

Mikey made his way over to me then, and I wrapped him in a bear hug as chaos ensued.

First it was the sound of sirens, and then Patrick being hauled away while more cameras and reporters showed up at the Scooter residence. It would have been comical, watching him struggle against the officers, throwing a fit in their grips and saying, "*Do you know who I am?*" over and over again, had I not been in shock. He even tried to throw a punch at one of them when they finally shoved his head into the squad car, the rest of him following suit, and then they slammed the door shut.

My brothers and I were clinging to each other in the front yard when our mother showed up, wide-eyed and riddled with worry, until we told her everything.

It was over.

It was all over.

And *finally*, we had justice for Dad.

A quiet, calm kind of numbness settled over me as we talked to police officers and reporters and filed statements. It wasn't the relief I thought we'd find, because as much as we'd finally found answers, we still didn't have our father.

He'd still died a horrible death, at the hands of a monstrous group of men.

I didn't know how late it was when the yard finally started to clear, and Sydney slipped her arms around my waist, and I held her against my chest, resting my cheek on the crown of her head.

"You okay?" I asked her.

She nodded, hands fisting in my shirt. "I'm shaken up," she admitted. "And confused. And heartbroken. And I still have no idea what I'll tell Paige, but... I'm relieved that it's over. I'm relieved that we can finally all find peace."

I kissed her forehead as my chest tightened, because peace seemed so far from my grasp.

"Are *you* okay?" she asked, and I knew she could feel my anxiety.

I just held her tighter in response, willing her without words to not let me go.

Because I *wasn't* okay.

I was far from it.

One weight had been lifted, but another had crashed down in its place, and while I was filled with exhaustion and joy and relief at the solving of my father's mysterious death, I was plagued with questions and betrayal at the discovery of my biological mother.

A million questions had been answered.

A million more had taken their place.

And as I locked eyes with my mother's — my *real* mother, not the biological one I'd just discovered — I had a feeling the answers I would find would be just as hard to hear as the ones we'd found tonight were.

"I'm right here," Sydney whispered, hugging me tight, and I tore my eyes from Mom's and closed them, instead. "No matter what happens next, you have me, okay? And we'll get through it. Together."

My throat tightened, and I held her even tighter, surrounding my aching heart with her words.

If I had her, I could face anything.

That much, at least, I was sure of.

TWENTY-FOUR

SYDNEY

The week that followed that emotional Monday night was the longest of my entire life.

So much happened that it felt like being in the middle of the Daytona 500 raceway track while cars zipped by, but at the same time, it all seemed to somehow move in slow motion.

Neither Jordan nor I went to work — which was not contested by anyone, least of all Principal Hanley. The entire town was abuzz once the story broke, and we all had eyes on us — eyes of pity, eyes of sympathy, eyes of suspicion. Everyone had their thoughts, and everyone wanted to see what we'd do next.

Randy was locked up that Monday night along with Patrick, and then slowly, each day, more and more men were silently taken into custody for questioning. There were lawyers, police officers, firemen, prominent men on the Scooter Whiskey Distillery board. And as more and more information came out, more and more people being tied to the heinous crime, it felt like our entire town was a live wire, buzzing and zapping and tense.

Jordan and I were handling our own personal matters while also trying to be there for each other, and we'd found the task difficult. There was just *so* much going on. It seemed that we were away from each other every day, and when we finally came together at night, all we could do was hold each other, and be silent, and listen to each other's heartbeat as if that steady rhythm was the only thing keeping us holding on.

I had to sit Paige down that very next day — *before* anyone else had the chance to tell her what happened. It was perhaps the most difficult thing I'd ever done as a mother, to have a real discussion with her about her father, about what he'd done, about what would happen to him next.

She took the news better than I imagined, which I attributed to her seeing her father's true colors that day he showed up at our door drunk and belligerent. Still, she cried, and held me, and said she missed him and she didn't want him to go to jail. I knew it wouldn't be an overnight thing to get her to understand, nor would this be something she would ever fully let go of.

It would be a part of *her* story just as much as it would be a part of mine. It was my job now as her mother to help her through it, each step of the way, from now until forever.

Thankfully, when my sister heard what had happened, she flew in to take care of Paige while I dealt with everything else. If I was being honest, I don't think anyone wanted to see Randy rot in prison more than Gabby did. And I was thankful for her help, for her presence, for her love — especially when I had a hundred things to take care of.

Like making sure Jordan was okay.

I knew he wasn't — not after everything that came to light that night at the Scooter's house. Sure, he'd landed the justice his family had been seeking for his father for a decade, but in the process, he discovered a dark past he didn't know he had.

His biological mother was Mary Scooter.

Laurelei and John had hid that from him his entire life.

And, the latest development which had knocked him breathless... Mary had told him who his father was.

So, on Friday night, I sat next to Jordan on Elijah Braxton's back porch with my hand in his, squeezing it every now and then for comfort, as he told his biological father everything.

It was a cold December night, but Eli had a fire going, and we sat around it with our coats and scarves and blankets over our laps. Eli and Jordan were sharing a bottle of whiskey and trying to share a lifetime of what they'd missed, too.

It turned out that Mary had never even told Eli about Jordan.

He had no idea he was a father.

He had no idea that he'd been watching his *son* coach the high school team all this time.

For hours, they swapped stories, and asked questions, and looked at each other in a way that I could never describe in words. I was quiet for most of the night, just there for support, witnessing a beautiful moment I was sure Jordan never thought he'd have.

"I can't believe she never told you about me," Jordan mused as the fire died down, shaking his head with his eyes on the weakening flames. "I mean, I guess I *can* now that I've discovered the other secrets that family has been hoarding but... I'm just so lost as to how she could have lived with herself, knowing what she'd done, what she'd hidden."

Eli adjusted his beanie over his ears, tossing another log onto the fire and poking at it before he sat back in his chair. "Mary was a complicated girl," he said. "I knew it when we were in high school, and I knew it when she gave me that first look when I went over to her place to work on the plumbing in their housing extension. That was when it all started. She was bored, or felt mistreated, or maybe both. But... she was also lovely, and kind, and innocent in her own way. She just wanted to be loved," he said with a shrug, as if it was obvious. "And she's not the only guilty one here, either," he pointed out. "I knew she was married, and I fell into temptation with her, anyway."

"The affair is one thing," Jordan said. "But, not telling you that you had a child?"

"I know," he said, letting out a slow breath. "Trust me, it pains me as much as I imagine it pains you. But, something I've learned in my years is not to spend time or energy being angry about the past, or letting someone else's actions dictate how I handle my own life." He looked at Jordan then with a small smile. "We didn't know about each other before, but we know now. And I bet we still have a lot of life yet to spend together as father and son." At that, his smile fell, and he swallowed. "That is, if you want to."

"Of course, I want to," Jordan answered, frowning. "I've been wondering who you were my entire life. I just... I don't know how to handle knowing Mary is my mother." He made a face, one that passed over him every time the subject came up. "I'm... I don't know. I feel a little lost, if I'm being honest."

"I think anyone would be, if they were in your shoes," Eli offered, and I squeezed Jordan's hand where I held it under the blanket over my lap, letting him know I agreed.

"It's funny," Jordan mused. "I always thought if I found out who my real parents were, I'd feel complete, whole, like a missing puzzle piece had finally been found. But... I feel the exact opposite. I feel like an imposter in the family I've always known, and like I don't know where I belong."

My heart broke with his admission, and I squeezed his hand again, leaning my head on his shoulder.

Eli leaned toward him, too, balancing his elbows on his knees as he locked eyes with his son. "You listen to me. That family — Laurelei, your brothers — they are still your family. They always have been, and they always will be. You hear me?" He paused. "And furthermore, John will always be your father. And I can tell you with absolute certainty that if he were here, he'd tell you right now how proud he is of you, and how much he loves you."

Jordan's eyes filled with tears, but not a single one fell.

"You and I, we got some time to make up for. And our relationship will not be like the relationship that other sons and fathers have. It won't be *anything* like the one you had with John. And that's okay, Son. What we have will be different, but it will be our own. And I know it feels impossible right now, but you might even find a relationship with Mary one day, too. And *that* will be different. It will be nothing like your relationship with Laurelei." He leaned down until Jordan's eyes met his again. "And that's okay, too."

Jordan nodded, but he still seemed so torn up, and I wished I could take away all the confusion and pain. I wondered if he was thinking about Mallory, too — about his half-sister. With all the chaos since Monday night, I knew they hadn't had a moment together yet, either.

"You know, I think a part of me must have known," Eli said. "I mean, obviously I couldn't have known that you were my son, but I've always felt tied to you. I watched you grow up as a kid, and watched you play football in high school, watched you take over as coach. I never felt so invested in anyone else in this town, but there was something about you that I was drawn to."

Jordan smiled. "I felt the same way. The gang of moms at every practice and game drove me crazy, and I didn't like to talk about football with anyone else in town — at the barbershop, the post office, none of it. But with you?" He shrugged. "I don't know. I just felt comfortable."

"Sounds like God was going to make sure we were in each other's life in some way, whether we knew why or not."

They shared a smile, and then Eli stood, squeezing Jordan's shoulder before excusing himself inside to use the restroom.

When he returned, it was with more wood for the fire, and we spent hours in that backyard with Eli, talking and laughing and crying a little, too. It was too much to try to talk about everything in one night, but I could tell on the ride back to Jordan's house that he already felt a little lighter.

When we finally crawled into bed that night, Jordan opened his arms for me to slide in and rest my head on his chest, and we held each other tightly, silent for a long time.

"This has been the wildest week of my life," he said on a breath after a while.

I chuckled. "Yeah... to say the least."

"Are you doing okay?"

I sighed, considering his question — one that we'd continued asking each other all week long. It wasn't so much of a demand to *be* okay, but rather a reminder that someone cared, that the other wasn't alone.

"Yeah," I finally answered. "Yeah, I think I really am. I mean, I'm worried about Paige, but... like you said. She's tougher than I give her credit for a lot of the time."

"She is. And she has you," he reminded me, kissing my forehead. "Which means she can get through anything."

"I guess I'm kind of in shock," I admitted. "I mean... who knows what will happen with Randy and Patrick and everyone. I'm glad we have lawyers, because I don't know about you, but I don't understand any of it."

"No, I don't either," he said with a deep exhale. "The only comfort I'm taking in any of it is that with Miranda's story being out there, there's no way Patrick or Randy can use their power or their money to get out of it this time."

"What do you think will happen?" I asked, leaning up on my elbow to look down at him in the soft moonlight streaming in from the blinds.

He thought for a moment. "I think Patrick will be charged with murder. Randy and the board members and the firemen who were in on it, the lawyers... I imagine they'll be charged with either being accomplices or at the very least, covering up the crime. At least, from what the lawyers are saying."

My heart jumped. "Do you think Randy will get out of doing time?"

"No," he answered quickly, smoothing his hand over where mine was on his chest. "He knew about it. He helped cover it up. They burned my father alive, for God's sake," he said, and we both shivered. "I don't think any judge would let them get away without doing life in prison. If everyone else gets off with lesser sentences, that would make sense. But... Randy is an accomplice. He might as well have lit the fire."

I nodded, resting my head on his chest again. "This is all so much... I can't digest it all."

"Me, either."

"How's your mom?"

He sighed. "She's shaken up, too. I mean, of course she's relieved we found out what happened, we got proof for what we'd known all along, but... it's also her worst nightmare, you know? Now she *knows* the love of her life was murdered, and all because of a jealous man who loved her and wanted her to love him, in return."

I shook my head. "I don't know how he can live with himself."

"Me either."

"Do you think they'll give you half of the company now? I mean, your family?"

"I'm not sure," he confessed. "Mary said she wants to talk to Mom about that this week, but... to be honest, it's the last thing on my mind right now."

"I get that. Are your brothers okay?"

"For the most part. I mean, they're all worried about Mom, mostly. And about me."

I leaned up again. "And are *you* okay?"

Jordan kept his eyes on the ceiling, thinking for a while before he answered with a small smile. "Yeah... I am."

"You are?"

He nodded, sweeping my bed hair out of my face and holding my cheek as I leaned into the touch. "I still have a lot of questions, and a lot of feelings — especially regarding my biological parents. But... mostly, I feel at peace. I feel like my dad can finally rest, that my family can finally heal, that we can finally have justice and resolution that we have wanted for so long." He paused, tapping my nose. "And I have you," he whispered. "Which, honestly, is what makes me feel the best right now."

I smiled. "Yeah?"

"Yeah," he said on a nod, leaning up to kiss me gently before he rolled us so he was nestled between my legs, and my head was flush against the pillow. "I know we still have a lot to figure out, but... hearing that you love me? I think that gave me the sense that nothing else matters."

My heart squeezed. "I wanted to tell you before all of this. You know that, right?"

"I wanted to tell you, too. At Thanksgiving, actually. But then everything happened with Mallory, and you were so upset, and I didn't want to put any pressure on you."

"I seem to remember you putting a *lot* of pressure on me that night," I teased, rolling my hips up to meet where he rested between my thighs.

He groaned, pinning me with a kiss before he pulled back and smiled. "It's just crazy. My entire life, I watched Mom and Dad love each other and wondered if I'd ever find someone like that. And honestly, I'd given up. My brothers found their girls, and I watched from the background, just imagining that I would never be able to open myself up like that, or to have someone who would open up to *me* like that, either."

"And then I came along."

"Yep. And you put my ass in place."

"Someone had to."

He chuckled. "Well, you were perfect for the job."

"I knew I was in trouble after that first game," I confessed. "When we fought in my office, and you were all up in my space, and you looked at my mouth like you wanted to kiss me."

"I *did* want to kiss you," Jordan groaned, and he kissed up and down my neck like a feverish mad man as I laughed and shoved him off. "And I've wanted to kiss you every moment since, too."

"We broke all the rules."

"I'm sure we'll break a few more."

He hovered over me, eyes searching mine as I played with the hair at the back of his neck.

"I love you," I mouthed.

"I love you, too," he mouthed back.

Then, his head disappeared under the covers, his lips trailing a path down my navel to the band of my flannel pajama pants.

And we were done talking for the night.

— ● —

JORDAN

The next day, Sydney and I gathered with the rest of my family at Mom's house before the parade.

It was tradition in Stratford — which I found pride in, seeing as how it could only be tradition if we *won*. The town had thrown one the past two years after we'd won the State Championship, with the team being the focal point.

I knew this one would hold more weight.

The entire town was buzzing with what had happened with Patrick Scooter and Randy Kelly, with more and more accomplices to my father's murder being outed each day.

And this would be the first time my family and I would make a public appearance.

Ruby Grace and Mallory made a giant breakfast for everyone at Mom's, and I sat at the table, mostly playing with my food and watching everyone who sat around it. Everyone was there — my brothers and their significant others, Mom, Betty, Sydney, Paige, and even Sydney's sister, Gabby, who was visiting from out of town to help with Paige.

She'd already pulled me to the side to threaten me within an inch of my life if I hurt her little sister.

But I know she believed me when I swore I never would.

"You look like you're about to *play* the championship game," she teased me. "Not go to a parade celebrating the fact that you already won it."

"Oh, that's just his permanent state of being," Betty chimed in. "He's the quiet type. Sydney didn't tell you?" Betty clucked her tongue. "Could be in a romance movie with all that broodiness."

Gabby laughed at that, and Betty steered the conversation away from me and onto Gabby's job, which Betty seemed to be interested in. She was *especially* interested in Gabby's hot doctor boss. And Betty winked at me as the conversation turned, as if she knew I just wanted to be alone.

I thanked her with a nod.

Gabby looked so much like Sydney, and I loved watching them together. They had that familiar comfort that I had with *my* brothers. It was in the way they spoke, the way there were so many things they didn't have to even speak out loud for the other to understand.

Sisters.

And when I glanced at Mallory from across the table, it hit me for the hundredth time that week that I now had one, too.

"Jordan," Mom said after breakfast, standing as Logan and Noah worked on clearing the dishes from the table. "Can we talk outside?"

Sydney and I exchanged glances, and she nodded encouragingly before I grabbed my coffee and made my way out onto the front porch with Mom. She sat in her favorite rocking chair, cupping her mug of tea between her hands, her favorite shawl wrapped tight around her shoulders as her eyes swept over the yard.

I took the seat next to her, and for a long time, we were both silent.

"Do you know why I named you Jordan?" she asked.

My stomach was in knots, because though we'd talked a lot since what happened at Patrick's home on Monday night, we hadn't been completely alone. And though she was still the same mom she'd always been to me, and I was still her son, there was a new, foreign cloud that hung between us — one with a lifetime of her hiding a secret from me that I found out in the worst way.

"I don't," I answered.

"In the *New Testament,* the River Palestine is where Jesus Christ is baptized by John the Baptist," she explained. "And *Jordan* comes from the Hebrew term, *Yarden*, which means to flow down. To descend."

I frowned, but Mom looked at me then with a soft smile.

"That's what you had done," she said. "You had flowed down to us from the heavens we were praying to every night to help us get pregnant. Descended, as if God himself had placed you in our arms. And we never could have known then that he would bless us later in life with three crazy, but amazing little boys to be your brothers," she said on a chuckle. "At the time, Jordan — you were it for us. You were our only one, and we thought that maybe you would *always* be our only one."

The corner of my mouth lifted, and I reached over to place my hand on hers for a moment before I held my coffee mug again.

Mom held my gaze. "I'm sorry, Son. I'm sorry it wasn't me who you learned your true past from." She looked grim. "I know it may not make sense to you, and I understand if you're angry with me. But... I made a promise to a woman who used to be one of my best friends. And, honestly, I swear, I didn't know who your father was," she added. "But, in my mind, as your mother, I was protecting you as much as I was protecting Mary by hiding the truth. In my eyes, you were never hers, anyway." Her eyes welled with tears. "You are, always have been, and always will be mine and John's son."

I set my coffee down and stood, extending a hand for Mom to do the same. She set her tea down, too, and then she was in my arms, and I hugged her tight as her little shoulders shook in my grasp.

"It's okay, Mom," I told her. "I understand. If Sydney has taught me anything, it's that parents sacrifice for their children, and they make tough decisions that affect their lives, too. But, I know you and Dad love me, and that everything you've done in your life has been with my best interests at heart."

"You don't hate us?"

I chuckled, hugging her tighter. "I could never."

She pulled back, looking up at me with a sniff.

"I was upset at first," I admitted. "Mostly because I was hurt by the truth, and confused, and I'll admit, a bit sad to know that I'm related to a family I've spent most of my life hating. But... I understand. Not just you and Dad, but Mary, too. And maybe one day we can have some sort of relationship," I offered. "Not now, but maybe one day."

"And what about Eli?"

I smiled. "I went over to his place last night and we talked about everything. He's in shock, of course, but said he kind of always knew, in a way. So... yeah, maybe I'll have a second father, too." I shrugged. "But, I feel the same way you do. You and Dad have always been and always will be my parents. This doesn't change that for me, either."

A few tears slipped free when she smiled, the edges of her eyes crinkling, and she hugged me tight again.

"Sydney is a good woman," she said when we finally pulled away. "I'm very glad you two found each other."

I smiled, glancing inside where I could see her, her sister, and Paige in the living room with my brothers. "Me, too, Mom."

"Don't mess it up," she warned, poking my chest.

I chuckled. "I'll do my best." Then, I held her arms in my hands for a moment, locking eyes with her. "Are *you* okay, Mom?"

She smiled. "I am. John is finally resting, and I think that means I can finally rest, too. I know we still have a long road ahead of us with all these lawyers and court dates and..." She paused, pressing a hand to her forehead as she looked back over the yard. "At least... we finally know the truth." She looked at me pointedly then. "And, as always, my sons have proven to me how stubborn and determined they can be."

"We should be detectives."

She laughed, and then I hooked an arm around her shoulder and led us both inside.

Before I could get all the way in, Mallory swung an arm through mine that wasn't holding Mom and turned me around.

"My turn, Brother."

Mom winked at me, letting me go, and I ignored the funny feeling in my stomach at Mallory calling me brother, letting her guide me back out onto the porch. When we were alone, she leaned against the railing, wrapping her long sweater around her tight as she appraised me.

"You going to just pretend forever like we aren't related?"

I sighed, tucking my hands in my pockets. "No, that wasn't the plan, but I'll admit, I've been trying to figure out what to say to you."

"How about we don't make a plan," she offered. "How about we just be us — the same us we've always been. Except now, maybe a little closer." She paused, smiling. "I'd like to get to know my oldest brother. Especially since the brother I've always *known* about isn't exactly my favorite human being."

I blanched at that, because for the first time, I realized that her brother, Malcolm, was also *my* brother now, too. He'd always been a huge pain in the ass for me and my brothers, and Noah had even nearly fought him in Buck's bar not too far back.

I ran a hand over my head, looking out over the yard. "It's so much to take in."

Mallory pushed off the railing. "Hey, one thing at a time, alright?" She patted my shoulder. "I just wanted to clear the air and tell you that I'm here when you're ready to talk more about it. Maybe we can sit down and go through family tree stuff." She shrugged. "You know, I'm not in the best place right now either, so I'm fine with us both taking a little time."

"It has to be hard for you," I said. "Your dad being locked away like that, and everything he admitted to."

She nodded, her gaze distant. "I knew he was a crooked man," she said quietly. "I found that out the hard way when I was in high school. But... I don't know. I guess I just never thought he could do something like *that*. And then Mom and Eli..." She paused, looking at me again. "And you."

"I know," I told her, and I didn't have to say much else. Because she knew I did.

"I will say, I'm glad to have Mom back in my life." She laughed to herself. "Maybe we'll actually have a real relationship now, one where Dad isn't running her like a puppet." Mallory's eyes were sincere when she found mine. "I think you'll like her, when you're ready to get to know her more. Something tells me my — er, *our* — mom has been through more than we give her credit for."

I frowned on a nod, but didn't reply. I wasn't ready to embrace Mary with open arms, but I did open them to Mallory, pulling her in for a long hug before we headed back inside.

Later, on the Main Street drag, I stood on top of a float with my team, all of us donned in our school colors and passing the State Championship trophy around as our town cheered in victory. We tossed out beads and candy, signed autographs as if we were the superstars we felt like, and slipped into that bittersweet mindset of knowing we accomplished our biggest goal, but also that the season was over.

It felt like that in my life, too.

One season had ended, a new one beginning, and I knew without a doubt I would not be the same man I was in the last one.

It was a new beginning, a new era — for me, for my brothers, for my mom, and for this entire town.

Sydney stood beside me at the top of the float, smiling and throwing out candy, until she realized I was staring at her.

"What?" she asked with a flushed smile.

The corner of my mouth ticked up, but I didn't answer her — not with words, anyway. Instead, I reached for her hips, turning her to face me as her face went ashen white. Then, I trailed my hands up over her arms, her neck, sliding them back to cradle her head. Her soft eyes were wide, searching mine, and in the next breath, I lowered my mouth to hers.

For what felt like a lifetime, everything slipped away. The crowd was gone, the parade in another universe, and it was just me and Sydney. I felt her like the piece of me that had always been missing had finally come home, or like *she* was my home, and now that I'd found her, I could finally find peace and meaning.

She was hesitant in my arms at first, but then she melted into me, kissing me back with purpose and pressing up onto her toes to deepen her affection. I could have stayed in that moment with her forever, but the roar of the crowd around us, and a few players knocking me on the back in congratulations, zapped me back to the moment.

When we broke the kiss, the cheers that met our ears were deafening. Sydney looked around with the fiercest blush I'd ever seen before she hid her face in my chest, and I chuckled, looking around at the town below us and my team on the float with a shit-eating grin.

Then, I lifted one fist into the air, as if I'd just won the girl and the battle of my life, too.

And in more ways than anyone there realized — I had.

Sydney leaned into my side, still blushing but taking up her post and throwing candy once again. And as the band played on in front of our float, I let my eyes wander the faces looking up at us from below.

I saw my brothers, with their loved ones tucked into their sides, their smiles knowing as our eyes met. We weren't just brothers in life, now, but brothers in war, too — and we had come out on the other side victorious, but not without the striking sadness of casualties. We were bonded together closer than ever, and I knew that though we'd lived such a long life together already, our new lives were only beginning.

And they would be even better than the last.

I saw my mother, too — her eyes shining with pride as she waved me past. I waved back, blowing her a kiss that she caught in the air and tucked into her heart for safe keeping. I hoped what she'd said to me on the porch was true, that she could finally rest, that she could finally find peace.

Mary Scooter didn't show at the parade — and I knew she was hurting in her own ways right now, too. I hoped one day to build a bridge of understanding between us, though I knew it would take time.

But I did see Eli on the sidewalk, who tipped his hat at me with his wide, crooked grin. I nodded back, and in my chest I felt a tug of both sadness and joy. I was sad for having missed the first three decades of my life with the man who gave it to me, but thankful for the chance to get to know him now, and to have him in whatever years we had left to come.

I saw Gabby and Paige — who was holding up a giant sign that read *Go Wild Cats!* — and I realized with a pinch of my heart that they were my family now, too. I would protect them just like I'd protected my mom and my brothers.

And still wrapped under my right arm was Sydney — the woman who barreled into my life like a shooting star, bright and breathtaking and completely unexpected.

She turned to look at me and smiled, making my heart pinch again, and her eyes reflected the emotion surging through me in that moment. When I'd given up hope, when I'd been nothing but a numb, shell of a man walking through life and trying to find meaning in it, she'd swung in and knocked me on my ass, away from everything I'd ever known before and into an era I never saw coming.

In the darkest hour of my life, I'd somehow managed to find love.

I marveled at how ironic this life could be.

As the confetti cannons blasted, shooting a river of color into the blue sky above us, I followed those little ribbons up, casting my face to the sun.

And I felt the warmth of it as an embrace from my father — his life finally avenged, his legacy finally bestowed.

I smiled up at him, my heart light for the first time since he'd left us, and he seemed to reach out for me as sun rays on my shoulders to let me know it was time to grab this life and live it fully.

Sydney watched me from where she stood at my side, and when I met her gaze, she smiled knowingly.

It turned out, our scarred hearts beat in the same rhythm. And without a word being exchanged, we both sighed — because we knew that now, they'd never have to beat alone.

In the confetti rain, and in front of everyone I loved, I kissed her again.

And we walked into our new life, hand in hand, heart in heart, soul in soul.

Together.

EPILOGUE

JORDAN – THREE YEARS LATER

"In your dreams, sucker!" Paige yelled, juking my little brother before sprinting toward the opposite side of Mom's backyard. She paused when she was a few feet from the line we'd drawn in the grass to indicate the touchdown zone, and then she turned, walking backward in a kind of moonwalk dance with her tongue stuck out.

Mikey was in her dust, hands on his knees, panting.

I laughed, calling out from where I had just thrown her the ball. "Atta girl!"

"She's a freak of nature," Mikey panted.

"I told you she was the best one on her team."

"Yeah, but you didn't tell me she played like an NFL player instead of a twelve-year-old."

"Shouldn't sleep on me just because I'm a girl, Mikey," Paige said, patting him on the back as she jogged back over to me. "Need me to get you some water?"

He side-eyed her while I held back another laugh.

"You still getting your butt whooped over here, little brother?" Logan asked, balancing a smiling Tamara on his shoulders. His daughter, named after one of Mallory's favorite painters — Tamara De Lempicka — had giant green eyes and white-blonde hair, tied into a tiny ponytail on top of her head that looked more like one single feather than a gathering of hair. She was giggling as he bounced her — a deep belly laugh that made me smile, too.

"Sure is," Paige answered for Mikey, high fiving me as she passed. "Pouting about it, too."

Mikey laughed, finally standing straight and hanging his hands on his hips as he caught his breath. "I would argue with her, but she ain't wrong."

"Guess you should stick to playing guitar and leave the football to Paige, huh?" Logan teased.

Mikey flipped him off, but smiled as he passed, anyway, taking our niece from Logan's shoulders and putting her on his own before he outstretched her arms like an airplane and took off running across the yard to where Mom had set up multiple folding tables for dinner.

It was Thanksgiving Day, and we were all together for the first time in months. It seemed to be harder to get us all in the same place now that life was running full speed, so when we did get the chance, we made the most of it.

Paige paused long enough to stretch out her quads and hamstrings before jogging back across the yard, and she threw me the ball, a perfect spiral. We fell into an easy rhythm of catch, but I knew she could tell even from the distance that I was nervous.

"Mikey looks good," I said to Logan to distract my thoughts.

He nodded. "He does. I think he and Kylie have really found their groove in New York City."

"Especially now that he's in that band," I said. "I knew he wouldn't be able to go without music for very long."

"Well, as he so grossly reminds us, Kylie brought back the music in his life."

"Such a sap."

"I know, right?" Logan shook his head. "And he's the only one. The rest of us aren't hopeless romantics at *all*."

"No way," I agreed. "I don't know if we even have feelings."

We shared a grin, and Logan clapped me on the back before I heaved the ball back to Paige. "She really is good," he mused. "How's she doing on the team?"

"She's easily the best at any position she plays," I answered. "But, just like we imagined, she's met some opposition along the way."

"Coach?"

"A little," I said. "But mostly the other players. They don't like being outperformed by a girl, and sometimes they're rougher with her than they need to be. But, she's tough," I said with pride, like she was my own daughter. In many ways, it felt like she was. "And when she's out there practicing twice as long and working twice as hard as them, I don't think it leaves them with much room to talk shit."

"I wonder what will happen when she gets to high school."

"Oh, God," Sydney said, joining us with two bottles of water in her hands. She tossed me one before calling for her daughter to come get the other, then she turned back to Logan. "Please, don't even get my anxiety spiral going on that front. She's twelve. I still have two years of pre-teen bliss before she'll be too cool for me."

"I'm already too cool for you, Mom," Paige teased, but kissed her mother's cheek anyway before taking the water from her hands. "Besides, at least when I'm in high school, you and Jordan can watch over me."

"*She* can watch over you," I said, putting an arm around Sydney. "But *I* will be your coach, and I'll likely be harder on you than on any of the other players."

"I can handle it," she said, chin high.

"Oh, I don't doubt that for a minute." I held up my hand, and we did our secret handshake that lasted a full sixty seconds and ended with me throwing an imaginary ball to her and her throwing it down to the ground in a victorious touchdown dance.

Sydney rolled her eyes, ruffling her daughter's wild curls once she was upright again. "We're about ready to eat," she said to all of us, then she turned back to her daughter. "Go wash your hands and help me bring the food out of the kitchen."

Paige saluted, giving me a knowing smirk before she ran off toward the house.

My nerves came back at once.

It was a beautiful day for November — the sun high and warm, a few clouds floating by to give us brief moments of shade, and a cool breeze sweeping over the yard. It wasn't too cold to be outside, though — which was a blessing, considering we had grown so much that we wouldn't fit *inside* anymore.

I took a seat at one of the folding tables, pulling out the chair next to Eli. He was in the middle of a riveting story that had Noah and Ruby Grace wide-eyed and leaning over the table toward him, anxious to know more.

I'd learned over the last few years that *all* his stories felt like that.

It had been easy, getting to know Eli and falling into a relationship with him. We spent a lot of time together, eating dinner or hanging out at football practice or me spending days on the job with him. He was getting older and needed the help, and I loved to see him in his element, helping people no matter their circumstances.

We'd been building our relationship for three years, and though I felt closer to him than I ever imagined I could be, I also learned something new every day.

What I loved learning *most* was about his family, *my* family, our ancestors and more. Because in addition to discovering him, I'd found that I had two aunts and five cousins who lived in Virginia, ones who I'd met *last* Thanksgiving when we joined them. I was finally able to explore all the pieces of what and *who* made me the man I was today.

At the table behind us, chatting with Mom, was Mary Scooter — my *other* mom.

Our relationship was a little more rocky.

We were trying, though it was stickier with us. She struggled with how she had left me with my adopted parents, though I'd assured her time and time again that it was the best thing she ever did for me. I loved my family, and I was blessed to have them — no matter the circumstances that landed me in their arms.

Still, Mary was in a dark place for a long time after Patrick was arrested. Everything fell into her lap then — the distillery, the Will, the flurry of court dates that had her testifying against the man she had loved and had children with. She was torn, there was no doubt about it, and we'd had little time to talk about *us* when so much of our focus had been on Patrick and Randy and everyone else involved in my father's murder.

Slowly, things were getting better — especially since the case had finally been closed. Patrick, Randy, three firefighters, and four members of the distillery board were all serving prison sentences of varying lengths — Patrick for life, Randy for forty years which might as *well* have been life. And as much as it broke Mary's heart that Patrick had been put away, I knew it brought her peace, too.

Mallory and Logan having little Tamara had sewed Mary even tighter into our family, and she and Mom worked well together as grandmothers. There was no way to say that little girl was anything less than spoiled by those two women. And the more time they spent together, the more we all saw their old friendship blooming again — one that had been tainted by a man no longer in our lives.

As for the distillery, Mary had been given charge of it, and after the history she'd had with the place, she wanted little to do with it in the end. She kept ten percent of the shares to live on and to remain on the board, but she signed the other ninety percent of the shares over to my family.

It's what Robert would have wanted, she'd said.

Now, Mom sat on the board, too — along with Noah and Logan. Noah served as President, with Logan as Vice, Mom as Secretary, and Mary as Treasurer. Together, they named the other members of the board — those they could trust — and were steering Scooter Whiskey into a new direction, a new era, born of the Beckers.

"Mallory, are you ready for the big grand opening of your studio next week?" Ruby Grace asked as we all started to gather around the tables. Mom had lined them up into one long one that spread half the yard, and Paige and Sydney were delivering giant dishes of food from the kitchen. Mom and Mary had hopped up to help while the rest of us got settled.

"More than ready," Logan answered for her, squeezing her knee with pride in his eyes. "She can't shut up about it."

Mallory pinched his side, leaning into his embrace next as they looked lovingly at each other. They'd morphed since becoming parents, and somehow dadhood had softened my brother. He wasn't wound as tight as he used to be — probably because he realized no matter what he did, his daughter was going to get dirty and messy and probably mess up everything else in her wake, too.

As was the beauty of being a parent.

He and Mallory had just bought land on the west edge of town to build their first home together, and Mallory had also purchased the same spot on Main Street that her dad had once owned. It was where her first shop had been set up and then ripped away from her a month later, and it was where she would be re-opening again next week.

On her own, this time.

"He's right," Mallory admitted on a sigh. "I'm excited, to say the least. Although, it's been a bit more challenging to get everything set up and ready to go with that little girl keeping me busy." She nodded down the table to where Tamara sat on Kylie's lap, Mikey playing peek-a-boo with her.

"Want me to come help this week?" Ruby Grace offered, then she rubbed her extremely swollen belly. "Honestly, anything to be moving and keep my mind off the fact that I'm about to pop is welcome."

Mallory chuckled. "As long as you don't pop on my new studio floor."

"No promises. His due date is two weeks from now, but I have a high suspicion we won't make it that long."

Noah smirked, rubbing her belly, too, with a mixture of love and complete terror in his eyes. I knew he had to be shitting himself on the brink of being a father, but Logan squeezed his shoulder reassuringly, as if to say, *you're going to be great.*

"I'll help, too," Sydney chimed in when she delivered the sweet potato casserole.

"I'd love that," Mallory replied. They shared a smile, and my heart beamed at the relationship my sister and my girlfriend had formed over the last few years. I knew a big part of it was standing up and testifying against Randy together. It hadn't been easy for either one of them, but it had brought them closer together.

Once everyone was seated and the food was on the table, Mom had us all gather hands, and she said grace. We all went around the table saying what we were thankful for, and after dinner, before the pie was brought out, we lit a candle in Betty's honor.

The old woman who had become such an integral part of our family and our lives had passed away that summer, leaving peacefully in her sleep on the Fourth of July. Kylie had joked that she'd planned it, wanting to *go out with a bang*. The news had been especially hard on her and Ruby Grace, who were by far the closest with Betty, but Mom had suffered, too, as they had become close friends over the years.

Betty had lived a long and full life, which was one comfort we found in her passing. More than that, she had been a light in our lives, too — helping so many of us out of the dark when we couldn't see even a ray of light that promised a way out.

The truth was we *all* missed her dearly, but the impression she'd left on our hearts was one that could never be forgotten. And we all knew she was dancing with *Mr.* Collins in heaven now.

Kylie and Mikey told us over dessert about the trip they were planning to Asia for the following summer, but I could barely listen, because my heart was ticking up a notch faster with every passing moment, beating loud and hard in my ears as I rehearsed what I'd been practicing for months. Before the plates could be cleared, Paige found her way over to me, clamping her hands down hard on my shoulders.

"Let's play catch, Coach," she said.

I swallowed, standing on shaking legs as Sydney smiled up at us.

"Do you two *ever* get tired of football?" she asked, laughing.

"Never," Paige answered, and she was already shoving me back toward the open yard where we'd been playing earlier.

When we were safely out of earshot, she put her hands on my shoulders again — which had her standing on her toes — leveling her eyes with me as best she could. "Alright, Coach," she said, seriously. "This is the big game. Your big moment. The play of your lifetime. You gotta focus, alright? Don't mess this up."

My palms were sweating, but I managed a laugh. "Gee, thanks for reminding me that there's nothing to worry about."

"Always here for you," she said, clapping her hands down on my shoulders once more before she pointed at me and started jogging backward toward the tables. "You've got this."

She turned, taking off in a slow jog as I forced as steady of a breath as I could manage. Then, I looked down at the football in my hands, and I pulled a small, navy blue, velvet box out of my pocket, fastening it to the ball with the sports tape Paige and I had tested a hundred times.

When it was safely in place, I looked up, finding Paige waiting in her designated spot behind her mom. Everyone was in conversation, still, and oblivious to what we were doing.

At least, until I took a breath and launched the ball, and Paige cried out, *"Heads up, Mom!"*

Sydney looked up just in time to notice the ball spiraling toward her, and her hands went up instinctively, catching it before it hit her chest. She screamed, though, and then laughed, looking back at Paige before her eyes found me and she pointed. "That was on purpose, you jerk!" She laughed again. "You're lucky I caught that!"

"What exactly did you catch?" Paige baited behind her, and Sydney looked back, confused, before her eyes fell to the ball in her hands.

And the little box strapped to the side of it.

I jogged over with my heart still pounding in my ears, and everyone fell silent, Sydney's eyes widening as she fingered the box out of the tape hold and held it between two fingers. She looked at it, looked at me, looked at it again, looked at me.

I swallowed, rounding the table until I was next to her chair, and lowering down onto one, shaky knee.

"Sydney Clark," I said, taking the box from her trembling fingers and holding it in my own.

Her eyes found mine, wide with surprise, her lips slightly parted as she waited for me to continue. From somewhere behind her I heard Ruby Grace whisper, *"I can't believe Betty is missing this."*

"All my life, I watched my dad and mom love each other, and I wondered if I'd ever find someone to share my life with the way they had," I said, and I heard my mom sniff from where she watched us at her end of the table. But my focus was on Sydney, and I grabbed her hand in mine, squeezing gently. "I decided at a pretty young age that I wouldn't, that it was rare and, in most ways, impossible. And I settled into a life alone, content to just be a brother, a son, and a football coach."

"A damn good one, too," Eli said, and a soft chuckle found the tables.

"And I was happy," I said. "I was. I didn't think anything was missing." I leveled my gaze with hers. "Not until you walked into my life, and my heart realized long before my brain did that I could never go back to life without you — not once I knew what it was like with you in it."

She smiled, her eyes glossing over with a sheen of tears.

"I know I'm not perfect," I started. "I know we will have mountains to climb. But if I've learned anything from the ones we've already overcome together, it's that there isn't one high enough to defeat us — and that there's no one I want to be standing with at the top more than you."

I fumbled, clumsily opening the box in my hand until the modest ring I'd bought her caught the sunlight. She gasped at the sight, covering her mouth as her eyes flooded even more.

"Sydney, I want to spend the rest of my life with you. I want to be a father to Paige, and a husband to you. I want to help you in the garden and watch you do yoga on the porch."

"Gross," Paige chimed in.

I laughed, and Sydney did, too, freeing two parallel tears down each cheek.

"I want to come home to you, every night, and I want to wake up to you every morning. I want to dream together, and accomplish together, and fight together, and *love* together. And I want to grow old with you, with the family we've built, with a love story only we could write."

Sydney was already nodding when I pulled the ring from its place in the box, lining it up with her ring finger on her left hand.

"Will you take me as the scarred, damaged, football-crazed man that I am and trust me to love you, to protect you, and to care for you, until our days on this Earth are done and we pass into our next life?" I asked, and I slipped the ring onto her finger, because I already knew the answer. "Sydney, will you marry me?"

She nodded more vigorously, wrapping her arms around my neck and lowering to kiss me as our family erupted into a burst of cheers around us. They clapped and whistled and my heart swelled to the size of a hot air balloon in my chest, relief finding me in a wave that nearly knocked me off balance where I was still on one knee.

"This calls for champagne!" Mary announced, and already she was up out of her chair and heading toward the house, Mom calling out to her where she could find some.

And when Sydney finally pulled back from our kiss, we were both swarmed, my brothers and family congratulating me while my mother and Mallory and Kylie and Ruby Grace surrounded Sydney, hugging her and begging to see the ring.

Paige high-fived me, pretending to be tough when she didn't know I'd seen the tears in her eyes, too.

"Nailed it, Coach," she said, proudly.

"Thanks for your help," I said back, then I opened my arms, and her eyes welled with tears again as she leaned in and let me wrap her in a hug.

"I'm so glad you found us," she whispered.

I nodded, holding her tight with a pang of something I only felt for that little girl tightening my chest. It was a longing to protect her, to fight for her, and to be a good man in her life — even if I wasn't her real dad.

Champagne was poured and toasts were made, and when the sun began to set, we made a fire in the pit and gathered around to listen to Mikey play guitar while we all sang the words to our favorite songs.

Surrounded by my family — *all* of my family — I held my fiancée's hand in mine and kissed her knuckles from time to time, both of us smiling at each other like a couple of love-sick loons. And for the first time in a long time, everything felt good and right and true.

From across the fire, I locked eyes with Noah, and we shared a nod, both of us smiling. We looked to Logan, then, who nodded to both of us, too — bouncing Tamara in his lap. Then, we all looked at Mikey, and he smiled at each of us, still keeping time on his guitar as he sang along to one of Betty's favorite country songs.

We made it, we all seemed to say.

And in my heart, I knew there was nothing the Becker brothers couldn't face together.

Slowly, Mikey changed the way he was strumming, slowly shifting until a soft, familiar melody met all of us. Mom's smile dropped, but only for a moment, and then she smiled, tears in her eyes as Mikey began singing the first words of "Wonderful Tonight."

I kissed Sydney's knuckles again before releasing them, and then I stood, walking over to where Mom sat and extending my hand down for hers. She took it with a knowing grin, and then she was in my arms, and we swayed like we had so many nights in the living room of that old house.

It wasn't long before Noah tapped my shoulder to cut in, and I danced with Sydney, instead — watching as one by one, each of my brothers took a turn with Mom on the makeshift dance floor.

"I think I'm marrying into the best family there is," Sydney whispered as we watched Mikey attempting to dance with Mom while still playing the guitar. They were laughing, even though Mom was crying, too — and the love and joy surrounding that fire was strong enough to be seen and felt, like a warm blanket or a perfect summer day.

"You'll make it even better," I whispered back, and Sydney smiled, her brown eyes shining in the firelight.

Then, I kissed my bride-to-be, whispering that she looked wonderful tonight as I pulled her closer, and knowing I'd be singing those words for years to come.

For an entire lifetime, if I was lucky.

And I swore I'd never blink, so as to never miss a single moment of it.

THE END

ACKNOWLEDGEMENTS

Sitting here at the end of this series, I am a mess of emotions. As I did my final read through and edits of the last twenty percent, I found myself tearing up time and time again. The truth is, this series has been alive in my heart for years now, taking up space and filling me with adventure and love, and now that it's come to an end, it is so, *so* bittersweet.

I have so many people to thank for helping bring these boys to life.

First and foremost, I want to thank my mother — LaVon Allen. You have been my rock my entire life, always pushing me to chase my dreams and follow my heart. You've fallen in love with these boys and their family just as much as I have. Thank you for always being the voice in my ear, and the inspiration for the amazing advice from both Betty and Laurelei in this series. I love you so much.

To Staci, my hype man and anchor, thank you for keeping me grounded. You're one of the first people I text when I wake up and one of the last before my head hits the pillow. I love that we check in all day every day and keep each other accountable — not only in our writing goals, but in our mental health, too. Our friendship is one I cherish so deeply. Thank you for believing in this series as much as I did and pushing me to make each book better (even if I did want to kill you during edits). I love you MTT.

My beta readers for *Old Fashioned* and for this entire series were hands down the A Team. Without them, these books would have been mediocre. They helped elevate them to some of the best work I've ever delivered and that I am most proud of. So, thank you to Trish QUEEN

MINTNESS, Kellee Fabre, Sarah Green, Danielle Lagasse, Kathryn Andrews, Carly Wilson, and Natalie Bailey. Your feedback was so instrumental in this last installment. Thank you for reading and re-reading and answering my pestering questions. I appreciate you all so, so much!

This project was different from any I've ever done before in that both the H *and* the h were POC. I took this responsibility of writing outside my culture seriously, and I could not have done it without my incredible team of Sensitivity Readers. Thank you so much Imani Blake, Chelé Walker, and Tiffanie Shipp. I believe your job was the most difficult, and I truly appreciate your time and attention to my work to ensure *Old Fashioned* was accurate and respectful and well-written.

Sasha Erramouspe, thank you for always being my last set of eyes on every project — especially in this series. You help catch last-minute edits and even more than that, you get just as emotional as I do over these boys and I LIVE for it. Love you!

The biggest shout out goes to my amazing friend and personal assistant, Tina Stokes. Tina, you are the glittery unicorn in my universe and I could not, *would* not do this without you. I am not sure how I ever survived without you on my team, but I'm so very thankful we found each other and have developed our special friendship. Thank you for helping me with everything from beta reading and edits to promotion when it came to this series. You are the wind beneath my wings and I love you!

I had some special help from a long-distance friend with *Old Fashioned,* and that friend is the incredible head football coach for the Brentwood, MO, high school team — Tim Kuhn (TK). Thank you SO MUCH for getting on the phone with me before I began this project and for answering my flurry of text messages as I made my way through it. Your insight and knowledge were absolutely invaluable and I could not have written this bad boy without your help. Thank you so much!

To Kendra Parker, congratulations on winning the 20k prize to name Sydney's daughter in *Old Fashioned* (who completely stole the show!). I loved that you used your own middle name, and it fit her perfectly. Thank you!

As always, a HUGE thank you to Lauren Perry of Perrywinkle Photography who helped bring my vision to life for *Old Fashioned*'s cover. Your talent is above and beyond and without you, I wouldn't have the magic covers that I do.

To Elaine York of Allusion Graphics, thank you for always working with my crazy timelines for editing, formatting, and more. My projects are never complete without your last spit shine and polish, and I cannot imagine not having you on my team.

To the lovely ladies at Social Butterfly PR: Nina, Brittany, Kelley and the entire team — thank you for helping me find special ways to promote this special series and finale. And thank you for always having my back. I adore you all!

Another huge shout out goes to all the bloggers and authors who read ARCs of *Old Fashioned* and went absolutely NUTS. I know reading time is limited, so I appreciate you picking my book among the noise. Thank you for spreading the word and for loving this series as much as I do!

To the BEST ladies on the interwebs who hang out with me in Kandiland, THANK YOU and I love you all so much! You are seriously the yin to my yang, the PB to my J, and the apple of my eye. I'm so happy to have our little corner of the internet to hang out in. Here's to many more adventures together!

To you, the reader who not only read this book and maybe the entire series but also ALL THE WAY TO THE ACKNOWLEDGEMENTS... thank you. Thank you for reading indie, for picking my books out of the millions out there, and for loving my words. I am so eternally grateful for you.

MORE FROM KANDI STEINER

The Red Zone Rivals Series
Fair Catch
Blind Side
Quarterback Sneak
Hail Mary

The Becker Brothers Series
On the Rocks
Neat (book 2)
Manhattan (book 3)
Old Fashioned (book 4)
Four brothers finding love in a small Tennessee town that revolves around a whiskey distillery with a dark past — including the mysterious death of their father.

The Best Kept Secrets Series
(AN AMAZON TOP 10 BESTSELLER)
What He Doesn't Know (book 1)
What He Always Knew (book 2)
What He Never Knew (book 3)
Charlie's marriage is dying. She's perfectly content to go down in the flames, until her first love shows back up and reminds her the other way love can burn.

Close Quarters
A summer yachting the Mediterranean sounded like heaven to Jasmine after finishing her undergrad degree. But her boyfriend's billionaire boss always gets what he wants. And this time, he wants her.

Make Me Hate You
Jasmine has been avoiding her best friend's brother for years, but when they're both in the same house for a wedding, she can't resist him — no matter how she tries.

The Wrong Game
(AN AMAZON TOP 10 BESTSELLER)
Gemma's plan is simple: invite a new guy to each home game using her season tickets for the Chicago Bears. It's the perfect way to avoid getting emotionally attached and also get some action. But after Zach gets his chance to be her practice round, he decides one game just isn't enough. A sexy, fun sports romance.

The Right Player
She's avoiding love at all costs. He wants nothing more than to lock her down. Sexy, hilarious and swoon-worthy, The Right Player is the perfect read for sports romance lovers.

On the Way to You
It was only supposed to be a road trip, but when Cooper discovers the journal of the boy driving the getaway car, everything changes. An emotional, angsty road trip romance.

A Love Letter to Whiskey
(AN AMAZON TOP 10 BESTSELLER)
An angsty, emotional romance between two lovers fighting the curse of bad timing.
Read Love, Whiskey – Jamie's side of the story and an extended epilogue – in the new Fifth Anniversary Edition!

Weightless
Young Natalie finds self-love and romance with her personal trainer, along with a slew of secrets that tie them together in ways she never thought possible.
Revelry
Recently divorced, Wren searches for clarity in a summer cabin outside of Seattle, where she makes an unforgettable connection with the broody, small town recluse next door.

Say Yes
Harley is studying art abroad in Florence, Italy. Trying to break free of her perfectionism, she steps outside one night determined to Say Yes to anything that comes her way. Of course, she didn't expect to run into Liam Benson...

Washed Up
Gregory Weston, the boy I once knew as my son's best friend, now a man I don't know at all. No, not just a man. A doctor. And he wants me...

The Christmas Blanket
Stuck in a cabin with my ex-husband waiting out a blizzard? Not exactly what I had pictured when I planned a surprise visit home for the holidays...

Black Number Four
A college, Greek-life romance of a hot young poker star and the boy sent to take her down.

The Palm South University Series
Rush (book 1) FREE if you sign up for my newsletter!
Anchor, PSU #2
Pledge, PSU #3
Legacy, PSU #4
Ritual, PSU #5
Hazed, PSU #6
Greek, PSU #7
#1 NYT Bestselling Author Rachel Van Dyken says, "If Gossip Girl and Riverdale had a love child, it would be PSU." This angsty college series will be your next guilty addiction.

Tag Chaser
She made a bet that she could stop chasing military men, which seemed easy — until her knight in shining armor and latest client at work showed up in Army ACUs.

Song Chaser
Tanner and Kellee are perfect for each other. They frequent the same bars, love the same music, and have the same desire to rip each other's clothes off. Only problem? Tanner is still in love with his best friend.

Kandi Steiner is a bestselling author and whiskey connoisseur living in Tampa, FL. Best known for writing "emotional rollercoaster" stories, she loves bringing flawed characters to life and writing about real, raw romance — in all its forms. No two Kandi Steiner books are the same, and if you're a lover of angsty, emotional, and inspirational reads, she's your gal.

ABOUT THE AUTHOR

KANDI STEINER is a bestselling author and whiskey connoisseur living in Tampa, FL. Best known for writing "emotional rollercoaster" stories, she loves bringing flawSed characters to life and writing about real, raw romance — in all its forms. No two Kandi Steiner books are the same, and if you're a lover of angsty, emotional, and inspirational reads, she's your gal.

An alumna of the University of Central Florida, Kandi graduated with a double major in Creative Writing and Advertising/PR with a minor in Women's Studies. She started writing back in the 4th grade after reading the first Harry Potter installment. In 6th grade, she wrote and edited her own newspaper and distributed to her classmates. Eventually, the principal caught on and the newspaper was quickly halted, though Kandi tried fighting for her "freedom of press." She took particular interest in writing romance after college, as she has always been a die hard hopeless romantic, and likes to highlight all the challenges of love as well as the triumphs.

When Kandi isn't writing, you can find her reading books of all kinds, talking with her extremely vocal cat, and spending time with her friends and family. She enjoys live music, traveling, anything heavy in carbs, beach days, movie marathons, craft beer and sweet wine — not necessarily in that order.

CONNECT WITH KANDI:

➜ NEWSLETTER: bit.ly/NewsletterKS
➜ FACEBOOK: facebook.com/kandisteiner
➜ FACEBOOK READER GROUP (Kandiland): facebook.com/groups/kandischasers
➜ INSTAGRAM: Instagram.com/kandisteiner
➜ TWITTER: twitter.com/kandisteiner
➜ PINTEREST: pinterest.com/kandicoffman
➜ WEBSITE: www.kandisteiner.com

Kandi Steiner may be coming to a city near you! Check out her "events" tab to see all the signings she's attending in the near future:

➜ www.kandisteiner.com/events

www.ingramcontent.com/pod-product-compliance
Lightning Source LLC
Chambersburg PA
CBHW032147190726
48290CB00005BB/1443